"DON'T START READING THIS BOOK UNLESS YOU HAVE A FREE EVENING, FOR YOU WON'T WANT TO LAY IT ASIDE UNTIL THE VERY END."

—*Seattle Post-Intelligencer*

The *Dolphin*, pride of America's nuclear fleet, is the only submarine capable of attempting the daring rescue of a British meteorological team trapped on a polar ice cap.

The officers aboard the *Dolphin* know well the hazards of such an assignment. What they do not know is that the rescue attempt is really a cover-up for one of the most desperate espionage missions of the Cold War—and that the *Dolphin* is heading straight for sub-zero disaster—facing hidden sabotage, murder ... and a deadly, invisible enemy. ...

"Exciting, suspenseful, mysterious, gripping ..."

—*St. Petersburg Times*

Fawcett Books
by Alistair MacLean:

- ☐ THE GUNS OF NAVARONE 14171 $2.50
- ☐ SOUTH BY JAVA HEAD   14023 $2.25
- ☐ THE SECRET WAYS   14010 $1.95
- ☐ NIGHT WITHOUT END   14129 $2.25
- ☐ FEAR IS THE KEY   14011 $2.25
- ☐ THE BLACK SHRIKE   14199 $1.95
- ☐ THE SATAN BUG   14212 $2.25
- ☐ ICE STATION ZEBRA   23885 $2.25
- ☐ WHEN EIGHT BELLS TOLL   23893 $2.50
- ☐ PUPPET ON A CHAIN   24056 $1.95
- ☐ CARAVAN TO VACCARES   24082 $2.25
- ☐ BEAR ISLAND   23560 $2.25
- ☐ BREAKHEART PASS   24092 $2.25
- ☐ CIRCUS   22875 $2.25
- ☐ THE GOLDEN GATE   23177 $2.50
- ☐ SEAWITCH   23597 $2.25

To Lachlan, Michael, and Alistair

1

COMMANDER JAMES D. SWANSON of the U.S. Navy was short, plump and crowding forty. He had jet-black hair topping a pink, cherubic face, and with the deep permanent creases of laughter lines radiating from his eyes and curving around his mouth, he was a dead ringer for the cheerful, happy-go-lucky extrovert who is the life and soul of the party where the guests park their brains along with their hats and coats. That, anyway, was how he struck me at first glance, but on the reasonable assumption that I might very likely find some other qualities in the man picked to command the latest and most powerful nuclear submarine afloat I took a second and closer look at him and this time I saw what I should have seen the first time if the dank gray fog and winter dusk settling down over the Firth of Clyde hadn't made seeing so difficult. His eyes. Whatever his eyes were, they weren't those of the glad-handing, wisecracking *bon vivant*. They were the coolest, clearest gray eyes I'd ever seen, eyes that he used as a dentist might his probe, a surgeon his lancet, or a scientist his electronic microscope. Measuring eyes. They measured first me and then the paper he held in his hand but gave no clue at all as to the conclusions arrived at on the basis of measurements made.

"I'm sorry, Dr. Carpenter." The south-of-the-Mason-Dixon-line voice was quiet and courteous, but without any genuine regret that I could detect, as he folded the telegram back into its envelope and handed it to me. "I can accept neither this telegram as sufficient authorization nor yourself as a passenger. Nothing personal, you know that: but I have my orders."

"Not sufficient authorization?" I pulled the telegram from its envelope and pointed to the signature. "Who do you think this is—the resident window cleaner at the Admiralty?"

It wasn't funny, and as I looked at him in the failing light I thought maybe I'd overestimated the depth of the laughter lines in the face. He said precisely, "Admiral Hewson is commander of the Nato Eastern Division. On Nato exercises I come under his command. At all other times I am responsible only to Washington. This is one of those other times. I'm sorry. And I must point out, Dr. Carpenter, that you could have arranged for anyone in London to send this telegram. It's not even on a naval message form."

He didn't miss much, that was a fact, but he was being suspicious about nothing. I said: "You could call him up by radio telephone, Commander."

"So I could," he agreed. "And it would make no difference. Only accredited American nationals are allowed aboard this vessel—and the authority must come from Washington."

"From the Director of Underseas Warfare or Commander Atlantic Submarines?" He nodded, slowly, speculatively, and I went on: "Please radio them and ask them to contact Admiral Hewson. Time is very short, Commander." I might have added that it was beginning to snow and that I was getting colder by the minute, but I refrained.

He thought for a moment, nodded, turned and walked a few feet to a portable dock-side telephone that was connected by a looping wire to the long, dark shape lying at our feet. He spoke briefly, keeping his voice low, and hung up. He barely had time to rejoin me when three duffel-coated figures came hurrying up an adjacent gangway, turned in our direction and stopped when they reached us. The tallest of the three tall men, a lean, rangy character with wheat-colored hair and the definite look of a man who ought to have had a horse between his legs, stood slightly in advance of the other two. Commander Swanson gestured toward him.

"Lieutenant Hansen, my executive officer. He'll look after you till I get back." The commander certainly knew how to choose his words.

"I don't need looking after," I said mildly. "I'm all grown up now and I hardly ever feel lonely."

"I shall be as quick as I can, Dr. Carpenter," Swanson said. He hurried off down the gangway, and I gazed thoughtfully after him. I put out of my mind any idea I might have had about the Commander U. S. Atlantic Submarines picking his captains from the benches in Central Park. I had tried to effect an entrance aboard Swanson's ship, and if such an entrace was unauthorized he didn't want me taking off till he'd found out why. Hansen and his two men, I guessed, would be the three biggest sailors on the ship.

The ship. I stared down at the great black shape lying almost at my feet. This was my first sight of a nuclear-engined submarine, and the *Dolphin* was like no submarine I had ever seen. She was about the same length as a World

War II long-range ocean-going submarine, but there all resemblance ceased. Her diameter was at least twice that of any conventional submarine. Instead of having the vaguely boat-shaped lines of her predecessors, the *Dolphin* was almost perfectly cylindrical in design; instead of the usual V-shaped bows, her fore end was completely hemispherical. There was no deck, as such: the rounded sheer of sides and bows rose smoothly to the top of the hull then fell as smoothly away again, leaving only a very narrow fore and aft working space so treacherous in its slippery convexity that it was permanently railed off in harbor. About a hundred feet back from the bows the slender yet massive conning tower reared over twenty feet above the deck, for all the world like the great dorsal fin of some monstrous shark; halfway up the sides of the conning tower and thrust out stubbily at right angles were the swept-back auxiliary diving planes of the submarine. I tried to see what lay further aft but the fog and the thickening snow swirling down from the north of Loch Long defeated me. Anyway, I was losing interest. I'd only a thin raincoat over my clothes and I could feel my skin start to gooseflesh under the chill fingers of that winter wind.

"Nobody said anything about us having to freeze to death," I said to Hansen. "That naval canteen there. Would your principles prevent you from accepting a cup of coffee from Dr. Carpenter, that well-known espionage agent?"

He grinned and said: "In the matter of coffee, friend, I have no principles. Especially tonight. Someone should have warned us about those Scottish winters." He not only looked like a cowboy, he talked like one. I was an expert on cowboys, as I was sometimes too tired to rise to switch off the TV set. "Rawlings, go tell the captain that we are sheltering from the elements."

While Rawlings went to the dock-side phone Hansen led the way to the nearby neon-lit canteen. He let me precede him through the door, then made for the counter while the other sailor, a red-complexioned character about the size and shape of a polar bear, nudged me gently into an angled bench seat in one corner of the room. They weren't taking too many chances with me. Hansen came and sat on the other side of me, and when Rawlings returned he sat squarely in front of me across the table.

"As neat a job of corralling as I've seen for a long time," I said approvingly. "You've got nasty, suspicious minds, haven't you?"

"You wrong us," Hansen said sadly. "We're just three friendly sociable guys carrying out our orders. It's Commander Swanson who has the nasty, suspicious mind, isn't that so, Rawlings?"

"Yes indeed, Lieutenant," Rawlings said gravely. "Very security-minded, the captain is."

I tried again. "Isn't this very inconvenient for you?" I asked. "I mean, I should have thought that every man would have been urgently required aboard if you're due to sail in less than two hours' time."

"You just keep on talking, Doc," Hansen said encouragingly. There was nothing encouraging about his cold blue Arctic eyes. "I'm a right good listener."

"Looking forward to your trip up to the ice pack?" I inquired pleasantly.

They operated on the same wave length, all right. They didn't even look at one another. In pefect unison they all hitched themselves a couple of inches closer to me, and there was nothing imperceptible about the way they did it, either. Hansen waited, smiling in a pleasantly relaxed fashion until the waitress had deposited four steaming mugs of coffee on the table, then said in the same encouraging tone: "Come again, friend. Nothing we like to hear better than top-classified information being bandied about in canteens. How the hell do *you* know where we're going?"

I reached up my hand beneath my coat lapel and it stayed there, my right wrist locked in Hansen's right hand. "We're not suspicious or anything," he said apologetically. "It's just that we submariners are very nervous on account of the dangerous life we lead. Also, we've a very fine library of movies aboard the *Dolphin*, and every time a character in one of those movies reaches up under his coat it's always for the same reason, and that's not just because he's checking to see if his wallet's still there."

I took his wrist with my free hand, pulled his arm away and pushed it down on the table. I'm not saying it was easy —the U. S. Navy clearly fed its submariners on a high-protein diet—but I managed it without bursting a blood vessel. I pulled a folded newspaper out from under my coat and laid it down. "You wanted to know how the hell I knew where you were going," I said. "I can read, that's why. That's a Glasgow evening paper I picked up in Renfrew airport half an hour ago."

Hansen rubbed his wrist thoughtfully, then grinned. "What did you get your doctorate in, Doc? Weight-lifting? About that paper—how could you have got it in Renfrew half an hour ago?"

"I flew down here. Helicopter."

"A whirly-bird, eh? I heard one arriving a few minutes ago. But that was one of ours."

"It had 'U. S. Navy' written all over it in four-foot letters," I conceded, "and the pilot spent all his time chewing gum and praying out loud for a quick return to California."

"Did you tell the skipper this?" Hansen demanded.

"He didn't give me the chance to tell him anything."

"He's got a lot on his mind and far too much to see to," Hansen said. He unfolded the paper and looked at the front page. He didn't have far to look to find what he wanted: the two-inch-banner headlines were spread over seven columns.

"Well, would you look at this." Lieutenant Hansen made no attempt to conceal his irritation and chagrin. "Here we are, pussy-footing around in this God-forsaken dump, tape all over our mouths, sworn to eternal secrecy about mission and destination—and then what? I pick up this damned limey newspaper and here are all the top-secret details plastered right across the front page."

"You are kidding, Lieutenant," said the man with the red face and the general aspect of a polar bear. His voice seemed to come from his boots.

"I am not kidding, Zabrinski," Hansen said coldly, "as you would appreciate if you had ever learned to read. 'Nuclear submarine to the rescue,' it says. 'Dramatic dash to the North Pole.' God help us, the North Pole. And a picture of the *Dolphin*. And of the skipper. Good God, there's even a picture of me."

Rawlings reached out a hairy paw and twisted the paper to have a better look at the blurred and smudged representation of the man before him. "So there is. Not very flattering, is it, Lieutenant? But a speaking likeness, mind you, a speaking likeness. The photographer has caught the essentials perfectly."

"You are utterly ignorant of the first principles of photography," Hansen said witheringly. "Listen to this piece. 'The following joint statement was issued simultaneously a few minutes before noon (G.M.T.) today in both London and Washington: "In view of the critical condition of the survivors of Drift Ice Station Zebra and the failure either to rescue or contact them by conventional means, the U. S. Navy has willingly agreed that the U. S. nuclear submarine *Dolphin* be dispatched with all speed to try to effect contact with the survivors.

" ' "The *Dolphin* returned to its base in the Holy Loch, Scotland, at dawn this morning after carrying out extensive exercises with the Nato naval forces in the eastern Atlantic. It is hoped that the *Dolphin* (Commander James D. Swanson,

11

U.S.N., commanding) will sail at approximately seven p.m. (G.M.T.) this evening."

" 'The laconic understatement of this communique heralds the beginning of a desperate and dangerous rescue attempt which must be without parallel in the history of the sea or the Arctic. It is now sixty hours—' "

" 'Desperate,' you said, Lieutenant?" Rawlings frowned heavily. " 'Dangerous,' you said? The captain will be asking for volunteers?"

"No need. I told the captain that I'd already checked with all eighty-eight enlisted men and that they'd volunteered to a man."

"You never checked with me."

"I must have missed you. Now, kindly shut up, your executive officer is talking. 'It is now sixty hours since the world was electrified to learn of the disaster that had struck Drift Ice Station Zebra, the only British meteorological station in the Arctic, when an English-speaking ham-radio operator in Bodö, Norway, picked up the faint S.O.S. from the top of the world.

" 'A further message, picked up less than twenty-four hours ago by the British trawler *Morning Star* in the Barents Sea, makes it clear that the position of the survivors of the fuel-oil fire that destroyed most of Drift Ice Station Zebra in the early hours of Tuesday morning is desperate in the extreme. With their oil-fuel reserves completely destroyed and their food stores all but wiped out, it is feared that those still lying cannot long be expected to survive in the twenty-below temperatures—fifty degrees of frost—at present being experienced in that area.

" 'It is not known whether all the prefabricated huts, in which the expedition members lived, have been destroyed.

" 'Drift Ice Station Zebra, which was established only in the late summer of this year, is at present in an estimated position of 85° 40′N., 21° 30′E., which is only about three hundred miles from the North Pole. Its position cannot be known with certainty, because of the clockwise drift of the polar ice pack.

" 'For the past thirty hours long-range supersonic bombers of the American, British and Russian air forces have been scouring the polar ice pack searching for Station Zebra. Because of the uncertainty about the drift station's actual position, the complete absence of daylight in the Arctic at this time of year and the extremely bad weather conditions, they were unable to locate the station and forced to return.' "

"They didn't have to locate it," Rawlings objected. "Not visually. With the instruments those bombers have nowadays,

12

they could home-in on a hummingbird a hundred miles away. The radio operator at the drift station had only to keep on sending and they could have used that as a beacon."

"Maybe the radio operator is dead," Hansen said heavily. "Maybe his radio has broken down on him. Maybe the fuel that was destroyed was essential for running the radio. All depends what source of power he used."

"Diesel-electric generator," I said. "He had a standby battery of Nife cells. Maybe he's conserving the batteries, using them only for emergencies. There's also a hand-cranked generator, but its range is pretty limited."

"How do you know that?" Hansen asked quietly. "About the type of power used?"

"I must have read it somewhere."

"You must have read it somewhere." He looked at me without expression, then turned back to his paper. " 'A report from Moscow states that the atomic-engined *Dvina*, the world's most powerful ice-breaker, sailed from Murmansk some twenty hours ago and is proceeding at high speed toward the Arctic pack. Experts are not hopeful about the outcome, for at this late period of the year the ice pack has already thickened and compacted into a solid mass which will almost certainly defy the efforts of any vessel, even those of the *Dvina*, to smash its way through.

" 'The use of the submarine *Dolphin* appears to offer the only slender hope of life for the apparently doomed survivors of Station Zebra. The odds against success must be regarded as heavy in the extreme. Not only will the *Dolphin* have to travel several hundred miles continuously submerged under the polar ice cap, but the possibilities of its being able to break through the ice cap at any given place or to locate the survivors are very remote. But undoubtedly if any ship in the world can do it, it is the *Dolphin*, the pride of the U.S. Navy's nuclear submarine fleet.' "

Hansen broke off and read on silently for a minute. Then he said: "That's about all. A story giving all the known details of the *Dolphin*. That, and a lot of ridiculous rubbish about the enlisted men in the *Dolphin's* crew being the elite of the cream of the U. S. Navy."

Rawlings looked wounded. Zabrinski, the polar bear with the red face, grinned, fished out a pack of cigarettes and passed them around. Then he became serious again and said: "What are those crazy guys doing up there at the top of the world, anyway?"

"Meteorological, lunkhead," Rawlings informed him. "Didn't you hear the lieutenant say so? A big word, mind you," he conceded generously, "but he made a pretty fair stab at it. 'Weather station' to you, Zabrinski."

"I still say they're crazy guys," Zabrinski rumbled. "Why do they do it, Lieutenant?"

"I suggest you ask Dr. Carpenter about it," Hansen said dryly. He stared through the plate-glass windows at the snow whirling grayly through the gathering darkness, his eyes bleak and remote, as if he were already visualizing the doomed men drifting to their death in the frozen immensity of the polar ice cap. "I think he knows a great deal more about it than I do."

"I know a little," I admitted. "There's nothing mysterious or sinister about what I know. Meteorologists now regard the Arctic and the Antarctic as the two great weather factories of the world, the areas primarily responsible for the weather that affects the rest of the hemispheres. We already know a fair amount about Antarctic conditions, but practically nothing about the Arctic. So we pick a suitable ice floe, fill it with huts crammed with technicians and all sorts of instruments, and let them drift around the top of the world for six months or so. Your own people have already set up two or three of those stations. The Russians have set up at least ten, to the best of my knowledge, most of them in the East Siberian Sea."

"How do they establish those camps, Doc?" Rawlings asked.

"Different ways. Your people prefer to establish them in wintertime, when the pack freezes up enough for plane landings to be made. Someone flies out from, usually, Point Barrow in Alaska and searches around the polar pack till they find a suitable ice floe—even when the ice is compacted and frozen together into one solid mass an expert can tell which pieces are going to remain as good-sized floes when the thaw comes and the break-up begins. Then they fly out all huts, equipment, stores and men by ski plane and gradually build the place up.

"The Russians prefer to use a ship in summertime. They generally use the *Lenin,* a nuclear-engined ice-breaker. It just batters its way deep into the summer pack, dumps everything and everybody on the ice, and takes off before the big freeze-up starts. We used the same technique for Drift Ice Station Zebra—our one and only ice station. The Russians lent us the *Lenin*—all countries are only too willing to concentrate on meteorological research, since everyone benefits by it—and took us pretty deep into the ice pack north of Franz Josef Land. Zebra has already moved a good bit from its original position—the polar ice cap, just sitting on top of the Arctic Ocean, can't quite manage to keep up with the west-

14

east spin of the earth, so that it has a slow westward movement in relation to the earth's crust. At the present moment
it's about four hundred miles due north of Spitsbergen."

"They're still crazy," Zabrinski said. He was silent for a
moment, then looked speculatively at me. "You in the limey
Navy, Doc?"

"You must forgive Zabrinski's manners, Dr. Carpenter,"
Rawlings said coldly. "But he's been denied the advantages
that the rest of us take for granted. I understand he was
born in the Bronx."

"No offense," Zabrinski said equably. "Royal Navy, I
meant. Are you, Doc?"

"Attached to it, you might say."

"Loosely, no doubt." Rawlings nodded. "Why so keen on
an Arctic holiday, Doc? Mighty cool up there, I can tell
you."

"Because the men on Drift Station Zebra are going to
be badly in need of medical aid. If there are any survivors, that is."

"We got our own medic on board and he's no slouch with
a stethoscope, or so I've heard from several who have survived his treatment. A well-spoken-of quack."

" 'Doctor,' you ill-mannered lout," Zabrinski said severely.

"That's what I meant," Rawlings apologized. "It's not often
that I get the chance to talk to an educated man like
myself, and it just kinda slipped out. The point is, the *Dolphin's* already all buttoned up on the medical side."

"I'm sure it is," I smiled, "but any survivors we might
find are going to be suffering from advanced exposure, frostbite, and probably gangrene. The treatment of those is rather
a specialty of mine."

"Is it now?" Rawlings surveyed the depths of his coffee cup.
"I wonder how a man gets to be a specialist in those things?"

Hansen stirred and withdrew his gaze from the darkly white
world beyond the canteen windows.

"Dr. Carpenter is not on trial for his life," he said mildly.
"The counsel for the prosecution will kindly shut up."

This air of easy familiarity between officer and men, the
easy camaraderie, the mutually tolerant disparagement with
the deceptively misleading overtones of music-hall comedy,
was something very rare in my experience but not unique. I'd
seen it before, in first-line R.A.F. bomber crews, a rela-
tionship found only among a close-knit, close-living group of
superbly trained experts, each of whom is keenly aware of
his complete interdependence on the others. The casually
informal and familiar attitude was a token not of the lack of
discipline but the complete reverse, it was the badge of a

15

very high degree of self-discipline, of the regard one man held for another not only as a highly skilled technician in his own field but also as a human being. It was clear, too, that a list of unwritten rules governed their conduct. Offhand and frequently completely lacking in outward respect though Rawlings and Zabrinski were in their attitude toward Lieutenant Hansen, there was an invisible line of propriety over which it was inconceivable that they would ever step: for Hansen's part, he scrupulously avoided any use of his authority when making disparaging remarks at the expense of the two enlisted men. It was also clear, as now, who was boss.

Rawlings and Zabrinski had stopped questioning me and had just embarked upon an enthusiastic discussion of the demerits of the Holy Loch in particular and Scotland in general as a submarine base, when a jeep swept past the canteen windows, the snow whirling whitely, thickly, through the swathe of the headlights. Rawlings jumped to his feet in mid-sentence, then subsided slowly and thoughtfully into his chair.

"The plot," he announced, "thickens."

"You saw who it was?" Hansen asked.

"I did indeed. Andy Bandy, no less."

"I didn't hear that, Rawlings," Hansen said coldly.

"Vice-Admiral John Garvie, U. S. Navy, sir."

"Andy Bandy, eh?" Hansen said pensively. He grinned at me. "Admiral Garvie. Officer Commanding U. S. Naval Forces in Nato. Now, this is very interesting, I submit. I wonder what he's doing here."

"World War III has just broken out," Rawlings announced. "It's just about time for the admiral's first Martini of the day, and no lesser crisis—"

"He didn't by any chance fly down with you in that chopper from Renfrew this afternoon?" Hansen interrupted shrewdly.

"No."

"Know him, by any chance?"

"Never even heard of him until now."

"Curiouser and curiouser," Hansen murmured.

A few minutes passed in desultory talk—the minds of Hansen and his two men were obviously very much on the reason for the arrival of Admiral Garvie—and then a snow-filled gust of chilled air swept into the canteen as the door opened and a blue-coated sailor came in and crossed to our table.

"The captain's compliments, Lieutenant. Would you bring Dr. Carpenter to his cabin, please?"

Hansen nodded, rose to his feet and led the way outside. The snow was beginning to lie now, the darkness was coming down fast and the wind from the north was bitingly cold. Hansen made for the nearest gangway, halted at its head as he saw seamen and dockyard workers, insubstantial and spectral figures in the swirling, flood-lit snow, carefully easing a slung torpedo down the for'ard hatch, turned and headed toward the after gangway. We clambered down and at the foot Hansen said: "Watch your step, Doc. It's a little slippery hereabouts."

It was all that, but with the thought of the ice-cold waters of the Holy Loch waiting for me if I put a foot wrong I made no mistake. We passed through the hooped canvas shelter covering the after hatch and dropped down a steep metal ladder into a warm, scrupulously clean and gleaming engine room packed with a baffling complexity of gray-painted machinery and instrument panels, its every corner brightly illuminated with shadowless fluorescent lighting.

"Not going to blindfold me, Lieutenant?" I asked.

"No need." He grinned. "If you're on the up and up, it's not necessary. If you're not on the up and up, it's still not necessary, for you can't talk about what you've seen—not to anyone that matters—if you're going to spend the next few years staring out from behind a set of prison bars."

I saw his point. I followed him for'ard, our feet soundless on the black rubber decking, past the tops of a couple of huge machines readily identifiable as turbo-generator sets for producing electricity. More heavy banks of instruments, a door, then a thirty-foot-long very narrow passageway. As we passed along its length I was conscious of a heavy vibrating hum from beneath my feet. The *Dolphin's* nuclear reactor had to be somewhere. This would be it, here. Directly beneath us. There were circular hatches on the passageway deck and those could only be covers for the heavily leaded glass windows, inspection ports that would provide the nearest and only approach to the nuclear furnace far below.

The end of the passage, another heavily clamped door, and then we were into what was obviously the control center of the *Dolphin*. To the left was a partitioned-off radio room, to the right a battery of machines and dialed panels of incomprehensible purpose, and straight ahead, a big chart table. Beyond that again, in the center, were massive mast housings and, still further on, the periscope stand with its twin periscopes. The whole control room was twice the size of any I'd ever seen in a conventional submarine but, even so, every square inch of bulkhead space seemed to be taken up by one type or another of highly complicated looking machines or instrument banks: even the deckhead was almost invisible, lost to sight above thickly twisted festoons of wires, cables and pipes of a score of different kinds.

The for'ard port side of the control room was for all the world like a replica of the flight deck of a modern multi-engined jet airliner. There were two separate yoke aircraft-type control columns, facing on to banks of hooded calibrated dials. Behind the yokes were two padded leather chairs, each chair, I could see, fitted with a safety belt to hold the helmsman in place. I wondered vaguely what type of violent maneuvers the *Dolphin* might be capable of when such safety belts were obviously considered essential to strap the helmsman down.

Opposite the control platform, on the other side of the passageway leading forward from the control room, was a second partitioned-off room. There was no indication what this might be and I wasn't given time to wonder. Hansen hurried down the passage, stopped at the first door on his left, and knocked. The door opened and Commander Swanson appeared.

"Ah, there you are. Sorry you've been kept waiting, Dr. Carpenter. We're sailing at six thirty, John"—this to Hansen. "You can have everything set up by then?"

"Depends how quickly the loading of the torpedoes goes, Captain."

"We're taking only six aboard."

Hansen lifted an eyebrow but made no comment. He said, "Loading them into the tubes?"

"In the racks. They have to be worked on."

"No spares?"

"No spares."

Hansen nodded and left. Swanson led me into his cabin and closed the door behind him.

Commander Swanson's cabin was bigger than a telephone booth, I'll say that for it, but not all that much bigger to shout about. A built-in bunk, a folding washbasin, a small writing desk and chair, a folding camp stool, a locker, some calibrated repeater-instrument dials above the bunk, and that was it. If you'd tried to perform the twist in there, you'd have fractured yourself in a dozen places without ever moving your feet from the center of the floor.

"Dr. Carpenter," Swanson said, "I'd like you to meet Admiral Garvie, Commander U. S. Nato naval forces."

Admiral Garvie put down the glass he was holding in his hand, rose from the only chair, and stretched out his hand.

18

As he stood with his feet together, the far from negligible clearance between his knees made it easy to understand the latter part of his "Andy Bandy" nickname: like Hansen, he'd have been at home on the range. He was a tall, florid-faced man with white hair, white eyebrows and a twinkle in the blue eyes below; he had that certain indefinable something about him common to all senior naval officers the world over, irrespective of race or nationality.

"Glad to meet you, Dr. Carpenter. Sorry for the—um—lukewarm reception you received, but Commander Swanson was perfectly within his rights in acting as he did. His men have looked after you?"

"They permitted me to buy them a cup of coffee in the canteen."

He smiled. "Opportunists all, those nuclear men. I feel that the good name of American hospitality is in danger. Whisky, Dr. Carpenter?"

"I thought American naval ships were dry, sir."

"So they are, my boy, so they are. Except for a little medicinal alcohol, of course. My personal supply." He produced a hip flask about the size of a canteen and reached for a convenient shot glass. "Before venturing into the remoter fastnesses of the Highlands of Scotland, the prudent man takes the necessary precautions. I have to make an apology to you, Dr. Carpenter. I saw your Admiral Hewson in London last night and had intended to be here this morning to persuade Commander Swanson here to take you aboard. But I was delayed."

"Persuade, sir?"

"Persuade." He sighed. "Our nuclear-submarine captains, Dr. Carpenter, are a touchy and difficult bunch. From the proprietary attitude they adopt toward their submarines you'd think that each one of them was a majority shareholder in the Electric Boat Company of Groton, where most of those boats are built." He raised his glass. "Success to the commander and yourself. I hope you manage to find those poor devils. But I don't give you one chance in a thousand."

"I think we'll find them, sir. Or Commander Swanson will."

"What makes you so sure?" he asked slowly. "Hunch?"

"You could call it that."

He laid down his glass and his eyes were no longer twinkling. "Admiral Hewson was most evasive about you, I must say. Who are you, Carpenter? *What* are you?"

"Surely he told you, Admiral? Just a doctor attached to the Navy to carry out—"

"A naval doctor?"

"Well, not exactly. I—"

"A civilian?"

I nodded, and the admiral and Swanson exchanged looks that they were at no pains at all to conceal from me. If they were happy at the prospect of having aboard America's latest and most secret submarine a man who was not only a foreigner but a civilian to boot, they were hiding it well. Admiral Garvie said: "Well, go on."

"That's all. I carry out environmental health studies for the services. How men react to extremes of environmental conditions, such as in the Arctic or the tropics, how they react to conditions of weightlessness in simulated space flight or to extremes of pressure when having to escape from submarines. Mainly—"

"Submarines." Admiral Garvie pounced on the word. "You have been to sea in submarines, Dr. Carpenter? Really sailed in them, I mean?"

"I had to. We found that simulated tank escapes were no substitute for the real thing."

The admiral and Swanson looked unhappier than ever. A foreigner—bad. A foreign civilian—worse. But a foreign civilian with at least a working knowledge of submarines—terrible. I didn't have to be beaten over the head to see their point of view. I would have felt just as unhappy in their shoes.

"What's your interest in Drift Ice Station Zebra, Dr. Carpenter?" Admiral Garvie asked bluntly.

"The Admiralty asked me to go there, sir."

"So I gather, so I gather," Garvie said wearily. "Admiral Hewson made that quite plain to me already. Why you, Carpenter?"

"I have some knowledge of the Arctic, sir. I'm supposed to be an expert on the medical treatment of men subjected to prolonged exposure, frostbite and gangrene. I might be able to save lives or limbs that your own doctor aboard might not."

"I could have half a dozen such experts here in a few hours," Garvie said evenly. "Regular officers of the U. S. Navy, at that. That's not enough, Carpenter."

This was becoming difficult. I tried again. I said, "I know Drift Station Zebra. I helped select the site. I helped establish the camp. The commandant, a Major Halliwell, has been my closest friend for many years." The last was only half the truth, but I felt that this was neither the time nor the place for overelaboration.

20

"Well, well," Garvie said thoughtfully. "And you still claim you're just an ordinary doctor?"

"My duties are flexible, sir."

"I'll say they are. Well, then, Carpenter, if you're just a common garden-variety sawbones, how do you explain this?" He picked up a signal form from the table and handed it to me. "This has just arrived in reply to Commander Swanson's radioed query to Washington about you."

I looked at the signal. It read: "Dr. Neil Carpenter bona fide beyond question. He may be taken into your fullest, repeat, fullest confidence. He is to be extended every facility and all aid short of actually endangering the safety of your submarine and the lives of your crew." It was signed by the Chief of Naval Operations.

"Very civil of the Chief of Naval Operations, I must say." I handed back the telegram. "With a character reference like this, what are you worrying about? That ought to satisfy anyone."

"It doesn't satisfy me," Garvie said heavily. "The ultimate responsibility for the safety of the *Dolphin* is mine. This message more or less gives you carte blanche to behave as you like, to ask Commander Swanson to act in ways that might be contrary to his better judgment. I can't have that."

"Does it matter what you can or can't have? You have your orders. Why don't you obey them?"

He didn't hit me. He didn't even bat an eyelid. He wasn't activated by pique about the fact that he wasn't privy to the reason for the seeming mystery of my presence there; he was genuinely concerned about the safety of the submarine. He said: "If I think it more important that the *Dolphin* should remain on an active war footing rather than go haring off on a wildgoose chase to the Arctic, or if I think you constitute a danger to the submarine, I can countermand the C.N.O.'s orders. I'm the Commander-in-Chief on the spot. And I'm not satisfied."

This was damnably awkward. He meant every word he said, and he didn't look the type who would give a hoot for the consequences if he believed himself to be in the right. I looked at both men, looked at them slowly and speculatively, the unmistakable gaze, I hoped, of a man who was weighing others in the balance; what I was really doing was thinking up a suitable story that would satisfy both. After I had given enough time to my weighing-up—and my thinking—I dropped my voice a few decibels and said: "Is that door sound-proof?"

"More or less," Swanson said. He'd lowered his own voice to match mine.

21

"I won't insult either of you by swearing you to secrecy or any such rubbish," I said quietly. "I want to put on record the fact that what I am about to tell you I am telling you under duress, under Admiral Garvie's threat to refuse me transport if I don't comply with his wishes."

"There will be no repercussions," Garvie said.

"How do you know? Not that it matters now. Well, gentlemen, the facts are these. Drift Ice Station Zebra is officially classed as an Air Ministry meteorological station. Well, it belongs to the Air Ministry, all right, but there's not more than a couple of qualified meteorologists among its entire personnel."

Admiral Garvie refilled the glass and passed it to me without a word, without a flicker of change in his expression. The old boy certainly knew how to play it cool.

"What you will find there," I went on, "are some of the most highly skilled men in the world in the fields of radar, radio, infrared, and electronic computers, operating the most advanced instruments ever used in those fields. We know now, never mind how, the count-down succession of signals the Russians use in the last minute before launching a missile. There's a huge dish aerial in Zebra that can pick up and amplify any such signals within seconds of its beginning. Then long-range radar and infrared home-in on that bearing and within three minutes of the rocket's lift-off they have its height, speed, and course pinpointed to an infinitesimal degree of error. The computers do this, of course. One minute later the information is in the hands of all the antimissile stations between Alaska and Greenland. One minute more and solid-fuel infrared homing antimissile rockets are on their way: then the enemy missiles will be intercepted and harmlessly destroyed while still high over the Arctic regions. If you look at a map, you will see that in its present position Drift Ice Station Zebra is sitting practically on Russia's missile doorstep. It's hundreds of miles in advance of the present DEW line —the 'distant early warning' system. Anyway, it renders the DEW line obsolete."

"I'm only the office boy around those parts," Garvie said quietly. "I've never heard of any of this before."

I wasn't surprised. I'd never heard of any of it myself, either, not until I'd just thought it up a moment ago. Commander Swanson's reactions, if and when we ever got to Drift Station Zebra, were going to be very interesting. But I'd cross that bridge when I came to it. At present, my only concern was to get there.

"Outside the drift station itself," I said, "I doubt if a

22

dozen people in the world know what goes on there. But now you know. And you can appreciate how vitally important it is to the free world that this base be maintained in being. If anything has happened to it, we want to find out just as quickly as possible *what* has happened so that we can get it operating again."

"I still maintain that you're not an ordinary doctor," Garvie smiled. "Commander Swanson, how soon can you get under way?"

"Finish loading the torpedoes, move alongside the *Hunley,* load some final food stores, pick up extra Arctic clothing, and that's it, sir."

"Just like that? You said you wanted to make a slow-time dive out in the loch to check the planes and adjust the underwater trim—those missing torpedoes up front are going to make a difference, you know."

"That's before I heard Dr. Carpenter. Now I want to get up there just as fast as he does, sir. I'll see if immediate trim checks are necessary: if not, we can carry them out at sea."

"It's your boat," Garvie acknowledged. "I'd give my two remaining back teeth to come with you, Commander. Where are you going to accommodate Dr. Carpenter, by the way?"

"There's space for a cot in the exec's and engineer's cabin." He smiled at me. "I've already had your suitcase put in there."

"Did you have much trouble with the lock?" I inquired.

He had the grace to color slightly. "It's the first time I've ever seen a combination lock on a suitcase," he admitted. "It was that more than anything else—and the fact that we couldn't open it—that made the admiral and myself so suspicious. I've still one or two things to discuss with the admiral, so I'll take you to your quarters now. Dinner's at eight."

"I'd rather skip dinner, thanks."

"No one ever gets seasick on the *Dolphin,* I can assure you," Swanson smiled.

"I'd appreciate the chance to sleep instead. I've had no sleep for almost three days and I've been traveling non-stop for the past fifty hours. I'm just tired, that's all."

"That's a fair amount of traveling," Swanson smiled. He seemed to be smiling almost always, and I supposed vaguely that there would be some people foolish enough to take that smile always at its face value. "Where were you fifty hours ago, Doctor?"

"In the Antarctic."

Admiral Garvie gave me a very old-fashioned look indeed, but he let it go at that.

23

2

WHEN I AWOKE I was still heavy with sleep, the heaviness of a man who has slept for a long time. My watch said 9:30, and I knew it must be the next morning, not the same evening: I had been asleep for fifteen hours.

The cabin was quite dark. I rose, fumbled for the light switch, found it, and looked around. Neither Hansen nor the engineer officer was there; they must have come in after I had gone to sleep and left before I woke up. I looked around some more and then I listened. I was suddenly conscious of the almost complete quiet, the stillness, the entire lack of any perceptible motion. I might have been in the bedroom of my own house. What had gone wrong? What hold-up had occurred? Why in God's name weren't we under way? I'd have sworn the previous night that Commander Swanson had been just as conscious of the urgency as I had been.

I had a quick wash in the folding Pullman-type basin, passed up the need for a shave, pulled on shirt, trousers and shoes, and went outside. A few feet away a door opened to starboard off the passage. I went along and walked in. The officers' wardroom, without a doubt, with one of them still at breakfast, slowly munching his way through a huge plateful of steak, eggs and French fries, glancing at a magazine in a leisurely fashion and giving every impression of a man enjoying life to the luxurious full. He was about my own age, big, inclined to fat—a common condition, I was to find, among the entire crew, who ate so well and exercised so little—with close-cropped black hair already graying at the temples, and a cheeful, intelligent face. He caught sight of me, rose and stretched out a hand.

"Dr. Carpenter, it must be. Welcome to the wardroom. I'm Benson. Take a seat, take a seat."

I said something, appropriate but quick, then asked,

24

"What's wrong? What's been the hold-up? Why aren't we under way?"

"That's the trouble with the world today," Benson said mournfully. "Rush, rush, rush. And where does all the hurry get them? I'll tell you——"

"Excuse me. I must see the captain." I turned to leave but he laid a hand on my arm.

"Relax, Dr. Carpenter. We *are* at sea. Take a seat."

"At sea? On the level? I don't feel a thing."

"You never do when you're three hundred feet down. Maybe four hundred. I don't," he said expansively, "concern myself with those trifles. I leave them to the mechanics."

"Mechanics?"

"The captain, the engineer officer, people like that." He waved a hand in a generously vague gesture to indicate the largeness of the concept he understood by the term "mechanics." "Hungry?"

"We've cleared the Clyde?"

"Unless the Clyde extends to well beyond the north of Scotland, the answer to that is, yes, we have."

"Come again?"

He grinned. "At the last check we were well into the Norwegian Sea, about the latitude of Bergen."

"This is still only Tuesday morning?" I don't know if I looked stupid: I certainly felt it.

"It's still only Tuesday morning," he laughed. "And if you can work out from that what kind of speed we've been making in the last fifteen hours, we'd all be obliged if you'd keep it to yourself." He leaned back in his seat and lifted his voice. "Henry!"

A steward, white-jacketed, appeared from what I took to be the pantry. He was a tall, thin character with a dark complexion and the long lugubrious face of a dyspeptic spaniel. He looked at Benson and said in a meaningful voice: "*Another* plate of French fries, Doc?"

"You know very well that I never have more than one helping of that carbohydrated rubbish," Benson said with dignity. "Not, at least, for breakfast. Henry, this is Dr. Carpenter."

"Howdy," Henry said agreeably.

"Breakfast, Henry," Benson said. "And, remember, Dr. Carpenter is a Britisher. We don't want him leaving with a low opinion of the chow served in the U. S. Navy."

"If anyone aboard this ship has a low opinion of the food," Henry said darkly, "they hide it pretty well. Breakfast. The works. Right away."

"Not the works, for heaven's sake," I said. "There are

25

some things we decadent Britishers can't face up to first thing in the morning. One of them is French fries."

He nodded approvingly and left.

I said, "Dr. Benson, I gather."

"Resident medical officer aboard the *Dolphin*, no less," he admitted. "The one who's had his professional competence called into question by having a competing practitioner called in."

"I'm along for the ride. I assure you I'm not competing with anyone."

"I know you're not," he said quickly. Too quickly. Quickly enough so that I could see Swanson's hand in this, could see him telling his officers to lay off quizzing Carpenter too much. I wondered again what Swanson was going to say when and if we ever arrived at the drift station and he found out just how fluent a liar I was. Benson went on, smiling: "There's no call for even one medico aboard this boat, much less two."

"You're not overworked?" From the leisurely way he was going about his breakfast, it seemed unlikely.

"Overworked! I've sick-bay call once a day and no one ever turns up—except the morning after we arrive in port with a long cruise behind us, and then there are liable to be a few sore heads around. My main job, and what is supposed to be my specialty, is checking on radiation and atmospheric pollution of one kind or another. In the old submarine days, the atmosphere used to get pretty foul after only a few hours submerged but we have to stay down for months, if necessary." He grinned. "Neither job is very exacting. We issue each member of the crew with a dosimeter and periodically check a film badge for radiation dosage—which is invariably less than you'd get sitting on the beach on a moderately warm day.

"The atmospheric problem is even easier. Carbon dioxide and carbon monoxide are the only things we have to worry about. We have a scrubbing machine that absorbs the breathed-out carbon dioxide from the atmosphere and pumps it out into the sea. Carbon monoxide—which we could more or less eliminate if we forbade cigarette smoking, only we don't want a mutiny on our hands when we're three hundred feet down—is burned to monoxide by a special heater and then scrubbed as usual. And even that hardly worries me, I've a very competent engineman who keeps those machines in tip-top condition." He sighed. "I've a surgery here that will delight your heart, Dr. Carpenter. Operating table, dentist's chair, the works, and the biggest crisis I've had yet is a cigarette burn between the fingers sustained by a cook who fell asleep during one of my lectures."

26

"Lectures?"

"I've got to do something if I'm not to go off my rocker. I spend a couple of hours a day keeping up with all the latest medical literature, but what good is that if you don't get a chance to practice it? So I lecture. I read up on places we're going to visit, and everyone listens to those talks. I give lectures on general health and hygiene, and some of them listen to those. I give lectures on the perils of overeating and underexercise, and no one listens to those. I don't listen to them myself. It was during one of those that the cook got burned. That's why our friend Henry, the steward, adopts his superior and critical attitude toward the eating habits of those who should obviously be watching their eating habits. He eats as much as any two men aboard but owing to some metabolic defect he remains as thin as a rail. Claims it's all due to dieting."

"It all sounds a bit less rigorous than the life of the average G.P."

"It is, it is." He brightened. "But I've got one job—a hobby to me—that the average G.P. can't have. The ice machine. I've made myself an expert on that."

"What does Henry think about it?"

"What? Henry?" He laughed. "Not that kind of ice machine. I'll show you later."

Henry brought food, and I'd have liked the maîtres d'hôtel of some allegedly five-star hotels in London to be there to see what a breakfast should be like. When I'd finished and told Benson that I didn't see that his lectures on the dangers of overweight were going to get him very far, he said: "Commander Swanson said you might like to look over the ship. I'm at your complete disposal."

"Very kind of you both. But first I'd like to shave, dress and have a word with the captain."

"Shave if you like. No one insists on it. As for dress, shirt and pants are the uniform of the day here. And the captain told me to tell you that he'd let you know immediately if anything that could possibly be of any interest to you came through."

So I shaved and then had Benson take me on a conducted tour of this city under the sea. The *Dolphin*, I had to admit, made any British submarine I'd ever seen look like a relic from the Ice Age.

To begin with, the sheer size of the vessel was staggering. So big had the hull to be to accommodate the huge nuclear reactor that it had internal accommodation equivalent to that of a 3,000-ton surface ship, with three decks instead of the usual one and lower hold found in the conventional submarine. The size, combined with the clever use of pastel paints for all the accommodation spaces, working spaces, and passageways, gave an overwhelming impression of lightness, airiness, and, above all, spaciousness.

He took me first, inevitably, to his sick bay. It was at once the smallest and most comprehensively equipped surgery I'd ever seen; whether a man wanted a major operation or just a tooth filled, he could have himself accommodated there. Neither clinical nor utilitarian, however, was the motif Benson had adopted for the decoration of the one bulkhead in his surgery completely free from surgical or medical equipment of any kind—a series of film stills in color featuring every cartoon character I'd ever seen, from Popeye to Pinnochio, with, as a two-foot-square centerpiece, an immaculately cravatted Yogi Bear industriously sawing off from the top of a wooden sign post the first word of a legend that read: "Don't feed the bears." From deck to deckhead, the bulkhead was covered with them.

"Makes a change from the usual pin-ups," I observed.

"I got inundated with those, too," Benson said regretfully. "Film librarian, you know. Can't use them, supposed to be bad for discipline. However. Lightens the morgue-like atmosphere, doesn't it? Cheers up the sick and the suffering, I like to think—and distracts their attention while I turn to page 217 in the old textbook to find out what's the matter with them."

From the surgery we passed through the wardroom and officers' quarters and dropped down a deck to the crew's living quarters. Benson took me through the gleaming tiled washrooms, the immaculate bunkroom, then into the crew's mess hall.

"The heart of the ship," he announced. "Not the nuclear reactor, as the uninformed maintain, but here. Just look at it. Hi-fi, juke box, record player, coffee machine, ice-cream machine, movie theater, library, and the home of all the cardsharps on the ship. What chance has a nuclear reactor against this layout? The old-time submariners would turn in their graves if they could see this: compared to the prehistoric conditions they lived in we must seem completely spoiled and ruined. Maybe we are, then again maybe we're not: the old boys never had to stay submerged for months at a time. . . . This is also where I send them to sleep with my lectures on the evils of overeating." He raised his voice for the benefit of seven or eight men who were sitting around the tables drinking coffee, smoking and reading. "You can observe for yourself, Dr. Carpenter, the effects of my

28

lectures on dieting and keeping fit. Did you ever see a bunch of more out-of-condition fat-bellied slobs in your life?"

The men grinned cheerfully. They were obviously well used to this sort of thing: Benson was exaggerating and they knew it. Each of them looked as if he knew what to do with a knife and fork when he got them in his hands, but that was about as far as it went. All had a curious similarity, big men and small men, the same characteristic I'd seen in Zabrinski and Rawlings—an air of relaxed competence, a cheerful imperturbability that marked them out as being the men apart they undoubtedly were.

Benson conscientiously introduced me to everyone, telling me exactly what their function aboard ship was and in turn informing them that I was a Royal Navy doctor along for an acclimatization trip. Swanson would have told him to say this; it was near enough the truth and would stop speculation on the reason for my presence there.

Benson turned into a small compartment leading off the mess hall. "The air-purification room. This is Engineman Harrison. How's our box of tricks, Harrison?"

"Just fine, Doc, just fine. CO reading steady on thirty parts a million." He entered some figures in a log book, Benson signed it with a flourish, exchanged a few more remarks and left.

"Half my day's toil done with one stroke of the pen," he observed. "I take it you're not interested in inspecting sacks of wheat, sides of beef, bags of potatoes, and about a hundred different varieties of canned goods."

"Not particularly. Why?"

"The entire for'ard half of the deck beneath our feet—a storage hold, really—is given up mainly to that. Seems an awful lot, I know, but then a hundred men can get through an awful lot of food in three months, which is the minimum time we must be prepared to stay at sea if the need arises. We'll pass up the inspection of the stores, the sight of all that food just makes me feel I'm fighting a losing battle all the time, and have a look at where the food's cooked."

He led the way for'ard into the galley, a small square room all tiles and glittering stainless steel. A tall, burly white-coated cook turned at our entrance and grinned at Benson. "Come to sample today's lunch, Doc?"

"I have not," Benson said coldly. "Dr. Carpenter, the chief cook and my arch enemy, Sam MacGuire. What form does the excess of calories take that you are proposing to thrust down the throats of the crew today?"

"No thrusting required," said MacGuire happily. "Cream soup, sirloin of beef no less, roast potatoes and as much

29

apple pie as a man can cope with. All good, nourishing food."

Benson shuddered. He was just about to leave the galley when he stopped and pointed at a heavy bronze ten-inch tube that stood about four feet above the deck of the galley. It had a heavy hinged lid and screwed clamps to keep the lid in position. "This might interest you, Dr. Carpenter. Guess what?"

"A pressure cooker?"

"Looks like it, doesn't it? This is our garbage-disposal unit. In the old days, when a submarine had to surface every few hours, garbage disposal was no problem: you just tipped the stuff over the side. But when you spend weeks on end cruising at three hundred feet, you can't just walk up to the upper deck and tip the waste over the side: garbage disposal becomes quite a problem. This tube goes right down to the bottom of the *Dolphin*. There's a heavy water-tight door at the lower end corresponding to this one, with interlocking controls that make it impossible for both doors to be open at the same time: it would be curtains for the *Dolphin* if they were. Sam here, or one of his henchmen, sticks the garbage into nylon mesh or polythene bags, weighs them with bricks—"

" 'Bricks,' you said?"

"Bricks. Sam, how many bricks aboard this ship?"

"Just over a thousand at the latest count, Doc."

"Regular builder's yard, aren't we?" Benson grinned. "Those bricks are to make sure the garbage bags sink to the bottom of the sea and not float to the surface. Even in peacetime we don't want to give our position away to anyone. In go three or four bags, the top door is clamped shut, and the bags are pumped out under pressure. Then the outer door is closed again. Simple."

"Yes." For some reason or other this odd contraption held a curious fascination for me. Days later I was to remember my inexplicable interest in it and wonder whether, after all, I wasn't becoming psychic with advancing years.

"It's not worth all that attention," Benson said good-humoredly. "Just an up-to-date version of the old rubbish chute. Come on, a long way to go yet."

He led the way from the galley to a heavy steel door set in a transverse bulkhead. Eight massive clamps to release and then replace after we had passed through the doorway.

"The for'ard torpedo storage room." Benson's voice was lowered, for at least half of the sixteen or so bunks that lined the bulkheads or were jammed up close to the torpedoes and racks were occupied and every man occupying them was sound asleep. "Only six torpedoes, as you can see. Normally there's stowage for twelve plus another six constantly kept loaded in the torpedo tubes. But those six are all we have just now. We had a malfunction in two of our torpedoes—the newest and more or less untested radio-controlled type—during the Nato exercises just ended, and Admiral Garvie ordered them all to be removed for inspection when we got back to the Holy Loch. The *Hunley*—that's our depot ship —carries experts for working on those things. However, they were no sooner taken off yesterday morning than this drift-station operation came our way, and Commander Swanson insisted on having at least six of them put back on right away." Benson grinned. "If there's one thing a submarine skipper hates it's putting to sea without his torpedoes. He feels he might just as well stay at home."

"Those torpedoes are still not operational?"

"I don't know whether they are or not. Our sleeping warriors here will do their best to find out when they come to."

"Why aren't they working on them now?"

"Because before our return to the Clyde, they were working on them for nearly sixty hours non-stop trying to find out the cause of the malfunction—and if it existed in the other torpedoes. I told the skipper that if he wanted to blow up the *Dolphin*, as good a way as any was to let those torpedomen keep on working—they were starting to stagger around like zombies, and a zombie is the last person you want to have working on the highly complicated innards of a torpedo. So he pulled them off."

He walked the length of the gleaming torpedoes and halted before another steel door in a cross bulkhead. He opened this, and beyond, four feet away, was another such heavy door set in another such bulkhead. The sills were about eighteen inches above deck level.

"You don't take many chances in building those boats, do you?" I asked. "It's like breaking into the Bank of England."

"Being a nuclear sub doesn't mean that we're not as vulnerable to underwater hazards as the older ships," Benson said. "We are. Ships have been lost before because the collision bulkhead gave way. The hull of the *Dolphin* can withstand terrific pressures, but a relatively minor tap from a sharp-edged object can rip us wide open like an electric can opener. The biggest danger is surface collision, which nearly always happens at the bows. So, to make doubly sure in the event of a bows collision, we have those double-collision bulkheads—the first submarine ever to have them. Makes fore and aft movement here a bit difficult, but you've no idea how much more soundly we all sleep at night."

He closed the after door behind him and opened the for'ard

31

one. We found ourselves in the for'ard torpedo room, a narrow, cramped compartment barely long enough to permit torpedoes to be loaded or withdrawn from their tubes. Those tubes, with their heavy hinged rear doors, were arranged close together in two vertical banks of three. Overhead were the loading rails, with heavy chain tackles attached. And that was all. No bunks in here and I didn't wonder: I wouldn't have liked to be the one to sleep for'ard of those collision bulkheads.

We began to work our way aft and had reached the mess hall when a sailor came up and said that the captain wanted to see me. I followed him up the wide central stairway into the control room, Dr. Benson a few paces behind to show that he wasn't being too inquisitive. Commander Swanson was waiting for me by the door of the radio room.

"Morning, Doctor. Sleep well?"

"Fifteen hours. What do you think? And breakfasted even better. What's up, Commander?" Something was up, that was for sure: for once, Commander Swanson wasn't smiling.

"Message coming through about Drift Station Zebra. Has to be decoded first, but that should take only minutes." Decoding or not, it seemed to me that Swanson already had a fair idea of the content of that message.

"When did we surface?" I asked. A submarine loses radio contact as soon as it submerges.

"Not since we left the Clyde. We're close to three hundred feet down right now."

"This is a *radio* message that's coming through?"

"What else? Times have changed. We still have to surface to transmit but we can receive down to our maximum depth. Somewhere in Connecticut is the world's largest radio transmitter, using an extremely low frequency, which can contact us at this depth far more easily than any other radio station can contact a surface ship. While we're waiting, come and meet the drivers."

He introduced me to some of his control-center crew—as with Benson, it seemed to be a matter of complete indifference to him whether it was officer or enlisted man—and finally stopped by an officer sitting just aft of the periscope stand, a youngster who looked as if he should still be in high school. "Will Raeburn," Swanson said. "Normally we pay no attention to him but after we move under the ice he becomes the most important man on the ship. Our navigation officer. Are we lost, Will?"

"We're just there, Captain." He pointed to a tiny pinpoint of light on the Norwegian Sea chart spread out beneath

32

the glass on the plotting table. "Gyro and sins are checking to a hair."

" 'Sins'?" I said.

"You may well look surprised, Dr. Carpenter," Swanson said. "Lieutenant Raeburn here is far too young to have any sins. He is referring to S.I.N.S.—Ship's Inertial Navigational System—a device once used for guiding intercontinental missiles and now adapted for submarine use, specifically nuclear submarines. No point in my elaborating: Will's ready to talk your head off about it if he manages to corner you." He glanced at the chart position. "Are we getting there quickly enough to suit you, Doctor?"

"I still don't believe it," I said.

"We cleared the Holy Loch a little earlier than I expected, before seven," Swanson admitted. "I had intended to carry out some slow-time dives to adjust trim, but it wasn't necessary. Even the lack of twelve torpedoes up in the nose didn't make her as stern-heavy as I'd expected. She's so damned big that a few tons more or less or here or there doesn't seem to make any difference to her. So we just came barreling on up—"

He broke off to accept a signal sheet from a sailor, and read through it slowly, taking his time about it. Then he jerked his head, walked to a quiet corner of the control center, and faced me as I came up to him. He still wasn't smiling.

"I'm sorry," he said. "Major Halliwell, the commandant of the drift station . . . You said last night he was a very close friend of yours?"

I felt my mouth begin to go dry. I nodded, and took the message from him. It read:

A further radio message, very broken and difficult to decipher, was received 0945 Greenwich Mean Time from Drift Ice Station Zebra by the British trawler *Morning Star*, the vessel that picked up the previous broadcast. Message stated that Major Halliwell, Officer Commanding, and three others, unnamed, critically injured or dead, no indication who or how many of the four are dead. Others, number again unknown, suffering severely from burns and exposure. Some message about food and fuel, atmospheric conditions and weakness in transmission made it quite indecipherable. Understood from very garbled signal that survivors in one hut unable to move because of weather. Words "ice storm" clearly picked up. Apparent details of wind speed and temperature, but unable to make out.

Morning Star several times attempted contact Drift

33

Station Zebra immediately afterward. No acknowledgment.

Morning Star, at request of British Admiralty, has abandoned fishing grounds and is moving closer in to Barrier to act as listening post. Message ends.

I folded the paper and handed it back to Swanson. He said again, "Sorry about this, Carpenter."

"Critically injured or dead," I said. "In a burnt-out station on the ice cap in winter, what's the difference?" My voice fell upon my ears as the voice of another man, a voice flat and lifeless, a voice empty of all emotion. "Johnny Halliwell and three of his men. Johnny Halliwell. Not the kind of man you would meet often, Commander. A remarkable man. Left school at fifteen, when his parents died, to devote himself to the support of a brother eight years younger than himself. He saved, he scraped, he sacrificed, he devoted many of the best years of his life to doing everything for his younger brother, including putting him through a six-year university course. Not till then did he think of himself, not till then did he get married. He leaves a lovely wife and three marvelous kids. Two nieces and a nephew not yet six months old."

"Two nieces—" He broke off and stared at me. "Good God, your brother? *Your* brother?" He didn't, for the moment, seem to find anything peculiar in the difference of surname.

I nodded silently. Young Lieutenant Raeburn approached us, an odd expression of anxiety on his face, but Swanson abruptly waved him away without even glancing in his direction. He shook his head slowly and was still shaking it when I said abruptly: "He's tough. He may be one of the survivors. He may live. We must get Drift Station Zebra's position. We *must* get it."

"Maybe they haven't got it themselves," Swanson said. I could see that he was grateful for something to talk about. "It *is* a drifting station, remember. The weather being what it is, it may have been days since they got their last fixes, and for all we know, their sextants, chronometers and radio direction finders have been lost in the fire."

"They must know what their latest fix was, even though it was a week ago. They must have a fairly accurate idea of the speed and direction of their drift. They'll be able to provide approximate data. The *Morning Star* must be told to keep transmitting non-stop with a continuous request for their position. If you surface now, can you contact the *Morning Star*?"

"I doubt it. The trawler must be the best part of a thousand miles north of us. His receiver wouldn't be big enough

34

to pull us in—which is another way of saying that our transmitter is too small."

"The B.B.C. have plenty of transmitters that are big enough. So have the Admiralty. Please ask one or the other to contact the *Morning Star* and ask it to make a continuous send for Zebra's position."

"They could do that themselves direct."

"Sure they could. But they couldn't hear the reply. The *Morning Star* can—if there's any reply. And she's getting closer to them all the time."

"We'll surface now," Swanson nodded. He turned away from the chart table we'd been standing beside and headed for the diving stand. As he passed the plotting table he said to the navigator: "What was it you wanted, Will?"

Lieutenant Raeburn turned his back on me and lowered his voice, but my hearing has always been a little abnormal. He whispered: "Did you see his face, Captain? I thought he was going to haul off and sock you."

"I thought the same thing myself," Swanson murmured. "For a moment. But I think I just happened to be in his line of vision, that's all."

I went forward to my cabin and lay down in the cot.

3

"THERE IT IS, THEN," said Swanson. "That's the Barrier."

The *Dolphin*, heading due north, her great cylindrical bulk at one moment completely submerged, the next showing clear as she rolled heavily through the steep quartering seas, was making less than three knots through the water, the great nuclear-powered engines providing just enough thrust to the big twin eight-foot propellers to provide steerage way and no more. Thirty feet below where we stood on the bridge the finest sonar equipment in the world was ceaselessly probing the waters all around us but even so Swanson was taking no chances on the effects of collision with a drifting ice block. The noon-day Arctic sky was so overcast that the light was no better than that of late dusk. The bridge thermometer showed the sea temperature to be 28°F., the air temperature—16°F. The gale-force wind from the northeast was snatching the tops off the rolling steel-gray waves and subjecting the steep-walled sides of the great conning tower—"sail," the crew called it—to the ceaseless battering of a bullet-driven spray that turned to solid ice even as it struck. The cold was intense.

Shivering uncontrollably, wrapped in a heavy duffel coat and oilskins and huddled against the illusory shelter of the canvas wind-dodger, I followed the line of Swanson's pointing arm; even above the high, thin, shrill whine of the wind and the drum-fire of the flying spray against the sail, I could hear the violent chattering of his teeth. Less than two miles away a long, thin, grayish-white line, at that distance apparently smooth and regular, seemed to stretch the entire width of the northern horizon. I'd seen it before and it wasn't much to look at but it was a sight a man never got used to, not because of itself but because of what it represented: the beginning of the polar ice cap that covered the top of the world, at this time of year a solid, compacted mass of ice that stretched clear from where we lay right across to Alaska on the other side of the world. And we had to go under that mass. We had to go under it to find men hundreds of miles away, men who might be already dying, men who might be already dead. Who probably were dead. Men, dying or dead, whom we had to seek out by guess and by God in that great wasteland of ice stretching out endlessly before us, for we did not know where they were.

The relayed radio message we had received just forty-nine hours ago had been the last. Since then, there had been only silence. The trawler *Morning Star* had been sending almost continuously in the intervening two days, trying to raise Drift Station Zebra, but out of that bleak desert of ice to the north had come nothing but silence. No word, no signal, no faintest whisper of sound had come out of that desolation.

Eighteen hours before, the Russian atomic-engined *Dvina* had reached the Barrier and had started on an all-out and desperate attempt to smash its way into the heart of the ice cap. In this early stage of winter the ice was neither so thick nor so compacted as it would be at the time of its maximum density, in March, and the very heavily armored and powerfully engined *Dvina* was reputed to be able to break through ice up to a thickness of eighteen feet: given fair conditions, the *Dvina* was widely believed to be capable of battering its way to the North Pole. But the conditions of the rafted ice had proved abnormal to a degree and the attempt a hopeless one. The *Dvina* had managed to crash its way over forty miles into the ice cap before being permanently stopped by a thick wall of rafter ice over twenty feet in height and probably more than a hundred deep. The *Dvina*, according to reports, had sustained heavy damage to its bows and was still in the process of extricating itself, with the greatest difficulty, from the pack. A very gallant effort that had achieved nothing except an improvement in East-West relations to an extent undreamed of for many years.

Nor had the Russians' efforts stopped there. Both they and the Americans had made several flights over the area with front-line long-range bombers. Through the deep overcast and driving ice- and snow-filled winds, those planes had criss-crossed the suspected area a hundred times searching with their fantastically accurate radar. But not one single radar sighting had been reported. Various reasons had been put forward to explain the failure, especially the failure of the Strategic Air Command's B52 bomber whose radar was known to be easily capable of picking out a hut against contrasting background from ten thousand feet and in pitch darkness. It had been suggested that the huts were no longer there:

that the radar's eye was unable to distinguish between an ice-sheathed hut and the thousands of ice hummocks that dot the polar cap in winter: and that they had been searching in the wrong area in the first place. The most probable explanation was that the radar waves had been blurred and deflected by the dense clouds of ice spicules blowing over the area. Whatever the reason, Drift Ice Station Zebra remained as silent as if no life had ever been there, as lost as if it had never existed.

"There's no percentage in staying up here and getting frozen to death." Commander Swanson's voice was a half-shout, it had to be to make him heard. "If we're going under that ice, we might as well go now." He turned his back to the wind and stared out to the west where a big, broad-beamed trawler was rolling heavily and sluggishly in the seas less than a quarter of a mile away. The *Morning Star*, which had closed right up to the edge of the ice pack over the last two days, listening, waiting, and all in vain, was about to return to Hull: her fuel reserves were running low.

"Send them this message," Swanson said to the seaman by his side. " 'We are about to dive and proceed under the ice. We do not expect to emerge for minimum four days, are prepared to remain maximum fourteen.' " He turned to me and said, "If we can't find them in that time—" and left the sentence unfinished.

I nodded, and he went on with the message: " 'Many thanks for your splendid co-operation. Good luck and a safe trip home.' " As the signalman's lamp started chattering out its message, he said wonderingly, "Do those fishermen trawl up in the Arctic the entire winter?"

"They do."

"The whole winter. Fifteen minutes and I'm about dead. Just a bunch of decadent limeys, that's what they are." A lamp aboard the *Morning Star* flickered for some seconds, and Swanson said, "What reply?"

" 'Mind your heads under that ice. Good luck and goodby.' "

"Everybody below," Swanson said. As the signalman began to strip the canvas dodger, I dropped down a ladder into a small compartment beneath, wriggled through a hatch and down a second ladder to the pressure hull of the submarine, another hatch, a third ladder, and then I was on the control deck of the *Dolphin*. Swanson and the signalman followed, then last of all Hansen, who had to close the two heavy water-tight doors above.

Commander Swanson's diving technique would have proved a vast disappointment to those brought up on a diet of movie submarines. No frenzied activity, no tense, steely-eyed men hovering over controls, no dramatic calls of "Dive, dive, dive," no blaring of klaxons. Swanson reached down a steel-spring microphone, said quietly, "This is the captain. We are about to move under the ice. Diving now," hung up and said: "Three hundred feet."

The chief electronics technician leisurely checked the rows of lights indicating all hatches, surface openings, and valves closed to the sea. The disc lights were out; the slot lights burned brightly. Just as leisurely he rechecked them, glanced at Swanson and said, "Straight line shut, sir." Swanson nodded. Air hissed loudly out of the ballast tanks, and that was it. We were on our way. It was about as wildly exciting as watching a man push a wheelbarrow. And there was something oddly reassuring about it all.

Ten minutes later Swanson came up to me. In the past two days I'd come to know Commander Swanson fairly well, like him a lot, and respect him tremendously. The crew had complete and implicit faith in him. I was beginning to have the same thing. He was a kindly, genial man with a vast knowledge of every aspect of submarining, a remarkable eye for detail, an even more remarkably acute mind and an imperturbability that remained absolute under all conditions. Hansen, his executive officer and clearly no respecter of persons, had said flatly that Swanson was the best submarine officer in the Navy. I hoped he was right; that was the kind of man I wanted around in conditions like these.

"We're about to move under the ice now, Dr. Carpenter," he said. "How do you feel about it?"

"I'd feel better if I could see where we were going."

"We can see," he said. "We've got the best eyes in the world aboard the *Dolphin*. We've got eyes that look down, around, ahead, and straight up. Our downward eye is the fathometer, or echo-sounder, which tells us just how deep the water below our keel is and as we have about five thousand feet of water below our keel at this particular spot, we're hardly likely to bump into underwater projections and its use right now is purely a formality. But no responsible navigation officer would ever think of switching it off. We have two sonar eyes for looking around and ahead, one sweeping the ship, another searching out a fifteen-degree path on either side of the bow. Sees everything, hears everything. You drop a wrench on a warship twenty miles away and we know all about it. Fact. Again it seems purely a formality. The sonar is searching for underwater ice stalactites forced down by the pressure of rafted ice above, but in five trips under the ice and two to the Pole, I've never seen under-

39

water stalactites or ridges deeper than two hundred feet, and we're at three hundred feet now. But we still keep them on."

"You might bump into a whale?" I suggested.

"We might bump into another submarine." He wasn't smiling. "And that would be the end of both of us. What with the Russian and our own nuclear submarines busy criss-crossing to and fro across the top of the world, the underside of the polar ice cap is getting more like Times Square every day."

"But surely the chances—"

"What are the chances of mid-air collision to the only two aircraft occupying ten thousand square miles of sky? On paper, they don't exist. There have been three such collisions this year already. So we keep the sonar pinging. But the really important eye, when you're under the ice, is the one that looks up. Come and have a look at it."

He led the way to the after-starboard end of the control room, where Dr. Benson and another man were busy studying a glassed-in eye-level machine that outwardly consisted of a seven-inch-wide moving ribbon of paper and an inked stylus that was tracing a narrow, straight black line along it. Benson was engrossed in adjusting some of the calibrated controls.

"The surface fathometer," Swanson said. "Better known as the ice machine. It's not really Dr. Benson's machine at all, we have two trained operators aboard, but as we see no way of separating him from it without actually court-martialing him, we take the easy way out and let him be." Benson grinned, but his eye didn't leave the line traced out by the stylus. "Same principle as the echo-sounding machine: it just bounces an echo back from the ice—when there is any. That thin black line you see means open water above. When we move under the ice, the stylus has an added vertical motion which not only indicates the presence of ice but also gives us its thickness."

"Ingenious," I said.

"It's more than that. Under the ice it can be life or death for the *Dolphin*. It certainly means life or death for Drift Station Zebra. If we ever get its position, we can't reach it until we break through the ice, and this is the only machine that can tell us where the ice is thinnest."

"No open water at this time of year? No leads?"

" 'Polynyas,' we call them. None. Mind you, the ice pack is never static, not even in winter, and surface-pressure changes can very occasionally tear the ice apart and expose open water. With air temperatures such as you get in winter, you can guess how long the open water stays in a liquid condition. There's a skin of ice on it in five minutes, an inch in an hour, and a foot inside two days. If we get to one of those frozen-over polynyas inside, say, three days, we've got a fair chance of breaking through."

"With the conning tower?"

"That's it. The sail. All new nuclear subs have specially strengthened sails designed for one purpose only: breaking through Arctic ice. Even so we have to go pretty gently as the shock, of course, is transmitted to the pressure hull."

I thought about this for a moment and then said, "What happens to the pressure hull if you come up too fast—as I understand may happen with a sudden change in salinity and sea temperature—and you find out at the last minute that you've drifted away from the indicated area of thin ice and have ten solid feet of the stuff above you?"

"That's it," he said. "Like you say, it's the last minute. Don't even think about such things, much less talk about them: I can't afford to have nightmares on this job." I looked at him closely, but he wasn't smiling any more. He lowered his voice. "I don't honestly think that there is one member of the crew of the *Dolphin* who doesn't get a little bit scared when we move in under the ice. I know I do. I think this is the finest ship in the world, Dr. Carpenter, but there are still a hundred things that can go wrong with it, and if anything happens to the reactor or the steam turbines or the electrical generators, then we're already in our coffin and the lid screwed down. The ice pack above is the coffin lid. In the open sea, most of those things don't matter a damn: we just surface or go to snorkel depth and proceed on our diesels. But for diesels you need air— and there's no air under the ice pack. So if anything happens we either find a polynya to surface in, one chance in ten thousand at this time of year, before our standby battery gives out, or . . . well, that's it."

"This is all very encouraging," I said.

"Isn't it?" He smiled, none too soon for me. "It'll never happen. What's the worthy Benson making all the racket about?"

"Here it is," Benson called. "The first drift block. And another. And another! Come and have a look, Doctor."

I had a look. The stylus, making a faint, soft hissing sound, was no longer tracing out a continuously horizontal line but was moving rapidly up and down across the paper, tracing out the outline of the block of ice passing astern above us. Another thin, straight line, more agitated vertical movements of the stylus, and again another block of ice

41

had gone. Even as I watched, the number of thin, horizontal lines became fewer and fewer and shorter and shorter until eventually they disappeared altogether.

"That's it, then," Swanson nodded. "We'll take her deep now, real deep, and open up all the stops."

When Commander Swanson had said he was going to hurry, he'd meant every word of it. In the early hours of the following morning I was awakened from a deep sleep by a heavy hand on my shoulder. I opened my eyes, blinked against the glare of the overhead light, then saw Lieutenant Hansen.

"Sorry about the beauty sleep, Doc," he said cheerfully. "But this is it."

"This is what?" I said irritably.

"85° 35′ north, 21°20′ east—the last estimated position of Drift Station Zebra. At least, the last estimated position with estimated correction for polar drift."

"Already?" I glanced at my watch, not believing it. "We're there already?"

"We have not," Hansen said modestly, "been idling. The skipper suggests you come along and watch us at work."

"I'll be right with you." When and if the *Dolphin* managed to break through the ice and began to try her one-in-a-million chance of contacting Drift Station Zebra, I wanted to be there.

We left Hansen's cabin and had almost reached the control room when I lurched, staggered, and would have fallen but for a quick grab at a hand rail that ran along one side of the passageway. I hung on grimly as the *Dolphin* banked violently sideways and around like a fighter plane in a tight turn. In my experience, no submarine had ever been able to begin to behave even remotely in that fashion. I understood now the reasons for the safety belts on the diving-control seats.

"What the hell's up?" I said to Hansen. "Avoiding some underwater obstruction ahead?"

"Must be a possible polynya. Some place where the ice is thin, anyway. As soon as we spot a possible like that, we come around like a dog chasing its own tail, just so we don't miss it. It makes us very popular with the crew, especially when they're drinking coffee or soup."

We went into the control room. Commander Swanson, flanked by the navigator and another man, was bent over the plotting table, examining something intently. Farther aft, a man at the surface fathometer was reading out ice-

42

thickness figures in a quiet, unemotional voice. Commander Swanson looked up from the chart.

"Morning, Doctor. John, I think we may have something here."

Hansen crossed to the plot and peered at it. There didn't seem to be much to peer at—a tiny pinpoint of light shining through the glass top of the plot and a squared sheet of chart paper marked by a most unseamanlike series of wavering black lines traced out by a man with a pencil following the track of the tiny moving light. There were three red crosses superimposed on the paper, two very close together, and just as Hansen was examining the paper the crewman manning the ice machine—Dr. Benson's enthusiasm for his toy did not, it appeared, extend to the middle of the night—called out " 'Mark!" Immediately the black pencil was exchanged for a red and a fourth cross made.

" 'Think' and 'may' are just about right, Captain," Hansen said. "It looks awfully narrow to me."

"It looks the same way to me, too," Swanson admitted. "But it's the first break in the heavy ice that we've had in an hour, almost. And the further north we go, the poorer our chances. Let's give it a try. Speed?"

"One knot," Raeburn said.

"All back one third," Swanson said. No sharp imperatives, not ever, in the way Swanson gave his orders, more a quiet and conversational suggestion, but there was no mistaking the speed with which one of the crewmen strapped into the diving-stand bucket seat leaned forward to telegraph the order to the engine room. "Left full rudder."

Swanson bent over to check the plot, closely watching the tiny pinpoint of light and the tracing pencil move back toward the approximate center of the elongated triangle formed by the four red crosses. "All stop," he went on. "Rudder amidships." A pause, then: "All ahead one third. No. All stop."

"Speed zero," Raeburn said.

"Twenty-one twenty feet," Swanson said to the diving officer. "But gently, gently."

A strong, steady hum echoed in the control center. I asked Hansen, "Blowing ballast?"

He shook his head. "Just pumping the stuff out. Gives a far more precise control of rising speed and makes it easier to keep the sub on an even keel. Bringing a stopped sub up on a dead even keel is no trick for beginners. Conventional subs never try this sort of thing."

The pumps stopped. There came the sound of water flood-

43

ing back into the tanks as the diving officer slowed up at the rate of ascent. The sound faded.

"Secure flooding," the diving officer said. "Steady on one hundred feet."

"Up periscope," Swanson said to the crewman by his side. An overhead lever was engaged, and we could hear the hiss of high-pressure oil as the hydraulic piston began to lift the starboard periscope off its seating. The gleaming cylinder rose slowly against the pressure of the water outside until finally the foot of the periscope cleared its well. Swanson opened the hinged hand grips and peered through the eye-piece.

"What does he expect to see in the middle of the night at this depth?" I asked Hansen.

"Never can tell. It's rarely completely dark, as you know. Maybe a moon, maybe only stars, but even starlight will show as a faint glow through the ice—if the ice is thin enough."

"What's the thickness of the ice above, in this rectangle?"

"The sixty-four-dollar question," Hansen admitted, "and the answer is that we don't know. To keep that ice machine to a reasonable size, the graph scale has to be very small. Anything between four and forty inches. Four inches we go through like the icing on a wedding cake: forty inches and we get a very sore head indeed." He nodded across to Swanson. "Doesn't look so good. That grip he's twisting is to tilt the periscope lens upward and that button is for focusing. Means he's having trouble in finding anything."

Swanson straightened. "Black as the earl of hell's waistcoat," he said conversationally. "Switch on hull and sail floodlights."

He stooped and looked again. For a few seconds only. "Pea soup. Thick and yellow and strong. Can't see a thing. Let's have the camera, shall we?"

I looked at Hansen, who nodded to a white screen that had just been unshuttered on the opposite bulkhead. "All mod cons, Doc. Closed-circuit TV. Camera is deck mounted under toughened glass and can be remote-controlled to look up or around."

"You could do with a new camera, couldn't you?" The TV screen was gray, fuzzy, featureless.

"Best that money can buy," Hansen said. "It's the water. Under certain conditions of temperature and salinity, it becomes almost completely opaque when flood-lit. Like driving into a heavy fog with your headlights full on."

"Floodlights off," Swanson said. The screen became quite

44

blank. "Floodlights on." The same drifting, misty gray as before. Swanson sighed and turned to Hansen. "Well, John?"

"If I were paid for imagining things," Hansen said carefully, "I could imagine I see the top of the sail in that left corner. Pretty murky out there, Captain. Blindman's buff, is that it?"

"Russian roulette, I prefer to call it." Swanson had the clear, unworried face of a man contemplating a Sunday afternoon in a deck chair. "Are we holding position?"

"I don't know." Raeburn looked up from the plot. "It's difficult to be sure."

"Sanders?" This to the man at the ice machine.

"Thin ice, sir. Still thin ice."

"Keep calling. Down periscope." He folded the handles up and turned to the diving officer. "Take her up like we were carrying a crate of eggs atop the sail and didn't want to crack even one of them."

The pumps started again. I looked around the control room. Swanson excepted, everyone was quiet and still and keyed-up. Raeburn's face was beaded with sweat, and Sanders' voice was too calm and impersonal by half as he kept repeating, "Thin ice, thin ice" in a low monotone. You could reach out and touch the tension in the air. I said quietly to Hansen, "Nobody seems very happy. There's still a hundred feet to go."

"There's forty feet," Hansen said shortly. "Readings are taken from keel level, and there's sixty feet between the keel and the top of the sail. Forty feet minus the thickness of the ice—and maybe a razor-sharp or needle-pointed stalactite sticking down ready to skewer the *Dolphin* through the middle. You know what that means?"

"That it's time I started getting worried too?"

Hansen smiled, but he wasn't feeling like smiling. Neither was I, not any more.

"Ninety feet," the diving officer said.

"Thin ice, thin ice," Sanders intoned.

"Switch off the deck flood, leave the sail flood on," Swanson said. "And keep that camera moving. Sonar?"

"All clear," the sonar operator reported. "All clear all around." A pause then: "No, hold it, hold it! Contact dead astern!"

"How close?" Swanson asked quickly.

"Too close to say. Very close."

"She's jumping!" the diving officer called out sharply. "Eighty, seventy-five." The *Dolphin* had hit a layer of colder water or extra salinity.

"Heavy ice, heavy ice!" Sanders called out urgently.

45

"Flood emergency!" Swanson ordered—and this time it was an order.

I felt the sudden build-up of air pressure as the diving officer vented the negative tank and tons of seawater poured into the emergency diving tank. But it was too late. With a shuddering, jarring smash that sent us staggering, the *Dolphin* crashed violently into the ice above, glass tinkled, lights went out and the submarine started falling like a stone.

"Blow negative to the mark!" the diving officer called. High-pressure air came boiling into the negative tank; at our rate of falling, we would have been flattened by the sea pressure before the pumps could even have begun to cope with the huge extra ballast load we had taken aboard in seconds. Two hundred feet, two hundred and fifty, and we were still falling. Nobody spoke; everybody just stood or sat in a frozen position staring at the diving stand. It required no gift for telepathy to know the thought in every mind. It was obvious that the *Dolphin* had been struck aft by some underwater pressure ridge at the same instant as the sail had hit the heavy ice above. If the *Dolphin* had been holed aft, this descent wasn't going to stop until the pressure of a million tons of water crushed and flattened the hull and in a flicker of time snuffed out the life of every man inside it.

"Three hundred feet," the diving officer called out. "Three fifty—and she's slowing. She's slowing."

The *Dolphin* was still falling, sluggishly passing the four hundred-foot mark, when Rawlings appeared in the control room, tool kit in one hand, a crate of assorted lamps in the other.

"It's unnatural," he said. He appeared to be addressing the shattered lamp above the plot which he had immediately begun to repair. "Contrary to the laws of nature, I've always maintained. Mankind was never meant to probe beneath the depths of the ocean. Mark my words, these newfangled inventions will come to a bad end."

"So will you if you don't keep quiet," Commander Swanson said acidly. But there was no reprimand in his face; he appreciated as well as any of us the therapeutic breath of fresh air that Rawlings had brought into that tension-laden atmosphere. "Holding?" he said to the diving officer.

The diving officer raised a finger and grinned. Swanson nodded and swung the coiled-spring microphone in front of him. "Captain speaking," he said calmly. "Sorry about that bump. Report damage at once."

A green light flashed in the panel of a box beside him.

Swanson touched a switch and a loud-speaker in the deck-head crackled.

"Maneuvering room." The maneuvering room was in the after end of the upper-level engine room, toward the stern. "Hit was directly above us here. We could do with a box of candles, and some of the dials and gauges are out of kilter. But we still got a roof over our heads."

"Thank you, Lieutenant. You can cope?"

"Sure we can."

Swanson pressed another switch. "Stern room?"

"We still attached to the ship?" a cautious voice inquired.

"You're still attached to the ship," Swanson assured him. "Anything to report?"

"Only that there's going to be an awful lot of dirty laundry by the time we get back to Scotland. The washing machine's had a kind of fit."

Swanson smiled and switched off. His face was untroubled; he must have had a special sweat-absorbing mechanism on his face. I felt I could have done with a bath towel. He said to Hansen, "That was bad luck. A combination of a current where a current had no right to be, a temperature inversion where a temperature inversion had no right to be, and a pressure ridge where we least expected it. Not to mention the damned opacity of the water. What's required is a few circuits until we know this polynya like the backs of our hands, a small off-set to allow for drift and a little precautionary flooding as we approach the ninety-foot mark."

"Yes, sir. That's what's required. Point is, what are we going to do?"

"Just that. Take her up and try again."

I had my pride so I refrained from mopping my brow. They took her up and tried again. At two hundred feet and for fifteen minutes Swanson juggled propellers and rudder until he had the outline of the frozen polynya above as accurately limned on the plot as he could ever expect to have it. Then he positioned the *Dolphin* just outside one of the boundary lines and gave an order for a slow ascent.

"One hundred twenty feet," the diving officer said. "One hundred ten."

"Heavy ice," Saunders intoned. "Still heavy ice."

Sluggishly the *Dolphin* continued to rise. Next time in the control room, I promised myself, I wouldn't forget that bath towel. Swanson said, "If we've overestimated the speed of the drift, there's going to be another bump, I'm afraid." He turned to Rawlings, who was still repairing lights. "If I were you, I'd suspend operations for the present. You may have

47

to start all over again in a moment, and we don't carry all that number of spares aboard."

"One hundred feet," the diving officer said. He didn't sound as unhappy as his face looked.

"The water's clearing," Hansen said suddenly. "Look."

The water had cleared, not dramatically so, but enough. We could see the top corner of the sail clearly outlined on the TV screen. And then, suddenly, we could see something else again, heavy, ugly ridged ice not a dozen feet above the sail.

Water flooded into the tanks. The diving officer didn't have be to told what to do: we'd gone up like an express elevator the first time we'd hit a different water layer, and once like that was enough in the life of any submarine.

"Ninety feet," he reported. "Still rising." More water flooded in, and then the sound died away. "She's holding. Just under ninety feet."

"Keep her there." Swanson stared at the TV screen. "We're drifting clear and into the polynya—I hope."

"Me too," Hansen said. "There can't be more than a couple of feet between the top of the sail and that damned ugly stuff."

"There isn't much room," Swanson acknowledged. "Sanders?"

"Just a moment, sir. The graph looks kinda funny— No, we're clear." He couldn't keep the excitement out of his voice. "Thin ice!"

I looked at the screen. He was right. I could see the vertical edge of a wall of ice move slowly across the screen, exposing clear water above.

"Gently, now, gently," Swanson said. "And keep that camera on the ice wall at the side, then straight up, turn about."

The pumps began to throb again. The ice wall, less than ten yards away, began to drift slowly down past us.

"Eighty-five feet," the diving officer reported. "Eighty."

"No hurry," Swanson said. "We're sheltered from that drift by now."

"Seventy-five feet." The pumps stopped, and water began to flood into the tanks. "Seventy." The *Dolphin* was almost stopped now, drifting upward as gently as thistledown. The camera switched upward, and we could see the top corner of the sail clearly outlined with a smooth ceiling of ice floating down to meet it. More water gurgled into the tanks, the top of the sail met the ice with a barely perceptible bump, and the *Dolphin* came to rest.

"Beautifully done," Swanson said warmly to the diving officer. "Let's try giving that ice a nudge. Are we slewing?"

"Bearing constant."

Swanson nodded. The pumps hummed, poured out water, lightening ship, steadily increasing positive buoyancy. The ice stayed where it was. More time passed, more water pumped out, and still nothing happened. I said softly to Hansen, "Why doesn't he blow the main ballast? You'd get a few hundred tons of positive buoyancy in next to no time, and even if that ice is forty inches thick, it couldn't survive all that pressure at a concentrated point."

"Neither could the *Dolphin*," Hansen said grimly. "With a suddenly induced big positive buoyancy like that, once she broke through, she'd go up like a cork from a champagne bottle. The pressure hull might take it, I don't know, but sure as little apples the rudder would be squashed as flat as a piece of tin. Do you want to spend what little's left of your life traveling in steadily decreasing circles under the polar ice cap?"

I didn't want to spend what little was left of my life in traveling in steadily decreasing circles under the ice cap, so I kept quiet. I watched Swanson as he walked across to the diving stand and studied the banked dials in silence for some seconds. I was beginning to become a little apprehensive about what Swanson would do next. I was beginning to realize, and not slowly, either, that he was a man who didn't give up very easily.

"That's enough of that," he said to the diving officer. "If we go through now with all this pressure behind us, we'll be airborne. This ice is even thicker than we thought. We've tried the long, steady shove and it hasn't worked. A sharp tap is obviously what is needed. Flood her down, but gently, to eighty feet or so. A good sharp whiff of air into the ballast tanks, and we'll give our well-known imitation of a bull at a gate."

Whoever had installed the 240-ton air-conditioning unit in the *Dolphin* should have been prosecuted; it just wasn't working any more. The air was very hot and stuffy—what little there was of it, that was. I looked around cautiously and saw that everyone else appeared to be suffering from this same shortage of air, all except Swanson, who seemed to carry his own built-in oxygen cylinder around with him. I hoped Swanson was keeping in mind the fact that the *Dolphin* cost 120 million dollars to build. Hansen's narrowed eyes held a definite core of worry, and even the usually imperturbable Rawlings was rubbing a bristly blue chin with a hand the size and shape of a shovel. In the deep silence after Swanson had finished speaking the scraping noise

49

sounded unusually loud, then was lost in the noise of water flooding into the tanks.

We stared at the screen. Water continued to pour into the tanks until we could see a gap appear between the top of the sail and the ice. The pumps started up, slowly, to control the speed of descent. On the screen, the cone of light thrown on to the underside of the ice by the floodlight grew fainter and larger as we dropped, then remained stationary, neither moving nor growing in size. We had stopped.

"Now," said Swanson. "Before that current gets us again."

There came the hissing roar of compressed air under high pressure entering the ballast tanks. The *Dolphin* started to move sluggishly upward while we watched the cone of light on the ice slowly narrow and brighten.

"More air," Swanson said.

We were rising faster now, closing the gap to the ice all too quickly for my liking. Fifteen feet, twelve feet, ten feet.

"More air," Swanson said.

I braced myself, one hand on the plot, the other on an overhead grab bar. On the screen, the ice was rushing down to meet us. Suddenly the picture quivered and danced, the *Dolphin* shuddered, jarred, and echoed hollowly along its length, more lights went out, the picture came back on the screen, the sail was still lodged below the ice, then the *Dolphin* trembled and lurched and the deck pressed against our feet like an ascending elevator. The sail on the TV vanished, nothing but opaque white taking its place. The diving officer, his voice high with strain that had not yet found relief, called out, "Forty feet, forty feet." We had broken through.

"There you are, now," Swanson said mildly. "All it needed was a little perseverance." I looked at the short, plump figure, the round, good-humored face, and wondered for the hundredth time why the nerveless iron men of this world so very seldom look the part.

I let my pride have a holiday. I took my handkerchief from my pocket, wiped my face, and said to Swanson, "Does this sort of thing go on all the time?"

"Fortunately, perhaps, no," he smiled. He turned to the diving officer. "We've got our foothold on this rock. Let's make sure we have a good belay."

For a few seconds, more compressed air was bled into the tanks, then the diving officer said: "No chance of her dropping down now, Captain."

"Up periscope."

Again the long, gleaming silver tube hissed up from its

50

well. Swanson didn't even bother folding down the hinged handles. He peered briefly into the eyepiece, then straightened. "Down periscope."

"Pretty cold up top?" Hansen asked.

Swanson nodded. "Water on the lens must have frozen solid as soon as it hit that air. Can't see a thing." He turned to the diving officer. "Steady at forty?"

"Guaranteed. And all the buoyancy we'll ever want."

"Fair enough." Swanson looked at the quartermaster, who was shrugging his way into a heavy sheepskin coat. "How about a little fresh air, Ellis?"

"Right away, sir." Ellis buttoned his coat and added: "Might take some time."

"I don't think so," Swanson said. "You may find the bridge and hatchways jammed with broken ice but I doubt it. My guess is that that ice is so thick that it will have fractured into very large sections and fallen outside clear of the bridge."

I felt my ears pop with the sudden pressure change as the hatch swung up and open and snapped back against its standing latch. Another, more distant sound as the second hatch cover locked open, and then we heard Ellis on the voice tube.

"All clear up top."

"Raise the antennae," Swanson said. "John, have them start transmitting and keep transmitting until their fingers fall off. Here we are and here we stay—until we raise Drift Ice Station Zebra."

"If there's anyone left alive there," I said.

"There's that, of course," Swanson said. He couldn't look at me. "There's always that."

4

THIS, I THOUGHT, death's dreadful conception of a dreadful world, must have been what had chilled the hearts and souls of our far-off Nordic ancestors when life's last tide slowly ebbed and they had tortured their failing minds with fearful imaginings of a bleak and bitter hell of eternal cold. But it had been all right for the old boys, all they had to do was imagine it, we had to experience the reality of it, and I had no doubt at all in my mind as to which was easier. The latter-day Eastern conception of hell was altogether more comfortable, at least a man could keep reasonably warm there.

One thing sure, nobody could keep reasonably warm where Rawlings and I were, standing a half-hour watch on the bridge of the *Dolphin* and slowly freezing solid. It had been my own fault entirely that our teeth were chattering like frenzied castanets. Half an hour after the radio room had started transmitting on Drift Ice Station Zebra's wave length and all without the slightest whisper by way of reply or acknowledgment, I had suggested to Commander Swanson that Zebra might possibly be able to hear us without having sufficient power to send a reply but that they might just conceivably let us have an acknowledgment some other way. I'd pointed out that drift stations habitually carried rockets—the only way to guide home any lost members of the party if radio communication broke down—and radio sondes and rockoons. The sondes were radio-carrying balloons that could rise to a height of twenty miles to gather weather information; the rockoons, radio rockets fired from balloons, could rise even higher. On a moonlit night such as this, those balloons, if released, would be visible at least twenty miles away: if flares were attached to them, at twice that distance. Swanson had seen my point, called for volunteers for the first watch, and in the circumstances I hadn't had much choice. Rawlings had offered to accompany me.

It was a landscape—if such a bleak, barren, and featureless desolation could be called a landscape—from another and ancient world, weird and strange and oddly frightening. There were no clouds in the sky, but there were no stars, either: this I could not understand. Low on the southern horizon a milky, misty moon shed its mysterious light over the dark lifelessness of the polar ice cap. Dark, not white. One would have expected moonlit ice to shine and sparkle and glitter with the light of a million crystal chandeliers: but it was dark. The moon was so low in the sky that the dominating color on the ice cap came from the blackness of the long shadows cast by the fantastically ridged and hummocked ice; and where the moon did strike directly, the ice had been so scoured and abraded by the assaults of a thousand ice storms that it had lost almost all its ability to reflect light of any kind.

This ridged and hummocked ice cap had a strange quality of elusiveness, of impermanence, of evanescence: one moment there, definitively hard and harsh and repellent in its coldly contrasting blacks and whites; the next, ghost-like, blurring coalescing and finally vanishing like a shimmering mirage fading and dying in some ice-bound desert. But this was no trick of the eye or imagination; it was the result of a ground-level ice storm that rose and swirled and subsided at the dictates of an icy wind that was never less than strong and sometimes gusted up to gale force, a wind that drove before it a swirling rushing fog of billions of needle-pointed ice spicules. For the most part, standing as we were on the bridge twenty feet above the level of the ice—the rest of the *Dolphin* might never have existed, as far as the eye could tell—we were above this billowing ground swell of ice particles—but occasionally the wind gusted strongly, and the spicules lifted, drummed demoniacally against the already ice-sheathed starboard side of the sail, drove against the few exposed inches of our skin with all the painfully stinging impact of a sand blaster held at arm's length. But, unlike a sand blaster, the pain-filled shock of those spear-tipped spicules was only momentary; each wasp-like sting carried with it its own ice-cold anesthetic, and all surface sensation was quickly lost. Then the wind would drop, the furious rattling on the sail would fade and in the momentary contrast of near-silence we could hear the stealthy rustling as of a million rats advancing as the ice spicules brushed their blind way across the iron-hard surface of the polar cap. The bridge thermometer stood at —21°F. —53° of frost. If I were a promoter interested in developing a summer holiday resort, I thought, I wouldn't pay very much attention to this place.

Rawlings and I stamped our feet, flailed our arms across our chests, shivered non-stop, took what little shelter we could from the canvas wind-break, rubbed our goggles constantly to keep them clear, and never once, except when the ice spicules drove into our faces, stopped examining every quarter of the horizon. Somewhere out there on those frozen wastes was a lost and dying group of men whose lives might depend upon so little a thing as the momentary misting-up of our goggles. We stared out over those shifting ice sands until our eyes ached. But that was all we had for it: just aching eyes. We saw nothing, nothing at all. The ice cap remained empty of all signs of life. Dead.

When our relief came, Rawlings and I got below with all the speed our frozen and stiffened limbs would allow. I found Commander Swanson sitting on a canvas stool outside the radio room. I stripped off outer clothes, face coverings, and goggles, took a steaming mug of coffee that had appeared from nowhere, and tried not to hop around too much as the blood came pounding back into my arms and legs.

"How did you cut yourself like that?" Swanson asked, concern in his voice. "You've a half-inch streak of blood right across your forehead."

"Flying ice, it just looks bad." I felt tired and pretty low. "We're wasting our time transmitting. If the men on Zebra were without any shelter, it's no wonder all signals ceased long ago. Without food and shelter, no one could last more than a few hours in that place. Neither Rawlings nor I is a wilting hot-house flower but after half an hour up there we've both just about had it."

"I don't know," Swanson said thoughtfully. "Look at Amundsen. Look at Scott, at Peary. They *walked* all the way to the Poles."

"A different breed of men, Captain. Either that or the sun shone for them. All I know is that half an hour is too long to be up there. Fifteen minutes is enough for anyone."

"Fifteen minutes it shall be." He looked at me, his face carefully devoid of all expression. "You haven't much hope?"

"If they're without shelter, I've none."

"You told me they had an emergency power pack of Nife cells for powering their transmitter," he murmured. "You also said those batteries will retain their charge indefinitely—years, if necessary—irrespective of the weather conditions under which they are stored. They must have been using that battery a few days ago when they sent out their first S.O.S. It wouldn't be finished already."

His point was so obvious that I didn't answer. The battery wasn't finished; the men were.

"I agree with you," he went on quietly. "We're wasting our time. Maybe we should just pack up and go home. If we can't raise them, we'll never find them."

"Maybe not. But you're forgetting your directive from Washington, Commander."

"How do you mean?"

"Remember? I'm to be extended every facility and all aid short of actually endangering the safety of the submarine and the lives of the crew. At the present moment we're doing neither. If we fail to raise them, I'm prepared for a twenty-mile sweep on foot around this spot in the hope of locating them. If that fails, we could move to another polynya and repeat the search. The search area isn't all that big, there's a fair chance, but a chance, that we might locate the station eventually. I'm prepared to stay up here all winter till we do find them."

"You don't call that endangering the lives of my men? Making extended searches of the ice cap, on foot, in mid-winter?"

"Nobody said anything about endangering the lives of your men."

"You mean—you mean you'd go it alone?" Swanson stared down at the deck and shook his head. "I don't know what to think. I don't know whether to say you're crazy or whether to say I'm beginning to understand why they—whoever 'they' may be—picked you for the job, Dr. Carpenter." He sighed, then regarded me thoughtfully. "One moment you say there's no hope, the next that you're prepared to spend the winter here, searching. If you don't mind my saying so, Doctor, it just doesn't make sense."

"Stiff-necked pride," I said. "I don't like throwing my hand in on a job before I've even started it. I don't know what the attitude of the U. S. Navy is on that sort of thing."

He gave me another speculative glance; I could see that he believed me the way a fly believes the spider on the web who has just offered him safe accommodation for the night. He smiled. He said: "The U. S. Navy doesn't take offense all that easily, Dr. Carpenter. I suggest you catch a couple of hours' sleep while you can. You'll need it if you're going to start walking toward the North Pole."

"How about yourself? You haven't been to bed at all tonight."

"I think I'll wait a while." He nodded toward the door of the radio room. "Just in case anything comes through."

"What are they sending? Just the call sign?"

55

"Plus request for position and a rocket, if they have either. I'll let you know immediately anything comes through. Good night, Dr. Carpenter. Or, rather, good morning."

I rose heavily and made my way to Hansen's cabin.

The atmosphere around the 8:00 a.m. breakfast table in the wardroom was less than festive. Apart from the officer on deck and the engineer lieutenant on watch, all the *Dolphin*'s officers were there, some just risen from their bunks, some just heading for them, none of them talking in anything more than monosyllables. Even the ebullient Dr. Benson was remote and withdrawn. It seemed pointless to ask whether any contact had been established with Drift Station Zebra; it was painfully obvious that it hadn't. And that after almost five hours of continuous sending. The sense of despondency and defeat, the unspoken knowledge that time had run out for the survivors of Drift Station Zebra hung heavy over the wardroom.

No one hurried over his meal—there was nothing to hurry for—but by and by they rose one by one and drifted off, Dr. Benson to his sick-bay call, the young torpedo officer, Lieutenant Mills, to supervise the efforts of his men who had been working twelve hours a day for the past two days to iron out the faults in the suspect torpedoes, a third to relieve Hansen, who had the watch, and three others to their bunks. That left only Swanson, Raeburn and myself. Swanson, I knew, hadn't been to bed at all the previous night, but for all that he had the rested, clear-eyed look of a man with eight solid hours behind him.

The steward, Henry, had just brought in a fresh pot of coffee when we heard the sound of running footsteps in the passageway outside and the quartermaster burst into the wardroom. He didn't quite manage to take the door off its hinges, but that was only because the Electric Boat Company put good, solid hinges on the doors of their submarines.

"We got it made!" he shouted, and then, perhaps recollecting that enlisted men were expected to conduct themselves with rather more decorum in the wardroom, "We've raised them, Captain, we've raised them!"

"What!" Swanson could move twice as fast as his comfortable figure suggested, and he was already half out of his chair.

"We are in radio contact with Drift Ice Station Zebra, sir," Ellis said formally.

Commander Swanson got to the radio room first, but only because he had a head start on Raeburn and myself. Two operators were on watch, both leaning forward toward their transmitters, one with his head bent low, the other with his cocked to one side, as if those attitudes of concentrated listening helped them to isolate and amplify the slightest sound coming through the earphones clamped to their heads. One of them was scribbling away mechanically on a message pad. "DSY," he was writing down, *"DSY"* repeated over and over and over again. DSY. The answering call sign of Drift Station Zebra. He stopped writing as he caught sight of Swanson out of the corner of his eye.

"We've got 'em, Captain, no question. Signal very weak and intermittent, but—"

"Never mind the signal!" It was Raeburn who made this interruption without any by-your-leave from Swanson. He tried, and failed, to keep the rising note of excitement out of his voice, and he looked more than ever like a youngster playing hooky from high school. "The bearing? Have you got their bearing? That's all that matters."

The other operator swiveled in his seat, and I recognized my erstwhile guard, Zabrinski. He fixed Raeburn with a sad and reproachful eye.

"Course we got their bearing, Lieutenant. First thing we did. Oh forty-five, give or take a whisker. Northeast, that is."

"Thank you, Zabrinski," Swanson said dryly. "Oh forty-five is northeast. The navigating officer and I wouldn't have known. Position?"

Zabrinski shrugged and turned to his watchmate, a man with a red face, leather neck and a shining, polished dome where his hair ought to have been. "What's the word, Curly?"

"Nothing. Just nothing." Curly looked at Swanson. "Twenty times I've asked for his position. No good. All he does is send out his call sign. I don't think he's hearing us at all, he doesn't even know we're listening, he just keeps sending his call sign over and over again. Maybe he hasn't switched his aerial in to receive."

"It isn't possible," Swanson said.

"It is with this guy," Zabrinski said. "At first Curly and I thought it was the signal that was weak, then we thought it was the operator who was weak or sick, but we were wrong: he's just a ham-handed amateur."

"You can tell?" Swanson asked.

"You can always tell. You can—" he broke off, stiffened and touched his watchmate's arm.

Curly nodded. "I got it," he said matter-of-factly. "Position unknown, the man says."

Nobody said anything, not just then. It didn't seem important that he couldn't give us his position; all that mattered was that we were in direct contact. Raeburn turned and ran forward across the control room. I could hear him speaking rapidly on the bridge telephone. Swanson turned to me.

"Those balloons you spoke of earlier. The ones on Zebra. Are they free or captive?"

"Both."

"How do the captive ones work?"

"A free-running winch, nylon cord marked off in hundreds and thousands of feet."

"We'll ask them to send a captive balloon up to five thousand feet," Swanson decided. "With flares. If they're within thirty or forty miles, we ought to see it, and if we get its elevation and make an allowance for the effect of wind on it, we should get a fair estimate of distance.... What is it, Brown?" This to the man Zabrinski called "Curly."

"They're sending again," Curly said. "Very broken, fades a lot. 'God's sake hurry.' Just like that, twice over. 'God's sake hurry.'"

"Send this," Swanson said. He dictated a brief message about the balloons. "And send it real slow."

Curly nodded and began to transmit. Raeburn came running back into the radio room.

"The moon's not down yet," he said quickly to Swanson. "Still a degree or two above the horizon. I'm taking a sextant up top and taking a moon-sight. Ask them to do the same. That'll give us the latitude difference, and if we know they're oh forty-five of us, we can pin them down to a mile."

"It's worth trying," Swanson said. He dictated another message to Brown. Brown transmitted the second message immediately after the first. We waited for the answer. For all of ten minutes we waited. I looked at the men in the radio room: they all had the same remote, withdrawn look of men who are there only physically, men whose minds are many miles away. They were all at the same place and I was too, wherever Drift Ice Station Zebra was.

Brown started writing again, not for long. His voice this time was still matter-of-fact but with overtones of emptiness. He said, "'All balloons burned. No moon.'"

"'No moon.'" Raeburn couldn't hide the bitterness, the sharpness of his disappointment. "Damn! Must be pretty heavy overcast up there. Or a bad storm."

"No," I said. "You don't get local weather variations like that on the ice cap. The conditions will be the same over fifty thousand square miles. The moon is down. For them, the moon is down. Their latest estimated position must have been pure guesswork, and bad guesswork at that. They must be at least a hundred miles farther north and east than we had thought."

"Ask them if they have any rockets," Swanson said to Brown.

"You can try," I said. "It'll be a waste of time. If they're as far off as I think, their rockets would never get above our horizon. Even if they did, we wouldn't see them."

"It's always a chance, isn't it?" Swanson asked.

"Beginning to lose contact, sir," Brown reported. "Something there about food but it faded right out."

"Tell them if they have any rockets to fire them at once," Swanson said. "Quickly, now, before you lose contact."

Four times in all Brown sent the message before he managed to pick up a reply. Then he said: "Message reads 'Two minutes.' Either this guy is pretty far gone or his transmitter batteries are. That's all. 'Two minutes,' he said."

Swanson nodded wordlessly and left the room. I followed. We picked up coats and binoculars and clambered up to the bridge. After the warmth and comfort of the control room, the cold seemed glacial, the flying ice spicules more lancet-like than ever. Swanson uncapped the gyro-repeater compass, gave us the line of 045, and told the two men who had been keeping watch what to look for and where.

A minute passed, two minutes, five. My eyes began to ache from staring into the ice-filled dark; the exposed part of my face had gone completely numb, and I knew that when I removed those binoculars I was going to take a fair amount of skin with them.

A phone bell rang. Swanson lowered his glasses, leaving two peeled and bloody rings around his eyes—he seemed unaware of it; the pain wouldn't come until later—and picked up the receiver. He listened briefly, hung up.

"Radio room," he said. "Let's get below. All of us. The rockets were fired three minutes ago."

We went below. Swanson caught sight of his face reflected in a glass gauge and shook his head. "They must have shelter," he said quietly. "They must. Some hut left. Or they would have been gone long ago." He went into the radio room. "Still in contact?"

"Yeah." It was Zabrinski. "Off and on. It's a funny thing. When a bum contact like this starts to fade, it usually gets lost and stays lost. But this guy keeps coming back. Funny."

"Maybe he hasn't even got batteries left," I said. "Maybe all they have is a hand-cranked generator. Maybe there's no one left with the strength to crank it for more than a few moments at a time."

"Maybe," Zabrinski agreed. "Tell the captain that last message, Curly."

59

" 'Can't late many tours,' " Brown said. "That's how the message came through. 'Can't late many tours.' I think it should read 'Can't last many hours.' Don't see what else it could have been."

Swanson looked at me briefly, and glanced away again. I hadn't told anyone else that the commandant of the base was my brother and I knew he hadn't told anyone, either. He said to Brown: "Give them a time check. Ask them to send their call signs five minutes every hour on the hour. Tell them we'll contact them again within six hours at the most, maybe only four. Zabrinski, how accurate was that bearing?"

"Dead accurate, Captain. I've had plenty of rechecks. Oh forty-five exactly."

Swanson moved out into the control center. "Drift Station Zebra can't see the moon. If we take Dr. Carpenter's word for it that weather conditions are pretty much the same all over, that's because the moon is below their horizon. With the elevation we have of the moon, and knowing their bearing, what's Zebra's minimum distance from us?"

"A hundred miles, as Dr. Carpenter said," Raeburn confirmed after a short calculation. "At least that."

"So. We leave here and take a course oh forty. Not enough to take us very far from their general direction, but it will give us enough off-set to take a good cross-bearing eventually. We will go exactly a hundred miles and try for another polynya. Call the executive officer, secure for diving." He smiled at me. "With two cross-bearings and an accurately measured base line, we can pin them down to a hundred yards."

"How do you intend to measure a hundred miles under the ice? Accurately, I mean?"

"Our inertial-navigation computer does it for me. It's very accurate: you wouldn't believe just how accurate. I can dive the *Dolphin* off the eastern coast of the United States and surface again in the eastern Mediterranean within five hundred yards of where I expect to be. Over a hundred miles I don't expect to be twenty yards out."

Radio aerials were lowered, hatches screwed down, and within five minutes the *Dolphin* had dropped down from her hole in the ice and was on her way. The two helmsmen at the diving stand sat idly smoking, doing nothing: the steering controls were in automatic interlock with the inertial-navigation system, which steered the ship with a degree of accuracy and sensitivity impossible to human hands. For the first time I could feel a heavy jarring vibration rumbling throughout the length of the ship. "Can't last many hours," the message had said. The *Dolphin* was under full power.

I didn't leave the control room that morning. I spent most

60

of the time peering over the shoulder of Dr. Benson, who had passed his usual five minutes in the sick bay waiting for the patients who never turned up and then had hurried to his seat by the ice machine. The readings on that machine meant living or dying to the Zebra survivors. We had to find another polynya to surface in to get a cross-bearing on Zebra's position: no polynya, no cross-bearing; no cross-bearing, no hope. I wondered for the hundredth time how many of the survivors of the fire were still alive. From the quiet desperation of the few garbled messages that Brown and Zabrinski had managed to pick up, I couldn't see that there would be many.

The pattern traced out by the hissing stylus on the chart was hardly an encouraging sight. Most of the time it showed the ice overhead to be of a thickness of ten feet or more. Several times the stylus dipped to show thicknesses of thirty to forty feet, and once it dipped down almost clear of the paper, showing a tremendous inverted ridge of at least 150 feet in depth. I tried to imagine what kind of fantastic pressures created by piled-up log jams of rafted ice on the surface must have been necessary to force ice down to such a depth; but I just didn't have the imagination to cope with that sort of thing.

Only twice in the first eighty miles did the stylus trace out the thin black line that meant thin ice overhead. The first of those polynyas might have accommodated a small row boat, but it would certainly never have looked at the *Dolphin;* the other had hardly been any bigger.

Shortly before noon the hull vibration died away as Swanson gave the order for a cut-back to a slow cruising speed. He said to Benson, "How does it look?"

"Terrible. Heavy ice all the way."

"Well, we can't expect a polynya to fall into our laps right away," Swanson said reasonably. "We're almost there. We'll make a grid search. Five miles east, five miles west, a quarter mile farther to the north each time."

The search began. An hour passed, two, then three. Raeburn and his assistant hardly ever raised their heads from the plotting table, where they were meticulously tracing every movement the *Dolphin* was making in her criss-cross search under the sea. Four o'clock in the afternoon. The normal background buzz of conversation, the occasional small talk from various groups in the control center, died away completely. Benson's occasional "Heavy ice, still heavy ice," growing steadily quieter and more dispirited, served only to emphasize and deepen the heavy, brooding silence that had fallen. Only a case-hardened undertaker could have felt perfectly at home in that atmosphere. At the moment, undertakers were the last people I wanted to think about.

Five o'clock in the afternoon. People weren't looking at each other any more, much less talking. Heavy ice, still heavy ice. Defeat, despair hung heavy in the air. Heavy ice, still heavy ice. Even Swanson had stopped smiling. I wondered if he had in his mind's eye what I now constantly had in mine: the picture of a haggard, emaciated, bearded man with his face all but destroyed with frostbite, a frozen, starving, dying man draining away the last few ounces of his exhausted strength as he cranked the handle of his generator and tapped out his call sign with lifeless fingers, his head bowed as he strained to listen above the howl of the ice storm for the promise of aid that never came. Or maybe there was no one tapping out a call sign any more. They were no ordinary men who had been sent to man Drift Ice Station Zebra, but there comes a time when even the toughest, the bravest, the most enduring will abandon all hope and lie down to die. Perhaps he had already lain down to die. Heavy ice, still heavy ice.

At half-past five Commander Swanson walked across to the ice machine and peered over Benson's shoulder. He said, "What's the average thickness of that stuff above?"

"Twelve to fifteen feet," Benson said. His voice was low and tired. "Nearer fifteen, I would say."

Swanson picked up a phone. "Lieutenant Mills? Captain here. What is the state of readiness of those torpedoes you're working on? Four? Ready to go? Good. Stand by to load. I'm giving this search another thirty minutes, then it's up to you. Yes, that is correct. We shall attempt to blow a hole through the ice." He replaced the phone.

Hansen said thoughtfully, "Fifteen feet of ice is a helluva lot of ice. And that ice will have a tamping effect and will direct ninety per cent of the explosive force down the way. You think we *can* blow a hole through fifteen feet of ice, Captain?"

"I've no idea," Swanson admitted. "How can anyone know until we try it?"

"Nobody ever tried to do this before?" I asked.

"No. Not in the U.S. Navy, anyway. The Russians may have tried it, I wouldn't know. They don't," he added dryly, "keep us very well informed on those matters."

"Aren't the underwater shock waves liable to damage the *Dolphin?*" I asked. I didn't care for the idea at all, and that was a fact.

"If they do, the Electric Boat Company can expect a pretty strong letter of complaint. We shall explode the warhead electronically about a thousand yards after it leaves the ship: it has to travel eight hundred yards anyway before a safety device unlocks and permits the warhead to be armed. We shall be bows on to the detonation, and with a hull designed to withstand the pressures this one is, the shock effects should be negligible."

"Very heavy ice," Benson intoned. "Thirty feet, forty feet, fifty feet. Very, very heavy ice."

"Just too bad if your torpedo ended up under a pile like the stuff above us just now," I said. "I doubt if it would even chip off the bottom layer."

"We'll take care that doesn't happen. We'll just find a suitably large layer of ice of normal thickness, kind of back off a thousand yards, and then let go."

"Thin ice!" Benson's voice wasn't a shout, it was a bellow. "Thin ice. No, by God, clear water! Clear water! Lovely, clear, clear water!"

My immediate reaction was that either the ice machine or Benson's brain had blown a fuse. But the officer at the diving panel had no such doubts, for I had to grab and hang on hard as the *Dolphin* heeled over violently to port and came curving around, engines slowing, in a tight circle to bring her back to the spot where Benson had called out. Swanson watched the plot, spoke quietly, and the big bronze propellers reversed and bit into the water to bring the *Dolphin* to a stop.

"How's it looking now, Doc?" Swanson called out.

"Clear, clear water," Benson said reverently. "I got a good picture of it. It's pretty narrow, but wide enough to hold us. It's long, with a sharp left-hand dogleg, for it followed us around through the first forty-five degrees of our curve."

"One fifty feet," Swanson said.

The pumps hummed. The *Dolphin* drifted gently upward like an airship rising from the ground. Briefly, water flooded back into the tanks. The *Dolphin* hung motionless.

"Up periscope," Swanson said.

The periscope hissed up slowly into the raised position. Swanson glanced briefly through the eyepiece, then beckoned to me. "Take a look," he beamed. "As lovely a sight as you'll ever see."

I took a look. If you'd made a picture of what could be seen above and framed it, you couldn't have sold the result even if you added Picasso's name to it; but I could see what he meant. Solid black masses on either side with a scarcely lighter strip of dark jungle green running between them on a line with the fore-and-aft direction of the ship. An open lead in the polar pack.

Three minutes later we were lying on the surface of the Arctic Ocean, just under 250 miles from the Pole.

The rafted, twisted ice pack reared up into contorted ridges almost fifty feet in height, towering twenty feet above the top of the sail, so close you could almost reach out and touch the nearest ridge. Three or four of those broken and fantastically hummocked ice hills stretching off to the west, and then the light of the floodlight failed and we could see no more. Beyond that there was only blackness.

To the east, we could see nothing at all. To have stared out to the east with opened eyes would have been to be blinded for life in a very few seconds: even goggles became clouded and scarred after the briefest exposure. Close in to the *Dolphin's* side you could, with bent head and hooded eyes, catch, for a fleeting part of a second, a glimpse of black water, already freezing over; but it was more imagined than seen.

The wind, shrieking and wailing across the bridge and through raised antennae, showed at consistently over sixty mph on the bridge anemometer. The ice storm was no longer the gusting, swirling fog of that morning but a driving wall of stiletto-tipped spears, near-lethal in its ferocity, high-speed ice-spicule lances that would have skewered their way through the thickest cardboard or shattered in a second a glass held in your hand. Over and above the ululating threnody of the wind we could hear an almost constant grinding, crashing, and deep-throated booming as millions of tons of racked and tortured ice, under the influence of the gale and some mighty pressure center heaven knew how many hundreds of miles away, reared and twisted and tore and cracked, one moment forming another rafted ridge as a layer of ice, perhaps ten feet thick, screeched and roared and clambered on to the shoulders of another and then another, the next rending apart in indescribably violent cacophony to open up a new lead, black, wind-torn water that started to skim over with ice almost as soon as it was formed.

"Are we both mad? Let's get below." Swanson cupped his hands to my ear and had to shout, but, even so, I could hardly hear him above that hellish bedlam of sound.

We clambered down into the comparatively sudden stillness of the control room. Swanson untied his parka hood and pulled off the scarf and goggles that had completely masked his face. He looked at me and shook his head wonderingly.

"And some people talk about the white silence of the Arctic. My God, a boilermaker's shop is like a library reading room compared to that." He shook his head again. "We stuck our noses out a few times above the ice pack last year, but we never saw anything like this. Or heard it. Winter, too. Cold, sure, damned cold, and windy, but never so bad that we couldn't take a brief stroll on the ice, and I used to wonder about those stories of explorers being stuck in their tents for days on end, unable to move. But I know now why Captain Scott died."

"It is pretty nasty," I admitted. "How safe are we here, Commander?"

"That's anybody's guess." Swanson shrugged. "The wind's got us jammed hard against the west wall of this polynya, and there's maybe fifty yards of open water to starboard. For the moment we're safe. But you can hear and see that that pack is on the move, and not slowly, either. The lead we're in was torn open less than an hour ago. How long? Depends on the configuration of the ice, but those polynyas can close up damned quickly at times, and while the hull of the *Dolphin* can take a good deal of pressure, it can't take a million tons of ice leaning against it. Maybe we can stay here for hours, maybe only for minutes. Whichever it is, as soon as that east wall comes within ten feet of the starboard side, we're dropping down out of it. You know what happens when a ship gets caught in the ice."

"I know. It gets squeezed flat, is carried around the top of the world for a few years, and then one day it's released and drops to the bottom, two miles straight down. The U. S. government wouldn't like it, Commander."

"The prospects of further promotion for Commander Swanson would be poor," Swanson admitted. "I think—"

"Hey!" The shout came from the radio room. "Hey, come 'ere."

"I think Zabrinski wants me," Swanson murmured. He moved off with his usual deceptive speed, and I followed him into the radio room. Zabrinski was sitting half turned in his chair, an ear-to-ear beam on his face, the earphones extended in his left hand. Swanson took them, listened briefly, then nodded.

"DSY," he said softly. "DSY, Dr. Carpenter. We have them. Got the bearing? Good." He turned to the quartermaster. "Ellis, ask the navigating officer to come here as soon as possible."

"We'll pick 'em all up yet, Captain," Zabrinski said jovially. The smile on the big man's face, I could see now, didn't extend as far as his eyes. "They must be a pretty tough bunch of boys out there."

"Very tough, Zabrinski," Swanson said absently. His eyes

were remote, and I knew he was listening to the metallic cannonading of the ice spicules, a billion tiny pneumatic chisels drumming away continuously against the outer hull of the submarine, a sound loud enough to make low speech impossible. "Very tough. Are you in two-way contact?"

Zabrinski shook his head and turned away. He'd stopped smiling. Raeburn came in, and was handed a sheet of paper, and left for his plotting table. We went with him. After a minute or two he looked up and said, "If anyone likes a Sunday afternoon's walk, this is it."

"So close?" Swanson asked.

"So very close. Five miles due east, give or take half a mile. Pretty fair bloodhounds, aren't we?"

"We're just lucky," Swanson said shortly. He walked back to the radio room. "Talking to them yet?"

"We've lost them altogether."

"Completely?"

"We only had 'em a minute, Captain. Then they faded. Got weaker and weaker. I think Doc Carpenter here is right: they're using a hand-cranked generator." He paused, then said idly, "I've a six-year-old daughter who could crank one of those machines for five minutes without turning a hair."

Swanson looked at me, then turned away without a word. I followed him to the unoccupied diving stand. From the bridge-access hatch we could hear the howl of the storm, the grinding ice with its boom and scream that spanned the entire register of hearing. Swanson said, "Zabrinski put it very well. . . . I wonder how long this damned storm is going to last?"

"Too long. I have a medical kit in my cabin, a fifty-ounce flask of medicinal alcohol, and cold-weather clothes. Could you supply me with a thirty-pound package of emergency rations, high-protein, high-calory concentrates? Benson will know what I mean."

"Do you mean what I think you mean?" Swanson said slowly. "Or am I just going nuts?"

"What's this about going nuts?" Hansen had just come through the doorway leading to the for'ard passageway, and the grin on his face was clear enough indication that though he'd caught Swanson's last words, he'd caught neither the intonation nor the expression on the captain's face. "Very serious state of affairs, going nuts. I'll have to assume command and put you in irons, Captain. Something about it in regulations, I daresay."

"Dr. Carpenter is proposing to sling a bag of provisions on his back and proceed to Drift Station Zebra on foot."

"You've picked them up again?" For the moment, Hansen had forgotten me. "You really got them? And a cross-bearing?"

"Just this minute. We've hit it almost on the nose. Five miles, Raeburn says."

"My God! Five miles. Only five miles!" Then the elation vanished from voice and face as if an internal switch had been touched. "In weather like this, it might as well be five hundred. Even old Amundsen couldn't have moved ten yards through this stuff."

"Dr. Carpenter evidently thinks he can improve on Amundsen's standards," Swanson said dryly. "He's talking about walking there."

Hansen looked at me for a long and considering moment, then turned back to Swanson. "I think maybe it's Doc Carpenter we should be locking up in irons."

"I think maybe it is," Swanson said.

"Look," I said. "There are men out there on Drift Station Zebra. Maybe not many, not now, but there are some. One, anyway. Men a long way past being sick. Dying men. To a dying man, it takes only the very smallest thing to spell out the difference between life and death. I'm a doctor, I know. The smallest thing. An ounce of alcohol, a few ounces of food, a hot drink, some medicine. Then they'll live. Without those little things, they will surely die. They're entitled to what smallest aid they can get, and I'm entitled to take whatever risks I care to to see they get it. I'm not asking anyone else to go, all I'm asking is that you implement the terms of your orders from Washington to give me all possible assistance without endangering the *Dolphin* or its crew. Threatening to stop me is not my idea of giving assistance. And I am not asking you to endanger your submarine or the lives of your men."

Swanson gazed at the floor. I wondered what he was thinking: the best way to stop me, his orders from Washington, or the fact that he was the only man who knew that the commandant on Zebra was my brother. He said nothing.

"You must stop him, Captain," Hansen said urgently. "Any other man you saw putting a pistol to his head or a razor to his throat, you'd stop that man. This isn't any different. He's out of his mind: he wants to commit suicide." He tapped the bulkhead beside him. "Good God, Doc, why do you think we have the sonar operators in here on duty even when we're stopped. So that they can tell us when the ice wall on the far side of the polynya starts to close in on us, that's why. And *that's* because it's impossible for any man to last thirty seconds on the bridge or see an inch against the

67

ice storm up there. Just take a quick twenty-second trip up there, up on the bridge, and you'll change your mind fast enough, I guarantee."

"We've just come down from the bridge," Swanson said matter-of-factly.

"And he still wants to go? It's like I say, he's crazy."

"We could drop down now," Swanson said. "We have the position. Perhaps we can find a polynya within a mile or half a mile of Zebra. That would be a different proposition altogether."

"Perhaps you could find a needle in a haystack," I said. "It took you six hours to find this one, and even at that we were lucky. And don't talk about torpedoes: the ice in this area is rafted anything up to a hundred feet in depth. Pretty much all over. You'd be as well trying to blast your way through with a twenty-two. Might be twelve hours, might be days before we could break through again. I can get there in two, three hours."

"*If* you don't freeze to death in the first hundred yards," Hansen said. "*If* you don't fall down a ridge and break your leg. *If* you don't get blinded in a few minutes. *If* you don't fall into a newly opened polynya that you can't see, where you'll either drown or, if you manage to get out, freeze solid in thirty seconds. And even if you do survive all those things, I'd be grateful if you'd explain to me exactly how you propose to find your way blind to a place five miles away. You can't carry a damn great gyro weighing about half a ton on your back, and a magnetic compass is useless in those latitudes. The magnetic north pole is a good deal *south* of where we are now and a long way to the west. Even if you *did* get some sort of bearing from it, in the darkness and the ice storm you could still miss the camp —or what's left of it—by only a hundred yards and never know it. And even if by one chance in a million you do manage to find your way there, how on earth do you ever expect to find your way back again? Leave a paper trail? A five-mile ball of twine? 'Crazy' is hardly the word for it."

"I may break a leg, drown or freeze," I conceded. "I'll take my chance on that. Finding my way there and back is no great trick. You have a radio bearing on Zebra and know exactly where it lies. You can take a radio bearing on any transmitter. All I have to do is tote a receiver-transmitter radio along with me, keep in touch with you, and you can keep me on the same bearing as Zebra. It's easy."

"It would be," Hansen said, "except for one little thing. We don't have any such radio."

"I have a twenty-mile walkie-talkie in my case," I said.

"Coincidence, coincidence," Hansen murmured. "Just happened to bring it along, no doubt. I'll bet you have all sorts of funny things in that case of yours, haven't you, Doc?"

"What Dr. Carpenter has in his case is really no business of ours," Swanson said in mild reproof. He hadn't thought so earlier. "What does concern us is his intention to do away with himself. You really can't expect us to consent to this ridiculous proposal, Dr. Carpenter."

"No one's asking you to consent to anything," I said. "Your consent is not required. All I'm asking you to do is stand to one side. And to arrange for that food-provision package for me. If you won't I'll have to manage without it."

I left and went to my cabin. Hansen's cabin, rather. But even though it wasn't my cabin that didn't stop me from turning the key in the lock as soon as I had passed through the door.

Working on the likely supposition that if Hansen did come down soon he wasn't going to be very pleased to find the door of his own cabin locked against him, I wasted no time. I spun the combination lock on my suitcase and opened the lid. At least three quarters of the available space was taken up by Arctic survival clothing, the very best that money could buy. It hadn't been my money that had bought it.

I stripped off the outer clothes I was wearing, pulled on long underwear, a wool shirt and corduroy trousers, then a triple-knit wool parka lined with pure silk. The parka wasn't quite standard; it had a curiously shaped suede-lined pocket below and slightly to the front of the left armpit, and a differently shaped suede-lined pocket on the right-hand side. I dug swiftly to the bottom of my case and brought up three separate items. The first of these, a nine-millimeter Mannlicher-Schoenauer automatic, fitted into the left-hand pocket as securely and strongly as if the pocket had been specially designed for it, which indeed it had; the other items, spare magazine clips, fitted as neatly into the right-hand pocket.

The rest of the dressing didn't take long. Two pairs of heavy-knit woollen socks, felt undershoes, and then the furs—caribou for the outer parka and trousers, wolverine for the hood, sealskin for the boots, and reindeer for the gloves, which were pulled on over other layers of silk gloves and woollen mittens. Maybe a polar bear would have had a slight edge over me when it came to being equipped to survive an Arctic blizzard, but there wouldn't have been much in it.

I hung snow mask and goggles around my neck, stuck a rubberized water-proof flashlight into the inside pocket of my fur parka, unearthed my walkie-talkie, and closed the case. I set the combination again. There was no need to set the combination any more, not now that I had the Mannlicher-Schoenauer under my arm, but it would give Swanson something to do while I was away. I shoved my medicine case and a steel flask of alcohol in a rucksack and unlocked the door.

Swanson was exactly where I'd left him in the control room. So was Hansen. So were two others who had not been there when I had left: Rawlings and Zabrinski. Hansen, Rawlings, and Zabrinski, the three biggest men in the ship. The last time I'd seen them together was when Swanson had summoned them up from the *Dolphin* in the Holy Loch to see to it that I didn't do anything he didn't want me to do. Maybe Commander Swanson had a one-track mind. Hansen, Rawlings and Zabrinski. They looked bigger than ever.

I said to Swanson, "Do I get those iron rations or not?"

"One last formal statement," Swanson said. His first thoughts, as I came waddling into the control center, must have been that a grizzly bear was loose inside his submarine, but he hadn't batted an eyelid. "For the record. Your intentions are suicidal, your chances nonexistent. I cannot give my consent."

"All right, your statement is on record, witnesses and all. The iron rations."

"I cannot give my consent because of a new and dangerous development. One of our electronics technicians was carrying out a routine calibration test on the ice machine just now and an overload coil didn't function. Electric motor burnt out. No spares: it will have to be rewired. You realize what that means. If we're forced to drop down, I can't find my way to the top again. Then it's curtains for everybody—everybody left above the ice, that is."

I didn't blame him for trying, but I was vaguely disappointed in him: he'd had time to think up a better one than that. I said, "The iron rations, Commander. Do I get them?"

"You intend to go through with this? After what I've said?"

"Oh, for God's sake. I'll do without the food."

"My executive officer, torpedoman Rawlings and radioman Zabrinski," Swanson said formally, "don't like this."

"I can't help what they like or don't like."

"They feel that they can't let you go through with it," he persisted.

They were more than big. They were huge. I could get past them the way a lamb gets past a starving lion. I had a gun, all right, but with that one-piece parka I was wearing I'd practically have to undress myself to get at it, and Hansen, in that Holy Loch canteen, had shown just how quickly he could react when he saw anyone making a suspicious move.

And even if I did get my gun out, what then? Men like Hansen, like Rawlings and Zabrinski, didn't scare. I couldn't bluff them with a gun. And I couldn't use the gun. Not against men who were just doing their duty.

"They *won't* let you go through with it," Swanson went on, "unless, that is, you permit them to accompany you, which they have volunteered to do."

"Volunteered." Rawlings sniffed. "You, you and you."

"I don't want them," I said.

"Gracious, ain't he?" Rawlings asked of no one in particular. "You might at least have said thanks, Doc."

"You are putting the lives of your men in danger, Commander Swanson. You know what your orders said."

"Yes. I also know that in Arctic travels, as in mountaineering and exploring, a party always has double the chances of the individual. I also know that if it became known that we had permitted a civilian doctor to set off on his own for Drift Station Zebra while we were all too scared to stir from our nice warm sub, the name of the U. S. Navy would become pretty muddy."

"What do your men think of your making them risk their lives to save the good name of the submarine service?"

"You heard the captain," Rawlings said. "We're volunteers. Look at Zabrinski there: anyone can see that he's a man cast in a heroic mold."

"Have you thought of what happens," I said, "if the ice closes in when we're away and the captain has to take the ship down?"

"Don't even mention it," Zabrinski urged. "I'm not all that heroic."

I gave up. I'd no option but to give up. Besides, like Zabrinski, I wasn't all that heroic and I suddenly realized that I would be very glad indeed to have those three men along with me.

5

LIEUTENANT HANSEN was the first man to give up. Or perhaps "give up" is wrong: the meaning of the words was quite unknown and the thought totally alien to Hansen. It would be more accurate to say that he was the first of us to show any glimmerings of common sense. He caught my arm, brought his head close to mine, pulled down his snow mask, and shouted, "No farther, Doc. We must stop."

"The next ridge," I yelled back. I didn't know whether he'd heard me or not, as soon as he'd spoken he'd pulled his mask back up into position again to protect the momentarily exposed skin against the horizontally driving ice storm, but he seemed to understand for he eased his grip on the rope around my waist and let me move ahead again. For the past two and a half hours Hansen, Rawlings and I had each taken our turn at being the lead man on the end of the rope, while the other three held on to it some ten yards behind, the idea being not that the lead man should guide the others but that the others should save the life of the lead man, should the need arise. And the need had already arisen, just once. Hansen, slipping and scrambling on all fours across a fractured and upward-sloping raft of ice, had reached gropingly forward with his arms into the blindness of the night and the storm and found nothing there. He had fallen eight vertical feet before the rope had brought him up with a vicious jerk that had been almost as painful for Rawlings and myself, who had taken the brunt of the shock, as it had been for Hansen. For nearly two minutes he'd dangled above the wind-torn black water of a freshly opened lead before we'd managed to drag him back to safety. It had been a close thing, far too close a thing, for in far sub-zero temperatures with a gale-force wind blowing, even a few seconds' submersion in water makes the certainty of death absolute, the process of dissolution as swift as it is irreversible. In those conditions the clothes of a man pulled from the water become a frozen and impenetrable suit of armor inside seconds, an armor that can neither be removed nor chipped away. Petrified inside this ice shroud, a man just simply and quickly freezes to death—in the unlikely event, that is, of his heart's having withstood the thermal shock of the body's surface being exposed to an almost instantaneous hundred-degree drop in temperature.

So now I stepped forward very cautiously, very warily indeed, feeling the ice ahead of me with a probe we'd devised after Hansen's near-accident—a chopped-off five-foot length of rope which we'd dipped into the water of the lead and then exposed to the air until it had become as rigid as a bar of steel. At times I walked, at times I stumbled, at times, when a brief lull in the gale-force wind, as sudden as it was unexpected, would catch me off balance, I'd just fall forward and continue on hands and knees, for it was quite as easy that way. It was during one of those periods when I was shuffling blindly forward on all fours that I realized that the wind had, for the time being, lost nearly all of its violence and that I was no longer being bombarded by that horizontally driving hail of flying ice spicules. Moments later my probe made contact with some solid obstacle in my path: the vertical wall of a rafted ice ridge. I crawled thankfully into its shelter, raised my goggles, and pulled out and switched on my flashlight as the others came blindly up to where I lay.

Blindly. With arms outstretched they pawed at the air before them like sightless men, which for the past two and a half hours was exactly what they had been. For all the service our goggles had given us, we might as well have stuck our heads in gunny sacks before leaving the *Dolphin*. I looked at Hansen, the first of the three to come up. Goggles, snow mask, hood, clothing—the entire front part of his body from top to toe was deeply and solidly encrusted in a thick and glittering layer of compacted ice, except for some narrow cracks caused by joint movements of legs and arms. As he drew close to me, I could hear him splintering and crackling a good five feet away. Long ice feathers streamed back from his head, shoulders, and elbows: as an extra-terrestrial monster from one of the chillier planets, such as Pluto, he'd have been a sensation in any horror movie. I suppose I looked much the same.

We huddled close together in the shelter of the wall. Only four feet above our heads the ice storm swept by in a glittering gray-white river. Rawlings, sitting on my left, pushed up his goggles, looked down at his ice-sheathed furs, and started to beat his chest with his fist to break up the covering. I reached out a hand and caught his arm.

"Leave it alone," I said.

"Leave it alone?" Rawlings' voice was muffled by his snow

73

mask, but not so muffled that I couldn't hear the chattering of his teeth. "This damn suit of armor weighs a ton. I'm out of training for this kind of weight-lifting, Doc."

"Leave it alone. If it weren't for that ice, you'd have frozen to death by this time: it's insulating you from that wind and the ice storm. Let's see the rest of your face. And your hands."

I checked him and the two others for frostbite, while Hansen checked me. We were still lucky. Blue and mottled and shaking with the cold, but no frostbite. The furs of the other three might not have been quite as fancy as mine, but they were very adequate indeed. Nuclear subs always got the best of everything, and Arctic clothing was no exception. But although they weren't freezing to death, I could see from their faces and hear from their breathing that they were pretty far gone in exhaustion. Thrusting into the power of that ice storm was like wading upstream against the current of a river of molasses; that was energy-sapping enough, but the fact that we had to spend most of our time clambering over, slipping on, sliding and falling across fractured ice or making detours around impassable ridges while being weighed down with forty-pound packs on our backs and heaven only knew how many additional pounds of ice coating our furs in front, had turned our trudge across that contorted, treacherous ice into a dark and frozen nightmare.

"The point of no return, I think," Hansen said. His breathing, like Rawlings', was very quick, very shallow, almost gasping. "We can't take much more of this, Doc."

"You ought to listen to Dr. Benson's lectures a bit more," I said reprovingly. "All this ice cream and apple pie and lolling around in your bunks is no training for this sort of thing."

"Yeah?" He peered at me. "How do *you* feel?"

"A mite tired," I admitted. "Nothing much to speak of." Nothing much to speak of! My legs felt as if they were falling off, that was all, but the goad of pride was always a useful one to have at hand. I slipped off my rucksack and brought out the medicinal alcohol. "I suggest fifteen minutes' break. Any more and we'll just start stiffening up completely. Meantime, a little drop of what we fancy will help keep the old blood corpuscles trudging around."

"I thought medical opinion was against alcohol in low temperatures," Hansen said doubtfully. "Something about opening the pores."

"Name me any form of human activity," I said, "and I'll find you a group of doctors against it. Spoilsports. Besides, this isn't alcohol, it's very fine Scotch whisky."

74

"You should have said so in the first place. Pass it over. Not too much for Rawlings and Zabrinski: they're not used to the stuff. Any word, Zabrinski?"

Zabrinski, with the walkie-talkie's aerial up and one earphone tucked in below the hood of his parka, was talking into the microphone through cupped hands. As the radio expert, Zabrinski had been the obvious man to handle the walkie-talkie, and I'd given it to him before leaving the submarine. This was also the reason why Zabrinski wasn't at any time given the position of lead man in our trudge across the ice. A heavy fall or immersion in water would have finished the radio he was carrying slung on his back; and if the radio were finished, so would we be, for without the radio, not only had we no hope of finding Drift Station Zebra; we wouldn't have a chance in a thousand of ever finding our way back to the *Dolphin* again. Zabrinski was built on the size and scale of a medium-sized gorilla and was about as durable; but we couldn't have treated him more tenderly had he been made of Dresden china.

"It's difficult," Zabrinski said. "Radio's okay, but this ice storm causes such damn distortion and squeaking—no, wait a minute, though, wait a minute."

He bent his head over the microphone, shielding it from the sound of the storm, and spoke again through cupped hands. "Zabrinski speaking ... Zabrinski. Yeah, we're all kinda tuckered out, but Doc here seems to think we'll make it. ... Hang on, I'll ask him."

He turned to me. "How far do you think we've come, they want to know."

"Four miles." I shrugged. "Three and a half, four and a half. You guess it."

Zabrinski spoke again, looked interrogatively at Hansen and me, saw our head shakes, and signed off. He said: "Navigating officer says we're four, five degrees north of where we should be and that we'll have to cut south if we don't want to miss Zebra by a few hundred yards."

It could have been worse. Over an hour had passed since we'd received the last bearing position from the *Dolphin*, and, between radio calls, our only means of navigating had been by judging the strength and direction of the wind in our faces. When a man's face is completely covered and largely numb, it's not a very sensitive instrument for gauging wind direction—and, for all we knew, the wind might be either backing or veering. It could have been a lot worse, and I said so to Hansen.

"It could be worse," he agreed heavily. "We could be traveling in circles or we could be dead. Barring that, I don't see how it could be worse." He gulped down the whisky, coughed, and handed the flask top back to me. "Things look brighter now. You honestly think we can make it?"

"A little luck, that's all. You think maybe our packs are too heavy? That we should abandon some of it here?" The last thing I wanted to was to abandon any of the supplies we had along with us: eighty pounds of food, a stove, thirty pounds of compressed-fuel tablets, a hundred ounces of alcohol, a tent, and a very comprehensive medical kit. But if it was to be abandoned, I wanted it to be their suggestion, and I was sure they wouldn't make it.

"We're abandoning nothing," Hansen said. Either the rest or the whisky had done him good; his voice was stronger, his teeth hardly chattering at all.

"Let the thought die still-born," Zabrinski said. When I'd first seen him in Scotland, he had reminded me of a polar bear, and now out here on the ice cap, huge and crouched in his ice-whitened furs, he resembled one even more. He had the physique of a bear, too, and seemed completely tireless; he was in far better shape than any of us. "This weight on my bowed shoulders is like a bad leg: an old friend that gives me pain, but I wouldn't be without it."

"You?" I asked Rawlings.

"I'm conserving my energy," Rawlings announced. "I expect to have to carry Zabrinski later on."

We pulled the scarred, abraded and now thoroughly useless snow goggles over our eyes again, hoisted ourselves stiffly to our feet and moved off to the south to find the end of and round the high ridge that had blocked our path. It was by far the longest and most continuous ridge we'd encountered yet, but we didn't mind; we needed to make a good offing to get us back on course, and not only were we doing just that, but we were doing it in comparative shelter and saving our strength by so doing. After perhaps four hundred yards the ice wall ended so abruptly, leading to so sudden and unexpected an exposure to the whistling fury of the ice storm that I was bowled completely off my feet. An express train couldn't have done it any better. I hung on to the rope with one hand, clawed and scrambled my way back to my feet with the help of the others, shouted a warning to the others, and then we were fairly into the wind again, holding it directly in our faces and leaning far forward to keep our balance.

We covered the next mile in less than half an hour. The going was easier now, much easier than it had been, although we still had to make small detours around rafted, compacted and broken ice: on the debit side, all of us, Zabrinski excepted, were near complete exhaustion, stumbling and falling far more often than was warranted by the terrain and the strength of the ice gale. For myself, my leaden, dragging legs felt as if they were on fire; each step now sent a shooting pain stabbing from my ankle clear to the top of my thigh. For all that, I think I could have kept going longer than any of them, even Zabrinski, for I had the motivation, the driving force that would have kept me going hours after my legs would have told me that it was impossible to carry on a step further. Major John Halliwell. My elder, my only brother. Alive or dead. Was he alive or was he dead, this one man in the world to whom I owed everything I had or had become? Was he dying, at that very moment when I was thinking of him, was he dying? His wife, Mary, and his three children, who spoiled and ruined their bachelor uncle as I spoiled and ruined them: whatever way it was, they would have to know, and only I could tell them. Alive or dead? My legs weren't mine; the stabbing fire that tortured them belonged to some other man, not to me. I had to know, I had to know, and if I had to find out by covering whatever miles lay between me and Drift Ice Station Zebra on my hands and knees, then I would do just that. I would find out. And over and above the tearing anxiety as to what had happened to my brother there was yet another powerful motivation, a motivation that the world would regard as of infinitely greater importance than the life or death of the commandant of the station. As infinitely more important than the living or dying of the score of men who manned that desolate polar outpost. Or so the world would say.

The demented drumming of the spicules on my mask and ice-sheathed furs suddenly eased, the gale wind fell away, and I found myself standing in the shelter of an ice ridge even higher than the last one we'd used for shelter. I waited for the others to come up, asked Zabrinski to make a position check with the *Dolphin*, and doled out some more of the medicinal alcohol. More of it than on the last occasion. We were in more need of it. Both Hansen and Rawlings were in a very distressed condition, their breath whistling in and out of their lungs in the rapid, rasping, shallow panting of a long-distance runner in the last tortured moments of his final exhaustion. I became gradually aware that the speed of my own breathing matched theirs almost exactly; it required a concentrated effort of willpower to hold my breath even for the few seconds necessary to gulp down my drink. I wondered vaguely if perhaps Hansen hadn't been right after all; maybe the alcohol wasn't good for us. But it certainly tasted as if it were.

Zabrinski was already talking through cupped hands into the microphone. After a minute or so he pulled the earphone out from under his parka and buttoned up the walkie-talkie set. He said: "We're either good or lucky or both. The *Dolphin* says we're exactly on the course we ought to be on." He drained the glass I handed him and sighed in satisfaction. "Well, that's the good part of the news. Here comes the bad part. The sides of the polynya the *Dolphin* is lying in are beginning to close together. They're closing pretty fast. The captain estimates he'll have to get out of it in two hours. Two at the most." He paused, then finished slowly: "And the ice machine is still on the blink."

"The ice machine," I said stupidly. Well, anyway, I felt stupid, I don't know how I sounded. "Is the ice—"

"It sure is, brother," Zabrinski said. He sounded tired. "But you didn't believe the skipper, did you, Dr. Carpenter? You were too clever for that."

"Well, that's a help," Hansen said heavily. "That makes everything just dandy. The *Dolphin* drops down, the ice closes up, and there we are, the *Dolphin* below, us on top, and the whole of the polar ice cap between us. They'll almost certainly never manage to find us again, even if they do fix the ice machine. Shall we just lie down and die now or shall we first stagger around in circles for a couple of hours and then lie down and die?"

"It's tragic," Rawlings said gloomily. "Not the personal aspect of it, I mean the loss to the U.S. Navy. I think I may fairly say, Lieutenant, that we are—or were—three promising young men. Well, you and me, anyway. I think Zabrinski there had reached the limit of his potentialities. He reached them a long time ago."

Rawlings got all this out between chattering teeth and still painful gasps of air. Rawlings, I reflected, was very much the sort of person I would like to have by my side when things began to get awkward, and it looked as if things were going to become very awkward indeed. He and Zabrinski had, as I'd found out, established themselves as the homespun if slightly heavy-handed humorists on the *Dolphin*. For reasons known only to themselves, both men habitually concealed intelligences of a high order and advanced education under a cloak of genial buffoonery.

"Two hours yet," I said. "With this wind at our backs we can be back in the sub in well under an hour. We'd be practically blown back there."

"And the men on Drift Station Zebra?" Zabrinski asked.

78

"We'd have done our best. Just one of those things."

"We are profoundly shocked, Dr. Carpenter," Rawlings said. The tone of genial buffoonery was less noticeable than usual.

"Deeply dismayed," Zabrinski added, "by the very idea." The words were light, but the lack of warmth in the voice had nothing to do with the bitter wind.

"The only dismaying thing around here is the level of intelligence of certain simple-minded sailors," Hansen said with some asperity. He went on, and I wondered at the conviction in his voice: "Sure, Dr. Carpenter thinks we should go back. That doesn't include him. Dr. Carpenter wouldn't turn back now for all the gold in Fort Knox." He pushed himself wearily to his feet. "Can't be much more than half a mile to go now. Let's get it over with."

In the backwash of light from my flashlight I saw Rawlings and Zabrinski glance at each other, saw them shrug their shoulders at the same moment. Then they, too, were on their feet and we were on our way again.

Three minutes later Zabrinski broke his ankle.

It happened in an absurdly simple fashion, but for all its simplicity it was a wonder that nothing of the same sort had happened to any of us in the previous three hours. After starting off again, instead of losing our bearing by working to the south or north until we had rounded the end of the ice ridge blocking our path, we elected to go over it. The ridge was all of ten feet high but by boosting and pulling each other we reached the top without much difficulty. I felt my way forward cautiously, using the ice probe; the flashlight was useless in that ice storm, and my goggles completely opaque. After twenty feet of crawling across the gently downward-sloping surface, I reached the far side of the ridge and stretched down with the probe.

"Five feet," I called to the others as they came up. "It's only five feet." I swung over the edge, dropped down, and waited for the others to follow. Hansen came first, then Rawlings, both sliding down easily beside me. What happened to Zabrinski was impossible to see: he either misjudged his distance from the edge or a sudden easing of the wind made him lose his footing. Whatever the cause, I heard him call out, the words whipped away and lost by the wind, as he jumped down beside us. He seemed to land squarely and lightly enough on his feet, then cried out sharply and fell heavily to the ground.

I turned my back to the ice storm, raised the useless snow goggles, and pulled out my flashlight. Zabrinski was half sitting, half lying on the ice, propped up on his right elbow

79

and cursing steadily and fluently and, as far as I could tell, because of the muffling effect of his snow mask, without once repeating himself. His right heel was jammed in a four-inch crack in the ice, one of the thousands of such fractures and fissures that criss-crossed the pressure areas of the pack; his right leg was bent over at an angle to the outside, an angle normally impossible for any leg to assume. I didn't need to have a medical diploma hung around my neck to tell that the ankle was gone: either that or the lowermost part of the tibia, for the ankle was so heavily encased in a stout boot with lace binding that most of the strain must have fallen on the shinbone. I hoped it wasn't a compound fracture, but it was an unreasonable hope: at that acute angle the snapped bone could hardly have failed to pierce the skin. Compound or not, it made no immediate difference; I'd no intention of examining it. A few minutes' exposure of the lower part of his leg in those temperatures was as good a way as any of ensuring that Zabrinski went through the rest of his life with one foot missing.

We lifted his massive bulk, eased the useless foot out of the crack in the ice, and lowered him gently to a sitting position. I unslung the medical kit from my back, knelt beside him and asked: "Does it hurt badly?"

"No, it's numb, I hardly feel a thing." He swore disgustedly. "What a crazy thing to do. A little crack like that. How stupid can a man get?"

"You wouldn't believe me if I told you," Rawlings said acidly. He shook his head. "I prophesied this, I prophesied this. I said it would end up with me carrying this gorilla here."

I laid splints to the injured leg and taped them as tightly as possible over the boot and the furs, trying not to think of the depth of trouble we were in now. Two major blows in one: not only had we lost the indispensable services of the strongest man in our party, we now had an extra 220 pounds —at least—of weight, of deadweight, to carry along with us. Not to mention his forty-pound pack. Zabrinski might almost have read my thoughts.

"You'll have to leave me here, Lieutenant," he said to Hansen. His teeth were rattling with shock and cold. "We must be almost there now. You can pick me up on the way back."

"Don't talk rubbish," Hansen said shortly. "You know damn well we'd never find you again."

"Exactly," Rawlings said. His teeth were like Zabrinski's, stuttering away irregularly like an asthmatic machine gun. He knelt on the ice to support the injured man's bulk. "No medals for morons. It says so in the ship's articles."

"But you'll never get to Zebra," Zabrinski protested. "If you have to carry me—"

"You heard what I said," Hansen interrupted. "We're not leaving you."

"The lieutenant is perfectly correct," Rawlings agreed. "You aren't the hero type, Zabrinski. You haven't got the face for it, for one thing. Now shut up while I get some of this stuff off my back."

I finished tightening the splints and pulled mittens and fur gloves back on my silk-clad but already frozen hands. We divided Zabrinski's load among the three of us, pulled goggles and snow masks back into position, hoisted Zabrinski to his one sound leg, turned into the wind, and went on our way again. It would be truer to say that we staggered on our way again.

But now, at last and when we most needed it, luck was with us. The ice cap stretched away beneath our feet as level and smooth as the surface of a frozen river. No ridges, no hummocks, no crevasses, not even the tiny cracks one of which had crippled Zabrinski. Just billiard-flat unbroken ice and not even slippery, for its surface had been scoured and abraded by the flying ice storm.

Each of us took turns at being lead man, the other two supporting a Zabrinski who hopped along in uncomplaining silence on one foot. After maybe three hundred yards of this smooth ice, Hansen, who was in the lead at the moment, stopped so suddenly and unexpectedly that we bumped into him.

"We're there!" he yelled above the wind. "We've made it. We're there! Can't you smell it?"

"Smell what?"

"Burnt fuel oil. Burnt rubber. Don't you get it?"

I pulled down my snow mask, cupped my hands to my face, and sniffed cautiously. One sniff was enough. I hitched up my mask again, pulled Zabrinski's arm more tightly across my shoulder, and followed Hansen.

The smooth ice ended in another few feet. The ice sloped up sharply to a level plateau, and it took the three of us all of what pitifully little strength remained to drag Zabrinski up after us. The acrid smell of burning seemed to grow more powerful with every step we took. I moved forward, away from the others, my back to the storm, goggles down, and sweeping the ice with semicircular movements of my flashlight. The smell was strong enough now to make my nostrils wrinkle under the mask. It seemed to be coming from directly ahead. I turned around into the wind, protectively cupped hand over my eyes, and, as I did, my flashlight struck something hard and solid and metallic. I lifted my flashlight and vaguely, through the driving ice, I could just make out the ghostly hooped-steel skeleton, ice-coated on the windward side, fire-charred on the leeward side, of what had once been a Nissen-shaped hut.

We had found Drift Ice Station Zebra.

I waited for the others to come up, guided them past the gaunt and burnt-out structure, then told them to turn backs to wind and lift their goggles. For maybe ten seconds we surveyed the ruin in the beam of my flashlight. No one said anything. Then we turned around into the wind again.

Drift Station Zebra had consisted of eight separate huts, four in each of two parallel rows, thirty feet separating the two rows, twenty feet between each two huts in the rows— this to minimize the hazard of fire spreading from hut to hut. But the hazard hadn't been minimized enough. No one could be blamed for that. No one, except in the wildest flights of nightmarish imagination, could have envisaged what must indeed have happened: exploding tanks and thousands of gallons of blazing oil being driven through the night by a gale-force wind. And, by a double inescapable irony, fire, without which human life on the polar ice cap cannot survive, is there the most dreaded enemy of all: for although the entire ice cap consists of water, frozen water, there is nothing that can melt that water and so put out the fire. Except fire itself. I wondered vaguely what had happened to the giant chemical fire extinguishers housed in every hut.

Eight huts, four in each row. The first two on either side were completely gutted. No trace remained of the walls, which had been of two layers of weather-proofed bonded ply that had enclosed the insulation of shredded glass fiber and kapok; on all of them even the aluminum sheeted roofs had disappeared. In one of the huts we could see charred and blackened generator machinery, ice-coated on the windward side, bent and twisted and melted almost out of recognition: one could only wonder at the furnace ferocity of the heat responsible.

The fifth hut—the third on the right-hand side—was a gutted replica of the other four, the framing even more savagely twisted by the heat. We were just turning away from this, supporting Zabrinski and too sick at heart even to speak to each other, when Rawlings called out something unintelligible. I leaned closer to him and pulled back my parka hood.

"A light!" he shouted. "A light. Look, Doc—across there!"

And a light there was, a long, narrow, strangely white vertical strip of light from the hut opposite the charred wreck by which we stood. Leaning sideways into the storm, we dragged

Zabrinski across the intervening gap. For the first time my flashlight showed something that was more than a bare framework of steel. This was a hut. A blackened, scorched, and twisted hut with a roughly nailed-on sheet of plywood where its solitary window had been, but nevertheless a hut. The light was coming from a door standing just ajar at the sheltered end. I laid my hand on the door, the one unscorched thing I'd seen so far in Drift Station Zebra. The hinges creaked like a rusty gate in a cemetery at midnight and the door gave beneath my hand. We went inside.

Suspended from a hook in the center of the ceiling, a hissing Coleman lamp threw its garish light, amplified by the glittering aluminum ceiling, over every corner and detail of that eighteen-by-ten hut. A thick but transparent layer of ice sheathed the aluminum roof except for a three-foot circle directly above the lamp, and the ice spread from the ceiling down the plywood walls all the way to the floor. The wooden floor, too, was covered with ice, except where the bodies of the men lay. There may have been ice under them as well. I couldn't tell.

My first thought, conviction rather, and one that struck at me with a heart-sapping sense of defeat, with a chill that even the polar storm outside had been unable to achieve, was that we had arrived too late. I had seen many dead men in my life, I knew what dead men looked like, and now I was looking at just that many more. Shapeless, huddled, lifeless forms lying under a shapeless mass of blankets, mackinaws, duffels and furs; I wouldn't have bet a cent on my chances of finding one heartbeat among the bunch. Lying packed closely together in a rough semicircle at the end of the room, far from the door, they were utterly still, as unmoving as men would be if they had been lying that way for a frozen eternity. Apart from the hissing of the pressure lamp, there was no sound inside the hut other than the metallic drumfire of the ice spicules against the ice-sheathed eastern wall of the hut.

Zabrinski was eased down into a sitting position against a wall. Rawlings unslung the heavy load he was carrying on his back, unwrapped the stove, pulled off his mittens, and started fumbling around for the fuel tablets. Hansen pulled the door to behind him, slipped the buckles of his rucksack, and wearily let his load of tinned food drop to the floor of the shack.

For some reason, the voice of the storm outside and the hissing of the Coleman inside served only to heighten the deathly stillness in the hut, and the unexpected metallic clatter of the falling cans made me jump. It made one of the dead men jump, too. The man nearest me by the left-hand wall suddenly moved, rolled over and sat up, bloodshot eyes staring out unbelievingly from a frost-bitten, haggard and cruelly burned face, the burns patchily covered by a long, dark stubble of beard. For long seconds he looked at us unblinkingly; then, some obscure feeling of pride making him ignore the offer of my outstretched arm, he pushed himself shakily and with obvious pain to his feet. Then the cracked and peeling lips broke into a grin.

"You've been a bleedin' long time getting here." The voice was hoarse and weak and as cockney as the Bow Bells themselves. "My name's Kinnaird. Radio operator."

"Whisky?" I asked.

He grinned again, tried to lick his cracked lips, and nodded. The stiff shot of whisky went down his throat like a man in a barrel going over Niagara Falls: one moment there, the next gone forever. He bent over, coughing harshly until the tears came to his eyes, but when he straightened, life was coming back into those same lackluster eyes and color touching the pale, emaciated cheeks.

"If you go through life saying 'Hallo' in this fashion, mate," he observed, "then you'll never lack for friends." He bent and shook the shoulder of the man beside whom he had been lying. "C'mon, Jolly, old boy, where's your bleedin' manners. We got company."

It took quite a few shakes to get Jolly old boy awake, but when he did come to he was completely conscious and on his feet with remarkable speed and nimbleness. He was a short, chubby character with china-blue eyes, and although he was in as much need of a shave as Kinnaird, there was still color in his face, and the round, good-humored face was far from emaciated; but frostbite had made a bad mess of both mouth and nose. The china-blue eyes, flecked with red and momentarily wide in surprise, crinkled into a grin of welcome. Jolly old boy, I guessed, would always adjust fast to circumstances.

"Visitors, eh?" His deep voice held a rich Irish brogue. "And damned glad we are to see you, too. Do the honors, Jeff."

"We haven't introduced ourselves," I said. "I'm Dr. Carpenter and this—"

"Regular meeting of the B.M.A., old boy," Jolly said. I was to find out later that he used the phrase "old boy" in every second or third sentence, a mannerism that went strangely with his Irish accent.

"Dr. Jolly?"

"The same. Resident medical officer, old boy."

84

"I see. This is Lieutenant Hansen, of the U. S. Navy submarine *Dolphin*—"

"Submarine?" Jolly and Kinnaird stared at each other, then at us. "You said 'submarine,' old top?"

"Explanations can wait. Torpedoman Rawlings. Radioman Zabrinski." I glanced down at the huddled men on the floor, some of them already stirring at the sound of voices, one or two propping themselves up on their elbows. "How are they?"

"Two or three pretty bad burn cases," Jolly said. "Two or three pretty far gone with cold and exhaustion, but not so far gone that food and warmth wouldn't have them right as rain in a few days. I made them all huddle together like this for mutual warmth."

I counted them. Including Jolly and Kinnaird, there were twelve all told. I said: "Where are the others?"

"The others?" Kinnaird looked at me in momentary surprise, then his face went bleak and cold. He pointed a thumb over his shoulder. "In the next hut, mate."

"Why?"

"Why?" He rubbed a weary forearm across bloodshot eyes. "Because we don't fancy sleeping with a roomful of corpses, that's why."

"Because you don't—" I broke off and stared down at the men at my feet. Seven of them were awake now, three of them propped on elbows, four still lying down, all seven registering various degrees of dazed bewilderment. The three who were still asleep—or unconscious—had their faces covered by blankets. I said slowly, "There were nineteen of you."

"Nineteen of us," Kinnaird echoed emptily. "The others— well, they never had a chance."

I said nothing. I looked carefully at the faces of the conscious men, hoping to find among them the one face I wanted to see, hoping that perhaps I had not immediately recognized it because frostbite or hunger or burns had made it temporarily unrecognizable. I looked very carefully indeed, and I knew that I had never seen any of those faces before.

I moved over to the first of the three still sleeping figures and lifted the blanket covering the face. The face of a stranger. I let the blanket drop. Jolly said in puzzlement: "What's wrong? What do you want?"

I didn't answer him. I picked my way around recumbent men, all staring uncomprehendingly at me, and lifted the blanket from the face of the second sleeping man. Again I let the blanket drop and I could feel my mouth go dry, the slow, heavy pounding of my heart. I crossed to the third man, then stood there hesitating, knowing I must find out, dreading what I must find. Then I stooped quickly and lifted the blanket. A man with a heavily bandaged face. A man with a broken nose and a thick blond beard. A man I had never seen in my life before. Gently I spread the blanket back over his face and straightened up. Rawlings, I saw, already had the solid-fuel stove going.

"That should bring the temperature up to close to freezing," I said to Dr. Jolly. "We've plenty of fuel. We've also brought food, alcohol, a complete medical kit. If you and Kinnaird want to start in on those things now, I'll give you a hand in a minute. Lieutenant, that was a polynya, that smooth stretch we crossed just before we got here? A frozen lead?"

"Couldn't be anything else." Hansen was looking at me peculiarly, a wondering expression on his face. "These people are obviously in no fit state to travel a couple of hundred yards, much less four or five miles. Besides, the skipper said he was going to be squeezed down pretty soon. So we call the *Dolphin* and have them surface at the back door?"

"Can he find that polynya—without the ice machine, I mean?"

"Nothing simpler. I'll take Zabrinski's radio, move a measured two hundred yards to the north, send a bearing signal, move two hundreds to the south, and do the same. They'll have our range to a yard. Take a couple of hundred yards off that and the *Dolphin* will find itself smack in the middle of the polynya."

"But still under it. I wonder how thick that ice is. You had an open lead to the west of the camp some time ago, Dr. Jolly. How long ago?"

"A month. Maybe five weeks. I can't be sure."

"How thick?" I asked Hansen.

"Five feet, maybe six. Couldn't possibly break through it. But the captain's always had a hankering to try out his torpedoes." He turned to Zabrinski. "Still able to operate that radio of yours?"

I left them to it. I'd hardly been aware of what I'd been saying, anyway. I felt sick and old and empty and sad and deathly tired. I had my answer now. I'd come 12,000 miles to find it; I'd have gone a million to avoid it. But the inescapable fact was there and now nothing could ever change it. Mary, my sister-in-law, and her three wonderful children—she would never see her husband again; they would never see their father again. My brother was dead, and no one was ever going to see him again. Except me. I was going to see him now.

I went out, closing the door behind me, moved around the corner of the hut, and lowered my head against the storm.

Ten seconds later I reached the door of the last hut in the line. I used the flashlight to locate the handle, twisted it, pushed and walked inside.

Once it had been a laboratory; now it was a charnel house, a house of the dead. The laboratory equipment had all been pushed roughly to one side and the cleared floor space covered with the bodies of dead men. I knew they were dead men, but only because Kinnaird had told me so: hideously charred and blackened and grotesquely misshapen as they were, those carbonized and contorted lumps of matter could have been any form of life or, indeed, no form of life at all. The stench of incinerated flesh and burnt diesel fuel was dreadful. I wondered which of the men in the other hut had had the courage, the iron resolution, to bring those grisly burdens, the shockingly disfigured remains of their former comrades, into this hut. They must have had strong stomachs.

Death must have been swift, swift for all of them. Theirs had not been the death of men trapped by fire; it had been the death of men who had themselves been on fire. Caught, drenched, saturated by a gale-borne sea of burning oil, they must have spent the last few seconds of life as incandescently blazing human torches before dying in insane, screaming agony. They must have died as terribly as men can ever die.

Something about one of the bodies close to me caught my attention. I stooped and focused the flashlight beam on what had once been a right hand, now no more than a blackened claw with the bone showing through. So powerful had been that heat that it had warped, but not melted, the curiously shaped gold ring on the third finger. I recognized that ring; I had been with my sister-in-law when she had bought it.

I was conscious of no grief, no pain, no revulsion. Perhaps, I thought dully, those would come later when the initial shock had worn off. But I didn't think so. This wasn't the man I remembered so well, the brother to whom I owed everything, a debt that could now never be repaid. This charred mass of matter before me was a stranger, so utterly different from the man who lived on in my memory, so changed beyond all possibility of recognition that my numbed mind in my exhausted body just could not begin to bridge the gap.

As I stood there, staring down, something ever so slightly off-beat about the way the body lay caught my professional attention. I stooped low, very low, and remained bent over for what seemed a long time. I straightened, slowly, and as I did I heard the door behind me open. I whirled around and saw that it was Lieutenant Hansen. He pulled down his snow mask, lifted up his goggles, and looked at me and then at the man at my feet. I could see shock draining expression and color from his face. Then he looked up at me.

"So you lost out, Doc?" I could hardly hear the husky whisper above the voice of the storm. "God, I'm sorry."

"What do you mean?"

"Your brother?" He nodded at the man at my feet.

"Commander Swanson told you?"

"Yeah. Just before we left. That's why we came." His gaze moved in horrified fascination over the floor of the hut, and his face was gray, like old parchment. "A minute, Doc, just a minute." He turned and hurried through the doorway.

When he came back he looked better, but not much. He said, "Commander Swanson said that that was why he had to let you go."

"Who else knows?"

"Skipper and myself. No one else."

"Keep it that way, will you? As a favor to me."

"If you say so, Doc." There was curiosity in his face now, and puzzlement, but horror was still the dominant expression. "My God, have you ever seen anything like it?"

"Let's get back to the others," I said. "We're doing nobody any good by staying here."

He nodded without speaking. Together we made our way back to the other hut. Apart from Dr. Jolly and Kinnaird, three other men were on their feet now: Captain Folsom, an extraordinarily tall, thin man, with savagely burnt face and hands, who was second in command of the base; Hewson, a dark-eyed taciturn character, a tractor driver and engineer who had been responsible for the diesel generators; and a cheerful Yorkshireman, Naseby, the camp cook. Jolly, who had opened my medical kit and was applying fresh bandages to the arms of one of the men still lying down, introduced them, then turned back to his job. He didn't seem to need my help—not for the moment, anyway. I heard Hansen say to Zabrinski: "In contact with the *Dolphin?*"

"Well, no." Zabrinski stopped sending his call sign and shifted slightly to ease his broken ankle. "I don't quite know how to put this, Lieutenant, but the fact is that this little ole set here seems to have blown a fuse."

"Well, now," Hansen said heavily. "That *is* clever of you, Zabrinski. You mean you can't raise them?"

"I can hear them, but they can't hear me." He shrugged apologetically. "Me and my clumsy feet, I guess. It wasn't only my ankle that went when I took that tumble out there."

"Well, can't you repair the damn thing?"

"I don't think so, Lieutenant."

"Damn it, you're supposed to be a radioman."

88

"That's so," Zabrinski acknowledged reasonably. "But I'm not a magician. And with a couple of numbed and frozen hands, no tools, an old-type set without a printed circuit, and the code signs in Japanese—well, even Marconi would have called it a day."

"*Can* it be repaired?" Hansen insisted.

"It's a transistor set. No valves to smash. I suppose it could be repaired. But it might take hours, Lieutenant. I'd even have to find a set of tools first."

"Well, find them. Anything you like. Only get that thing working."

Zabrinski said nothing. He held out the headphones to Hansen. Hansen looked at Zabrinski, then at the phones, took them without a word and listened briefly. Then he shrugged, handed back the phones, and said, "Well, I guess there *is* no hurry to repair that radio."

"Yeah," Zabrinski said. "Awkward, you might say, Lieutenant."

"What's awkward?" I asked.

"Looks as if *we're* going to be next on the list for a rescue party," Hansen said heavily. "They're sending a more or less continuous message: 'Ice closing rapidly, return at once.' "

"I was against this madness from the very beginning," Rawlings intoned from the floor. He stared down at the already melting lumps of frozen tinned soup and stirred it moodily with a fork. "A gallant attempt, man, but fore-doomed to failure."

"Keep your filthy fingers out of that soup and kindly shut up," Hansen said coldly. He turned suddenly to Kinnaird. "How about *your* radio set? Of course—that's it. We have men here to crank your generator and—"

"I'm sorry." Kinnaird smiled the way a ghost might smile. "It's not a hand-powered generator—that was destroyed—it's a battery set. The batteries are dead. Completely dead."

"A battery set, you said?" Zabrinski looked at him in mild surprise. "Then what caused all the power fluctuations when you were transmitting?"

"We kept changing over the nickle cadmium cells to try to make the most of what little power was left in them: we'd only fifteen left altogether: most of them were lost in the fire. That caused the power fluctuations. But even Nife cells don't last forever. They're dead, mate. The combined power left in those cells wouldn't light a pencil torch."

Zabrinski didn't say anything. No one said anything. The ice spicules drummed incessantly against the east wall, the Coleman hissed, the solid fuel stove purred softly, but the sole effect of those three sounds was to make the silence inside seem that little bit more absolute. No one looked at his neighbors; everyone stared down at the floor with the fixed and steadfast gaze of an entomologist hunting for traces of woodworm. Any newspaper printing a picture taken at that instant wouldn't have found it any too easy to convince its readers that the men on Drift Ice Station Zebra had been rescued just ten minutes previously, and rescued from certain death at that. The readers would have pointed out that one might have expected a little more jubilation in the atmosphere, a touch, perhaps, of light-hearted relief, and they wouldn't have been far wrong at that, there wasn't very much gaiety around.

After the silence had gone on just that little too long I said to Hansen: "Well, that's it, then. We don't have to hire any electronic computer to work this one out. Someone's got to get back to the *Dolphin* and get back there now. I'm nominating myself."

"No!" Hansen said violently, then more quietly, "Sorry, friend, but the skipper's orders didn't include giving permission to anyone to commit suicide. You're staying here."

"So I stay here," I nodded. This wasn't the time to tell him I didn't need his permission for anything; much less was it the time to start flourishing the Mannlicher-Schoenauer. "So we all stay here. And then we all die here. Quietly, without any fighting, without any fuss, we just lie down and die here. I suppose you reckon that comes under the heading of inspiring leadership. Amundsen would have loved that." It wasn't fair, but then I wasn't feeling fair-minded at the moment.

"Nobody's going anyplace," Hansen said. "I'm not my brother's keeper, Doc, but, even so, I'll be damned if I let you kill yourself. You're not fit, none of us is fit to make the return trip to the *Dolphin*—not after what we've just been through. That's the first thing. The next is that without a transmitter from which the *Dolphin* can pick up our directional bearings, we could never hope to find the *Dolphin* again. The third is that the closing ice will probably have forced the *Dolphin* to drop down before anyone could get halfway there. And the last is that if we failed to find the *Dolphin*, either because we missed her or because she was gone, we could never make our way back to Zebra again: we wouldn't have the strength and we would have nothing to guide us back, anyway."

"The odds offered aren't all that attractive," I admitted. "What odds are you offering on the ice machine being repaired?"

Hansen shook his head, said nothing. Rawlings started stirring his soup again, carefully not looking up, he didn't want to meet the anxious eyes, the desperate eyes, in that circle of haggard and frost-bitten faces any more than I did. But he looked up as Captain Folsom pushed himself away from the support of a wall and took a couple of unsteady steps toward us. It didn't require any stethoscope to see that Folsom was in a pretty bad way.

"I am afraid that we don't understand," he said. His voice was slurred and indistinct, the puffed and twisted lips had been immobilized by the savage charring of his face: I wondered bleakly how many months of pain would elapse, how many visits to the surgeon's table, before Folsom could show that face to the world again. In the very remote event, that was, of our ever getting him to a hospital. "Would you please explain? What is the difficulty?"

"Simply this," I said. "The *Dolphin* has an ice fathometer, a device for measuring the thickness of the overhead ice. Normally, even if Commander Swanson—the captain of the *Dolphin*—didn't hear from us, we could expect him on our doorstep in a matter of hours. He has the position of this drift station pinned down pretty closely. All he would have to do is drop down, come under us here, start a grid search with his ice fathometer, and it would be only minutes before he located the relatively thin ice out in that lead there. But things aren't normal. The ice machine has broken down, and if it stays that way he'll never find that lead. That's why I want to go back there. Now. Before Swanson's forced to dive by the closing ice."

"Don't see it, old boy," Jolly said. "How's that going to help? Can *you* fix this ice whatyoumaycallit?"

"I don't have to. Commander Swanson knows his distance from this camp, give or take a hundred yards. All I have to do is tell him to cover the distance less quarter of a mile and fire a torpedo. That ought—"

"Torpedo?" Jolly asked. "Torpedo? To break through the ice from beneath?"

"That's it. It's never been tried before. I suppose there's no reason why it shouldn't work if the ice is thin enough, and it won't be all that thick in the lead out there. I don't really know."

"They'll be sending planes, you know, Doc," Zabrinski said quietly. "We started transmitting the news as soon as we broke through, and everybody will know by now that Zebra has been found—at least, they'll know exactly where it is. They'll have the big bombers up here in a few hours."

"Doing what?" I asked. "Sculling around uselessly in the darkness up above? Even if they do have the exact position, they still won't be able to see what's left of this station because of the darkness and the ice storm. Perhaps they can with radar, it's unlikely, but even if they do, what then? Drop supplies? Maybe. But they won't dare drop supplies directly on us for fear of killing us. They'd have to drop them some distance off—and even a quarter mile would be too far away for any chance we'd ever have of finding stuff in those conditions. As for landing—even if weather conditions were perfect, no plane big enough to have the range to fly here could ever hope to land on the ice cap. You know that."

"What's your middle name, Doc?" Rawlings asked dolefully. "Jeremiah?"

"The greatest good of the greatest number," I said. "The old yardstick, but there's never been a better one. If we just hole up here without making any attempt to help ourselves and the ice machine remains useless, then we're all dead. All sixteen of us. If I make it there safely, then we're all alive. Even if I don't, the ice machine may be fixed and there would only be one lost then." I started pulling on my mittens. "One is less than sixteen."

"We might as well make it two," Hansen sighed and began to pull on his own gloves. I was hardly surprised, when he'd last spoken he'd talked at first of "you" having no chance and finished by saying that "we" had none, and it hadn't required any psychiatrist to follow his quick shift in mental orientation: whatever men like Hansen were hand-picked for, it wasn't for any predilection for shifting the load to others' shoulders when the going became sticky.

I didn't waste any time arguing with him.

Rawlings got to his feet.

"One skilled volunteer for the soup-stirring," he requested. "Those two wouldn't get as far as that door without my holding their hands. I'll probably get a medal for this. What's the highest decoration awarded in peacetime, Lieutenant?"

"There are no medals given for soup-stirring, Rawlings," Hansen said, "which is what you are going to keep on doing. You're staying right here."

"Uh-uh." Rawlings shook his head. "Prepare yourself to deal with your first mutiny, Lieutenant. I'm coming with you. I can't lose. If we get to the *Dolphin*, you'll be too damned glad and happy to have made it to dream of reporting me, apart from being a fair-minded man who will have to admit that our safe arrival back at the ship will be entirely due to torpedoman Rawlings." He grinned. "And if we don't make it—well, you can't very well report it, can you, Lieutenant?"

Hansen walked across to him. He said quietly: "You know that there's more than an even chance that we won't reach the *Dolphin*. That would leave twelve pretty sick men here, not to mention Zabrinski with a broken ankle, and with no one to look after them. They've got to have one able man to look after them. You couldn't be that selfish, now, could you, Rawlings? Look after them, will you? As a favor to me?"

Rawlings looked at him for long seconds, then squatted down and started stirring the soup again. "As a favor to me, you mean," he said bitterly. "Okay, I'll stay. As a favor to me. Also to prevent Zabrinski from tripping over his legs again and breaking another ankle." He stirred the soup viciously. "Well, what are you waiting for? The skipper may be making up his mind to dive any minute."

He had a point. We brushed off protests and attempts to stop us made by Captain Folsom and Dr. Jolly and were ready to leave in thirty seconds. Hansen was through the door first. I turned and looked at the sick and emaciated and injured survivors of Drift Station Zebra. Folsom, Jolly, Kinnaird, Hewson, Naseby and seven others. Twelve men altogether. They couldn't all be in cahoots together, so it had to be a single man, maybe two, acting in concert. I wondered who those men might be, those men I would have to kill, that person or persons who had murdered my brother and six other men on Drift Ice Station Zebra.

I pulled the door to behind me and followed Hansen out into the dreadful night.

6

WE HAD BEEN TIRED, more than tired, even before we had
set out. We had been leaden-legged, bone-weary, no more
than a short handspan from total exhaustion. But, for all
that, we flitted through the howling darkness of that night
like two great white ghosts across the dimly seen whiteness
of a nightmare lunar landscape. We were no longer bowed
under the weight of heavy packs. Our backs were to that
gale-force wind, so that for every laborious plodding step we
had made on our way to Zebra we now covered five, with so
little a fraction of our earlier toil that at first it seemed all
but effortless. We had no trouble in seeing where we were
going, no fear of falling into an open lead or of crippling
ourselves against some unexpected obstacle, for with our useless goggles removed and powerful flashlight beams dancing
erratically ahead of us as we jog-trotted along, visibility was
seldom less than five yards, more often nearer ten. Those
were the physical aids that helped us on our way but even
more sharply powerful as a spur to our aching legs was that
keen and ever-growing fear that dominated our minds to
the exclusion of all else, the fear that Commander Swanson
had already been compelled to drop down and that we would
be left to die in that shrieking wasteland: with our lacking
both shelter and food, the old man with the scythe would
not be keeping us waiting too long.

We ran, but we did not run too fast, for to have done that
would have been to have the old man tapping us on the
shoulder in very short order indeed. In far sub-zero temperatures, there is one thing that the Eskimo avoids as he would
the plague—overexertion, in those latitudes more deadly,
even, than the plague itself. Too much physical effort while
wearing heavy furs inevitably results in sweat, and when the
effort ceases, as eventually cease it must, the sweat freezes
on the skin: the only way to destroy that film of ice is by
further exertion, producing even more sweat, the beginnings

of a vicious and steadily narrowing circle that can have only one end. So though we ran it was only at a gentle jog-trot, hardly more than a fast walk; we took every possible precaution against overheating.

After half an hour, perhaps a little more, I called for a brief halt in the shelter of a steep ice wall. Twice in the past two minutes Hansen had stumbled and fallen where there hadn't appeared to be any reason to stumble and fall: and I had noticed that my own legs were more unsteady than the terrain warranted.

"How are you making out?" I asked.

"Pretty bushed, Doc." He sounded it, too, his breathing quick and rasping and shallow. "But don't write me off yet. How far do you think we've come?"

"Three miles, near enough." I patted the ice wall behind us. "When we've had a couple of minutes, I think we should try climbing this. Looks like a pretty tall hummock to me."

"To try to get into the clear above the ice storm?" I nodded my head and he shook his. "Won't do any good, Doc. This ice storm must be at least twenty feet thick, and even if you do get above it the *Dolphin* will still be below it. She's only got the top of her sail clear above the ice."

"I've been thinking," I said. "We've been so lost in our own woes and sorrows that we've forgotten about Commander Swanson. I think we've been guilty of underestimating him pretty badly."

"It's likely enough. Right now I'm having a fulltime job worrying about Lieutenant Hansen. What's on your mind?"

"Just this. The chances are better than fifty-fifty that Swanson believes we're on our way back to the *Dolphin*. After all, he's been ordering us to return for quite some time. And if he thinks we didn't get the order because something has happened to us or to the radio, he'll still figure that we will be returning."

"Not necessarily. Radio or not, we might still be heading for Drift Station Zebra."

"No. Definitely not. He'll be expecting us to be smart enough to figure it the way he would, and smart enough to see that that is the way *he* would figure it. He would know that if our radio broke down before we got to Zebra, it would be suicidal for us to try to find it without radio bearing—but that it *wouldn't* be suicidal for us to try to make it back to the *Dolphin*, for he would be hoping that we would have sufficient savvy to guess that he would put a lamp in the window to guide the lost sheep home."

"My God, Doc, I think you've got it! Of course he would,

of course he would. God, what am I using for brains?" He straightened and turned to face the ice wall.

Pushing and pulling, we made it together to the top. The summit of the rafted ice hummock was less than twenty feet above the level of the ice pack and not quite high enough. We were still below the surface of that gale-driven river of ice spicules. Occasionally, for a brief moment of time, the wind force would ease fractionally and let us have a brief glimpse of the clear sky above: but only occasionally and for a fraction of a second. And if there was anything to be seen in that time, we couldn't see it.

"There'll be other hummocks," I shouted in Hansen's ear. "Higher hummocks." He nodded without answering. I couldn't see the expression on his face but I didn't have to see it. The same thought was in both our minds: we could see nothing because there was nothing to see. Commander Swanson hadn't put a lamp in the window, for the window was gone, the *Dolphin* forced to dive to avoid being crushed by the ice.

Five times in the next twenty minutes we climbed hummocks, and five times we climbed down, each time more dejected, more defeated. By now I was pretty far gone, moving in a pain-filled nightmare: Hansen was in even worse shape, lurching and staggering around like a drunken man. As a doctor, I knew well the hidden and unsuspected resources that an exhausted man could call on in times of desperate emergency; but I knew too that those resources are not limitless and that we were pretty close to the end. And when that end came we would just lie down in the lee of an ice wall and wait for the old man to come along: he wouldn't keep us waiting long.

Our sixth hummock all but defeated us. It wasn't that it was hard to climb—it was well ridged with foot and hand holds—but the sheer physical effort of climbing came very close to defeating us. And then I dimly began to realize that part of the effort was owing to the fact that this was by far the highest hummock we had found yet. Some colossal pressures had concentrated on this one spot, rafting and logjamming the ice pack until it had risen a clear thirty feet above the general level; the giant underwater ridge beneath must have stretched down close to two hundred feet toward the black floor of the Arctic.

Eight feet below the summit our heads were in the clear: on the summit itself, holding on to each other for mutual support against the gale, we could look down on the ice storm whirling by just beneath our feet, a fantastic sight: a great gray-white sea of undulating turbulence, a giant rushing river that stretched from horizon to horizon. Like so much else in the high Arctic, the scene had an eerie and terrifying strangeness about it, a mindless desolation that belonged not to earth but to some alien and long-dead planet.

We scanned the horizon to the west until our eyes ached. Nothing. Nothing at all. Just that endless desolation. From due north to due south, through 180°, we searched the surface of that great river: and still we saw nothing. Three minutes passed. Still nothing. I began to feel the ice running in my blood.

On the remote off-chance that we might already have bypassed the *Dolphin* to the north or south, I turned and peered toward the east. It wasn't easy, for that gale of wind brought tears to the eyes in an instant of time, but at least it wasn't impossible; we no longer had to contend with the needle-pointed lances of the ice spicules. I made another slow 180° sweep of the eastern horizon, and again, and again. Then I caught Hansen's arm.

"Look there," I said. "To the northeast. Maybe a quarter of a mile away, maybe half. Can you see anything?"

For several seconds Hansen squinted along the direction of my outstretched hand, then shook his head. "I see nothing. What do you think you see?"

"I don't know. I'm not sure. I can imagine I see a very faint touch of luminescence on the surface of the ice storm there, maybe just a fraction of a shade whiter than the rest."

For a full half-minute Hansen stared out through cupped hands. Finally he said, "It's hopeless. I don't see it. But then my eyes have been acting up on me for the past half-hour. But I can't even *imagine* I see anything."

I turned away to give my streaming eyes a rest from that icy wind and then looked again. "Damn it," I said, "I can't be sure that there is anything there, but I can't be sure that there isn't, either."

"What do you think it would be?" Hansen's voice was dispirited, with overtones of hopelessness. "A light?"

"A searchlight shining vertically upward. A searchlight that's not able to penetrate that ice storm."

"You're kidding yourself, Doc," Hansen said wearily. "The wish father to the thought. Besides, that would mean that we had already passed the *Dolphin*. It's not possible."

"It's not impossible. Ever since we started climbing those damned ice hummocks I've lost track of time and space. It *could* be."

"Do you still see it?" The voice was empty, uninterested, he didn't believe me and he was just making words.

"Maybe my eyes are acting up, too," I admitted. "But, damn it, I'm still not sure that I'm not right."

97

"Come on, Doc, let's go."

"Go where?"

"I don't know." His teeth chattered so uncontrollably in that intense cold that I could scarcely follow his words. "I guess it doesn't matter very much where—"

With breath-taking abruptness, almost in the center of my imagined patch of luminescence and not more than 400 yards away, a swiftly climbing rocket burst through the rushing river of ice spicules and climbed high into the clear sky trailing behind it a fiery tail of glowing red sparks. Five hundred feet it climbed, perhaps 600, then burst into a brilliantly incandescent shower of crimson stars, stars that fell lazily back to earth again, streaming away to the west on the wings of the gale and dying as they went, till the sky was colder and emptier than ever before.

"You still say it doesn't matter very much where we go?" I asked Hansen. "Or maybe you didn't see that little lot?"

"What I just saw," he said reverently, "was the prettiest ole sight that Ma Hansen's little boy ever did see—or ever will see." He thumped me on the back, so hard that I had to grab him to keep my balance. "We got it made, Doc!" he shouted. "We got it made. Suddenly I have the strength of ten. Home sweet home, here we come."

Ten minutes later we were home.

"God, this is wonderful," Hansen sighed. He stared in happy bemusement from the captain to me to the glass in his hand to the water dripping from the melting ice on his furs onto the corticene decking of the captain's tiny cabin. "The warmth, the light, the comfort and home sweet home. I never thought I'd see any of it again. When that rocket went up, skipper, I was just looking around to pick a place to lay me down and die. And don't think I'm joking, because I'm not."

"And Dr. Carpenter?" Swanson smiled.

"Defective mental equipment somewhere," Hansen said. "He doesn't seem to know how to go about giving up. I think he's just mule-headed. You get them like that."

Hansen's slightly off-beat, slightly irrational talk had nothing to do with the overwhelming relief and relaxation that come after moments of great stress and tension. Hansen was too tough for that. I knew that and I knew that Swanson knew it, too. We'd been back for almost twenty minutes now, we'd told our story, the pressure was off, a happy ending for all seemed in sight, and normalcy was again almost the order of the day. But when the strain is off and conditions are back to normal, a man has time to start thinking about things again. I knew only too well what was in Hansen's mind's eye: that charred and huddled shapelessness that had once been my brother. He didn't want me to talk about him, and for that I didn't blame him; he didn't want me even to think about him, although he must have known that that was impossible. The kindest men nearly always are like that, hard and tough and cynical on the outside, men who have been too kind and showed it.

"However it was," Swanson smiled, "you can consider yourselves two of the luckiest men alive. That rocket you saw was the third last we had, it's been a regular fourth of July for the past hour or so. And you think Rawlings, Zabrinski, and the survivors on Zebra are safe for the present?"

"Nothing to worry about for the next couple of days," Hansen nodded. "They'll be okay. Cold, mind you, and a good half of them desperately in need of hospital treatment, but they'll survive."

"Fine. Well, this is how it is. This lead here stopped closing in about half an hour ago, but it doesn't matter now: we can drop down any time and still hold our position. What does matter is that we have located the fault in the ice machine. It's a damned tricky and complicated job, and I expect it will take several hours yet to fix. But I think we'll wait until it is fixed before we try anything. I'm not too keen on this idea of making a dead-reckoning approach to this lead near Zebra, then letting off a shot in the dark. Since there's no desperate hurry, I'd rather wait till we got the ice fathometer operating again, make an accurate survey of this lead then fire a torpedo up through the middle. If the ice is only four or five feet thick there, we shouldn't have much trouble blowing a hole through."

"That would be best," Hansen agreed. He finished off his medicinal alcohol—an excellent bourbon—rose stiffly to his feet, and stretched. "Well, back to the old treadmill again. How many torpedoes in working order?"

"Four, at the last count."

"I may as well go help young Mills load them up now. If that's okay by you, skipper."

"It is not okay by me," Swanson said mildly, "and if you'll take a quick gander at that mirror there, you'll understand why. You're not fit to load a slug into an air rifle, much less a torpedo into its tube. You haven't just been on a Sunday-afternoon stroll, you know. A few hours' sleep, John, then we'll see."

Hansen didn't argue. I couldn't imagine anyone arguing

99

with Commander Swanson. He made for the door. "Coming, Doc?"

"In a moment. Sleep well."

"Yeah. Thanks." He touched me lightly on the shoulder and smiled through bloodshot and exhausted eyes. "Thanks for everything. Good night, all."

When he was gone Swanson said, "It was pretty wicked out there tonight?"

"I wouldn't recommend it for an old ladies' home Sunday-afternoon outing."

"Lieutenant Hansen seems to imagine he's under some kind of debt to you," he went on inconsequentially.

"Imagination, as you say. They don't come any better than Hansen. You're damned lucky to have him as an exec."

"I know that." He hesitated, then said quietly: "I promise you I won't mention this again, but, well, I'm damned sorry, Doctor."

I looked at him and nodded slowly. I knew he meant it, I knew he had to say it, but there's not much you can say in turn to anything like that. I said: "Six others died with him, Commander."

He hesitated again. "Do we—do we take the dead back to Britain with us?"

"Could I have another drop of that excellent bourbon, Commander? Been a very heavy run on your medicinal alcohol in the past few hours, I'm afraid." I waited till he had filled my glass, then went on: "We don't take them back with us. They're not dead men, they're just unrecognizable and unidentifiable lumps of charred matter. Let them stay here."

His relief was unmistakable and he was aware of it, for he went on hurriedly, for something to say: "All this equipment for locating and tracking the Russian missiles. Destroyed?"

"I didn't check." He'd find out for himself soon enough that there had been no such equipment. How he'd react to that discovery in light of the cock-and-bull story I'd spun to him and Admiral Garvie in the Holy Loch I couldn't even begin to guess. At the moment I didn't even care. It didn't seem important; nothing seemed important, not any more. All at once I felt tired, not sleepy, just deathly tired, so I pushed myself stiffly to my feet, said good night, and left.

Hansen was in his bunk when I got back to his cabin, his furs lying where he had dropped them. I checked that he was no longer awake, slipped off my own furs, hung them up, and replaced the Mannlicher-Schoenauer in my case. I lay

100

down in my cot to sleep, but sleep wouldn't come. Exhausted though I was, I had never felt less like sleep in my life.

I was too restless and unsettled for sleep, too many problems coming all at once were causing a first-class log jam in my mind. I got up, pulled on a shirt and denim pants, and made my way to the control room. I spent the better part of what remained of the night there, pacing up and down, watching two technicians repairing the vastly complicated innards of the ice machine, reading the messages of congratulation which were still coming in, talking desultorily to the officer on deck, and drinking endless cups of coffee. It passed the night for me, and although I hadn't closed an eye I felt fresh and almost relaxed by the time morning came.

At the wardroom breakfast table that morning everyone seemed quietly cheerful. They knew they had done a good job, the whole world was telling them they had done a magnificent job, and you could see that they all regarded that job as being as good as over. No one appeared to doubt Swanson's ability to blow a hole through the ice. If it hadn't been for the presence of the ghost at the feast, myself, they would have been positively jovial.

"We'll pass up the extra cups of coffee this morning, gentlemen," Swanson said. "Drift Station Zebra is still waiting for us, and even though I'm assured everyone there will survive, they must be feeling damned cold and miserable. The ice machine has been in operation for almost an hour now, at least we hope it has. We'll drop down right away and test it, and after we've loaded the torpedoes—two should do it, I think—we'll blow our way up into this lead at Zebra."

Twenty minutes later the *Dolphin* was back where she belonged, 150 feet below the surface of the sea—or the ice cap. After ten minutes' maneuvering, with a close check being kept on the plotting table to maintain our position relative to Drift Station Zebra, it was clear that the ice machine was behaving perfectly normally again, tracing out the inverted ridges and valleys in the ice with its usual magical accuracy. Commander Swanson nodded his satisfaction.

"That's it, then." He nodded to Hansen and Mills, the torpedo officer. "You can go ahead now. Maybe you'd like to accompany them, Dr. Carpenter. Or is loading torpedoes old hat to you?"

"Never seen it," I said truthfully. "Thanks, I'd like to go along." Swanson was as considerate toward men as he was toward his beloved *Dolphin*, which was why every man in the ship swore by him. He knew, or suspected, that apart from the shock I felt at my brother's death, I was worried stiff about other things. He would have heard, although he hadn't mentioned it to me and hadn't even asked me how I had slept, that I'd spent the night prowling aimlessly and restlessly about the control room; he knew I would be grateful for any distraction, for anything that would relieve my mind, however temporarily, of whatever it was that was troubling it. I wondered just how much that extraordinarily keen brain knew or guessed. But that was an unprofitable line of thought so I put it out of my mind and went along with Hansen and Mills. Mills was another like Raeburn, the navigation officer; he looked to me more like a college undergraduate than the highly competent officer he was, but I supposed it was just another sign that I was growing old.

Hansen crossed to a panel by the diving console and studied a group of lights. The night's sleep had done him a great deal of good and, apart from the abraded skin on his forehead and around the cheekbones where the ice spicules of last night had done their work, he was again his normal, cheerfully cynical, relaxed self, fresh and rested and fit. He waved his hand at the panel.

"The torpedo safety lights, Dr. Carpenter. Each green light represents a closed torpedo tube door. Six doors that open to the sea—bow caps, we call them—six rear doors for loading the torpedoes. Only twelve lights, but we study them very, very carefully—just to make sure that all the lights are green. For if any of them were red—any of the top six, that is, which represent the sea doors—well, that wouldn't be so good, would it?" He looked at Mills. "All green?"

"All green," Mills echoed.

We moved for'ard along the wardroom passage and dropped down the wide companionway into the crew's mess. From there we moved into the for'ard torpedo-storage room. Last time I'd been there, on the morning after our departure from the Clyde, nine or ten men had been sleeping in their bunks; now all the bunks were empty. Five men were waiting for us: four seamen and a petty officer, Bowen, whom Hansen, no stickler for protocol, addressed as Charlie.

"You will see now," Hansen observed to me, "why officers are more highly paid than enlisted men, and deservedly so. While Charlie and his gallant men skulk here behind two sets of collision bulkheads, we must go and test the safety of the tubes. Regulations. Still, a cool head and an iron nerve: we do it gladly for our men."

Bowen grinned and unlatched the first collision-bulkhead door. We stepped over the eighteen-inch sill, leaving the five men behind, and waited until the door had been latched again before opening the for'ard collision-bulkhead door and stepping over the second sill into the cramped torpedo room.

This time the door was swung wide open and hooked back on a heavy standing catch.

"All laid down in the book of rules," Hansen said. "The only time the two doors can be opened at the same time is when we're actually loading the torpedoes." He checked the position of metal handles at the rear of the tubes, reached up, swung down a steel-spring microphone, and flicked a switch. "Ready to test tubes. All manual levers shut. All lights showing green?"

"All lights still green." The answering voice from the overhead squawk box was hollow, metallic, queerly impersonal.

"You already checked," I said mildly.

"So we check again. Same old book of rules." He grinned. "Besides, my grandpa died at ninety-seven and I am out to beat his record. Take no chances and you run no risks. What are they to be, George?"

"Three and four."

I could see the brass plaques on the circular rear doors of the tubes, 2, 4, and 6 on the port side, 1, 3, and 5 on the starboard. Lieutenant Mills was proposing to use the central tubes on each side.

Mills unhooked a rubberized flashlight from the bulkhead and approached number 3 first. Hansen said, "Still no chances. First of all George opens the test cock in the rear door, which will show if there is any water at all in the tubes. Shouldn't be, but sometimes a little gets past the bow caps. If the test cock shows nothing, then he opens the door and shines his light up to examine the bow cap and see that there is no obstruction in the tube. How is it, George?"

"Okay, number 3." Three times Mills lifted the test-cock handle and no trace of water appeared. "Opening the door now."

He hauled on the big lever at the rear, pulled it clear, and swung back the heavy circular door. He shone his kam up the gleaming inside length of the tube, then straightened. "Clean as a whistle and dry as a bone."

"That's not the way he was taught to report it," Hansen said sorrowfully. "I don't know what the young officers are coming to these days. Right, George, number 4."

Mills grinned, secured the rear door on number 3, and crossed to number 4. He lifted the test-cock handle and said, "Oh-oh."

"What is it?" Hansen asked.

"Water," Mills said tersely.

"Is there much? Let's see."

"Just a trickle."

"Is that bad?" I asked.

"It happens," Hansen said briefly. He joggled the handle up and down and another spoonful of water appeared. "You can get a slightly imperfect bow cap, and if you go deep enough to build up sufficient outside pressure you can get a trickle of water coming in. Probably what has happened in this case. If the bow cap was open, friend, at this depth the water would come out of that spout like a bullet. But no chances, no chances." He reached for the microphone again. "Number four bow cap still green? We have a little water here."

"Still green."

Hansen looked down at Mills. "How's it coming?"

"Not so much now."

"Control center," Hansen said into the microphone. "Check the trim chit, just to make sure."

There was a pause, then the box crackled again.

"Captain speaking. All tubes showing 'empty.' Signed by Lieutenant Hansen and the foreman engineer."

"Thank you, sir." Hansen switched off and grinned. "Lieutenant Hansen's word is good enough for me any day. How's it now?"

"Stopped."

Mills tugged the heavy lever. It moved an inch or two, then struck. "Pretty stiff," he commented.

"You torpedomen never heard of anything called lubricating oil?" Hansen demanded. "Weight, George, weight."

Mills applied more weight. The lever moved another couple of inches. Mills scowled, shifted his feet to get maximum leverage, and heaved just as Hansen shouted, "No! Stop! For God's sake, stop!"

He was too late. He was a lifetime too late. The lever snapped clear, the heavy circular rear door smashed open as violently as if it had been struck by some gigantic battering ram, and a roaring torrent of water burst into the for'ard torpedo room. The sheer size, the enormous power and frightening speed of that almost horizontally traveling column of water was staggering. It was like a giant hose pipe, like one of the outlet pipes of the Boulder Dam. It caught up Lieutenant Mills, already badly injured by the flailing sweep of that heavy door, and swept him back across the torpedo room to smash heavily against the after bulkhead; for a moment he half stood there, pinned by the power of that huge jet, then slid down limply to the deck.

"Blow all main ballast!" Hansen shouted into the microphone. He was hanging on a rear-torpedo door to keep from being carried away, and, even above the thunderous roar of the waters, his voice carried clearly. "Emergency. Blow all main ballast. Number 4 tube open to the sea. Blow all main ballast!" He released his grip and staggered across the deck, trying to keep his balance in the madly swirling already foot-deep water. "Get out of here, for God's sake."

He should have saved his energy and breath. I was already on my way out of there. I had Mills under the arms and was trying to drag him over the high sill of the for'ard collision bulkhead and I was making no headway at all. The proper trim of a submarine is a delicate thing at the best of times, and even after those few seconds, the nose of the *Dolphin*, heavy with the tons of water that had already poured in, was beginning to cant sharply downward. Trying to drag Mills and at the same time keep my balance on that sloping deck with knee-high water boiling around me was more than I could do: but suddenly Hansen had Mills by the feet, and I stumbled off balance, tripped over the high sill, and fell backward into the confined space between the two collison bulkheads, dragging Mills after me.

Hansen was still on the other side of the bulkhead. I could hear him cursing steadily, monotonously, and as if he meant it as he struggled to unhook the heavy door from its standing catch. Because of the steep downward pitch of the *Dolphin's* deck, he had to lean all his weight against the massive steel door to free the catch, and with his insecure footing among the swirling waters on that sloping, slippery deck, he was obviously having the devil's own time trying to release it. I let Mills go, jumped over the sill, flung my shoulder against the door, and with the suddenly added pressure, the latch clicked free. The heavy door at once swung half shut, carrying us along with it and knocking us both off our feet into the battering-ram path of that torrent still gushing from number 4 tube. Coughing and spluttering, we scrambled upright again, crossed the sill, and, hanging on to a latch handle apiece, tried to drag the door shut.

Twice we tried and twice we failed. The water boiled in through the tube, and its level was now almost lipping the top of the sill. With every second that passed, the downward angle of the *Dolphin* increased, and with every extra degree of steepness the task of pulling that door uphill against the steadily increasing gravity became more and more difficult.

The water began to spill over the sill onto our feet.

Hansen grinned at me. At least I thought for a moment he was grinning, but the white teeth were clamped tightly together and there was no amusement at all in his eyes. He shouted above the roar of the water: "It's now or never."

A well-taken point. It was indeed now or never. At a signal from Hansen, we flung our combined weights on to those latch handles, each with one hand to a latch while the other braced against the bulkhead to give maximum leverage. We got the door to within four inches. It swung open. We tried again. Still four inches, and I knew that all our strength had gone into that one.

"Can you hold it for a moment?" I shouted.

He nodded. I shifted both hands to the lower corner latch, dropped to the deck, braced my feet against the sill, and straightened both legs in one convulsive jerk. The door crashed shut, Hansen jammed his latch home, I did the same with mine, and we were safe. For the moment we were safe.

I left Hansen to secure the remaining latches and started knocking those of the after collision-bulkhead door. I'd only got as far as the first one when the others started falling off by themselves. Petty officer Bowen and his men, on the other side of that door, needed no telling that we wanted out of there just as fast as possible. The door was pulled open and my eardrums popped with the abrupt fall in air pressure. I could hear the steady echoing roar of air blasting into the ballast tanks under high pressure. I hoisted Mills by the shoulders, strong, competent hands lifted him out and over the sill, and a couple of seconds later Hansen and I were beside him.

"In God's name!" Bowen said to Hansen. "What's gone wrong?"

"Number 4 tube open to the sea."

"Jesus!"

"Secure that door," Hansen ordered. "But good." He left at a dead run, clawing his way up the sharply sloping deck of the torpedo storage room. I took a look at Lieutenant Mills —one short look was all I needed—and followed after Hansen. Only I didn't run. Running wasn't going to help anybody now.

The roar of compressed air filled the ship, the ballast tanks were rapidly emptying, but still the *Dolphin* continued on its deadly dive, arrowing down for the dark depths of the Arctic. Not even the massive compressed-air banks of the submarine could hope to cope so soon with the effects of the scores of tons of sea water that had already flooded into the for'ard torpedo room: I wondered bleakly if they would ever be able to cope at all. As I walked along the wardroom passage, using the hand rail to haul myself up that crazily canted deck, I could feel the entire submarine shudder beneath my feet. No doubt about what that was: Swanson had the great turbines turning over at maximum revolutions, the big bronze propellers threshing madly in reverse, trying to bite deep into the water to slow up the diving submarine.

You can smell fear. You can smell it and you can see it, and I could do both as I hauled my way into the control center of the *Dolphin* that morning. Not one man as much as flickered an eye in my direction as I passed by the sonar room. They had no eyes for me. They had no eyes for anybody: tense, strained, immobile, with hunted faces, they had eyes for one thing only—the plummeting needle on the depth gauge.

The needle was passing the six-hundred-feet mark. Six hundred feet. No conventional submarine I'd ever been on could have operated at this depth. Could have survived at this depth. Six hundred and fifty. I thought of the fantastic outside pressure that represented and I felt far from happy. Someone else was feeling far from happy also: the young seaman manning the inboard diving seat. His fists were clenched till the knuckles showed, a muscle was jumping in his cheek, a nerve twitching in his neck, and he had the look of a man who sees the bony finger of death beckoning.

Seven hundred feet. Seven hundred and fifty. Eight hundred. I'd never heard of a submarine that had reached that depth and lived. Neither, apparently, had Commander Swanson.

"We have just set a new record, men," he said. His voice was calm and relaxed, and although he was far too intelligent a man not to be afraid, no trace of it showed in tone or manner. "Lowest recorded dive ever, as far as I am aware. Speed of descent?"

"No change."

"It will change soon. The torpedo room must be about full now—apart from the pocket of air compressed under high pressure." He gazed at the dial and tapped his teeth thoughtfully with a thumbnail—this, for Swanson, was probably the equivalent of going into hysterics. "Blow the diesel tanks: blow the fresh-water tanks." Imperturbable though he sounded, Swanson was close to desperation for this was the counsel of despair: thousands of miles from home and supplies, yet jettisoning all the diesel and drinking water, the lack of either of which could make all the difference between life and death. But, at that moment, it didn't matter; all that mattered was lightening the ship.

"Main ballast tank's empty," the diving officer reported. His voice was hoarse and strained.

Swanson nodded, said nothing. The volume of the sound of the compressed air had dropped at least seventy-five per cent and the sudden comparative silence was sinister, terrifying, as if it meant that the *Dolphin* was giving up the fight. Now we had only the slender reserves of the fresh water and diesel to save us; at the rate at which the *Dolphin* was still diving, I didn't see how it could.

Hansen was standing beside me. I noticed blood dripping from his left hand to the deck, and when I looked more closely, I could see that two of his fingers were broken. It must have happened in the torpedo room. At the moment, it didn't seem important. It certainly didn't seem important to Hansen. He was entirely oblivious of it.

The pressure gauge fell further and still further. I knew now that nothing could save the *Dolphin*. A bell rang. Swanson swung down a microphone and pressed a button.

"Engine room speaking," a metallic voice came through. "We must slow down. Main bearings beginning to smoke. She'll seize up any minute."

"Maintain revolutions." Swanson swung back the microphone. The youngster at the diving console, the one with the jumping cheek muscles and the nervous twitch, started to mumble, "Oh, dear God, oh, dear God," over and over again, softly at first, then the voice climbing up the scale to hysteria. Swanson moved two paces and touched him on the shoulder. "Do you mind, laddie? I can hardly hear myself think." The mumbling stopped and the boy sat quite still, his face carved from gray granite, the nerve in his neck going like a trip hammer.

"How much more of this will she take?" I asked casually. At least, I meant it to sound casual, but it came out like the croak of an asthmatic bullfrog.

"I'm afraid we're moving into the realms of the unknown," Swanson admitted calmly. "One thousand feet plus. If that dial is right, we passed the theoretical implosion point —where the hull should have collapsed—fifty feet ago. At the present moment she's being subjected to well over a million tons of pressure." Swanson's repose, his glacial calm, was staggering, they must have scoured the whole of America to find a man like that. If ever there was the right man in the right place at the right time, it was Commander Swanson in the control room of a runaway submarine diving to depths hundreds of feet below what any submarine had ever experienced before.

"She's slowing," Hansen whispered.

"She's slowing." Swanson nodded.

She wasn't slowing half fast enough for me. It was impossible that the pressure hull could hold out any longer. I wondered vaguely what the end would be like, then put the thought from my mind, I would never know anything about it, anyway. At that depth the pressure must have been about twenty tons to the square foot; we'd be squashed as flat as flounders before our senses could even begin to record what was happening to us.

The engine-room call-up bell rang again. The voice this time was imploring, desperate. "We must ease up, Captain. Switch gear is turning red hot. We can see it glowing."

"Wait till it's white hot, then you can complain about it," Swanson said curtly. If the engines were going to break down, they were going to break down: but until they did, he'd tear the life out of them in an attempt to save the *Dolphin*. Another bell rang.

"Control room?" The voice was harsh, high-pitched. "Crew's mess deck speaking. Water is beginning to come in." For the first time, every eye in the control room turned away from the depth gauge and fixed itself on that loudspeaker. The hull was giving at last under the fantastic pressure, the crushing weight. One little hole, one tiny, threadlike crack as a starting point, and the pressure hull would rip and tear and flatten like a toy under a steam hammer. A quick glance at the strained, shocked faces showed this same thought in every mind.

"Where?" Swanson demanded.

"Starboard bulkhead."

"How much?"

"A pint or two, just trickling down the bulkhead. And it's getting worse. It's getting worse all the time. For God's sake, Captain, what are we going to do?"

"What are you going to do?" Swanson echoed. "Mop the damn stuff up, of course. You don't want to live in a dirty ship, do you?" He hung up.

"She's stopped. She's stopped." Four words and a prayer. I'd been wrong about every eye being on that loud-speaker; one pair of eyes had never left the depth gauge, the pair belonging to the youngster at the console.

"She's stopped," the diving officer confirmed. His voice had a shake in it.

No one spoke. The blood continued to drip unheeded from Hansen's crushed fingers. I thought that I detected, for the first time, a faint sheen of sweat on Swanson's brow, but I couldn't be sure. The deck still shuddered beneath our feet as the giant engines strove to lift the *Dolphin* out of those deadly depths; the compressed air still hissed into the diesel and fresh-water tanks. I could no longer see the depth gauge; the diving officer had drawn himself up so close to it that he obscured most of it from me.

Ninety seconds passed, ninety seconds that didn't seem any longer than a leap year, ninety interminable seconds while we waited for the sea to burst in our hull and take us for its own, then the diving officer said. "Ten feet. *Up.*"

"Are you sure?" Swanson asked.

"A year's pay."

"We're not out of the woods yet," Swanson said mildly. "The hull can still go: it should have gone a damn long time ago. Another hundred feet—that means a couple of tons less pressure to the square foot—and I think we'll have a chance. At least a fifty-fifty chance. And after that the chances will improve with every foot we ascend, and as we ascend, the highly compressed air in the torpedo room will expand, driving out water and so lightening the ship."

"Still rising," the diving officer said. "Still rising. Speed of ascent unchanged."

Swanson walked across to the diving stand and studied the slow movement of the depth-gauge dial. "How much fresh water left?"

"Thirty per cent."

"Secure blowing fresh-water ballast. Engines all back two thirds."

The roar of compressed air fell away and the deck vibration eased almost to nothing as the engine revolutions fell from emergency power to two-thirds full speed.

"Speed of ascent unchanged," the diving officer reported. "One hundred feet up."

"Secure blowing diesel." The roar of compressed air stopped completely. "All back one third."

"Still rising. Still rising."

Swanson took a silk handkerchief from his pocket and wiped his face and neck. "I was a little worried there," he said to no one in particular, "and I don't much care who knows it." He reached for a microphone and I could hear his voice booming faintly throughout the ship.

"This is the captain. All right, you can all start breathing again. Everything is under control, we're on our way up. As a point of interest, we're still over three hundred feet deeper than the lowest previous submarine dive ever recorded."

I felt as if I had just been through the rollers of a giant mangle. We all looked as if we'd just been through the rollers of a giant mangle. A voice said: "I've never smoked in my life, but I'm starting now. Someone give me a cigarette." Hansen said: "When we get back to the States, do you know what I'm going to do?"

"Yes," Swanson said. "You're going to scrape together your last cent, go up to Groton, and throw the biggest, the most expensive party ever for the men who built this boat. You're too late, Lieutenant, I thought of it first." He stopped abruptly and said sharply: "What's happened to your hand?"

Hansen lifted his left hand and stared at it in surprise. "I never even knew I'd been scratched. Must have happened with that damn door in the torpedo room. There's a medical-supply box there, Doc. Would you fix this?"

"You did a damn fine job there, John," Swanson said warmly. "Getting that door closed, I mean. Couldn't have been easy."

"It wasn't. All pats on the back to our friend here," Hansen said. "He got it closed, not me. And if he hadn't got it closed—"

"Or if I'd let you load the torpedoes when you came back last night," Swanson said grimly. "When we were sitting on the surface and the hatches wide open. We'd have been eight thousand feet down now and very, very dead."

Hansen suddenly snatched his hand away. "My God!" he said remorsefully. "I'd forgotten. Never mind this damned hand of mine. George Mills, the torpedo officer. He took a pretty bad sock. You'd better see him first. Or Doc Benson."

I took his hand back. "No hurry for either of us. Your fingers first. Mills isn't feeling a thing."

"Good God!" Astonishment showed in Hansen's face, maybe shock at my callousness. "When he recovers consciousness—"

"He'll never recover consciousness again," I said. "Lieutenant Mills is dead."

"What!" Swanson's fingers bit deeply, painfully into my arm. " 'Dead,' did you say?"

"That column of water from number 4 tube came in like an express train," I said tiredly. "Flung him right back against the after bulkhead and smashed in the occiput—the back of his head—like an eggshell. Death must have been instantaneous."

"Young George Mills," Swanson whispered. His face had gone very pale. "Poor kid. His first trip on the *Dolphin*. And now, just like that—killed."

"Murdered," I said.

"What!" If Commander Swanson didn't watch out with his fingers, he'd have my upper arm all black and blue. "What was that you said?"

" 'Murdered,' I said. 'Murdered' I meant."

Swanson stared at me for a long moment, his face empty of expression but his eyes strained and tired and suddenly somehow old. He wheeled, walked across to the diving officer, spoke a few words to him, and returned. "Come on," he said abruptly. "You can fix up the lieutenant's hand in my cabin."

111

7

"YOU REALIZE THE SERIOUSNESS of what you are saying?" Swanson asked. "You are making a grave accusation—"

"Come off it," I said rudely. "This is not a court of law and I'm not accusing anyone. All I say is that murder has been done. Whoever left that bow-cap door open is directly responsible for the death of Lieutenant Mills."

"What do you mean 'left the door open'? Who says anyone left the door open? It could have been due to natural causes. And even if—I can't see it—that door had been left open, you can't accuse a man of murder because of carelessness or forgetfulness or because—"

"Commander Swanson," I said. "I'll go on record as saying that you are probably the best naval officer I have ever met. But being best at that doesn't mean that you're best at everything. There are noticeable gaps in your education, Commander, especially in the appreciation of the finer points of skulduggery. You require an especially low and devious type of mind for that, and I'm afraid that you just haven't got it. Doors left open by natural causes, you say. What natural causes?"

"We've hit the ice a few stiff jolts," Swanson said slowly. "That could have jarred it open. Or when we poked through the ice last night a piece of ice, a stalactite, say, could have—"

"Your tubes are recessed, aren't they? Mighty odd-shaped stalactite that would go down and then bend in at a right angle to reach the door—and even then it would only shut it more tightly."

"The doors are tested every time we're in harbor," Commander Swanson persisted quietly. "They're also opened when we open tubes to carry out surface-trimming tests in dock. Any dockyard has pieces of waste, rope, and other rubbish floating around that could easily have jammed a door open."

"The safety lights showed the doors shut."

"They could have been opened just a crack, not enough to disengage the safety contact."

"Open a crack! Why do you think Mills is dead? If you've ever seen the jet of water that hits the turbine blades in a hydro-electric plant, then you'll know how that water came in. A crack? My God! How are those doors operated?"

"Two ways. Remote control, hydraulic, just press a button: then there are manually operated levers in the torpedo room itself."

I turned to Hansen. He was sitting on the bunk beside me, his face pale as I splinted his broken fingers. I said, "Those hand-operated levers. Were they in the shut position?"

"You heard me say so in there. Of course they were. First thing we always check."

"Somebody doesn't like you," I said to Swanson. "Or somebody doesn't like the *Dolphin*. Or somebody knew that the *Dolphin* was going searching for the Zebra survivors and they didn't like that, either. So they sabotaged the ship. You will remember you were rather surprised you didn't have to correct the *Dolphin*'s trim? It had been your intention to carry out a slow-time dive to check the underwater trim because you thought that would have been affected by the fact that you had no torpedoes in the for'ard tubes. But surprise, surprise. She didn't need any correction."

"I'm listening," Swanson said quietly. He was with me now. He was with me all the way. He cocked an eyebrow as we heard water flooding back into the tanks. The repeater gauge showed 200 feet; Swanson must have ordered his diving officer to level off at that depth. The *Dolphin* was still canted nose downward at an angle of about 25°.

"She didn't need any correcting because some of her tubes were already full of water. For all I know, maybe number 3 tube. The one we tested and found okay is the only one that is *not* full of water. Our clever little pal left the doors open, disconnected the hand-operated levers so that they appeared to be in the shut position when they were actually open, and crossed over a few wires in a junction box so that the open position showed green while the closed showed red. A man who knew what he was about could have done it in a few minutes. Two men who knew what they were about could have done it in no time at all. I'll lay anything you like that when you're eventually in a position to check, you'll find the levers disconnected, the wires crossed, and the inlets of the test cocks blocked with sealing wax, quick-drying paint or even chewing gum, so that when the test cocks were

113

opened, nothing would show and you would assume the tubes to be empty."

"There was a trickle from the test cock in number 4 tube," Hansen objected.

"Low-grade chewing gum."

"The murderous swine," Swanson said calmly. His restraint was far more effective than the most thunderous denunciations could ever have been. "He could have murdered us all. But for the grace of God and the Groton boatyard shipwrights, he would have murdered us all."

"He didn't mean to," I said. "He didn't mean to kill anyone. You had intended to carry out a slow-time dive to check trim in the Holy Loch before you left that evening. You told me so yourself. Did you announce it to the crew, post it up in daily orders or something like that?"

"Both."

"So. Our pal knew. He also knew that you would carry out those checks when the boat was still awash or just under the surface. When you checked the tubes to see if they were okay, water would come in, too much water to permit the rear doors to be shut again, but not under such high pressure that you wouldn't have time and enough to spare to close the fo'ard collision-bulkhead door and make a leisurely retreat in good order. What would have happened? Not much. At the worst you would have settled down slowly to the bottom and stayed there. Not deep enough to worry the *Dolphin*. In a submarine of even ten years ago it might have been fatal for all, because of the limited air supply. Not today, when your air-purifying machines can let you stay down for months at a time. You just float up your emergency-indicator buoy and telephone, tell your story, sit around and drink coffee till a naval diver comes down and replaces the bow cap, pump out the torpedo room and surface again. Our unknown pal—or pals—didn't mean to kill anyone. But they did mean to delay you. And they would have delayed you. We know now that you could have got to the surface under your own steam, but, even so, your top brass would have insisted that you go into dock for a day or two to check that everything was okay."

"Why should anyone want to delay us?" Swanson asked. I thought he had an unnecessarily speculative look in his eyes, but it was hard to be sure; Commander Swanson's face showed exactly what Commander Swanson wanted it to show and no more.

"My God, do you think I know the answer to that one?" I said irritably.

"No. No, I don't think so." He could have been more

114

emphatic about it. "Tell me, Dr. Carpenter, do you suspect some member of the *Dolphin*'s crew to be responsible?"

"Do you really need an answer to that one?"

"I suppose not," he sighed. "Going to the bottom of the Arctic Ocean is not a very attractive way of committing suicide, and if any member of the crew had jinxed things, he'd damn soón have unjinxed them as soon as he realized that we weren't going to carry out trim checks in shallow water. Which leaves only the civilian dockyard workers in Scotland—and every one of them had been checked and rechecked and given a top-grade security clearance."

"Which means nothing. There are plushy Moscow hotels and British and American prisons full of people who had top-grade security clearances. . . . What are you going to do now, Commander? About the *Dolphin*, I mean?"

"I've been thinking about it. In the normal course of events the thing to do would be to close the bow cap of number 4 and pump out the torpedo room, then go in and close the rear door of number 4. But the bow-cap door won't close. Within a second of John's telling us that number 4 was open to the sea, the diving officer hit the hydraulic button— the one that closes it by remote control. You saw for yourself that nothing happened. It must be jammed."

"You bet your life it's jammed," I said grimly. "A sledge hammer might do some good, but pressing buttons won't."

"I could go back to that lead we've just left, surface again, and send a diver under the ice to investigate and see what he can do, but I'm not going to ask any man to risk his life doing that. I could retreat to the open sea, surface, and fix it there, but not only would it be a damned slow and uncomfortable trip with the *Dolphin* canted at this angle, it might take us days before we got back here again. And some of the Drift Station Zebra men are pretty far gone. It might be too late."

"Well, then," I said. "You have the man at hand, Commander. I told you when I first met you that environmental health studies were my specialty, especially in the field of pressure extremes when escaping from submarines. I've done an awful lot of simulated sub escapes, Commander. I do know a fair amount about pressures, how to cope with them and how I react to them myself."

"How do you react to them, Dr. Carpenter?"

"A high tolerance. They don't worry me much."

"What do you have in mind?"

"You know damn well what I have in mind," I said impatiently. "Drill a hole in the door of the after collision bulkhead, screw in a high-pressure hose, open the door, shove someone in the narrow space between the two collision bulkheads, and turn up the hose until the pressure between the collision bulkheads equals that in the torpedo room. You have the clips eased off the for'ard collision door. When the pressures are equalized, it opens at a touch, you walk inside, close number 4 rear door, and walk away again. That's what you had in mind, wasn't it?"

"More or less," he admitted. "Except that *you* are no part of it. Every man on this ship has made simulated escapes. They all know the effects of pressure. And most of them are a great deal younger than you."

"Suit yourself," I said. "But age has little to do with the ability to stand stresses. You didn't pick a teen-ager as the first American to orbit the earth, did you? As for simulated escapes, making a free ascent up a hundred-foot tank is a different matter altogether from going inside an iron box, waiting for the slow build-up of pressure, working under that pressure, then waiting for the slow process of decompression. I've seen young men, big, tough, very, very fit young men break up completely under those circumstances and almost go crazy trying to get out. The combination of physiological and psychological factors involved is pretty fierce."

"I think," Swanson said slowly, "that I'd sooner have you —what do the English say, 'batting on a sticky wicket'?—than almost any man I know. But there's a point you've overlooked. What would the Commander of Atlantic Submarines say to me if he knew I'd let a civilian go instead of one of my own men?"

"If you *don't* let me go, I know what he'll say. He'll say, 'We must reduce Commander Swanson to lieutenant, j.g., because he had on board the *Dolphin* an acknowledged expert in this specialty and refused, out of stiff-necked pride, to use him, thereby endangering the lives of his crew and the safety of his ship.' "

Swanson smiled, a pretty bleak smile, but with the desperately narrow escape we had just had, the predicament we were still in, and the fact that his torpedo officer was lying dead not so many feet away, I hardly expected him to break into gales of laughter. He looked at Hansen. "What do you say, John?"

"I've seen more incompetent characters than Dr. Carpenter," Hansen said. "Also, he gets about as nervous and panic-stricken as a bag of Portland cement."

"He has qualifications you don't expect to find in the average medical man," Swanson agreed. "I shall be glad to accept your offer. One of my men will go with you. That way the dictates of common sense and honor are both satisfied."

It wasn't all that pleasant, not by a long shot. but it wasn't all that terribly bad, either. It went off exactly as it could have been predicted it would go off. Swanson cautiously eased the *Dolphin* up until her stern was just a few feet beneath the ice; this reduced the pressure in the torpedo room to a minimum, but even at that the bows were still about a hundred feet down.

A hole was drilled in the after collision bulkhead door and an armored high-pressure hose screwed into position. Dressed in porous rubber suits and equipped with an aqualung apiece, a young torpedoman by the name of Murphy and I went inside and stood in the gap between the two collision bulkheads. High-powered air hissed into the confined space. Slowly the pressure rose: twenty, thirty, forty, fifty pounds to the square inch. I could feel the pressure on lungs and ears, the pain behind the ears, the slight wooziness that comes from the poisonous effect of breathing pure oxygen under such pressure. But I was used to it; I knew it wasn't going to kill me. I wondered if young Murphy knew that. This was the stage where the combined physical and mental effects became too much for most people, but if Murphy was scared or panicky or suffering from bodily distress, he hid it well. Swanson would have picked his best man, and to be the best man in a company like that, Murphy had to be something very special.

We eased off the clips on the for'ard collision bulkhead door, knocked them off cautiously as the pressures equalized. The water in the torpedo room was about two feet above the level of the sill, and as the door came ajar, the water boiled whitely through into the collision space while compressed air hissed out from behind us to equalize the lowering pressure of the air in the torpedo room. For about ten seconds we had to hang on grimly to hold the door and maintain our balance while water and air fought and jostled in a seething maelstrom to find their own natural levels. The door opened wide. The water level now extended from about thirty inches up on the collision bulkhead to the for'ard deckhead of the torpedo room. We crossed the sill, switched on our waterproof flashlights, and ducked under.

The temperature of that water was about 28°F.—4° below freezing. Those porous rubber suits were specially designed to cope with icy waters, but, even so, I gasped with the shock of it—as well as one can gasp when breathing pure oxygen under heavy pressure. But we didn't linger, for the longer we remained there, the longer we would have to spend decompressing afterward. We half walked, half swam toward the fore end of the compartment, located the rear door on number 4 tube, and closed it, but not before I had a quick look at the inside of the pressure cock. The door itself seemed undamaged: the body of the unfortunate Lieutenant Mills had absorbed its swinging impact and prevented it from being wrenched off its hinges. It didn't seem distorted in any way, and fitted snugly into place. We forced its retaining lever back into place and left.

Back in the collision compartment we gave the prearranged taps on the door. Almost at once we heard the subdued hum of a motor as the high-speed extraction pumps in the torpedo room got to work, forcing the water out through the hull. Slowly the water level dropped, and as it dropped, the air pressure as slowly decreased. Degree by degree the *Dolphin* began to come back on even keel. When the water was finally below the level of the for'ard sill, we gave another signal and the remaining over-pressure air was slowly bled out through the hose.

A few minutes later, as I was stripping off the rubber suit, Swanson asked, "Any trouble?"

"None. You picked a good man in Murphy."

"The best. Many thanks, Doctor." He lowered his voice. "You wouldn't by any chance—"

"You know damned well I would," I said. "I did. Not sealing wax, not chewing gum, not paint. Glue, Commander Swanson. That's how they blocked the test-cock inlet. The old-fashioned animal-hide stuff that comes out of a tube. Ideal for the job."

"I see," he said, and walked away.

The *Dolphin* shuddered along its entire length as the torpedo hissed out of its tube—number 3 tube, the only one in the submarine Swanson could safely rely upon.

"Count it down," Swanson said to Hansen. "Tell me when we should hit, when we should hear it hit."

Hansen looked at the stop watch in his bandaged hand and nodded. The seconds passed slowly. I could see Hansen's lips move silently. Then he said, "We should be hitting—now," and two or three seconds later, "We should be hearing—now."

Whoever had been responsible for the settings and time calculations on that torpedo had known what he was about. Just at Hansen's second "now" we felt as much as heard the clanging vibration along the *Dolphin*'s hull as the shock waves from the exploding warhead reached us. The deck shook briefly beneath our feet, but the impact was nowhere nearly as powerful as I had expected. I was relieved. I didn't have to be a clairvoyant to know that everyone was relieved. No submarine had ever before been in the vicinity of a torpedo detonating under the ice pack; no one had known to what extent the tamping effect of overhead ice might have increased the pressure and destructive effect of the lateral shock waves.

"Nicely," Swanson murmured. "Very nicely done indeed. Both ahead one third. I hope that bang had considerably more effect on the ice than it had on our ship." He said to Benson at the ice machine, "Let us know as soon as we reach that lead, will you?"

He moved to the plotting table. Raeburn looked up and said: "Five hundred yards gone, five hundred to go."

"All stop," Swanson said. The slight vibration of the engines died away. "We'll just mosey along very carefully. That explosion may have sent blocks of ice weighing a few tons apiece pretty far down into the sea. I don't want to be doing any speed at all if we meet any of them on the way up."

"Three hundred yards to go," Raeburn said.

"All clear. All clear all around," the sonar room reported.

"Still thick ice," Benson intoned. "Ah! That's it. We're under the lead. Thin ice. Well, five or six feet."

"Two hundred yards," Raeburn said. "It checks."

We drifted slowly onward. At Swanson's orders the propellers kicked over once or twice, then stopped again.

"Fifty yards," Raeburn said. "Close enough."

"Ice reading?"

"No change. Five feet, about."

"Speed?"

"One knot."

"Position?"

"One thousand yards exactly. Passing directly under target area."

"And nothing on the ice machine? Nothing at all?"

"Not a thing." Benson shrugged and looked at Swanson. The captain walked across and watched the inked stylus draw its swiftly etched vertical lines on the paper.

"Peculiar, to say the least," Swanson murmured. "Seven hundred pounds of very high-grade amatol in that torpedo. Must be unusually tough ice in those parts. Again, to say the least. We'll go up to ninety feet and make a few passes under the area. Floodlights on, TV on."

So we went up to ninety feet and made a few passes and nothing came of it. The water was completely opaque, the floods and camera useless. The ice machine stubbornly registered four to six feet—it was impossible to be more accurate—all the time.

"Well, that seems to be it," Hansen said. "We back off and try again?"

"Well, I don't know," Swanson said pensively. "What do you say we just try to shoulder our way up?"

" 'Shoulder our way up?' " Hansen wasn't with him; neither was I. "What kind of shoulder is going to heave five feet of ice to one side?"

"I'm not sure. The thing is, we've been working from unproved assumptions and that's always a dangerous basis. We've been assuming that if the torpedo didn't blow the ice to smithereens, it would at least blow a hole in it. Maybe it doesn't happen that way at all. Maybe there's just a big upward pressure of water distributed over a sizable area that heaves the ice up and breaks it into pretty big chunks that just settle back into the water again in their original position in the pattern of a dried-up mud hole with tiny cracks all around the isolated sections. But with cracks all around. Narrow cracks, but there. Cracks so narrow that the ice machine couldn't begin to register them even at the slow speed we were doing." He turned to Raeburn. "What's our position?"

"Still in the center of the target area, sir."

"Take her up till we touch the ice," Swanson said.

He didn't have to add any cautions about gentleness. The diving officer took her up like floating thistledown until we felt a gentle bump.

"Hold her there," Swanson said. He peered at the TV screen, but the water was so opaque that all definition vanished halfway up the sail. He nodded to the diving officer. "Kick her up—hard."

Compressed air roared into the ballast tanks. Seconds passed without anything happening; then all at once the *Dolphin* shuddered as something very heavy and very solid seemed to strike the hull. A moment's pause, another solid shock, and then we could see the edge of a giant segment of ice sliding down the face of the TV screen.

"Well, now, I believe I might have had a point there," Swanson remarked. "We seem to have hit a crack between two chunks of ice almost exactly in the middle. Depth?"

"Forty-five."

"Fifteen feet showing. And I don't think we can expect to lift the hundreds of tons of ice lying over the rest of the hull. Plenty of positive buoyancy?"

"All we'll ever want."

"Then we'll call it a day. Okay, quartermaster, away you go up top and tell us what the weather is like."

I didn't wait to hear what the weather was like. I was interested enough in it, but I was even more interested in making sure that Hansen didn't come along to his cabin in time to find me putting on the Mannlicher-Schoenauer along

120

with my furs. But this time I stuck it not in its special holster but in the outside pocket of my caribou trousers. I thought it might come in handier there.

It was exactly noon when I clambered over the edge of the bridge and used a dangling rope to slide down a great rafted chunk of ice that slanted up almost to the top of the sail. The sky had about as much light in it as a late twilight in winter when the sky is heavy with gray cloud. The air was as bitter as ever, but, for all that, the weather had improved. The wind was down now, backed around to the northeast, seldom gusting at more than twenty mph, the ice spicules rising no more than two or three feet above the ice cap. Nothing to tear your eyes out. To be able to see where you were going on that damned ice cap made a very pleasant change.

There were eleven of us altogether: Commander Swanson himself, Dr. Benson, eight enlisted men and myself. Four of the men were carrying stretchers with them.

Even 700 pounds of the highest grade conventional explosive on the market hadn't managed to do very much damage to the ice in that lead. Over an area of seventy yards square or thereabouts the ice had fractured into large fragments curiously uniform in size and roughly hexagonal in shape but fallen back so neatly into position that you couldn't have put a hand down most of the cracks between the adjacent fragments of ice: many of the cracks, indeed, were already beginning to come together. A poor enough performance for a torpedo warhead—until you remembered that though most of its disruptive power must have been directed downward, it had still managed to lift and fracture a chunk of the ice cap weighing maybe 5,000 tons. Looked at that way, it didn't seem such a puny effort after all. Maybe we'd been pretty lucky to achieve what we had.

We walked across to the eastern edge of the lead, scrambled up onto the ice pack proper, and turned around to get our bearings, to line up on the unwavering white finger of the searchlight that reached straight up into the gloom of the sky. No chance of getting lost this time. While the wind stayed quiet and the spicules stayed down, you could see that lamp in the window ten miles away.

We didn't even need to take any bearings. A few steps away and up from the edge of the lead and we could see it at once. Drift Station Zebra. Three huts, one of them badly charred, five blackened skeletons of what had once been huts. Desolation.

"So that's it," Swanson said in my ear. "Or what's left of it. I've come a long way to see this."

"You nearly went a damned sight longer and never saw it," I said. "To the floor of the Arctic, I mean. Pretty, isn't it?"

Swanson shook his head slowly and moved on. There were only a hundred yards to go. I led the way to the nearest intact hut, opened the door, and walked inside.

The hut was about thirty degrees warmer than the last time I had been there, but still bitterly cold. Only Zabrinski and Rawlings were awake. The hut smelled of burnt fuel, disinfectant, iodine, morphine and a peculiar aroma arising from a particularly repulsive-looking hash that Rawlings was industriously churning around in a large iron pot on the low stove.

"Ah, there you are," Rawlings said conversationally. He might have been greeting a neighbor who'd phoned a minute previously to see if he could come across to borrow the lawn mower, rather than greeting men he'd been fairly certain he'd never see again. "The timing is perfect—just about to ring the dinner bell, Captain. Care for some Maryland chicken—I think?"

"Not just at the moment, thank you," Swanson said politely. "Sorry about the ankle, Zabrinski. How is it?"

"Just fine, Captain, just fine. In a plaster cast." He thrust out a foot, stiffly. "The doc here—Dr. Jolly—fixed me up real nice. Had much trouble last night?" This was for me.

"Dr. Carpenter had a great deal of trouble last night," Swanson said. "And we've had a considerable amount since. But later. Bring that stretcher in here. You first, Zabrinski. As for you, Rawlings, you can stop making like Escoffier. The *Dolphin*'s less than a couple of hundred yards from here. We'll have you all aboard in half an hour."

I heard a shuffling noise behind me. Dr. Jolly was on his feet, helping Captain Folsom to his. Folsom looked even weaker than he had yesterday; his face, bandaged though it was, certainly looked worse.

"Captain Folsom," I said by way of introduction. "Dr. Jolly. This is Commander Swanson, captain of the *Dolphin*. Dr. Benson."

"'*Dr.*' Benson, you said, old boy?" Jolly lifted an eyebrow. "My word, the pill-rolling competition's getting a little fierce in these parts. And 'Commander.' By Jove, but we're glad to see you fellows." The combination of the rich Irish brogue and the English slang of the twenties fell more oddly than ever on my ear; he reminded me of educated Singhalese I'd met with their precise, lilting, standard southern English

122

interlarded with the catch phrases of forty years ago. Topping, old bean, simply too ripping for words.

"I can understand that." Swanson smiled. He looked around at the huddled, unmoving men on the floor, men who might have been living or dead but for the immediate and smoky condensation from their shallow breathing, and his smile faded. He said to Captain Folsom, "I cannot tell you how sorry I am. This has been a dreadful thing."

Folsom stirred and said something, but we couldn't make out what it was. Although his shockingly burnt face had been bandaged since I'd seen him last, it didn't seem to have done him any good; he was talking inside his mouth, all right, but the ravaged cheek and mouth had become so paralyzed that his speech didn't emerge as any recognizable language. The good side of his face, the left, was twisted and furrowed, and the eye above almost completely shut. This had nothing to do with any sympathetic neuro-muscular reaction caused by the wickedly charred right cheek. The man was in agony. I said to Jolly, "No morphine left?" I'd left him, I'd thought, with more than enough of it.

"Nothing left," he said tiredly. "I used it all. All of it."

"Dr. Jolly worked all through the night," Zabrinski said quietly. "Eight hours. Rawlings and himself and Kinnaird. They never stopped once."

Benson had his medical kit open. Jolly saw it and smiled, a smile of relief, a smile of exhaustion. He was in far worse shape than he'd been the previous evening. He hadn't had all that much in him when he'd started. But he'd worked. He'd worked a solid eight hours. He'd even fixed up Zabrinski's ankle. A good doctor. Conscientious. Hippocratic, anyway. He was entitled to relax. Now that there were other doctors here, he'd relax. But not before.

He began to ease Folsom into a sitting position and I helped him. He slid down himself, his back to the wall. "Sorry and all that, you know," he said. His bearded frost-bitten face twisted into the semblance of a grin. "A poor host."

"You can leave everything to us now, Dr. Jolly," Swanson said quietly. "You've got all the help that's going. One thing. All those men fit to be moved?"

"I don't know." Jolly rubbed an arm across bloodshot, smudged eyes. "I don't know. One or two of them slipped pretty far back last night. It's the cold. Those two. Pneumonia, I think. Something an injured man could fight off in a few days back home can be fatal here. It's the cold," he repeated. "Uses up ninety per cent of his energy, not in fighting illness and infection, but just generating enough heat to stay alive."

123

"Take it easy," Swanson said. "Maybe we'd better change our minds about that half-hour to get you all aboard. Who's first for the ambulance, Dr. Benson?" Not Dr. Carpenter. Dr. Benson. Well, Benson was his own ship's doctor. But pointed, all the same. A regrettable coolness, as sudden in its onset as it was marked in degree, had appeared in his attitude toward me, and I didn't have to be beaten over the head with a heavy club to guess at the reason for the abrupt change.

"Zabrinski, Dr. Jolly, Captain Folsom, and this man here," Benson said promptly.

"Kinnaird, radio operator," Kinnaird identified himself. "We never thought you'd make it, mate." This to me. He dragged himself somehow to his feet and stood there swaying. "I can walk."

"Don't argue," Swanson said curtly. "Rawlings, stop stirring that filthy mush and get to your feet. Go with them. How long would it take you to run a cable from the boat, fix up a couple of big electric heaters in here, some lights?"

"Alone?"

"All the help you want, man."

"Fifteen minutes. I could rig a phone, sir."

"That would be useful. When the stretcher bearers come back, bring blankets, sheets, hot water. Wrap the water containers in the blankets. Anything else, Dr. Benson?"

"Not now, sir."

"That's it, then. Away you go."

Rawlings lifted the spoon from the pot, tasted it, smacked his lips in appreciation, and shook his head sadly. "It's a crying shame," he said mournfully. "It really is." He went out in the wake of the stretcher bearers.

Of the eight men left lying on the floor, four were conscious. Hewson, the tractor driver, Naseby, the cook, and two others who introduced themselves as Harrington. Twins. They were as alike as two freshly minted pennies, they'd even been burnt and frost-bitten in the same places. The other four were either sleeping or in coma. Benson and I started looking them over, Benson much more carefully than myself, very busy with thermometer and stethoscope. Looking for signs of pneumonia. I didn't think he'd have to look very far. Commander Swanson looked speculatively around the cabin, occasionally throwing a very odd look in my direction, occasionally flailing his arms across his chest to keep the circulation going. He had to. He didn't have the fancy furs I had, and in spite of the solid-fuel stove, the place was like an icebox.

The first man I looked at was lying on his side in the far

right-hand corner of the room. He had half-open eyes, just showing the lower arcs of his pupils, sunken temples, marble-white forehead, and the only part of his face that wasn't bandaged was as cold as the marble in a winter graveyard. I said, "Who is this?"

"Grant. John Grant." Hewson, the dark, quiet tractor driver, answered me. "Radio operator. Kinnaird's sidekick. How's it with him?"

"He's dead. He's been dead quite some time."

"Dead?" Swanson said sharply. "You sure?" I gave him my aloof professional look and said nothing. He said to Benson, "Anybody too ill to be moved?"

"Those two here, I think," Benson said. He wasn't noticing the series of peculiar looks Swanson was letting me have, so he handed me his stethoscope. After a minute I straightened and nodded.

"Third-degree burns," Benson said to Swanson. "What we can see of them, that is. Both high temperatures, both very fast, very weak, and erratic pulses, both with lung fluids."

"They'd have a better chance inside the *Dolphin*," Swanson said.

"You'd kill them getting there," I said. "Even if you could wrap them up warmly enough to take them back to the ship, hauling them up to the top of the sail and then lowering them vertically through those hatchways would finish them off."

"We can't stay out in that lead indefinitely," Swanson said. "I'll take the responsibility for moving them."

"Sorry, Captain." Benson shook his head gravely. "I agree with Dr. Carpenter."

Swanson shrugged and said nothing. Moments later the stretcher bearers were back, followed soon after by Rawlings and three other enlisted men carrying cables, heaters, lamps, and a telephone. It took only a few minutes to connect the heaters and lamps on to the cable. Rawlings cranked the call-up generator of his field phone and spoke briefly into the mouthpiece. Bright lights came on and the heaters started to crackle and, after a few seconds, glow.

Hewson, Naseby, and the Harrington twins left by stretcher. When they'd gone, I unhooked the Coleman lantern. "You won't be needing this now," I said. "I won't be long."

"Where are you going?" Swanson's voice was quiet.

"I won't be long," I repeated. "Just looking around."

He hesitated, then stood to one side. I went out, moved around a corner of the hut, and stopped. I heard the whirr of the call-up bell, a voice on the telephone. It was only a mur-

mur to me, I couldn't make out what was being said. But I'd expected this.

The Coleman storm lantern flickered and faded in the wind but didn't go out. Stray ice spicules struck against the glass, but it didn't crack or break; it must have been one of those specially toughened glasses immune to a couple of hundred degrees' temperature range between the inside and the outside.

I made my way diagonally across to the only hut left on the south side. No trace of burning, charring, or even smoke-blackening on the outside walls. The fuel store must have been the one next to it, on the same side and to the west, straight downwind; that almost certainly must have been its position judging by the destruction of all the other huts, and the grotesquely buckled shape of its remaining girders made this strong probability a certainty. Here had been the heart of the fire.

Hard against the side of the undamaged hut was a lean-to shed, solidly built. Six feet high, six wide, eight long. The door opened easily. Wooden floor, gleaming aluminum for the sides and ceiling, big black heaters bolted to the inside and outside walls. Wires led from those, and it was no job for an Einstein to guess that they led—or had led—to the now destroyed generator house. This lean-to shed would have been warm night and day. The squat, low-slung tractor that took up nearly all the floor space inside would have started any time at the touch of a switch. It wouldn't start at the turn of a switch now; it would take three or four blowtorches and the same number of strong men even to turn the engine over once. I closed the door and went into the main hut.

It was packed with metal tables, benches, machinery, and every modern device for the automatic recording and interpretation of every conceivable observed detail of the Arctic weather. I didn't know what the functions of most of the instruments were and I didn't care. This was the meteorological office and that was enough for me. I examined the hut carefully but quickly, and there didn't seem to be anything odd or out of place that I could see. In one corner, on an empty wooden packing case, was a portable radio transmitter with listening phones—"transeivers," they called them nowadays. Near it, in a box of heavy oiled wood, were fifteen Nife cells connected up in series. Hanging from a hook on the wall was a two-volt test lamp. I touched its bare leads to the outside terminals of the battery formed by the cells. Had those cells left in them even a fraction of their original power, that test lamp should have burnt out in a white flash. It didn't even begin to glow. I tore a piece of flex from a near-

126

by lamp and touched its ends to the terminals. Not even the minutest spark. Kinnaird hadn't been lying when he had said that his battery had been completely dead. But, then, I hadn't for a moment thought he'd been lying.

I made my way to the last hut—the hut that held the charred remnants of the seven men who had died in the fire. The stench of charred flesh and burnt diesel seemed stronger, more nauseating than ever. I stood in the doorway and the last thing I wanted to do was to approach even an inch closer. I peeled off fur and woollen mittens, set the lamp on a table, pulled out my flashlight, and knelt by the first dead man.

Ten minutes passed and all I wanted was out of there. There are some things that doctors, even hardened pathologists, will go a long way to avoid. Bodies that have been too long in the sea is one; bodies that have been in the immediate vicinity of underwater explosion is another; and men who have literally been burned alive is another. I was beginning to feel more than slightly sick: but I wasn't going to leave there until I was finished.

The door creaked open. I turned and watched Commander Swanson come in. He'd been a long time, I'd expected him before then. Lieutenant Hansen, his damaged left hand wrapped in some thick woollen material, came in after him. That was what the phone call had been about—the Commander calling up reinforcements. Swanson switched off his flashlight, pushed up his snow goggles, and pulled down his mask. His eyes narrowed at the scene before him, his nostrils wrinkled in involuntary disgust, and color drained swiftly from his ruddy cheeks. Both Hansen and I had told him what to expect, but he hadn't been prepared for this: not often can the imagination encompass the reality. For a moment I thought he was going to be sick, but then I saw a slight tinge of color touch his cheekbones and I knew he wasn't.

"Dr. Carpenter," Swanson said in a voice in which the unsteady huskiness seemed only to emphasize the stilted formality, "I wish you to return at once to the ship, where you will remain confined to your quarters. I would prefer you went voluntarily, accompanied by Lieutenant Hansen here. I wish no trouble. I trust you don't, either. If you do, we can accommodate you. Rawlings and Murphy are waiting outside that door."

"Those are fighting words, Commander," I said, "and very unfriendly. Rawlings and Murphy are going to get uncommonly cold out there." I put my right hand in my caribou pants pocket—the one with the gun in it—and surveyed him unhurriedly. "Have you had a brainstorm?"

Swanson looked at Hansen and nodded in the direction of the door. Hansen half turned, then stopped as I said, "Very high-handed, aren't we. I'm not worth an explanation, is that it?"

Hansen looked uncomfortable. He didn't like any part of this. I suspected Swanson didn't, either, but he was going to do what he had to do and let his feelings look elsewhere.

"Unless you're a great deal less intelligent than I believe— and I credit you with a high intelligence—you know exactly what the explanation is. When you came aboard the *Dolphin* in the Holy Loch, both Admiral Garvie and myself were highly suspicious of you. You spun us a story about being an expert in Arctic conditions and of having helped set up this station here. When we wouldn't accept that as sufficient authority or reason to take you along with us, you told a highly convincing tale about this being an advanced missile- warning outpost, and even though it was peculiar that Admiral Garvie had never heard of it, we accepted it. The huge dish aerial you spoke of, the radar masts, the electronic computers—what's happened to them, Dr. Carpenter? A little insubstantial, weren't they? Like all figments of the imagination."

I looked at him, considering, and let him go on.

"There never were any of those things, were there? You're up to your neck in something very murky indeed, my friend. What it is I don't know, nor, for the moment, do I care. All I care for is the safety of the ship, the welfare of the crew, and bringing the Zebra survivors safely back home, and I'm taking no chances at all."

"The wishes of the British Admiralty, the orders from your own Director of Underseas Warfare—those mean nothing to you?"

"I'm beginning to have very strong reservations about the way those orders were obtained," Swanson said grimly. "You're altogether too mysterious for my liking, Dr. Carpenter—as well as being a fluent liar."

"Those are harsh, harsh words, Commander."

"The truth not infrequently sounds that way. Will you please come?"

"Sorry. I'm not through here yet."

"I see. John, will you—"

"I can give you an explanation. I see I have to. Won't you listen?"

"A third fairytale?" A head shake. "No."

"And I'm not ready to leave. Impasse."

Swanson looked at Hansen, who turned to go. I said,

"Well, if you're too stiff-necked to listen to me, call up the bloodhounds. Isn't it just luck, now, that we have three fully qualified doctors here?"

"What do you mean?"

"I mean this." Guns have different characteristics in appearance. Some look relatively harmless, some ugly, some businesslike, some wicked. The Mannlicher-Schoenauer in my hand just looked plain downright wicked. Very wicked indeed. The white light from the Coleman glittered off the blued metal, menacing and sinister. It was a great gun to terrify people with.

"You wouldn't use it," Swanson said flatly.

"I'm through talking. I'm through asking for a hearing. Bring on the bailiffs, friend."

"You're bluffing, mister," Hansen said savagely. "You don't dare."

"There's too much at stake for me not to dare. Find out now. Don't be a coward. Don't hide behind your enlisted men's backs. Don't order them to get themselves shot." I snapped off the safety catch. "Come and take it from me yourself."

"Stay right where you are, John," Swanson said sharply. "He means it. I suppose you have a whole armory in that combination-lock suitcase of yours," he added bitterly.

"That's it. Automatic carbines, six-inch naval guns, the works. But for a small-size situation, a small-size gun. Do I get my hearing?"

"You get your hearing."

"Send Rawlings and Murphy away. I don't want anyone else to know anything about this. Anyway, they're probably freezing to death."

Swanson nodded. Hansen went to the door, opened it, spoke briefly, and returned. I laid the gun on a table, picked up my flashlight, and moved some paces away. I said, "Come and have a look at this."

They came. Both of them passed by the table with the gun lying there and didn't even look at it. I stopped before one of the grotesquely misshapen charred lumps lying on the floor. Swanson came close and stared down. His face had lost whatever little color it had regained. He made a queer noise in his throat.

"That ring, that gold ring—" he began, then stopped short.

"I wasn't lying about that."

"No. No, you weren't. I—I don't know what to say. I'm most—"

"It doesn't matter," I said roughly. "Look here. At the back. I'm afraid I had to remove some of the carbon."

129

"The neck," Swanson whispered. "It's broken."

"Is that what you think?"

"Something heavy, I don't know, a beam from one of the huts, must have fallen—"

"You've just seen one of those huts. They have no beams. There's an inch and a half of the vertebrae missing. If anything sufficiently heavy to smash off an inch and a half of the backbone had struck him, the broken piece would be imbedded in his neck. It's not. It was blown out. He was shot from the front, through the base of the throat. The bullet went out the back of the neck. A soft-nosed bullet—you can tell by the size of the exit hole—from a powerful gun, something like a thirty-eight Colt or Luger or Mauser."

"Good God above!" For the first time, Swanson was badly shaken. He stared at the thing on the floor, then at me. "Murdered. You mean he was murdered."

"Who would have done this?" Hansen said hoarsely. "Who, man, who? And in God's name, why?"

"I don't know who did it."

Swanson looked at me, his eyes strange. "You just found this out?"

"I found out last night."

"You found out last night." The words were slow, far-spaced, a distinct hiatus between each two. "And all the time since, aboard the ship, you never said ... you never showed ... My God, Carpenter, you're inhuman."

"Sure," I said. "See that gun there? It makes a loud bang, and when I use it to kill the man who did this, I won't even blink. I'm inhuman, all right."

"I was speaking out of turn. Sorry." Swanson was making a visible effort to bring himself under normal control. He looked at the Mannlicher-Schoenauer, then at me, then back at the gun. "Private revenge is out, Carpenter. No one is going to take the law into his own hands."

"Don't make me laugh out loud. A morgue isn't a fit place for it. Besides, I'm not through showing you things yet. There's more. Something that I've just found out now. Not last night." I pointed to another huddled black shape on the ground. "Care to have a look at this man here?"

"I'd rather not," Swanson said steadily. "Suppose you tell us?"

"You can see from where you are. The head. I've cleaned it up. Small hole in the front, in the middle of the face and slightly to the right: larger exit hole at the back of the top of the head. Same gun. Same man behind the gun."

Neither man said anything. They were too sick, too shocked to say anything.

"Queer path the bullet took," I went on. "Ranged sharply upwards. As if the man who fired the shot had been lying or sitting down while his victim stood above him."

"Yes." Swanson didn't seem to have heard me. "Murder. Two murders. This is a job for the authorities, for the police."

"Sure," I said. "For the police. Let's just ring the sergeant at the local station and ask him if he would mind stepping this way for a few minutes."

"It's not a job for us," Swanson persisted. "As captain of an American naval vessel, with a duty to discharge, I am primarily interested in bringing my ship and the Zebra survivors back to Scotland again."

"Without endangering the ship?" I asked. "With a murderer aboard, the possibility of endangering the ship does not arise?"

"We don't know he is—or will be—aboard."

"You don't even begin to believe that yourself. You know he will be. You know as well as I do why this fire broke out and you know damn well that it was no accident. If there was any accidental element about it, it was just the size and extent of the fire. The killer may have miscalculated that. But both time and weather conditions were against him: I don't think he had very much option. The only possible way in which he could obliterate all traces of his crime was to have a fire of sufficient proportions to obliterate those traces. He would have got away with it, too, if I hadn't been here, if I hadn't been convinced before we left port that something was very much wrong indeed. But he would take very good care that he wouldn't obliterate himself in the process. Like it or not, Commander, you're going to have a killer aboard your ship."

"But all of those men have been burned, some very severely—"

"What the hell did you expect? That the unknown X would go about without a mark on him, without as much as a cigarette burn, proclaiming to the world that he had been the one who had been throwing matches about and had then thoughtfully stood to one side? Local color. He *had* to get himself burned."

"It doesn't necessarily follow," Hansen said. "How was he to know that anyone was going to get suspicious and start investigating?"

"You'd be well advised to join your captain in keeping out of the detecting racket," I said shortly. "The men behind this are top-flight experts with far-reaching contacts—part of a criminal octopus with tentacles so long that it can even

131

reach out and sabotage your ship in the Holy Loch. Why they did that, I don't know. What matters is that top-flight operators like those *never* take chances. They always operate on the assumption that they *may* be found out. They take every possible precaution against every possible eventuality. Besides, when the fire was at its height—we don't know the story of that yet—the killer would have had to pitch in and rescue those trapped. It would have seemed damned odd if he hadn't. And so he got burned."

"My God." Swanson's teeth were beginning to chatter with the cold but he didn't seem to notice it. "What a hellish set-up."

"Isn't it? I dare say there's nothing in your Navy regulations to cover this."

"But what—what are we going to do?"

"We call the cops. That's me."

"What do you mean?"

"What I say. I have more authority, more official backing, more scope, more power and more freedom of action than any cop you ever saw. You must believe me. What I say is true."

"I'm beginning to believe it *is* true," Swanson said in slow thoughtfulness. "I've been wondering more and more about you in the past twenty-four hours. I've kept telling myself I was wrong, even ten minutes before I kept telling myself. You're a policeman? Or detective?"

"Naval officer. Intelligence. I have credentials in my suit-case which I am empowered to show in an emergency." It didn't seem the time to tell him just how wide a selection of credentials I did have. "This is the emergency."

"But—but you are a doctor."

"Sure I am. A Navy doctor—on the side. My specialty is in-vestigating sabotage in the U.K. armed forces. The cover-up of research doctor is the ideal one. My duties are deliber-ately vague, and I have the power to poke and pry into all sorts of corners and situations and talk to all sorts of people on the grounds of being an investigating psychologist which would be impossible for the average officer."

There was a long silence; then Swanson said bitterly, "You might have told us before this."

"I might have broadcast it all over your tannoy system. Why the hell should I? I don't want to trip over blundering amateurs every step I take. Ask any cop. The biggest men-ace of his life is the self-appointed Sherlock. Besides, I couldn't trust you, and before you start getting all hot and bothered about that I might add that I don't mean you'd deliberately give me away or anything like that but that you

132

may inadvertently give me away. Now I've no option but to tell you what I can and chance the consequences. Why couldn't you just have accepted that directive from your Chief of Naval Operations and acted accordingly?"

"Directive?" Hansen looked at Swanson. "What directive?"

"Order from Washington to give Dr. Carpenter here carte blanche for practically everything. Be reasonable, Carpenter. I don't like operating in the dark and I'm naturally suspicious. You came aboard in highly questionable circumstances. You knew too damn much about submarines. You were as evasive as hell. You had this sabotage theory all cut and dried. Damn it, man, of course I had reservations. Wouldn't you have had, in my place?"

"I suppose so. I don't know. Me, I obey orders."

"Uh-huh. And your orders in this case?"

"Meaning what exactly is all this about?" I sighed. "It would have to come to this. You must be told now, and you'll understand why your Chief of Naval Operations was so anxious that you give me every help possible."

"We can believe this one?" Swanson asked.

"You can believe this one. The story I spun you back in the Holy Loch wasn't all malarkey. I just dressed it up a bit to make sure you'd take me along. They did indeed have a very special item of equipment here—an electronic marvel that was used for monitoring the count-down of Soviet missiles and pinpointing their locations. This machine was kept in one of the huts now destroyed—the second from the west in the south row. Night and day a giant captive radio-sonde balloon reached thirty thousand feet up into the sky—but it had no radio attached. It was just a huge aerial. Incidentally, I should think that this is the reason why the oil fuel appears to have been flung over so large an area—an explosion caused by the bursting of the hydrogen cylinders used to inflate the balloons. They were stored in the fuel hut."

"Did everybody in Zebra know about this monitoring machine?"

"No. Most of them thought it a device for investigating cosmic rays. Only four people knew what it really was—my brother and the three others who all slept in the hut that housed this machine. Now the hut is destroyed. The free world's most advanced listening post. You wonder why your C.N.O. was so anxious?"

"Four men?" Swanson looked at me, a faint speculation still in his eye. "Which four men, Dr. Carpenter?"

"Do you have to ask? Four of the seven men you see lying here, Commander."

He stared down at the floor, then looked quickly away. He said: "You mentioned that you were convinced even before we left port that something was wrong. Why?"

"My brother had a top-secret code. We had messages sent by him: he was an expert radio operator. One said that there had been two separate attempts to wreck the monitor. He didn't go into details. Another said that he had been attacked and left unconscious when making a midnight check and finding someone bleeding off the gas from the hydrogen cylinders: without the radio-sonde aerial, the monitor would have been useless. He was lucky, he was out for only a few minutes, as long again and he would have frozen to death. In the circumstances did you expect me to believe that the fire was unconnected with the attempts to sabotage the monitor?"

"But how would anyone *know* what it was?" Hansen objected. "Apart from your brother and the other three men, that is?" Like Swanson, he glanced at the floor and, like Swanson, looked as hurriedly away. "For my money, this is the work of a psycho. A madman. A coldly calculating criminal would—well, he wouldn't go in for wholesale murder like this. But a psycho would."

"Three hours ago," I said, "before you loaded the torpedo into number 3 tube, you checked the manually controlled levers and the warning lights for the tube bow caps. In the one case, you found that the levers had been disconnected in the open position: in the other, you found that the wires had been crossed in a junction box. Do you think that was the work of a psycho? Another psycho?"

He said nothing. Swanson said, "What can I do to help, Dr. Carpenter?"

"What are you willing to do, Commander?"

"I will not hand over command of the *Dolphin*." He smiled, but he wasn't feeling like smiling. "Short of that, I— and the crew of the *Dolphin*—am at your complete disposal. You name it, Doctor, that's all."

"This time you believe my story?"

"This time I believe your story."

I was pleased about that; I almost believed it myself.

8

THE HUT WHERE WE'D FOUND all the Zebra survivors huddled together was almost deserted when we got back to it; only Dr. Benson and the two very sick men remained. The hut seemed bigger now, somehow, bigger and colder, and very shabby and untidy, like the remnants of a church rummage sale where the housewives have trained for a couple of months before moving up to battle stations. Pieces of clothing, bedding, frayed and shredded blankets, gloves, plates, cutlery, and dozens of odds and ends of personal possessions lay scattered all over the floor. The sick men had been too sick—and too glad to be on their way—to worry much about taking too many of their various knickknacks out of there. All they had wanted out of there was themselves. I didn't blame them.

The two unconscious men had their scarred and frost-bitten faces toward us. They were either sleeping or in a coma. But I took no chances. I beckoned to Benson and he came and stood with us in the shelter of the west wall.

I told Benson what I'd told the commander and Hansen. He had to know. As the man who would be in the most constant and closest contact with the sick men, he had to know. I suppose he must have been pretty astonished and shaken, but he didn't show it. Doctors' faces behave as doctors tell them to; when they come across a patient in a pretty critical state of health, they don't beat their breasts and break into loud lamentations, as this tends to discourage the patient. This now made three men from the *Dolphin*'s crew who knew what the score was—well, half the score, anyway. Three was enough. I only hoped it wasn't too much.

Thereafter Swanson did the talking; Benson would take it better from him than he would from me. Swanson said, "Where were you thinking of putting the sick men we've sent back aboard?"

"In the most comfortable places I can find. Officers' quarters, crew's quarters, scattered all over so that no one is upset too much. Spread the load, so to speak." He paused. "I didn't know of the latest—um—development at the time. Things are somewhat different now."

"They are. Half of them in the wardroom, the other half in the crew's mess— No, the crew's quarters. No reason why they shouldn't be made comfortable. If they wonder at this, you can say it's for ease of medical treatment and that they can all be under constant medical watch, like heart patients in a ward. Get Dr. Jolly behind you in this. He seems a co-operative type. And I've no doubt he'll support you in your next move—that all patients are to be stripped, bathed and provided with clean pajamas. If they're too ill to move, a bed bath. Dr. Carpenter here tells me that prevention of infection is of paramount importance in cases of severe burn injuries."

"And their clothes?"

"You catch on more quickly than I did," Swanson grunted. "All their clothes to be taken away and labeled. All contents to be removed and labeled. The clothes, for anyone's information, are to be disinfected and laundered."

"It might help if I am permitted to know just what we are looking for," Benson suggested.

Swanson looked at me.

"God knows," I said. "Anything and everything. One thing certain—you won't find a gun. Be especially careful in labeling gloves—when we get back to Britain, we'll have the experts test them for nitrates from the gun used."

"If anyone has brought aboard anything bigger than a postage stamp, I'll find it," Benson promised.

"Are you sure?" I asked. "Even if you brought it aboard yourself?"

"What? Me? What the devil are you suggesting?"

"I'm suggesting that something may have been shoved inside your medical kit, even your pockets, when you weren't looking."

"Good Lord." He dug feverishly into his pockets. "The idea never even occurred to me."

"You haven't the right type of nasty, suspicious mind," Swanson said dryly. "Off you go. You too, John."

They left, and Swanson and I went inside. Once I'd checked that the two men really were unconscious, we went to work. It must have been many years since Swanson had policed a deck or parade ground, much less doubled as scavenger, but he took to it in the manner born. He was assiduous, painstaking and missed nothing. Neither did I. We cleared a corner of the hut and brought over there every single article that was either lying on the floor or attached to the still ice-covered walls. Nothing was missed. It was either shaken, turned over, opened or emptied according to what it was. Fifteen minutes and we were all through. If there was anything bigger than a match stick to be found in that room, we would have found it. But we found nothing. Then we scattered everything back over the floor again until the hut looked more or less as it had before our search. If either of the two unconscious men came to, I didn't want him knowing that we had been looking for anything.

"We're no great shakes in the detecting business," Swanson said. He looked slightly discouraged.

"We can't find what isn't here to be found. And it doesn't help that we don't know what we're looking for. Let's try for the gun now. May be anywhere, he may even have thrown it away on the ice cap, though I think that unlikely. A killer never likes to lose his means of killing—and he couldn't have been sure that he wouldn't require it again. There aren't so very many places to search. He wouldn't have left it here, for this is the main bunkhouse and in constant use. That leaves only the met office and the lab where the dead men are lying."

"He could have hidden it among the ruins of one of the burnt-out huts," Swanson objected.

"Not a chance. Our friend has been here for some months now, and he must know exactly the effect those ice storms have. The spicules silt up against any object that lies in their path. The metal frameworks at the bases of the destroyed buildings are still in position, and the floors of the huts—or where the wooden floors used to be—are covered with solid ice to a depth of from four to six inches. He would have done as well to bury his gun in quick-setting concrete."

We started on the meteorological hut. We looked in every shelf, every box, every cupboard, and had just started ripping the backs off the metal cabinets that housed the meteorological equipment when Swanson said abruptly, "I have an idea. Back in a couple of minutes."

He was better than his word. He was back in a minute flat, carrying in his hands four objects that glittered wetly in the lamplight and smelled strongly of petrol. A gun—a Mauser automatic—the haft and broken-off blade of a knife, and two rubber-wrapped packages that turned out to be spare magazines for the Mauser. He said: "I guess this was what you were looking for."

"Where did you find them?"

"The tractor. In the gas tank."

"What made you think of looking there?"

"Just luck. I got to thinking about your remark that the man who had used this gun might want to use it again. But if he was to hide it anywhere where it was exposed to the weather, it might have become jammed up with ice. Even if it didn't, he might have figured that the metal would contract, so that the shells wouldn't fit, or that the firing mechanism and lubricating oil would freeze solid. Only two things don't freeze solid in those sub-zero temperatures—alcohol and gasoline. You can't hide a gun in a bottle of gin."

"It wouldn't have worked," I said. "Metal would still contract—the petrol is as cold as the surrounding air."

"Maybe he didn't know that. Or if he did, maybe he just thought it was a good place to hide it, quick and handy." He looked consideringly at me as I broke the butt and looked at the empty magazine, then said sharply: "You're smearing that gun a little, aren't you?"

"Finger prints? Not after being in petrol. He was probably wearing gloves, anyway."

"So why did you want it?"

"Serial number. May be able to trace it. It's even possible that the killer had a police permit for it. It's happened before, believe it or not. And you must remember that the killer believed there would be no suspicion of foul play, much less that a search would be carried out for the gun.

"Anyway, this knife explains the gun. Firing guns is a noisy business, and I'm surprised—I was surprised—that the killer risked it. He might have waked the whole camp. But he had to take the risk because he'd gone and snapped off the business end of this little sticker here. This is a very slender blade, the kind it's very easy to snap unless you know exactly what you're doing, especially when extreme cold makes the metal brittle. He probably struck a rib or broke the blade trying to haul it out: a knife slides in easily enough but it can jam against cartilage or bone when you try to remove it."

"You mean—you mean the killer murdered a *third* man?" Swanson asked carefully. "With this knife?"

"The third man but the first victim," I nodded. "The missing half of the blade will be stuck inside someone's chest. But I'm not going to look for it: it would be pointless and take far too long."

"I'm not sure that I don't agree with Hansen," Swanson said slowly. "I know it's impossible to explain away the sabotage on the boat—but, my God, this looks like the work of a maniac. All this—all this senseless killing."

"All this killing," I agreed. "But not senseless—not from

138

the point of view of the killer. No, don't ask me, I don't know what his point of view was—or is. I know—you know—why he started the fire: what we don't know is why he killed those men in the first place."

Swanson shook his head, then said: "Let's get back to the other hut. I'll phone for someone to keep a watch over those sick men. I don't know about you, but I'm frozen stiff. And you had no sleep last night."

"I'll watch them meantime," I said. "For an hour or so. And I've some thinking to do, some very hard thinking."

"You haven't much to go on, have you?"

"That's what makes it so hard."

I'd said to Swanson that I didn't have much to go on, a less than accurate statement, for I didn't have anything to go on at all. So I didn't waste any time thinking. Instead I took a flashlight and went once again to the lab where the dead men lay. I was cold and tired and alone, and darkness was falling and I didn't very much fancy going there. Nobody would have fancied going there, a place of dreadful death which any sane person would have avoided like the plague. And that was why I was going there, not because I wasn't sane, but because it was a place that no man would ever voluntarily visit—unless he had an extremely powerful motivation, such as the intention of picking up some essential thing he had hidden there in the near certainty that no one else would ever go near the place. It sounded complicated, even to me. I was very tired. I made a fuzzy mental note to ask around, when I got back to the *Dolphin*, to find out who had suggested shifting the dead men in there.

The walls of the lab were lined with shelves and cupboards containing jars and bottles and retorts and test tubes and such-like chemical junk, but I didn't give them more than a glance. I went to the corner of the hut where the dead men lay most closely together, shone my light along the side of the room, and found what I was looking for in a matter of seconds—a floorboard standing slightly proud of its neighbors. Two of the blackened, contorted lumps that had once been men lay across that board. I moved them just far enough, not liking the job at all, then lifted one end of the loose floorboard.

It looked as if someone had had it in mind to start up a supermarket. In the six-inch space between the floor and the base of the hut were stacked dozens of neatly arranged cans—soup, beef, fruit, vegetables, a fine varied diet with all the proteins and vitamins a man could want. Someone had had no intention of going hungry. There was even a small pressure stove and a couple of gallons of kerosene to thaw out the cans. And to one side, lying flat, two rows of gleaming Nife cells—there must have been about forty in all.

I replaced the board, left the lab, and went across to the meteorological hut again. I spent over an hour there, unbuttoning the backs of metal cabinets and peering into their innards, but I found nothing. Not what I had hoped to find, that is. But I did come across one very peculiar item, a small green metal box six inches by four by two, with a circular control that was both switch and tuner, and two glassed-in dials with neither figures nor marking on them. On one side of the box was a brass-rimmed hole.

I turned the switch and one of the dials glowed green, a magic-eye tuning device with the fans spread well apart. The other dial stayed dead. I twiddled the tuner control but nothing happened. Both the magic eye and the second dial required something to activate them—something like a preset radio signal. The hole in the side would accommodate the plug of any standard telephone receiver. Not many people would have known what this was, but I'd seen one before—a transistorized homing device for locating the direction of a radio signal, such as emitted by the *Sarah* device on American space capsules which enables searchers to locate it once it has landed in the sea.

What legitimate purpose could be served by such a device in Drift Ice Station Zebra? When I'd told Swanson and Hansen of the existence of a console for monitoring rocket-firing signals from Siberia, that much of my story, anyway, had been true. But that had called for a giant aerial stretching far up into the sky: this comparative toy couldn't have ranged a twentieth of the distance to Siberia.

I had another look at the portable radio transmitter and the now exhausted Nife batteries that served them. The dialing counter was still tuned to the wave band on which the *Dolphin* had picked up the distress signals. There was nothing for me there. I looked more closely at the nickel-cadmium cells and saw that they were joined to one another and to the radio set by wire-cored rubber leads with very powerful spring-loaded sawtooth clips on the terminals: those last ensured perfect electrical contact, as well as being very convenient to use. I undid two of the clips, held my flashlight high, and peered closely at the terminals. The indentations made by the sharpened steel saw teeth were faint but unmistakable.

I made my way back to the laboratory hut, lifted the loose floorboard again, and shone my light on the Nife cells lying there. At least half of the cells had the same character-

140

istic markings. Cells that looked fresh and unused, yet had those same markings, and if anything was certain, it was that those cells had been brand new and unmarked when Drift Ice Station Zebra had been first set up. A few of the cells were tucked so far away under adjacent floorboards that I had to stretch my hand far in to reach them. I pulled out two, and in the space behind them, I seemed to see something dark and dull and metallic.

It was too dark to distinguish clearly what the object was but after I'd levered up another two floorboards, I could see without any trouble at all. It was a cylinder about thirty inches long and six in diameter with brass stopcock and mounted pressure gauge registering "Full," close beside it was a package about eighteen inches square and four thick stenciled with the words "Radio Sonde Balloons." Hydrogen, batteries, balloons, corned beef, and mulligatawny soup. A catholic enough assortment of stores by any standards: but there wouldn't have been anything haphazard about the choice of that assortment.

When I made it back to the bunkhouse, the two patients were still breathing. That was about all I could say for myself, too, I was shaking with cold, and even clamping my teeth together couldn't keep them from chattering. I thawed out under the big electric heaters until I was only half frozen; then I picked up my flashlight and moved out again into the wind and the cold and the dark. I was a sucker for punishment, that was for sure.

In the next twenty minutes I made half a dozen complete circuits of the camp, moving a few yards farther out with each circuit. I must have walked over a mile altogether and that was all I had for it, just the walk and a slight touch of frostbite high up on my cheekbones, the only part of my face other than my eyes exposed to that bitter cold. I knew I had frostbite, for my skin had suddenly ceased to feel cold any more and was quite dead to the touch. Enough was enough, and I had a hunch that I was wasting my time, anyway. I headed back to the camp.

I passed between the meteorological hut and the lab and was just level with the eastern end of the bunkhouse when I sensed as much as saw something odd out of the corner of my eye. I steadied my flashlight beam on the east wall and peered closely at the sheath of ice that had been deposited there over the days by the ice storm. Most of the encrustation was of a homogeneous grayish-white, very smooth and polished, but it wasn't all gray-white; here and there it was speckled with dozens of black flecks of odd shapes and sizes, none of them more than an inch square. I tried to touch them, but they were deeply imbedded in and showing through the gleaming ice. I went to examine the east wall of the meteorological hut, but it was quite innocent of any such black flecking. So was the east wall of the lab.

A short search inside the meteorological hut turned up a hammer and screw-driver. I chipped away a section of the black-flecked ice, brought it into the bunkhouse, and laid it on the floor in front of one of the big electrical heaters. Ten minutes later I had a small pool of water and, lying in it, the sodden remains of what had once been fragments of burnt paper. This was very curious indeed. It meant that there were scores of pieces of burnt paper imbedded in the east wall of the bunkhouse. Just there: nowhere else. The explanation, of course, could be completely innocuous: or not, as the case might be.

I had another look at the two unconscious men. They were warm enough and comfortable enough, but that was about all you could say for them. I knew they weren't well enough to be moved within the next twenty-four hours. I lifted the phone and asked for someone to relieve me, and when two seamen arrived I made my way back to the *Dolphin*.

There was an unusual atmosphere aboard ship that afternoon, quiet and dull and almost funereal. It was hardly surprising. As far as the crew of the *Dolphin* had been concerned, the men manning Drift Ice Station Zebra had been just so many ciphers, not even names, just unknowns. But now the burnt, frost-bitten, emaciated survivors that had come aboard ship, sick and suffering men each with a life and individuality of his own, and the sight of those wasted men still mourning the deaths of their eight comrades had suddenly brought home to every man on the submarine the full horror of what had happened on Zebra. And, of course, less than seven hours had elapsed since their own torpedo officer, Lieutenant Mills, had been killed. Now, even though the mission had been successful, there seemed little reason for celebration. Down in the crew's mess the hi-fi and the juke box were stilled. The ship was like a tomb.

I found Hansen in his cabin. He was sitting on the edge of his Pullman bunk, still wearing his fur trousers, his face bleak and hard and cold. He watched me in silence as I stripped off my parka, undid the empty holster tied around my chest, hung it up, and stuck inside it the automatic I'd pulled from my caribou pants. Then he said suddenly, "I wouldn't take them all off, Doc. Not if you want to come with us, that is." He looked at his own furs, and his mouth was bitter. "Hardly the uniform for a funeral, is it?"

"You mean—"

"Skipper's in his cabin. Boning up on the burial service. Tom Mills and that assistant radio operator—Grant, wasn't it?—who died out there today. A double funeral. Out on the ice. There's some men there already, chipping a place with crow bars and sledges at the base of a hummock."

"I saw no one."

"Port side. To the west."

"I thought Swanson would have taken young Mills back to the States. Or Scotland."

"Too far. And there's the psychological angle. You could hardly dent the morale of this bunch we have aboard here, much less shoot it to pieces, but carrying a dead man as a shipmate is an unhappy thing. He's had permission from Washington . . ." He broke off uncertainly, looked up at me and then away again. I didn't have any need of telepathy to know what was in his mind.

"The seven men on Zebra?" I shook my head. "No, no funeral service for them. How could you? I'll pay my respects some other way."

His eyes flickered up at the Mannlicher-Schoenauer hanging in its holster, then away again. He said in a quiet, savage voice, "Goddamn his black, murderous soul. That devil's aboard, Carpenter. Here. On our ship." He smacked a bunched fist hard against the palm of his other hand. "Have you no idea what's behind this, Doc? No idea who's responsible?"

"If I had, I wouldn't be standing here. Any idea how Benson is getting along with the sick and injured?"

"He's all through. I've just left him."

I nodded, reached up for the automatic, and stuck it in the pocket of my caribou pants. Hansen said quietly: "Even here?"

"Especially here."

I left him and went along to the surgery. Benson was sitting at his table, his back to his art gallery of technicolor cartoons, making entries in a book. He looked up as I closed the door behind me.

"Find anything?" I asked.

"Nothing I'd consider interesting. Hansen did most of the sorting. You may find something." He pointed to neatly folded piles of clothing on the deck, several small attaché cases, and a few polythene bags, each labeled. "Look for yourself. How about the two men left out on Zebra?"

"Holding their own. I think they'll be okay, but it's too early to say yet." I squatted on the floor, went carefully through all the pockets in the clothes, and found, as I had expected, nothing. Hansen wasn't the man to miss anything. I felt every square inch of the lining areas and came up with the same results. I went through the small cases and the polythene bags, small items of clothing and personal gear, shaving kits, letters, photographs, two or three cameras. I broke open the cameras and they were all empty. I said to Benson: "Dr. Jolly brought his medical case aboard with him?"

"Wouldn't even trust one of your own colleagues, would you?"

"No."

"Neither would I." He smiled with his mouth only. "Your evil influence. I went through every item in it. Not a thing. I even measured the thickness of the bottom of the case. Nothing there."

"Good enough for me. How are the patients?"

"Nine of them," Benson said. "The psychological effect of knowing that they're safe has done them more good than any medication ever could." He consulted cards on his desk. "Captain Folsom is the worst. No danger, of course, but his facial burns are pretty savage. We've arranged to have a plastic surgeon standing by in Glasgow when we return. The Harrington twins, both met officers, aren't so badly burned but they're very weak from cold and hunger. Food, warmth, and rest will have them on their feet in a couple of days again. Hassard, another met officer, and Jeremy, a lab technician, moderate burns, moderate frostbite, in the best shape of all otherwise. It's queer how different people react so differently to hunger and cold. The other four—Kinnaird, the senior radio operator, Dr. Jolly, Naseby, the cook, and Hewson, the tractor driver and man who was in charge of the generator—are much of a muchness: they're suffering most severely of all from frostbite, especially Kinnaird, all with moderate burns, weak, of course, but recovering fast. Only Folsom and the Harrington twins have consented to become bed patients. The rest we've provided with clothes of one sort or another. They're all lying down, of course, but they won't be lying down long. All of them are young, tough, and basically healthy. They don't pick children or old men to man places like Drift Station Zebra."

There was a knock on the door and Swanson's head appeared. He said "Hello, back again" to me, then turned to Benson. "A small problem of medical discipline here, Doctor." He stood aside to let us see Naseby, the Zebra cook, standing close behind him, dressed in a U. S. Navy's petty officer's uniform. "It seems that your patients have heard

144

about the funeral service. They want to go along—those who are able, that is—to pay their last respects to their colleagues. I understand and sympathize, of course, but their state of health—"

"I would advise against it, sir," Benson said. "Strongly."

"You can advise what you like, mate." The voice came from behind Naseby. It was Kinnaird, the cockney radio operator, who was also dressed in blue. "No offense. Don't want to be rude or ungrateful. But I'm going. Jimmy Grant was my mate."

"I know how you feel," Benson said. "I also know how *I* feel about it—your condition, I mean. You're in no state to do anything except lie down. You're making things very difficult for me."

"I'm the captain of this ship," Swanson put in mildly. "I can forbid it, you know. I can say no and make it stick."

"And you are making things difficult for us, sir," Kinnaird said. "I don't reckon it would advance the cause of Anglo-American unity very much if we started hauling off at our rescuers an hour or two after they'd saved us from certain death." He smiled faintly. "Besides, look at what it might do to our wounds and burns."

Swanson cocked an eyebrow at me. "Well, they're your countrymen."

"Dr. Benson is perfectly correct," I said. "But it's not worth a civil war. If they could survive five or six days on that damned ice cap, I don't suppose a few minutes more is going to finish them off."

"Well, if it does," Swanson said heavily, "we'll blame you."

If I ever had any doubt about it, I didn't have then, not after ten minutes out in the open. The Arctic ice cap was no place for a funeral; but I couldn't have imagined a more promising set-up for a funeral director who wanted to drum up some trade. After the warmth of the *Dolphin*, the cold seemed intense and within five minutes we were all shivering violently. The darkness was as nearly absolute as it ever becomes on the ice cap, the wind was lifting again, and thin flurries of snow came gusting through the night. The solitary floodlight served only to emphasize the ghostly unreality of it all: the huddled circle of mourners with bent heads, the two shapeless, canvas-wrapped forms lying huddled at the base of an ice hummock, Commander Swanson bent over his book, the wind and the snow snatching the half-heard mumble from his lips as he hurried through the burial service. I caught barely one word in ten of the committal and then it was all over: no meaningless rifle salutes, no empty blowing of bugles, just the service and the silence and the dark shapes of stumbling men hurriedly placing fragments of broken ice over the canvas-sheeted forms. And within twenty-four hours the eternally drifting spicules and blowing snow would have sealed them forever in their icy tomb, and there they might remain forever, drifting in endless circles about the North Pole; or someday, perhaps a thousand years from then, an ice lead might open up and drop them down to the uncaring floor of the Arctic, their bodies as perfectly preserved as if they had died only that day. It was a macabre thought.

Heads bent against the snow and ice, we hurried back to the shelter of the *Dolphin*. From the ice cap to the top of the sail it was a climb of over twenty feet up the almost vertically inclined huge slabs of ice that the submarine had pushed upward and sideways as she had forced her way through. Hand lines had been rigged from the top of the sail, but even then it was a fairly tricky climb. It was a set-up where, with the icy slope, the frozen slippery ropes, the darkness and the blinding effect of the snow and ice, an accident could all too easily happen. And happen it did.

I was about six feet up, giving a hand to Jeremy, the lab technician from Zebra, whose burnt hands made it almost impossible for him to climb alone, when I heard a muffled cry above me. I glanced up and had a darkly blurred impression of someone teetering on top of the sail, fighting for his balance, then jerked Jeremy violently toward me to save him from being swept away as that same someone lost his footing, toppled over backward, and hurtled down past us to the ice below. I winced at the sound of the impact—two sounds, rather: a heavy, muffled thud followed immediately by a sharper, crisper crack. First the body, then the head. I half imagined that I heard another sound afterward, but I couldn't be sure. I handed Jeremy over to the care of someone else and slithered down an ice-coated rope, not looking forward very much to what I must see. The fall had been the equivalent of a twenty-foot drop on to a concrete floor.

Hansen had got there before me and was shining his light, not on one prostrate figure, as I had expected, but on two. Benson and Jolly, both of them out cold.

I said to Hansen, "Did you see what happened?"

"No. Happened too quickly. All I know is that it was Benson that did the falling and Jolly that did the cushioning. Jolly was beside me only a few seconds before the fall."

"If that's the case, then Jolly probably saved your doctor's

146

life. We'll need to strap them in stretchers and haul them up and inside. We can't leave them out here."

"Stretchers? Well, yes, if you say so. But they might come around any minute."

"One of them might. But one of them is not going to come around for a long time. You heard that crack when a head hit the ice, it was like someone being clouted over the head with a fence post. And I don't know which it is yet."

Hansen left. I stooped over Benson and eased back the hood of the duffel coat he was wearing. A fence post was just about right. The side of his head, an inch above the right ear, was a blood-smeared mess, a three-inch-long gash in the purpling flesh with the blood already coagulating in the bitter cold. Two inches further forward and he'd have been a dead man; the thin bone behind the temple would have shattered under such an impact. For Benson's sake, I hoped the rest of his skull was pretty thick. No question but that this had been the sharp crack I'd heard.

Benson's breathing was very shallow, the movement of his chest barely discernible. Jolly's, on the other hand, was fairly deep and regular. I pulled back his anorak hood, probed carefully over his head, and encountered a slight puffiness far back, near the top on the left-hand side. The inference seemed obvious. I hadn't been imagining things when I thought I had heard a second sound after the sharp crack caused by Benson's head striking against the ice. Jolly must have been in the way of the falling Benson, not directly enough beneath him to break his fall in any way, but directly enough to be knocked backward on to the ice and bang the back of his head as he fell.

It took ten minutes to have them strapped in stretchers, taken inside, and placed in a couple of temporary cots in the sick bay. With Swanson waiting anxiously, I attended to Benson first, though there was little enough I could do. I had just started on Jolly when his eyes flickered and he slowly came back to consciousness, groaning a bit and trying to hold the back of his head. He made an effort to sit up in his cot, but I restrained him.

"Oh, Lord, my head." Several times he squeezed his eyes tightly shut, opened them wide, focused with difficulty on the bulkhead riotous with the color of Benson's cartoon characters, then looked away as if he didn't believe it. "Oh, my word, that must have been a dilly. Who did it, old boy?"

"Did what?" Swanson asked.

"Walloped me on the old bean. Who? Eh?"

"You mean to say you don't remember?"

"Remember?" Jolly said irritably. "How the devil should

I—" He broke off as his eye caught sight of Benson in the adjacent cot, a huddled figure under the blankets, with only the back of his head and a big gauze pack covering his wound showing. "Of course, of course. Yes, that's it. He fell on top of me, didn't he?"

"He certainly did," I said. "Did you try to catch him?"

"Catch him? No, I didn't try to catch him. I didn't try to get out of the way, either. It was all over in half a second. I just don't remember a thing about it." He groaned a bit more, then looked across at Benson. "Came a pretty nasty cropper, eh? Must have done."

"Looks like it. He's very severely concussed. There's X-ray equipment here and I'll have a look at his head shortly. Damned hard luck on you too, Jolly."

"I'll get over it," he grunted. He pushed my hand away and sat up. "Can I help you?"

"You may not," Swanson said quietly. "Early supper, then twelve hours solid for you and the other eight, Doctor, and those are *my* doctor's orders. You'll find supper waiting in the wardroom now."

"Aye-aye, sir." Jolly gave a ghost of a smile and pushed himself groggily to his feet. "That bit about the twelve hours sounds good to me."

After a minute or two, when he was steady enough on his feet, he left. Swanson said, "What now?"

"You might inquire around to see who was closest or close to Benson when he slipped climbing over the edge of the bridge. But discreetly. It might do no harm if at the same time you hinted around that maybe Benson had just taken a turn."

"What are *you* hinting at?" Swanson asked slowly.

"Did he fall or was he pushed? That's what I'm hinting at."

"Did he fall or—" He broke off then went on warily: "Why should anyone want to push Dr. Benson?"

"Why should anyone want to kill seven—eight, now—men on Drift Ice Station Zebra?"

"You have a point," Swanson acknowledged quietly. He left.

Making X-ray films wasn't very much in my line, but apparently it hadn't been very much in Dr. Benson's line, either, for he'd written down, for his own benefit and guidance, a detailed list of instructions for the taking and developing of X-ray films. I wondered how he would have felt if he had known that the first beneficiary of his meticulous thoroughness was to be himself. The two finished negatives I came

148

up with wouldn't have caused any furor in the Royal Photographic Society, but they were enough for my wants.

By and by, Commander Swanson returned, closing the door behind him. I said, "Ten gets one that you got nothing."

"You won't die a poor man," he nodded. "Nothing is what it is. So chief torpedoman Patterson tells me, and you know what he's like."

I knew what he was like. Patterson was the man responsible for all discipline and organization among the enlisted men, and Swanson had said to me that he regarded Patterson, and not himself, as the most indispensable man on the ship.

"Patterson was the man who reached the bridge immediately before Benson," Swanson said. "He said he heard Benson cry out, swung around and saw him already beginning to topple backward. He didn't recognize who it was at the time, it was too dark and snowy for that. He said he had the impression that Benson had already had one hand and one knee on the bridge coaming when he fell backward."

"A funny position in which to start falling backward," I said. "Most of his body weight must already have been inboard. And even if he did topple outward, he would surely still have had plenty of time to grab the coaming with both hands."

"Maybe he did take a turn," Swanson suggested. "And don't forget that the coaming is glass-slippery with its smooth coating of ice."

"As soon as Benson disappeared, Patterson ran to the side to see what had happened to him?"

"He did," Swanson said wearily. "And he said there wasn't a person within ten feet of the top of the bridge when Benson fell."

"And who *was* ten feet below?"

"He couldn't tell. Don't forget how black it was out there on the ice cap and that the moment Patterson had dropped into the brightly lit bridge he'd lost whatever night sight he'd built up. Besides, he didn't wait for more than a glance. He was off for a stretcher even before you or Hansen got to Benson. Patterson is not the sort of man who has to be told what to do."

"So it's a dead end there?"

"A dead end."

I nodded, crossed to a cupboard, and brought back the two X-rays, still wet, held in their metal clips. I held them up to the light for Swanson's inspection.

"Benson?" he asked, and when I nodded, he peered at them more closely and finally said, "That line there—a fracture?"

"A fracture. And not a hair-line one, either, as you can see. He really caught a wallop."

"How bad is it? How long before he comes out of this coma— He *is* in a coma?"

"He's all that. How long? If I were a lad fresh out of medical school I'd let you have a pretty confident estimate. If I were a top-flight brain surgeon I'd say anything from half an hour to a year or two, because people who really know what they are talking about are only too aware that we know next to nothing about the brain. Being neither, I'd guess at two or three days—and my guess could be hopelessly wrong. There may be cerebral bleeding. I don't know. I don't think so. Blood pressure, respiration, and temperature show no evidence of organic damage. And now you know as much about it as I do."

"Your colleagues wouldn't like that." Swanson smiled faintly. "This cheerful confession of ignorance does nothing to enhance the mystique of your profession. How about your other patients—the two men still out in Zebra?"

"I'll see them after supper. Maybe they'll be well enough to be brought here tomorrow. Meanwhile, I'd like to ask a favor of you. Could you lend me the services of your torpedoman Rawlings? And would you have any objections to his being taken into our confidence?"

"Rawlings? I don't know why you want him, but why Rawlings? The officers and petty officers aboard this ship are the pick of the U. S. Navy. Why not one of them? Besides, I'm not sure that I like the idea of passing on to an enlisted man secrets denied to my officers."

"They're strictly non-naval secrets. The question of hierarchy doesn't enter into it. Rawlings is the man I want. He's got a quick mind, quick reflexes, and a dead-pan, give-away-nothing expression that is invaluable in a game like this. Besides, in the event—the unlikely event, I hope—of the killer suspecting that we're on to him, he wouldn't look for any danger from one of your enlisted men because he'd be certain that we wouldn't let them in on it."

"What do you want him for?"

"To keep a night guard on Benson here."

"On Benson?" A fractional narrowing of the eyes that could have been as imagined as real was the only change in Swanson's impassive face. "So you don't think it was an accident, do you?"

"I don't honestly know. But I'm like you when you carry out a hundred and one different checks, most of which you know to be unnecessary, before you take your ship to sea: I'm taking no chances. If it wasn't an accident, then someone might have an interest in doing a really permanent job next time."

"But how can Benson represent a danger to anyone?" Swanson argued. "I'll bet anything, Carpenter, that Benson doesn't—or didn't—know a thing that could point a finger at anyone. If he did, he'd have told me right away. He's like that."

"Maybe he saw or heard something the significance of which he didn't then realize. Maybe the killer is frightened that if Benson has time enough to think about it, the significance will dawn on him. Or maybe it's all a figment of my overheated imagination: maybe he just fell. But I'd still like to have Rawlings."

"You'll have him." Swanson rose to his feet and smiled. "I don't want you quoting that Washington directive at me again."

Two minutes later Rawlings arrived. He was dressed in a light-brown shirt and overalls, obviously his own conception of what constituted the well-dressed submariner's uniform, and for the first time in our acquaintance he didn't smile a greeting. He didn't even glance at Benson on his cot. His face was still and composed, without any expression.

"You sent for me, sir?" *Sir*, not *Doc*.

"Take a seat, Rawlings." He sat, and as he did, I noticed the heavy bulge in the twelve-inch thigh pocket on the side of his overall pants. I nodded and said, "What have you got there? Doesn't do much for the cut of your natty suiting, does it?"

He didn't smile. He said: "I always carry one or two tools around with me. That's what the pocket is for."

"Let's see this particular tool," I said.

He hesitated briefly, shrugged and, not without some difficulty, pulled a heavy, gleaming drop-forged steel pipe wrench from the pocket. I hefted it in my hand.

"I'm surprised at you, Rawlings," I said. "What do you think the average human skull is made of—concrete? One little tap with this thing and you're up on a murder or manslaughter charge." I picked up a roll of bandage. "Ten yards of this wrapped around the business end will automatically reduce the charge to one of assault and battery."

"I don't know what you're talking about," he said mechanically.

"I'm talking about the fact that when Commander Swanson, Lieutenant Hansen and I were inside the laboratory this afternoon and you and Murphy were outside, you must have kind of leaned your ear against the door and heard more than was good for you. You know there's something

151

wrong, and though you don't know what, your motto is 'Be prepared.' Hence the cosh. Correct?"

"Correct."

"Does Murphy know?"

"No."

"I'm a naval-intelligence officer. Washington knows all about me. Want the captain to vouch for me?"

"Well, no." The first faint signs of a grin. "I heard you pull a gun on the skipper, but you're still walking around loose. You must be in the clear."

"You heard me threaten the captain and Lieutenant Hansen with a gun. But then you were sent away. You heard nothing after that?"

"Nothing."

"Three men have been murdered on Zebra. Two shot, one knifed. Their bodies were burned to conceal traces of the crime. Four others died in the fire. The killer is aboard this ship."

Rawlings said nothing. His eyes were wide, his face pale and shocked. I told him everything I'd told Swanson and Hansen and emphasized that he was to keep it all to himself. Then I finished, "Dr. Benson here has been seriously hurt. A deliberate attempt, God knows for what reason, may have been made on his life. We don't know. But if it was a deliberate attempt, then it's failed—so far."

Rawlings had brought himself under control. He said, his voice as empty of expression as his face: "Our little pal might come calling again?"

"He may. No member of the crew except the captain, the executive officer or I will come here. Anyone else—well, you can start asking him questions when he recovers consciousness."

"You recommended ten yards of this bandage, Doc?"

"It should be enough. And only a gentle tap, for God's sake. Above and behind the ear. You might sit behind that curtain there where no one can see you."

"I'm feeling lonesome tonight," Rawlings murmured. He broke open the bandage, started winding it around the head of the wrench, and glanced at the cartoon-decorated bulkhead beside him. "Even old Yogi Bear ain't no fit companion for me tonight. I hope I have some other company calling."

I left him there. I felt vaguely sorry for anyone who should come calling, killer or not. I felt, too, that I had taken every possible precaution. But when I left Rawlings there guarding Benson, I did make one little mistake. Just one. I left him guarding the wrong man.

The second accident of the day happened so quickly, so easily, so inevitably that it might almost have been just that—an accident.

At supper that evening I suggested that, with Commander Swanson's permission, I'd have a surgery at nine the next morning; because of enforced neglect, most of the burn wounds were suppurating pretty badly, requiring constant cleaning and changing of coverings. I also thought it about time that an X-ray inspection be made of Zabrinski's broken ankle. Medical supplies in the sick bay were running short: where did Benson keep his main supplies? Swanson told me and detailed Henry, the steward, to show me where it was.

About ten that night, after I'd returned from seeing the two men out on Zebra, Henry led me through the now deserted control room and down the ladder that led to the inertial-navigation room and the electronics space, which abutted on it. He undid the strong-back clamp on the square, heavy steel hatch in a corner of the electronics room and, with an assist from me—the hatch must have weighed about 150 pounds—swung it up and back until the hatch clicked home on its standing latch.

Three rungs welded onto the inside of the hatch cover led onto the vertical steel ladder that reached down to the deck below. Henry went down first, snapping on the light as he went, and I followed.

The medical storage room, though tiny, was equipped on the same superbly lavish scale as was everything else on the *Dolphin*. Benson, as thoroughly meticulous in this as he had been in his outlining of X-ray procedure, had everything neatly and logically labeled, so that it took me less than three minutes to find everything I wanted. I went up the ladder first, stopped near the top, stretched down, and took the bag of supplies from Henry, swung it up on the deck above, then reached up quickly with my free hand to grab the middle of the three rungs welded on the lower side of the hatch cover to haul myself up onto the deck of the electronics space. But I didn't haul myself up. What happened was that I hauled the hatch cover down. The retaining latch had become disengaged, and the 150-pound deadweight of that massive cover was swinging down on top of me before I could even begin to realize what was happening.

I fell half sideways, half backward, pulling the hatch cover with me. My head struck against the hatch coaming. Desperately I ducked my head forward—if it had been crushed between the coaming and the falling cover, the two sides of my skull would just about have met in the middle—and tried to snatch my left arm back inside. I was more or less successful with my head—I had it clear of the coaming and was ducking so quickly that the impact of the cover was no more than enough to give me a slight headache afterward—but my left arm was a different matter altogether. I almost got it clear—but only almost. If my left hand and wrist had been strapped to a steel block and a gorilla had had a go at it with a sledge hammer, the effect couldn't have been more agonizing. For a moment or two I hung there, trapped, dangling by my left wrist; then the weight of my body tore the mangled wrist and hand through the gap and I crashed down to the deck beneath. Then the gorilla seemed to have another go with the sledge hammer, and consciousness went.

"I won't beat about the bush, old lad," Jolly said. "No point in it with a fellow pill roller. Your wrist is a mess. I had to dig half your watch out of it. The middle and little fingers are broken, the middle in two places. But the permanent danger, I'm afraid, is to the back of your hand. The little- and ring-finger tendons have been sliced."

"What does that mean?" Swanson asked.

"It means that in his left hand he'll have to get by with two fingers and a thumb for the rest of his life," Jolly said bluntly.

Swanson swore softly and turned to Henry. "How in God's name could you have been so damned careless? An experienced submariner like you? You know perfectly well that you're required to make a visual check every time a hatch cover engages in a standing latch. Why didn't you?"

"I didn't need to, sir." Henry was looking more dyspeptic and forlorn than ever. "I heard it click and I gave a tug. It was engaged, all right. I can swear to it, sir."

"How could it have been engaged? Look at Dr. Carpenter's hand. Just a hair-line engagement and the slightest extra pressure— My God, why can't you people obey regulations?"

Henry stared at the desk in silence. Jolly, who was understandably looking about as washed-out as I felt, packed away the tools of his trade, advised me to take a couple of days off, gave me a handful of pills to take, said a weary good night, and climbed up the ladder leading from the electronics space, where he had been fixing my hand. Swanson said to Henry: "You can go now, Baker"—the first time I'd ever heard anyone address Henry by his surname, a sufficient enough token of what Swanson regarded as the enormity of his crime. "I'll decide what to do about this in the morning."

"I don't know about the morning," I said after Henry

154

was gone. "Maybe the next morning. Or the one after that. Then you can apologize to him. You and me both. That cover was locked on its standing latch. *I* checked it visually, Commander Swanson."

Swanson gave me his cool, impassive look. After a moment he said quietly, "Are you suggesting what I think you are suggesting?"

"Someone took a risk," I said. "Not all that much of a risk, though. Most of the men are asleep now, and the control room was deserted at the moment that mattered. Someone in the wardroom tonight heard me ask your permission to go down to the medical store and heard you giving your okay. Shortly after that, nearly everyone turned in. One man didn't—he kept awake and hung around patiently until I came back from the drift station. He followed me down below—he was lucky—Lieutenant Sims, your officer on deck, was taking star sights up on the bridge and the control room was empty—and he unhooked the latch but left the hatch cover in a standing position. There was a slight element of gambling as to whether I would come up first, but not all that much, it would have been a matter of elementary courtesy, he would have thought, for Henry to see me up first. Anyway, he won his gamble, slight though it was. After that, our unknown friend wasn't quite so lucky—I think he expected the damage to be a bit more permanent."

"I'll get inquiries under way immediately," Swanson said. "Whoever was responsible, someone must have seen him. Someone must have heard him leaving his cot—"

"Don't waste your time, Commander. We're up against a highly intelligent character who doesn't overlook the obvious. Not only that, but word of your inquiries is bound to get around, and you'd scare him under cover where I'd never get at him."

"Then I'll just keep the whole damned bunch under lock and key until we get back to Scotland," Swanson said grimly. "*That* way there'll be no more trouble."

"That way we'll *never* find out who the murderer of my brother and the six—seven—others are. Whoever it is has to be given sufficient rope to trip himself up."

"Good God, man, we can't just sit back and let things be done to us." There was a hint of testiness in the commander's voice, and I couldn't blame him. "What do we—what do *you*—propose to do now?"

"Start at the beginning. Tomorrow morning we'll hold a court of inquiry among the survivors. Let's find out all we can about that fire. Just an innocent, above-board, fact-finding inquiry, for the Ministry of Supply, let us say. I've an idea

155

we might turn up something very interesting indeed."

"You think so?" Swanson shook his head. "I don't believe it. I don't believe it for a moment. Look what's happened to you. It's obvious, man, that someone knows or suspects that you're on to them. They'll take damned good care to give nothing away."

"You think that's why I was clouted tonight?"

"What other reason could there be?"

"Was that why Benson was hurt?"

"We don't know that he was. Deliberately, I mean. May have been pure coincidence."

"Maybe it was," I agreed. "And then again, maybe it wasn't. My guess, for what it's worth, is that the accident or accidents have nothing at all to do with any suspicions the killer may have that we're on to him. Anyway, let's see what tomorrow brings."

It was midnight when I got back to my cabin. The engineer officer was on watch and Hansen was asleep, so I didn't put on any light lest I disturb him. I didn't undress, just removed my shoes, lay down on the cot, and pulled a cover over me.

I didn't sleep. I couldn't sleep. My left arm from the elbow down still felt as if it were caught in a bear trap. Twice I pulled from my pocket the pain killers and sleeping tablets that Jolly had given me and twice I put them away.

Instead I just lay there and thought, and the first and most obvious conclusion I came up with was that there was someone aboard the *Dolphin* who didn't care any too much for the members of the medical profession. Then I got to wondering why the profession was so unpopular, and after half an hour of beating my weary brain cells around, I got silently to my feet and made my way in my socks to the sick bay.

I passed inside and closed the door softly behind me. A red night light burnt dully in one corner, just enough to let me see Benson's huddled form on the cot. I switched on the overhead light, blinked in the sudden fierce wash of light, and looked at the curtain at the other end of the bay. Nothing stirred behind it. I said, "Just kind of take your itching fingers away from that pipe wrench, Rawlings. It's me, Carpenter."

The curtain was pulled to one side and Rawlings appeared, the pipe wrench, with its bandage-wrapped head, dangling from one hand. He had a disappointed look on his face.

"I was expecting someone else," he said reproachfully. "I

was kinda hoping— My God, Doc, what's happened to your arm?"

"Well may you ask, Rawlings. Our little pal had a go at me tonight. I think he wanted me out of the way. Whether he wanted me out of the way permanently or not I don't know but he near as a toucher succeeded." I told him what had happened, then asked, "Is there any man aboard you can trust absolutely?" I knew the answer before I had asked the question.

"Zabrinski," he said unhesitatingly.

"Do you think you could pussy-foot along to wherever it is that he's sleeping and bring him here without waking up anyone?"

He didn't ask any questions. He said, "He can't walk, Doc, you know that."

"Carry him. You're big enough."

He grinned and left. He was back with Zabrinski inside three minutes. Three quarters of an hour later, after telling Rawlings he could call off his watch, I was back in my cabin.

Hansen was still asleep. He didn't wake even when I switched on a side light. Slowly, clumsily, painfully, I dressed myself in my furs, unlocked my case, and drew out the Mauser, the two rubber-covered magazines and the broken knife that Commander Swanson had found in the tractor's gas tank. I put them in my pocket and left. On my way through the control room, I told the officer on deck that I was going out to check on the two patients still left out in the camp. As I had pulled a fur mitten over my injured hand, he didn't raise an eyebrow, doctors were a law unto themselves, and I was just the good healer en route to give aid and comfort to the sick.

I did have a good look at the two sick men, both of whom seemed to me to be picking up steadily, then said good night to the two *Dolphin* crewmen who were watching over them. But I didn't go straight back to the ship. First I went to the tractor shed and replaced the gun, magazines and broken knife in the tractor tank. Then I went back to the ship.

9

"I'M SORRY TO HAVE to bother you with all these questions," I said pleasantly. "But that's the way it is with all government departments. A thousand questions in quadruplicate and each of them more pointlessly irritating than the rest. But I have this job to do and the report to be radioed off as soon as possible, and I would appreciate all the information and co-operation you can give me. First of all, has anyone any idea at all how this damned fire started?"

I hoped I sounded like a Ministry of Supply official, which was what I'd told them I was, making a Ministry of Supply report. I'd further told them, just to nip any eyebrow-raising in the bud, that it was the Ministry of Supply's policy to send a doctor to report on any accident where loss of life was involved. Maybe this was the case. I didn't know and I didn't care.

"Well, I was the first to discover the fire, I think," Naseby, the Zebra cook, said hesitantly. His Yorkshire accent was very pronounced. He was still no picture of health and strength, but, for all that, he was a hundred per cent improved on the man I had seen yesterday. Like the other eight survivors of Drift Ice Station Zebra who were present in the ward-room that morning, a long night's warm sleep and good food had brought about a remarkable change for the better. More accurately, like seven others. Captain Folsom's face had been so hideously burned that it was difficult to say what progress he was making, though he had certainly had a good enough breakfast, almost entirely liquid, less than half an hour previously.

"It must have been about two o'clock in the morning," Naseby went on. "Well, near enough two. The place was already on fire. Burning like a torch, it was. I—"

"What place?" I interrupted. "Where were you sleeping?"

"In the cookhouse. That was also our dining hall. Furthest-west hut in the north row."

"You slept there alone?"

"No. Hewson, here, and Flanders and Bryce slept there also. Flanders and Bryce, they're—they were—lab technicians. Hewson and I slept at the very back of the hut, then there were two big cupboards, one on each side, that held all our food stores, then Flanders and Bryce slept in the dining hall itself, by a corner of the galley."

"They were nearest the door?"

"That's right. I got up, coughing and choking with smoke, very groggy, and I could see flames already starting to eat through the east wall of the hut. I shook Hewson, then ran for the fire extinguisher: it was kept by the door. It wouldn't work. Jammed solid with the cold, I suppose. I don't know. I ran back in again. I was blind by this time. You never saw smoke like it in your life. I shook Flanders and Bryce and shouted at them to get out; then I bumped into Hewson and told him to run and wake Captain Folsom here."

I looked at Hewson. "You woke Captain Folsom?"

"I went to wake him, but not right away. The whole camp was blazing like the biggest Fifth of November bonfire you ever saw, and flames twenty feet high were sweeping down the lane between the two rows of huts. The air was full of flying oil, a lot of it burning. I had to make a long swing to the north to get clear of the oil and the flames."

"The wind was from the east?"

"Not quite. Not that night. Southeast, I would say. East-southeast would be more like it. Anyway, I gave a very wide berth to the generator house—that was the one next to the dining hall in the north row—and reached the main bunkhouse. That was the one you found us in."

"Then you woke Captain Folsom?"

"He was already gone. Shortly after I'd left the dining hall, the fuel drums in the fuel-storage hut—that was the one directly south of the main bunkhouse—started exploding. Like bloody great bombs going off, they were, the noise they made. They would have waked the dead. Anyway, they woke Captain Folsom. He and Jeremy here"—he nodded at a man sitting across the table from him—"had taken the fire extinguisher from the bunkhouse and tried to get close to Major Halliwell's hut."

"That was the one directly west of the fuel store?"

"That's right. It was an inferno. Captain Folsom's extinguisher worked well enough, but he couldn't get close enough to do any good. There was so much flying oil in the air that even the extinguisher foam seemed to burn."

"Hold on a minute," I said. "To get back to my original question. How did the fire start?"

"We've discussed that a hundred times among ourselves," Dr. Jolly said wearily. "The truth is, old boy, we haven't a clue. We know *where* it started, all right: match the huts destroyed against the wind direction that night and it could only have been in the fuel store. But how? It's anybody's guess. I don't see that it matters a great deal now."

"I disagree. It matters very much. If we could find out how it started, we might prevent another such tragedy later on. That's why I'm here. Hewson, you were in charge of the fuel store and generator hut. Have you no opinion on this?"

"None. It *must* have been electrical, but how I can't guess. It's possible that there was a leakage from one of the fuel drums and that oil vapor was present in, the air. There were two black heaters in the fuel store, designed to keep the temperature up to zero Fahrenheit so that the oil would always flow freely. Arcing across the make and break of the thermostats might have ignited the gas. But it's only a wild guess, of course.

"No possibility of any smoldering rags or cigarette butts being the cause?"

Hewson's face turned a dusky red. "Look, mister, I know my job. Burning rags, cigarette butts, I know how to keep a bloody fuel store—"

"Keep your shirt on," I interrupted. "No offense. I'm only doing *my* job." I turned back to Naseby. "After you'd sent Hewson to rouse Captain Folsom, what then?"

"I ran across to the radio room—that's the hut due south of the cookhouse and west of Major Halliwell's—"

"But those two lab technicians—Flanders and Bryce, wasn't it?—surely you made sure they were awake and out of it before you left the dining hall?"

"God help me, I didn't." Naseby stared down at the deck, his shoulders hunched, his face bleak. "They're dead. It's my fault they're dead. But you don't know what it was like inside that dining hall. Flames were breaking through the east wall, the place was full of choking smoke and oil, I couldn't see, I could hardly breathe. I shook them both and shouted at them to get out. I shook them hard and I certainly shouted loud enough."

"I can bear him out on that," Hewson said quietly. "I was right beside him at the time."

"I didn't wait," Naseby went on. "I wasn't thinking of saving my own skin. I thought Flanders and Bryce were all right and that they would be out the door on my heels. I wanted to warn the others. It wasn't—it wasn't until minutes later that I realized there was no sign of them. And then—well, then it was too late."

160

"You ran across to the radio room. That's where you slept, Kinnaird, wasn't it?"

"That's where I slept, yes." His mouth twisted. "Me and my mate Grant, the boy that died yesterday. And Dr. Jolly slept in the partitioned-off east end of the hut. That's where he had his surgery and the little cubby hole where he carried out his tests on ice samples."

"So your end would have started to go on fire first?" I said to Jolly.

"Must have done," he agreed. "Quite frankly, old chap, my recollection of the whole thing is just like a dream—a nightmare, rather. I was almost asphyxiated in my sleep, I think. First thing I remember was young Grant bending over me, shaking me and shouting. Can't recall what he was shouting, but it must have been that the hut was on fire. I don't know what I said or did, probably nothing, for the next thing I clearly remember was being hit on both sides of the face, and not too gently, either. But, by Jove, it worked. I got to my feet, and he dragged me out of my office into the radio room. I owe my life to young Grant. I'd just enough sense left to grab the emergency medical kit that I always kept packed."

"What woke Grant?"

"Naseby here woke him," Kinnaird said. "He woke us both, shouting and hammering on the door. If it hadn't been for him, Dr. Jolly and I would both have been goners. The air inside that place was like poison gas, and I'm sure if Naseby hadn't shouted on us, we would never have woken up. I told Grant to wake the doctor while I tried to get the outside door open."

"It was locked?

"The damned thing was jammed. That was nothing unusual at night. During the day, when the heaters were going full blast to keep the huts at a decent working temperature, the ice around the doors tended to melt. At night, when we got into our sleeping bags, we turned our heaters down, and the melted ice froze hard around the door openings, sealing it solid. That happened most nights in most of the huts—usually had to break our way out in the morning. But I can tell you that I didn't take too long to burst it open that night."

"And then?"

"I ran out," Kinnaird said. "I couldn't see a thing for black smoke and flying oil. I ran maybe twenty yards to the south to get some idea of what was happening. The whole camp seemed to be on fire. When you're woken up like that at two in the morning, half blinded, half asleep and groggy with fumes, your mind isn't at its best but thank God I'd enough

161

left of my mind to realize that an S.O.S. radio message was the one thing that was going to save our lives. So I went back inside the radio hut."

"We all owe our lives to Kinnaird." Speaking for the first time was Jeremy, a burly, red-haired Canadian who had been chief technician on the base. "And if I'd been a bit quicker with my hands, we'd all have been dead."

"Oh, for Christ's sake, mate, shut up," Kinnaird growled.

"I won't shut up," Jeremy said soberly. "Besides, Dr. Carpenter wants a full report. I was the first out of the main bunkhouse after Captain Folsom. As Hewson said, we tried the extinguisher on Major Halliwell's hut. It was hopeless from the beginning, but we had to do it—after all, we knew there were four men trapped in there. But, like I say, it was a waste of time. Captain Folsom shouted that he was going to get another extinguisher and told me to see how things were in the radio room.

"The place was ablaze from end to end. As I came around as close as I could to the door at the west end I saw Naseby here bending over Dr. Jolly, who'd keeled over as soon as he had come out into the fresh air. He shouted to me to give him a hand to drag Dr. Jolly clear, and I was just about to when Kinnaird came running up. I saw that he was heading straight for the door of the radio room." He smiled without humor. "I thought he had gone off his rocker. I jumped in front of him to stop him. He shouted at me to get out of the way. I told him not to be crazy, and he yelled—you had to yell to make yourself heard above the roar of the flames—that he had to get the portable radio out, that all the oil was gone, and the generator and the cookhouse with all the food were burning up. He knocked me down, and the next thing I saw was him disappearing through that door. Smoke and flames were pouring through the doorway. I don't know how he ever got out alive."

"Was that how you got your face and hands so badly burned?" Commander Swanson asked quietly. He was standing in a far corner of the wardroom, having taken no part in the discussion up till now but missing nothing, all the same. That was why I had asked him to be present: just because he was a man who missed nothing.

"I guess so, sir."

"That should earn you a trip to Buckingham Palace," Swanson murmured.

"The hell with Buckingham Palace," Kinnaird said violently. "How about my mate, eh? How about young Jimmy Grant? Can he make the trip to Buckingham Palace? Not now he can't, the poor bastard. Do you know what he was doing?

He was still *inside* the radio room when I went back in, sitting at the main transmitter, sending out an S.O.S. on our regular frequency. His clothes were on fire. I dragged him off his seat and shouted to him to grab some Nife cells and get out. I caught up the portable transmitter and a nearby box of Nife cells and ran through the door. I thought Grant was on my heels, but I couldn't hear anything, what with the roar of flames and the bursting of fuel drums, the racket was deafening. Unless you'd been there, you just can't begin to imagine what it was like. I ran far enough clear to put the radio and cells in a safe place. Then I went back. I asked Naseby, who was still trying to bring Dr. Jolly round, if Jimmy Grant had come out. He said he hadn't. I started to run for the door again, and, well, that's all I remember."

"I clobbered him," Jeremy said with gloomy satisfaction. "From behind. I had to."

"I could have killed you when I came round," Kinnaird said morosely. "But I guess you saved my life at that."

"I certainly did, brother." Jeremy grimaced. "That was my big contribution that night. Hitting people. After Naseby had brought Dr. Jolly round, he suddenly started shouting, 'Where's Flanders and Bryce, where's Flanders and Bryce!' Those were the two who had been sleeping with him and Hewson in the cookhouse. A few others had come down from the main bunkhouse by that time, and the best part of a minute had elapsed before we realized that Flanders and Bryce weren't among them. Naseby started back for the cookhouse at a dead run. He was making for the doorway, only there was no doorway left, just a solid curtain of fire where the doorway used to be. I swung at him as he passed, and he fell and hit his head on the ice." He looked at Naseby. "Sorry again, Johnny, but you were quite crazy at the moment."

Naseby rubbed his jaw and grinned wearily. "I can still feel it. And God knows you were right."

"Then Captain Folsom arrived, along with Dick Foster, who also slept in the main bunkhouse," Jeremy went on. "Captain Folsom said he'd tried every other extinguisher on the base and that all of them were frozen solid. He'd heard about Grant being trapped inside the radio room and he and Foster were carrying a blanket apiece, soaked with water. I tried to stop them but Captain Folsom ordered me to stand aside." Jeremy smiled faintly. "When Captain Folsom orders people to stand aside ... well, they do just that."

"He and Foster threw the wet blankets over their heads and ran inside. Captain Folsom was out in a few seconds,

163

carrying Grant. I've never seen anything like it: they were burning like human torches. I don't know what happened to Foster, but he never came out. By that time the roofs of both Major Halliwell's hut and the cookhouse had fallen in. Nobody could get anywhere near either of those buildings. Besides, it was far too late by then. Major Halliwell and the three others inside the major's hut and Flanders and Bryce inside the cookhouse must have been dead already. Dr. Jolly doesn't think they would have suffered very much: asphyxiation would have got them, like enough, before the flames did."

"Well," I said slowly, "that's as clear a picture of what must have been a very confusing and terrifying experience as we're ever likely to get. It wasn't possible to get anywhere near Major Halliwell's hut?"

"You couldn't have gone within fifteen feet of it and hoped to live," Naseby said simply.

"And what happened afterward?"

"I took charge, old boy," Jolly said. "Wasn't much to take charge of, though, and what little there was to be done could be done only by myself—fixing up the injured, I mean. I made 'em all wait out there on the ice cap until the flames had died down a bit and there didn't seem to be any more likelihood of further fuel drums bursting. Then we all made our way to the bunkhouse, where I did the best I could for the injured men. Kinnaird here, despite pretty bad burns, proved himself a first-class assistant doctor. We bedded down the worst of them. Young Grant was in a shocking condition—'fraid there never really was very much hope for him. And—well, that was about all there was to it."

"You had no food for the next few days and nights?"

"Nothing at all, old boy. No heat, either, except for the stand-by Coleman lamps that were in the three remaining huts. We managed to melt a little water from the ice, that was all. By my orders everyone remained lying down and wrapped up in what was available in order to conserve energy and warmth."

"Bit rough on you," I said to Kinnaird. "Having to lose any hard-earned warmth you had every couple of hours in order to make those S.O.S. broadcasts."

"Not only me," Kinnaird said. "I'm no keener on frostbite than anyone else. Dr. Jolly insisted that everyone who could should take turns sending out the S.O.S.'s. Wasn't hard. There was a pre-set mechanical call-up, and all anyone had to do was to send this and listen in on the earphones. If any message came through, I was across to the met office in a flash.

It was actually Hewson here who contacted the ham operator in Bodö and Jeremy who got through to that trawler in the Barents Sea. I carried on from there, of course. Apart from them, there were Dr. Jolly and Naseby to give a hand, so it wasn't so bad. Hassard, too, took a turn after the first day—he'd been more or less blinded on the night of the fire."

"You remained in charge throughout, Dr. Jolly?" I asked.

"Bless my soul, no. Captain Folsom was in a pretty shocked condition for the first twenty-four hours, but when he'd recovered from that, he took over. I'm only a pill-roller, old boy. As a leader of men and a dashing man of action—well, no, quite frankly, old top, I don't see myself in that light at all."

"You did damned well all the same." I looked around at the company. "That most of you won't be scarred for life is due entirely to the quick and highly efficient treatment Dr. Jolly gave you under almost impossible circumstances. Well, that's all. Must be a pretty painful experience for all of you, having to relive that night again. I can't see that we can ever hope to find out how the fire started, just one of those chance-in-a-million accidents, what the insurance companies call an act of God. I'm certain, Hewson, that no shadow of negligence attaches to you and that your theory on the outbreak of the fire is probably correct. Anyway, although we've paid a hellishly high cost, we've learned a lesson: never again to site a main fuel store within a hundred yards of the camp."

The meeting broke up. Jolly bustled off to the sick bay, not quite managing to conceal his relish at being the only medical officer aboard who wasn't *hors de combat*. He had a busy couple of hours ahead of him: changing bandages on burns, checking Benson, X-raying Zabrinski's broken ankle and resetting the plaster.

I went to my cabin, unlocked my case, took out a small wallet, relocked my case, and went to Swanson's cabin. I noticed that he wasn't smiling quite so often now as when I'd first met him in Scotland. He looked up as I came in in answer to his call and said without preamble, "If those two men still out in the camp are in any way fit to be moved, I want them both aboard at once. The sooner we're back in Scotland and have some law in on this the happier I'll be. I warned you that this investigation of yours would turn up nothing. Lord knows how short a time it will be before someone else gets it. For God's sake, Carpenter, we have a murderer running loose."

"Three things," I said. "Nobody's going to get it any more, that's almost for certain. Secondly, the law, as you call it, wouldn't be allowed to touch it. And, in the third place, the meeting this morning was of some use. It eliminated three potential suspects."

"I must have missed something that you didn't."

"Not that. I knew something that you didn't. I knew that under the floor of the laboratory were about forty Nife cells in excellent condition—but cells that had been used."

"The hell you did," he said softly. "Sort of forgot to tell me, didn't you?"

"In this line of business I never tell anyone anything unless I think he can help me by having that knowledge."

"You must win an awful lot of friends and influence an awful lot of people," Swanson said dryly.

"It gets embarrassing. Now, who could have used those cells? Only those who left the bunkhouse from time to time to send out the S.O.S.'s. That cuts out Captain Folsom and the Harrington twins—there's no question of any of the three of them having left the bunkhouse at any time. They weren't fit to. So that leaves Hewson, Naseby, Dr. Jolly, Jeremy, Hassard and Kinnaird. Take your choice. One of them is a murderer."

"Why did they want those extra cells?" Swanson asked. "And if they had those extra cells why did they risk their lives by relying on those dying cells that they did use? Does it make sense to you?"

"There's sense in everything," I said. "If you want evasion, Carpenter has it." I brought out my wallet, spread cards before him. He picked them up, studied them and returned them to my wallet.

"So now we have it," he said calmly. "Took you quite a while to get around to it, didn't it? The truth, I mean. Officer of M.I.6. Counter-espionage. Government agent, eh? Well, I won't make any song and dance about it, Carpenter, I've known since yesterday what you must be: you couldn't be anything else." He looked at me in calm speculation. "You guys never disclose your identity unless you have to." He left the logical question unspoken.

"Three reasons why I'm telling you. You're entitled to some measure of my confidence. I want you on my side. And because of what I'm about to tell you, you'd have known anyway. Have you ever heard of the Perkin-Elmer Roti satellite missile-tracker camera?"

"Quite a mouthful," he murmured. "No."

"Heard of Samos? Samos III?"

"Satellite and Missile Observation System?" He nodded. "I have. And what conceivable connection could that have with a ruthless killer running rampant on Drift Station Zebra?"

So I told him what connection it could have. A connection that was not only conceivable, not only possible, not only probable, but absolutely certain. Swanson listened very carefully, very attentively, not interrupting even once, and at the end of it he leaned back in his chair and nodded. "You have the right answer, no doubt about that. The question is, who? I just can't wait to see this bastard under armed guard."

"You'd clap him in irons straight away?"

"Good God!" He stared at me. "Wouldn't you?"

"I don't know. Yes, I do. I'd leave him be. I think our friend is just a link in a very long chain, and if we give him enough rope, he'll not only hang himself, he'll lead us to the other members of the chain. Besides, I'm not all that sure that there *is* only one murderer: killers have been known to have accomplices before now, Commander."

"Two of them? You think there may be two killers aboard my ship?" He pursed his lips and squeezed his chin with a thoughtful hand, Swanson's nearest permissible approach to a state of violent agitation. Then he shook his head definitely. "There may only be one. If that was so, and I knew who he was, I'd arrest him at once. Don't forget, Carpenter, we've hundreds of miles to go under the ice before we're out into the open sea. We can't watch all six of them all the time, and there are a hundred and one things that a man with even only a little knowledge of submarines could do that would put us all in mortal danger. Things that wouldn't matter were we clear of the ice: things that would be fatal under it."

"Aren't you rather overlooking the fact that if the killer did us in, he'd also be doing himself in?"

"I don't necessarily share your belief in his sanity. All killers are a little crazy. No matter how excellent their reasons for killing, the very fact that they do kill makes them abnormal. You can't judge them by normal standards."

He was only half right, but unfortunately that half might apply in this case. Most murderers kill in a state of extreme emotional once-in-a-lifetime stress and never kill again. But our friend in this case had every appearance of being a stranger to emotional stress of any kind—and, besides, he'd killed a great deal more than once.

"Well," I said doubtfully, "perhaps. Yes, I think I do agree with you." I refrained from specifying our common ground for agreement. "Who's your candidate for the high jump, Commander?"

"I'm damned if I know. I listened to every word that was

167

said this morning. I watched the face of each man who spoke—and the faces of the ones who weren't speaking. I haven't stopped thinking about it since and I'm still damned if I have a clue. How about Kinnaird?"

"He's the obvious suspect, isn't he? But only because he's a skilled radio operator. I could train a man in a couple of days to send and receive in Morse. Slow, clumsy, he wouldn't know a thing about the instrument he was using, but he could still do it. Any of them may easily have been competent enough to operate a radio. The fact that Kinnaird is a skilled operator may even be a point in his favor."

"Nife cells were removed from the radio cabin and taken to the laboratory," Swanson pointed out. "Kinnaird had the easiest access to them. Apart from Dr. Jolly who had his office and sleeping quarters in the same hut."

"So that would point a finger at Kinnaird or Jolly?"

"Well, wouldn't it?"

"Certainly. Especially if you will agree that the presence of those tinned foods under the lab floor also points a finger at Hewson and Naseby, both of whom slept in the cook-house, where the food was stored, and that the presence of the radio-sonde balloon and the hydrogen in the lab also points a finger at Jeremy and Hassard, one a met officer and the other a technician who would have had the easiest access to those items."

"That's right, confuse things," Swanson said irritably. "As if they weren't confused enough already."

"I'm not confusing things. All I'm saying is that if you admit a certain possibility for a certain reason, then you must admit similar possibilities for similar reasons. Besides, there are points in Kinnaird's favor. He risked his life to go back into the radio room to bring out the portable transmitter. He risked almost certain suicide when he tried to go in the second time to bring out his assistant, Grant, and probably would have died if Jeremy hadn't clobbered him. Look what happened to that man Foster who went in there immediately afterward with a wet blanket over his head: *he* never came out.

"Again, would Kinnaird have mentioned the Nife cells if he had any guilt complex about them? But he did. That, incidentally, might have been why Grant, the assistant radio operator, collapsed in there and later died—Kinnaird had told him to bring out the other Nife cells, and he was overcome because he stayed there too long looking for things that had already been removed from the hut. And there's one final point: we have Naseby's word for it that the door of the radio room was jammed, presumably by ice. Had Kinnaird been playing with matches a few moments previously, that door wouldn't have had time to freeze up."

"If you rule Kinnaird out," Swanson said slowly, "you more or less have to rule Dr. Jolly out, too." He smiled. "I don't see a member of your profession running around filling people full of holes, Dr. Carpenter. Repairing holes is their line of business, not making them. Hippocrates wouldn't have liked it."

"I'm not ruling Kinnaird out," I said. "But I'm not going off half cocked and pinning a murder charge on him, either. As for the ethics of my profession, would you like a list of the good healers who have decorated the dock in the Old Bailey? True, we have nothing on Jolly. His part in the proceedings that night seems to have consisted in staggering out from the radio room, falling flat on his face, and staying there till pretty near the end of the fire. That, of course, has no bearing upon whatever part he might have taken in the proceedings prior to the fire. Though against that possibility there's the fact of the jammed door, the fact that Kinnaird or Grant would have been almost bound to notice if he had been up to something. Jolly's bunk was at the back of the radio room, and he would have had to pass Kinnaird and Grant to get out, not forgetting that he would also have to stop to pick up the Nife cells. And there is one more point in his favor—an apparent point, that is. I still don't think that Benson's fall was an accident, and if it was no accident it is difficult to see how Jolly could have arranged it while he was at the foot of the sail and Benson at the top, and it's even more difficult to see why he should have stood at the foot of the sail and let Benson fall on top of him."

"You're putting up a very good defense case for both Jolly and Kinnaird," Swanson murmured.

"No. I'm only saying what a defense lawyer would say."

"Hewson," Swanson said slowly. "Or Naseby, the cook. Or Hewson and Naseby. Don't you think it damned funny that those two, who were sleeping at the back or east side of the cookhouse, which was the first part of the hut to catch fire, should have managed to escape while the other two—Flanders and Bryce, wasn't it?—who slept in the middle should have suffocated in there? Naseby said he shouted at them and shook them violently. Maybe he could have shouted and shaken all night without result. Maybe they were already unconscious—or dead. Maybe they had seen Naseby or Hewson or both removing food supplies and had been silenced. Or maybe they had been silenced *before* anything had been removed. And don't forget the gun. It was hidden

169

in the gas tank of the tractor, a pretty damned funny place for a man to hide anything. But nothing funny about the idea occurring to Hewson, was there? He was the tractor driver. And he seems to have taken his time about getting around to warning Captain Folsom. He said he had to make a wide circuit to avoid the flames but apparently Naseby didn't find it so bad when he went to the radio room. Another thing—a pretty telling point, I think, he said that when he was on the way to the bunkhouse the oil drums in the fuel store started exploding. If they only started exploding then, how come all the huts—the five that were eventually destroyed, that is—were already uncontrollably on fire? They were uncontrollably on fire because they were saturated by flying oil so the first explosions must have come a long time before then. And, apart from warning Folsom—who had already been warned—Hewson doesn't seem to have done very much after the fire started."

"You'd make a pretty good prosecuting counsel yourself, Commander. But wouldn't you think there's just too *much* superficially against Hewson? That a clever man wouldn't have allowed so much superficial evidence to accumulate against him? You would have thought that at least he would have indulged in a little fire-fighting heroics to call attention to himself."

"No. You're overlooking the fact that he would never have had reason to expect that there would be any investigation into the causes of the fire. That the situation would never arise where he—or anyone else, for that matter— would have to justify his actions and behavior if accusations were to be leveled against him."

"I've said it before and I say it again. People like that *never* take a chance. They always act on the assumption that they *may* be found out."

"How could they be found out?" Swanson protested. "How could they possibly expect to have suspicion aroused?"

"You don't think it possible that they suspect we're on to them?"

"No, I don't."

"That wasn't what you were saying last night after that hatch fell on me," I pointed out. "You said it was obvious that someone was on to me."

"Thank God all I have to do is the nice, uncomplicated job of running a nuclear submarine," Swanson said heavily. "The truth is, I don't know what to think any more. How about this cook fellow—Naseby?"

"You think he was in cahoots with Hewson?"

"If we accept the premise that the men in the cookhouse

170

who were not in on this business had to be silenced, and Naseby wasn't, then he must have been, mustn't he? But, damn it, how about his attempt to rescue Flanders and Bryce?"

"May just have been a calculated risk. He saw how Jeremy flattened Kinnaird when he tried to go back into the radio room a second time and perhaps calculated that Jeremy would oblige again if he tried a similar but fake rescue act."

"Maybe Kinnaird's second attempt was also fake," Swanson said. "After all, Jeremy had already tried to stop him once."

"Maybe it was," I agreed. "But Naseby. If he's your man, why should he have said that the radio-room door was jammed with ice and that he had to burst it open? That gives Kinnaird and Jolly an out—and a murderer wouldn't do anything to put any other potential suspect in the clear."

"It's hopeless," Swanson said calmly. "I say let's put the whole damned crowd of them under lock and key."

"That would be clever," I said. "Yes, let's do just that. That way we'll never find out who the murderer is. Anyway, before you start giving up, remember it's even more complicated than that. Remember you're passing up the two most obvious suspects of all—Jeremy and Hassard—two tough, intelligent birds who, if they were the killers, were clever enough to see that *nothing* pointed the finger against them. Unless, of course; there might have been something about Flanders and Bryce that Jeremy didn't want anyone to see, so he stopped Naseby from going back into the cookhouse. Or not."

Swanson almost glared at me. Watching his submarine plummeting out of control beyond the 1,000-feet mark was something that rated maybe the lift of an eyebrow; but this was something else again. He said: "Very well, then, we'll let the killer run loose and wreck the *Dolphin* at his leisure. I must have very considerable confidence in you, Dr. Carpenter. I feel sure my confidence will not be misplaced. Tell me one last thing. I assume you are a highly skilled investigator. But I was puzzled by one omission in your questioning. A vital question, I should have thought."

"Who suggested moving the corpses into the lab, knowing that by doing so he would be making his hiding place for the cached material a hundred per cent fool-proof?"

"I apologize." He smiled faintly. "You had your reasons, of course."

"Of course. You're not sure whether or not the killer is on to the fact that we are on to him. I'm sure. I know he's not. But had I asked that question, he'd have known immediately that there could be only one reason for my asking it. Then

171

he would have known I was on to him. Anyway, it's my guess that Captain Folsom gave the order, but the original suggestion, carefully camouflaged so that Folsom may no longer be able to pin it down, would have come from another quarter."

Had it been a few months earlier, with the summer Arctic sun riding in the sky, it would have been a brilliant day. As it was, there was no sun, not in that latitude and so late in the year; but, for all that, the weather was about as perfect as it was possible for it to be. Thirty-six hours—the time that had elapsed since Hansen and I had made that savage trip back to the *Dolphin*—had brought about a change that seemed pretty close to miraculous. The knifing east wind had died completely. That flying sea of ice spicules was no more. The temperature had risen at least twenty degrees, and the visibility was as perfect as visibility on the winter ice pack ever is.

Swanson, sharing Benson's viewpoint on the crew's over-sedentary mode of existence and taking advantage of the fine weather, had advised everyone not engaged in actual watch-keeping to take advantage of the opportunity offered to stretch their legs in the fresh air. It said much for Swanson's powers of persuasion that by eleven that morning the *Dolphin* was practically deserted; and of course the crew, to whom Drift Ice Station Zebra was only so many words, were understandably curious to see the place, even the shell of the place, that had brought them to the top of the world.

I took my place at the end of the small line being treated by Dr. Jolly. It was close to noon before he got around to me. He was making light of his own burns and frostbite and was in tremendous form, bustling happily about the sick bay as if it had been his own private domain for years.

"Well," I said, "the pill-rolling competition wasn't so fierce after all, was it? I'm damned glad there was a third doctor around. How are things on the medical front?"

"Coming along not too badly, old boy," he said cheerfully. "Benson's picking up very nicely. Pulse, respiration, blood pressure close to normal, level of unconsciousness very slight now, I should say. Captain Folsom's still in considerable pain, but no actual danger, of course. The rest have improved a hundred per cent, little thanks to the medical fraternity. Excellent food, warm beds, and the knowledge that they're safe have done them more good than anything we could ever do. Anyway, it's done me a lot of good, by Jove!"

"And them," I agreed. "All your friends except Folsom

172

and the Harrington twins have followed most of the crew on to the ice, and I'll wager that if you had suggested to them forty-eight hours ago that they'd willingly go out there again in so short a time, they'd have called for a straitjacket."

"The physical and mental recuperative power of homo sapiens," Jolly said jovially. "Beyond belief at times, old lad, beyond belief. Now, let's have a look at that broken wing of yours."

So he had a look, and because I was a colleague and therefore inured to human suffering, he didn't spend any too much time in molly-coddling me, but by hanging on to the arm of my chair and the shreds of my professional pride, I kept the roof from falling in on me. When he was finished he said, "Well, that's the lot, except for Brownell and Bolton, the two lads out on the ice."

"I'll come with you," I said. "Commander Swanson is waiting pretty anxiously to hear what we have to say. He wants to get away from here as soon as possible."

"Me too," Jolly said fervently. "But what's the commander so anxious about?"

"Ice. You never know the hour or minute it starts to close in. Want to spend the next year or two up here?"

Jolly grinned, thought it over for a moment, then stopped grinning. He said apprehensively, "How long are we going to be under this damned ice? Before we reach the open sea, I mean?"

"Twenty-four hours, Swanson says. Don't look so worried, Jolly. Believe me, it's far safer under this stuff than among it."

With a very unconvinced look on his face, Jolly picked up his medical kit and led the way from the sick bay. Swanson was waiting for us in the control room. We climbed up the hatches, dropped down over the side, and walked over to the drift station.

Most of the crew had already made their way out there. We passed numbers of them on the way back; most of them looked grim or sick or both, and didn't even glance up as we passed. I didn't have to guess why they looked as they did; they'd been opening doors that they should have left closed.

With the sharp rise in outside temperature and the effect of the big electric heaters having been burning there for twenty-four hours, the bunkhouse hut was now, if anything, overheated, with the last traces of ice long vanished from walls and ceiling. One of the men, Brownell, had recovered consciousness and was sitting up, supported, drinking soup provided by one of the two men who had been keeping watch over him.

"Well," I said to Swanson, "here's one ready to go."

"No doubt about that," Jolly said briskly. He bent over the other, Bolton, for some seconds, then straightened and shook his head. "A very sick man, Commander, very sick. I wouldn't care to take the responsibility of moving him."

"I might be forced to take the responsibility myself," Swanson said bluntly. "Let's have another opinion on this." His tone and words, I thought, could have been more diplomatic and conciliatory; but if there were a couple of murderers aboard the *Dolphin*, there was a thirty-three and a third per cent chance that Jolly was one of them, and Swanson wasn't forgetting it for a moment.

I gave Jolly an apologetic half-shrug, bent over Bolton, and examined him as best I could with only one hand available for the task. I straightened and said, "Jolly's right. He is pretty sick. But I think he might just stand the transfer to the ship."

" 'Might just' is not quite the normally accepted basis for deciding the treatment of a patient," Jolly objected.

"I know it's not. But the circumstances are hardly normal, either."

"I'll take the responsibility," Swanson said. "Dr. Jolly, I'd be most grateful if you would supervise the transport of those two men back to the ship. I'll let you have as many men as you want right away."

Jolly protested some more, then gave in with good grace. He supervised the transfer, and very competent he was about it, too. I remained out there a little longer, watching Rawlings and some others dismantling heaters and lights and rolling up cables, and after the last of them was gone and I was alone, I made my way around to the tractor shed.

The broken shaft of the knife was still in the tank of the tractor. But not the gun and not the two magazines. Those were gone. And whoever had taken them, it hadn't been Dr. Jolly; he hadn't been out of my sight for two consecutive seconds between the time he'd left the *Dolphin* and the time of his return to it.

At three o'clock that afternoon we dropped down below the ice and headed south for the open sea.

10

THE AFTERNOON AND EVENING passed quickly and pleasantly enough. Closing our hatches and dropping down from our hardly won foothold in that lead had had a symbolic significance at least as important as the actual fact of leaving itself. The thick ceiling of ice closing over the hull of the *Dolphin* was a curtain being drawn across the eye of the mind. We had severed all physical connection with Drift Ice Station Zebra, a home of the dead that might continue to circle slowly around the Pole for mindless centuries to come; and with the severance had come an abrupt diminution of the horror and the shock that had hung pall-like over the ship and its crew for the past twenty-four hours. A dark door had swung to behind us, and we had turned our backs on it. Mission accomplished, duty done, we were heading for home again, and the sudden upsurge of relief and happiness among the crew to be on their way again, their high anticipation of port and leave, was an almost tangible thing. The mood of the ship was close to that of light-hearted gaiety. But there was no gaiety in my mind, and no peace: I was leaving too much behind. Nor could there be any peace in the minds of Swanson and Hansen, of Rawlings and Zabrinski: they knew we were carrying a killer aboard, a killer who had killed many times. Dr. Benson knew also, but for the moment Dr. Benson did not count: he still had not regained consciousness, and I held the very unprofessional hope that he wouldn't for some time to come. In the twilit world of emergence from coma, a man can start babbling and say all too much.

Some of the Zebra survivors had asked if they could look around the ship and Swanson agreed. In light of what I had told him in his cabin that morning, he must have agreed very reluctantly indeed, but no trace of this reluctance showed in his calmly smiling face. To have refused their request would have been rather a churlish gesture, for all the secrets of the *Dolphin* were completely hidden from the eye of the layman.

But it wasn't good manners that made Swanson give his consent: refusing a reasonable request could have been responsible for making someone very suspicious indeed.

Hansen took them around the ship and I accompanied them, less for the exercise or interest involved than for the opportunity it gave me to keep a very close eye indeed on their reactions to their tour. We made a complete tour of the ship, missing only the reactor room, which no one could visit anyway, and the inertial-navigation room, which had been barred to me also. As we moved around I watched them all, and especially two of them, as closely as it is possible to watch anyone without making him aware of your observation, and I learned precisely what I had expected to learn—nothing. I'd been crazy even to hope I'd learn anything; our friend with the gun was wearing a mask that had been forged into shape and riveted into position. But I'd had to do it anyway; playing in this league, I couldn't pass up the one chance in a million.

Supper over, I helped Jolly as best I could with his evening surgery. Whatever else Jolly was, he was a damned good doctor. Quickly and efficiently he checked and where necessary rebandaged the walking cases, examined and treated Benson and Folsom, then asked me to come right aft with him to the nucleonics laboratory in the stern room, which had been cleared of deck gear to accommodate the four other bed patients, the Harrington twins, Brownell, and Bolton. The sick bay itself had only two cots for invalids, and Benson and Folsom had those.

Bolton, despite Jolly's dire predictions, hadn't suffered a relapse because of his transfer from the hut to the ship—which had been due largely to Jolly's extremely skillful and careful handling of the patient and the stretcher into which he had been strapped. Bolton, in fact, was conscious now and complaining of severe pain in his badly burned right forearm. Jolly removed the burn covering. Bolton's arm was a mess, all right, no skin left worth speaking of, showing an angry violent red between areas of suppuration. Different doctors have different ideas as to the treatment of burns: Jolly favored a salve-coated aluminum foil which he smoothed across the entire burn area, then lightly bandaged in place. He then gave him a pain-killing injection and some sleeping pills and briskly informed the enlisted man who was keeping watch that he was to be informed immediately of any change or deterioration in Bolton's condition. A brief inspection of the three others, a changed bandage here and there, and he was through for the night.

So was I. For two nights now I had had practically no sleep; what little had been left for me the previous night had been ruined by the pain in my left hand. I was exhausted. When I got to my cabin, Hansen was already asleep and the engineer officer gone.

I didn't need any of Jolly's sleeping pills that night.

I awoke at two o'clock. I was sleep-drugged, still exhausted, and felt as if I had been in bed about five minutes. But I awoke in an instant and in that instant I was fully awake.

Only a dead man wouldn't have stirred. The racket issuing from the squawk box just above Hansen's bunk was appalling, a high-pitched, shrieking, atonic whistle, two-toned and altering pitch every half-second, it drilled stiletto-like against my cringing eardrums. A banshee in its death agonies could never have hoped to compete with that racket.

Hansen already had his feet on the deck and was pulling on clothes and shoes in desperate haste. I had never thought to see that slow-speaking laconic Texan in such a tearing hurry, but I was seeing it now.

"What in hell's name is the matter?" I demanded. I had to shout to make myself heard above the shrieking of the alarm whistle.

"Fire!" His face was shocked and grim. "The ship's on fire. And under this Goddamned ice!"

Still buttoning his shirt, he hurdled my cot, crashed the door back on its hinges, and was gone.

The atonic screeching of the whistle stopped abruptly and the silence fell like a blow. Then I was conscious of something more than silence—I was conscious of a complete lack of vibration throughout the ship. The great engines had stopped. And then I was conscious of something else again: feathery fingers of ice brushing up and down my spine.

Why had the engines stopped? What could make a nuclear engine stop so quickly and what happened once it did? My God, I thought, maybe the fire is coming from the reactor room itself. I'd looked into the heart of the uranium atomic pile through a heavily leaded glass-inspection port and seen the indescribable unearthly radiance of it, a nightmarish coalescence of green and violet and blue, the new "dreadful light" of mankind. What happened when this dreadful light ran wild? I didn't know, but I suspected I didn't want to be around when it happened.

I dressed slowly, not hurrying. My damaged hand didn't help me much but that wasn't why I took my time. Maybe the ship was on fire, maybe the nuclear power plant had gone out of kilter. But if Swanson's superbly trained crew couldn't cope with every emergency that could conceivably arise, then matters weren't going to be improved any by Carpenter running around in circles shouting: "Where's the fire?"

Three minutes after Hansen had gone I walked along to the control room and peered in: if I was going to be in the way, then this was as far as I was going to go. Dark, acrid smoke billowed past me and a voice—Swanson's—said sharply: "Inside and close that door."

I pulled the door to and looked around the control room. At least, I tried to. It wasn't easy. My eyes were already steaming as if someone had thrown a bag of pepper into them, and what little sight was left them didn't help me much. The room was filled with black evil-smelling smoke, denser by far and more throat-catching than the worst London fog. Visibility was no more than a few feet, but what little I could see showed me men still at their stations. Some were gasping, some were half choking, some were cursing softly, all had badly watering eyes, but there was no trace of panic.

"You'd have been better off on the other side of that door," Swanson said dryly. "Sorry to have barked at you, Doctor, but we want to limit the spread of the smoke as much as possible."

"Where's the fire?"

"In the engine room." Swanson could have been sitting on his front porch at home discussing the weather. "Where in the engine room we don't know. It's pretty bad. At least, the smoke is. The extent of the fire we don't know, because we can't locate it. Engineer officer says it's impossible to see your hand in front of your face."

"The engines," I said. "They've stopped. Has anything gone wrong—"

He rubbed his eyes with a handkerchief, spoke to a man who was pulling on a heavy rubber suit and a smoke mask, then turned back to me.

"We're not going to be vaporized, if that's what you mean." I could have sworn he was smiling. "The atomic pile can only fail safe no matter what happens. If anything goes wrong, the uranium rods slam down in very quick time indeed—a fraction under a thousandth of a second—stopping the whole reaction. In this case, though, we shut it off ourselves. The men in the maneuvering room could no longer see either the reactor dials or the governor for the control rods. No option but to shut it down. The engine-room crew have been forced to abandon the engine and maneuvering rooms and take shelter in the stern room."

Well, that was something at least. We weren't going to

178

be blown to pieces, ignobly vaporized on the altar of nuclear advancement: good old-fashioned suffocation, that was to be our lot. "So what do we do?" I asked.

"What we should do is surface immediately. With fourteen feet of ice overhead, that's not easy. Excuse me, will you?"

He spoke to the now completely masked and suited man, who was carrying a small dialed box in his hands. They walked together past the navigator's chart desk and ice machine to the heavy door opening on the passage that led to the engine room over the top of the reactor compartment. They unlatched the door, pushed it open. A dense, blinding cloud of dark smoke rolled into the room as the masked man stepped quickly into the passageway and swung the door to behind him. Swanson clamped the door shut, walked, temporarily blinded, back to the control position, and fumbled down a roof microphone.

"Captain speaking." His voice echoed emptily through the control center. "The fire is located in the engine room. We do not know yet whether it is electrical, chemical, or fuel oil: the source of the fire has not been pinpointed. Acting on the principle of being prepared for the worst, we are now testing for a radiation leak." So that was what the masked man had been carrying, a Geiger counter. "If that proves negative, we shall try for a steam leak, and if that is negative, we shall carry out an intensive search to locate the fire. It will not be easy, as I'm told visibility is almost zero. We have already shut down all electrical circuits in the engine room, lighting included, to prevent an explosion in the event of atomized fuel being present in the atmosphere. We have closed the oxygen-intake valves and isolated the engine room from the air-cleaning system in the hope that the fire will consume all available oxygen and burn itself out.

"All smoking is prohibited until further notice. Heaters, fans, and all electrical circuits other than communication lines to be switched off—and that includes the juke box and the ice-cream machine. All lights to be switched off except those absolutely essential. All movement is to be restricted to a minimum. I shall keep you informed of any progress we may make."

I became aware of someone standing by my side. It was Dr. Jolly, his normally jovial face puckered and woe-begone, the tears flowing down his face. Plaintively he said to me, "This *is* a bit thick, old boy, what? I'm not sure that I'm so happy now about being rescued. And all those prohibitions —no smoking, no power to be used, no moving around—do those mean what I take them to mean?"

"I'm afraid they do indeed." It was Swanson who answered

Jolly's question for him. "This, I'm afraid, is every nuclear-submarine captain's nightmare come true—fire under the ice. At one blow we're not only reduced to the level of a conventional submarine—we're two stages worse. In the first place, a conventional submarine wouldn't be under the ice anyway. In the second place, it has huge banks of storage batteries, and even if it were beneath the ice, it would have sufficient reserve power to steam far enough south to get clear of the ice. Our reserve storage battery is so small that it wouldn't take us a fraction of the way."

"Yes, yes," Jolly nodded. "But this no smoking, no moving—"

"That same very small battery, I'm afraid, is the only source left to us for power for the air-purifying machines, for lighting, ventilation, heating—I'm afraid the *Dolphin* is going to get very cold in a short time—so we have to curtail its expenditures of energy on those things. So no smoking, minimum movement—the less carbon dioxide breathed into the atmosphere, the better. But the real reason for conserving electric energy is that we need it to power the heaters, pumps and motors that have to be used to start up the reactor again. If that battery exhausts itself before we get the reactor going—well, I don't have to draw a diagram."

"You're not very encouraging, are you, Commander?" Jolly complained.

"No, not very. I don't see any reason to be," Swanson said dryly.

"I'll bet you'd trade in your pension for a nice open lead above us just now," I said.

"I'd trade in the pension of every flag officer in the U. S. Navy," he said matter-of-factly. "If we could find a polynya I'd surface, open the engine-room hatch to let most of the contaminated air escape, start up our diesel—it takes its air direct from the engine room—and have the rest of the smoke sucked out in nothing flat. As it is, that diesel is about as much use to me as a grand piano."

"And the compasses?" I asked.

"That's another interesting thought," Swanson agreed. "If the power out-put from our reserve battery falls below a certain level, our three Sperry gyro-compass systems and the N6A—that's the inertial-guidance machine—just go out of business. After that we're lost, completely. Our magnetic compass is quite useless in those latitudes—it just walks in circles."

"So we would go round and round in circles, too," Jolly said thoughtfully. "Forever and ever under the jolly old ice cap,

180

what? By Jove, Commander, I'm really beginning to wish we'd stayed up at Zebra."

"We're not dead yet, Doctor. . . . Yes, John?" This to Hansen, who had just come up.

"Sanders, sir. On the ice machine. Can he have a smoke mask? His eyes are watering pretty badly."

"Give him anything you like in the ship," Swanson said, "just so long as he can keep his eyes clear to read that graph. And double the watch on the ice machine. If there's a lead up there only the size of a hair, I'm going for it. Immediate report if the ice thickness falls below, say, eight or nine feet."

"Torpedoes?" Hansen asked. "There hasn't been ice thin enough for that in three hours. And at the speed we're drifting, there won't be for three months. I'll go keep the watch myself. I'm not much good for anything else, this hand of mine being the way it is."

"Thank you. First you might tell engineman Harrison to turn off the CO_2 scrubber and monoxide burners. Must save every amp of power we have. Besides, it will do this pampered bunch of ours a world of good to sample a little of what the old-time submariners had to experience when they were forced to stay below maybe twenty hours at a time."

"That's going to be pretty rough on our really sick men," I said. "Benson and Folsom in the sick bay, the Harrington twins, Brownell and Bolton in the nucleonics lab right aft. They've got enough to contend with without foul air as well."

"I know," Swanson admitted. "I'm damned sorry about it. Later on, when—and if—the air gets really bad, we'll start up the air-purifying systems again but blank off every place except the lab and the sick bay." He broke off and turned around as a fresh wave of dark smoke rolled in from the suddenly opened after door. The man with the smoke mask was back from the engine room, and even with my eyes streaming in that smoke-filled, acrid atmosphere, I could see he was in a pretty bad way. Swanson and two others rushed to meet him, two of them catching him as he staggered into the control room, the third quickly swinging the heavy door shut against the darkly evil clouds of smoke.

Swanson pulled off the man's smoke mask. It was Murphy, the man who had accompanied me when we'd closed the torpedo tube door. People like Murphy and Rawlings, I thought, always got picked for jobs like this.

His face was white and he was gasping for air, his eyes upturned in his head. He was hardly more than half conscious, but even that foul atmosphere in the control center must have seemed to him like the purest mountain air compared

181

to what he had just been breathing, for within thirty seconds his head had begun to clear and he was able to grin up painfully from where he'd been lowered into a chair.

"Sorry, Captain," he gasped. "This smoke mask was never meant to cope with the stuff that's in the engine room. Pretty hellish in there, I tell you." He grinned again. "Good news, Captain. No radiation leak."

"Where's the Geiger counter?" Swanson asked quietly.

"It's had it, I'm afraid, sir. I couldn't see what I was doing in there. Honest, sir, you can't see three inches in front of your face. I tripped and damn near fell down into the machinery space. The counter did fall down. But I'd a clear check before then. Nothing at all." He reached up to his shoulder and unclipped his film badge. "This'll show, sir."

"Have that developed immediately. That was very well done, Murphy," he said warmly. "Now get for'ard to the mess room. You'll find some really clear air there."

The film badge was developed and brought back in minutes. Swanson took it, glanced at it briefly, smiled, and let out his breath in a long, slow whistle of relief. "Murphy was right. No radiation leak. Thank God for that, anyway. If there had been—well, that was that, I'm afraid."

The for'ard door of the control room opened, a man came in, and the door was as quickly closed. I guessed who it was before I could see him properly.

"Permission from chief torpedoman Patterson to approach you, sir," Rawlings said with brisk formality. "We've just seen Murphy. He's pretty groggy, and both the chief and I think that youngsters like that shouldn't be—"

"Am I to understand that you are volunteering to go next, Rawlings?" Swanson asked. The screws of responsibility and tension were turned down hard on him, but I could see that it cost him some effort to keep his face straight.

"Well, not exactly volunteering, sir. But, well—who else is there?"

"The torpedo department aboard this ship," Swanson observed acidly, "always did have a phenomenally high opinion of itself."

"Let him try an underwater oxygen set," I said. "Those smoke masks seem to have their limitations."

"A steam leak, Captain?" Rawlings asked. "That what you want me to check on?"

"Well, you seem to have been nominated, voted for, and elected by yourself," Swanson said. "Yes, a steam leak."

"That the suit Murphy was wearing?" Rawlings pointed to the clothes on the deck.

"Yes. Why?"

"You'd have thought there would be some signs of moisture or condensation if there had been a steam leak, sir."

"Maybe. Maybe soot and smoke particles are holding the condensing steam in suspension. Maybe it was hot enough in there to dry off any moisture that did reach his suit. Maybe a lot of things. Don't stay too long in there."

"Just as long as it takes me to get things fixed up," Rawlings said confidently. He turned to Hansen and grinned. "You stopped me once back out there on the ice cap, Lieutenant, but sure as little apples I'm going to get that little old medal this time. Bring undying credit to the whole ship, I will."

"If torpedoman Rawlings will ease up with his ravings for a moment," Hansen said, "I have a suggestion to make, Captain. I know he won't be able to take off his mask inside there but if he gave a call-up signal on the engine telephone or rang through on the engine answering telegraph every four or five minutes we'd know he was okay. If he doesn't, someone can go in after him."

Swanson nodded. Rawlings pulled on suit and oxygen apparatus and left. That made it the third time the door leading to the engine compartment had been opened in a few minutes and each time fresh clouds of that black and biting smoke had come rolling in. Conditions were now very bad inside the control room, but someone had issued a supply of goggles all around and a few were wearing smoke masks.

A phone rang. Hansen answered, spoke briefly, and hung up.

"That was Jack Cartwright, skipper." Lieutenant Cartwright was the main-propulsion officer, who had been on watch in the maneuvering room and had been forced to retreat to the stern room. "Seems he was overcome by the fumes and was carried back into the stern room. Says he's okay now and could we send smoke masks or breathing apparatus for him and one of his men. They can't get at the ones in the engine room. I told him yes."

"I'd certainly feel a lot happier if Jack Cartwright was in there investigating in person," Swanson admitted. "Send a man, will you?"

"I thought I'd take them myself. Someone else can double on the ice machine."

Swanson glanced at Hansen's injured hand, hesitated, then nodded. "Right. But straight through the engine room and straight back."

Hanson was on his way in a minute. Five minutes later he

183

was back again. He stripped off his breathing equipment. His face was pale and covered with sweat.

"There's fire in the engine room, all right," he said grimly. "Hotter than the hinges of hell. No trace of sparks or flames, but that doesn't mean a thing, the smoke in there is so thick that you couldn't see a blast furnace a couple of feet away."

"See Rawlings?" Swanson asked.

"No. Hasn't he rung through?"

"Twice, but—" He broke off as the engine-room telegraph rang. "So. He's still okay. How about the stern room, John?"

"Damn sight worse than it is here. The sick men aft there are in a pretty bad way, especially Bolton. Seems the smoke got in before they could get the door shut."

"Tell Harrison to start up his air scrubbers. But for the lab only. Shut off the rest of the ship."

Fifteen minutes passed, fifteen minutes during which the engine-room telegraph rang three times, fifteen minutes during which the air became thicker and fouler and steadily less breathable, fifteen minutes during which a completely equipped fire-fighting team was assembled in the control center, then another billowing cloud of black smoke announced the opening of the after door.

It was Rawlings. He was very weak and had to be helped out of his breathing equipment and his suit. His face was white and streaming sweat, his hair and clothes so saturated with sweat that he might easily have come straight from an immersion in the sea. But he was grinning triumphantly.

"No steam leak, Captain, that's for certain." It took him three breaths to get that out. "But fire down below in the machinery space. Sparks flying all over the shop. Some flame, not much. I located it, sir. Starboard high-pressure turbine. The sheathing's on fire."

"You'll get that medal, Rawlings," Swanson said, "even if I have to make the damn thing myself." He turned to the waiting firemen. "You heard. Starboard turbine. Four at a time, fifteen minutes maximum. Lieutenant Raeburn, the first party. Knives, claw hammers, pliers, crow bars, CO_2. Saturate the sheathing first, then rip it off. Watch out for flash flames when you're pulling it off. I don't have to warn you about the steam pipes. Now, on your way."

They left. I said to Swanson: "Doesn't sound so much. How long will it take? Ten minutes, quarter of an hour?"

He looked at me somberly. "A minimum of three or four hours—if we're lucky. It's hell's own maze down in the machinery space there. Valves, tubes, condensers, and miles of that damned steam piping that would burn your hands off if

184

you touched it. Working conditions even normally are so cramped as to be almost impossible. Then there's that huge turbine housing with all that thick insulation sheathing wrapped all around it, and the engineers who fitted it meant it to stay there for keeps. Before they start, they have to douse the fire with the CO_2 extinguishers, and even that won't help much. Every time they rip off a piece of charred insulation, the oil-soaked stuff below will burst into flames again as soon as it comes into contact with the oxygen in the atmosphere."

" 'Oil-soaked'?"

"That's where the whole trouble must lie," Swanson explained. "Wherever you have moving machinery, you must have oil for lubrication. There's no shortage of machinery, down in the machine space—and no shortage of oil, either. And just as certain materials are strongly hygroscopic, so that damned insulation has a remarkable affinity for oil. Where there's any around, whether in its normal fluid condition or in fine suspension in the atmosphere, that sheathing attracts it as a magnet does iron filings. And it's as absorbent as blotting paper."

"But what could have caused the fire?"

"Spontaneous combustion. There have been cases before. We've gone over fifty thousand miles in this ship now, and in that time I suppose the sheathing has become thoroughly saturated. We've been going at top speed ever since we left Zebra, and the excess heat generated has set the damn thing off. . . . John, no word from Cartwright yet?"

"Nothing."

"He must have been in there for the better part of twenty minutes now."

"Maybe. But he was just beginning to put his suit on—he and Ringman—when I left, and maybe they didn't go into the engine room right away. I'll call the stern room." He did, then hung up, his face grave. "Stern room says they've been gone twenty-five minutes. Shall I investigate, sir?"

"You stay right here. I'm not—"

He broke off as the after door opened with a crash and two men came staggering out—rather, one staggering, the other supporting him. The door was heaved shut and the men's masks removed. One man I recognized as an enlisted man who had accompanied Raeburn; the other was Cartwright.

"Lieutenant Raeburn sent me out with the lieutenant here," the enlisted man said. "He's not so good, I think, Captain."

It was a pretty fair diagnosis. He wasn't so good and that was a fact. He was barely conscious but nonetheless fighting

185

grimly to hang on to what few shreds of consciousness were left him.

"Ringman," he jerked out. "Five minutes—five minutes ago. We were going back—"

"Ringman," Swanson prompted with a gentle insistence. "What about Ringman?"

"He fell. Down into the machinery space. I—I went after him, tried to lift him up the ladder. He screamed. God, he screamed. I—he—"

He slumped in his chair, was caught before he fell to the floor. I said: "Ringman. Either a major fracture or internal injuries."

"Damn!" Swanson swore softly. "Damn it all! A fracture. Down there. John, have Cartwright carried through to the crew's mess. A fracture!"

"Please have a mask and suit ready for me," Jolly said briskly. "I'll fetch Dr. Benson's emergency kit from the sick bay."

"You?" Swanson shook his head. "Damned decent, Jolly. I appreciate it, but I can't let you—"

"Just for once, old boy, the hell with your Navy regulations," Jolly said politely. "The main thing to remember, Commander, is that I'm aboard this ship, too. Let us remember that we all—um—sink or swim together. No joke intended."

"But you don't know how to operate those sets—"

"I can learn, can't I?" Jolly said with some asperity. He turned and left.

Swanson looked at me. He was wearing goggles, but they couldn't hide the concern in his face. He said, curiously hesitant: "Do you think—"

"Of course Jolly's right. You've no option. If Benson were fit you know very well you'd have him down there in no time. Besides, Jolly is a damned fine doctor."

"You haven't been down there, Carpenter. It's a metal jungle. There isn't room to splint a broken finger, much less—"

"I don't think Dr. Jolly will try to fix or splint anything. He'll just give Ringman a jab that will put him out so that he can be brought up here without screaming in agony all the way."

Swanson nodded, pursed his lips, and walked away to examine the ice fathometer. I said to Hansen, "It's pretty bad, isn't it?"

"You can say that again, friend. It's worse than bad. Normally, there should be enough air in the submarine to last us maybe sixteen hours. But well over half the air in this ship, from here right aft, is already practically unbreathable.

186

What we have left can't possibly last us more than a few hours. Skipper's boxed in on three sides. If he doesn't start the air purifiers up, the men working down in the machinery space are going to have a hell of a job doing anything. Working in near-zero visibility with breathing apparatus on, you're practically as good as blind: the floods will make hardly any difference. If he does start up the purifiers in the engine room, the fresh oxygen will cause the fire to spread. And when he starts them up, of course, that means less and less power to get the reactor working again."

"That's very comforting," I said. "How long will it take you to restart the reactor?"

"At least an hour. That's after the fire has been put out and everything checked for safety. At least an hour."

"And Swanson reckoned three or four hours to put the fire out. Say five, all told. It's a long time. Why doesn't he use some of his reserve power cruising around to find a lead?"

"An even bigger gamble than staying put and trying to put out the fire. I'm with the skipper. Let's fight the devil we know rather than the one we don't."

Medical case in hand, Jolly came coughing and spluttering his way back into the control center and started pulling on a suit and breathing apparatus. Hansen gave him instructions on how to operate it, and Jolly seemed to get the idea pretty quickly. Brown, the enlisted man who'd helped Cartwright into the control center, was detailed to accompany him: Jolly had no idea of the location of the ladder leading down from the upper engine room to the machinery space.

"Be as quick as you can," Swanson said. "Remember, Jolly, you're not trained for this sort of thing. I'll expect you back inside ten minutes."

They were back in exactly four minutes. They didn't have an unconscious Ringman with them, either. The only unconscious figure was that of Dr. Jolly, whom Brown half carried, half dragged over the sill into the control room.

"Can't say for sure what happened," Brown gasped. He was trembling from the effort he had just made; Jolly must have outweighed him by at least thirty pounds. "We'd just got into the engine room and shut the door. I was leading, and suddenly Dr. Jolly fell against me. I think he must have tripped over something. He knocked me down. When I got to my feet, he was lying there behind me. I put the flashlight on him. He was out cold. His mask had been torn loose. I put it on as best I could and pulled him out."

"My God," Hansen said reflectively. "The medical profession on the *Dolphin* *is* having a rough time." He gloomily surveyed the prone figure of Dr. Jolly as it was carried away toward the after door and relatively fresh air. "All three sawbones out of commission now. That's very handy, isn't it, skipper?"

Swanson didn't answer. I said to him, "The injection for Ringman. Would you know what to give, how to give it and where?"

"No."

"Would any of your crew?"

"I'm in no position to argue, Dr. Carpenter."

I opened Jolly's medical kit, hunted among the bottles on the lid rack until I found what I wanted, dipped a hypodermic and injected it in my left forearm, just where the bandage ended. "Pain-killer," I said. "I'm just a softy. But I want to be able to use the forefinger and thumb of that hand." I glanced across at Rawlings, as recovered as anyone could get in that foul atmosphere, and said: "How are you feeling now?"

"Just resting lightly." He rose from his chair and picked up his breathing equipment. "Have no fears, Doc. With torpedoman first class Rawlings by your side—"

"We have plenty of fresh men still available aft, Dr. Carpenter," Swanson said.

"No. Rawlings. It's for his own sake. Maybe he'll get two medals now for this night's work."

Rawlings grinned and pulled the mask over his head. Two minutes later we were inside the engine room.

It was stiflingly hot in there, and visibility, even with the powerful beam of our flashlights, didn't exceed eighteen inches; but for the rest it wasn't too bad. The breathing apparatus functioned well enough, and I was conscious of no discomfort. At first, that was.

Rawlings took my arm and guided me to the head of a ladder that reached down to the deck of the machinery space. I heard the penetrating hiss of a fire extinguisher and peered around to locate its source.

A pity they had no submarines in the Middle Ages, I thought; the sight of that little lot down there would have given Dante an extra fillip when he started in on his Inferno. Over on the starboard side, two very powerful floodlights had been slung above the huge turbine: the visibility they gave varied from three to six feet, according to the changing amount of smoke given off by the charred and smoldering insulation. At the moment, one patch of the insulation was deeply covered in a layer of white foam—carbon dioxide released under pressure immediately freezes anything with which it comes in contact. As the man with the extinguisher stepped back, three others moved forward in the swirling gloom and

188

started hacking and tearing away at the insulation. As soon as a sizable strip was dragged loose the exposed lagging below immediately burst into flame reaching the height of a man's head, throwing into sharp relief weird masked figures leaping backward to avoid being scorched by the flames. And then the man with the CO_2 would approach again, press his trigger, the blaze would shrink down, flicker, and die, and a coat of creamy white foam would bloom where the fire had been. Then the entire process would be repeated all over again. The whole scene with the repetitively stylized movements of the participants highlit against a smoky, oil-veined background of flickering crimson was somehow weirdly suggestive of the priests of a long-dead and alien culture offering up some burnt sacrifice on their blood-stained pagan altar.

It also made me see Swanson's point: at the painfully but necessarily slow rate at which those men were making progress, four hours would be excellent par for the course. I tried not to think what the air inside the *Dolphin* would be like in four hours' time.

The man with the extinguisher—it was Raeburn—caught sight of us, came across, and led me through a tangled maze of steam pipes and condensers to where Ringman was lying. He was on his back, very still, but conscious: I could see the movement of the whites of his eyes behind his goggles. I bent down till my mask was touching his.

"Your leg?" I shouted.

He nodded.

"Left?"

He nodded again, reached out gingerly, and touched a spot halfway down the shinbone. I opened the medical case, pulled out scissors, pinched the clothes on his upper arm between finger and thumb, and cut a piece of the material away. The hypodermic came next and within two minutes he was asleep. With Rawlings' help, I laid splints against his leg and bandaged them roughly in place. Two of the fire fighters stopped work long enough to help us drag him up the ladder, and then Rawlings and I took him through the passage above the reactor room. I became aware that my breathing was now distressed, my legs shaking, and my whole body bathed in sweat.

Once in the control center, I took off my mask and immediately began to cough and sneeze uncontrollably, tears streaming down my cheeks. Even in the few minutes we had been gone, the air in the control room had deteriorated to a frightening extent.

189

Swanson said, "Thank you, Doctor. What's it like in there?"

"Quite bad. Not intolerable, but not nice. Ten minutes is long enough for your fire fighters at one time."

"Fire fighters I have plenty of. Ten minutes it shall be."

A couple of burly enlisted men carried Ringman through to the sick bay. Rawlings had been ordered for'ard for rest and recuperation in the comparatively fresh air of the mess room, but he elected to stop off at the sick bay with me. He'd glanced at my bandaged left hand and said, "Three hands are better than one, even though two of them do happen to belong to Rawlings."

Benson was restless and occasionally murmuring but still below the level of consciousness. Captain Folsom was asleep, deeply so, which I found surprising until Rawlings told me that there were no alarm boxes in the sick bay and that the door was completely sound-proofed.

We laid Ringman down on the examination table, and Rawlings slit his trouser leg with a pair of heavy surgical scissors. It wasn't as bad as I had feared it would be: a clean fracture of the tibia, not compound. With Rawlings doing most of the work, we soon had his leg fixed up. I didn't try to put his leg in traction; when Jolly, with his two good hands, had completely recovered, he'd be able to make a better job of it than I could.

We'd just finished when a telephone rang. Rawlings lifted it quickly before Folsom could hear it, spoke briefly, and hung up.

"Control room," he said. I knew from the wooden expression on his face that whatever news he had for me, it wasn't good. "It was for you. Bolton, the sick man in the nucleonics lab, the one you brought back from Zebra yesterday afternoon. He's gone. About two minutes ago." He shook his head despairingly. "My God, another death."

"No," I said. "Another murder."

11

THE DOLPHIN WAS AN ICE-COLD TOMB. At half-past six that morning, four and a half hours after the outbreak of the fire, there was still only one dead man inside the ship—Bolton. But as I looked with bloodshot and inflamed eyes at the men sitting or lying about the control room—no one was standing any more—I knew that within an hour, two at the most, Bolton would be having company. By ten o'clock at the latest, under those conditions, the *Dolphin* would be no more than a steel coffin with no life left inside her.

As a ship the *Dolphin* was already dead. All the sounds we associated with the living vessel, the murmurous pulsation of great engines, the high-pitched whine of generators, the deep hum of the air-conditioning unit, the unmistakable transmission from the sonar, the clickety-clack from the radio room, the soft hiss of air, the brassy jingle from the juke box, the whirring of fans, the rattle of pots from the galley, the movement of men, the talking of men—all those were gone. All those vital sounds, the heartbeats of a living vessel, were gone; but in their place was not silence but something worse than silence, something that bespoke not living but dying, the frighteningly rapid, hoarse, gasping breathing of lung-tortured men fighting for air and for life.

Fighting for air. That was the irony of it. Fighting for air while there were still many days' supply of oxygen in the giant tanks. There were some breathing sets aboard, similar to the British Built-in Breathing System, which takes a direct oxynitrogen mixture from tanks, but only a few, and all members of the crew had had a chance at those, but only for two minutes at a time. For the rest, for the more than ninety per cent without those systems, there was only the panting, straining agony that leads eventually to death. Some portable closed-circuit sets were still left, but those were reserved exclusively for the fire fighters.

Oxygen was occasionally bled from the tanks directly into

the living spaces, and it just didn't do any good at all; the only effect it seemed to have was to make breathing even more cruelly difficult by heightening the atmospheric pressure. All the oxygen in the world was going to be of little avail as long as the level of carbon dioxide given off by our anguished breathing mounted steadily with the passing of each minute. Normally, the air in the *Dolphin* was cleaned and circulated throughout the ship every two minutes, but the giant 200-ton air conditioner responsible for this was a glutton for the electric power that drove it; and the electricians' estimate was that the reserve of power in the standby battery, which alone could reactivate the nuclear power plant, was already dangerously low. So the concentration of carbon dioxide increased steadily toward lethal levels, and there was nothing we could do about it.

Increasing, too, in what passed now for air, were the Freon fumes from the refrigerating machinery and the hydrogen fumes from the batteries. Worse still, the smoke was now so thick that visibility, even in the for'ard parts of the ship, was down to a few feet, but that smoke had to remain also; there was no power to operate the electrostatic precipitators, and even when those had been briefly tried, they had proved totally inadequate to cope with the concentration of billions of carbon particles held in suspension in the air. Each time the door to the engine room was opened—and that was progressively oftener as the strength of the fire fighters ebbed— fresh clouds of that evil acrid smoke rolled through the submarine. The fire in the engine room had stopped burning over two hours previously; but now what remained of the redly smoldering insulation around the starboard high-pressure turbine gave off far more smoke and fumes than flames ever could have.

But the greatest enemy of all lay in the mounting count of carbon monoxide, that deadly, insidious, colorless, tasteless, odorless gas with its murderous affinity for the red blood cells—500 times that of oxygen. On board the *Dolphin* the normal permissible tolerance of carbon monoxide in the air was thirty parts in a million. Now the reading was somewhere between 400 and 500 parts in a million. When it reached a thousand parts, none of us would have more than minutes to live.

And then there was the cold. As Commander Swanson had grimly prophesied, the *Dolphin*, with the steam pipes cooled down and all heaters switched off, had chilled down to the sub-freezing temperature of the sea outside, and was ice cold. In terms of absolute cold, it was nothing—a mere two degrees below zero on the centigrade scale. But in terms of cold as it

192

reacted on the human body, it was very cold indeed. Most of the crew were without warm clothing of any kind. In normal operating conditions the temperature inside the *Dolphin* was maintained at a steady 22°C. regardless of the temperature outside. The men were forbidden to move around, but even if they were allowed to, they now lacked the energy to counteract the effects of the cold, and what little energy was left in their rapidly weakening bodies was so wholly occupied in forcing their laboring chest muscles to gulp in more and ever more of that foul and steadily worsening air that they had none at all left to generate sufficient animal heat to ward off that dank and bitter cold. You could actually *hear* men shivering, could listen to their violently shaking limbs knocking and rat-tat-tatting helplessly against bulkheads and deck, could hear the chattering of their teeth, the sound of some of them, far gone in weakness, whimpering softly with the cold: but always the dominant sound was that harsh, strangled moaning, a rasping and frightening sound, as men sought to suck air down into starving lungs.

With the exception of Hansen and myself—both of whom were virtually one-handed—and the sick patients, every man in the *Dolphin* had taken his turn that night in descending into the machinery space and fighting that red demon that threatened to slay us all. The number in each fire-fighting group had been increased from four to eight and the time spent down there shortened to three or four minutes, so that efforts could be concentrated and more energy expended in a given length of time, but because of the increasingly Stygian darkness in the machinery space, the ever-thickening coils of oily black smoke, and the wickedly cramped and confined space in which the men had to work, progress had been frustratingly, maddeningly slow: and entered into it now, of course, was the factor of that dreadful weakness that now assailed us all, so that men with the strength only of little children were tugging and tearing at the smoldering insulation in desperate near-futility and seemingly making no progress at all.

I'd been down again in the machinery space, just once, at 5:30 a.m. to attend to Jolly, who had himself slipped, fallen, and laid himself out while helping an injured crewman up the ladder, and I knew I would never forget what I had seen there: dark and spectral figures in a dark and spectral and swirling world, lurching and staggering around like zombies in some half-forgotten nightmare, swaying and stumbling and falling to the deck or down into the bilges now deep-covered in great snow drifts of carbon-dioxide foam and huge, smoking, blackened chunks of torn-off sheathing. Men on the rack, men in the last stages of exhaustion. One little spark of fire, one little spark of an element as old as time itself, and all the brilliant technological progress of the twentieth century was set at nothing, the frontiers of man's striving translated in a moment from the nuclear age to the dark unknown of pre-history.

Every dark hour brings forth its man, and there was no doubt in the minds of the crew of the *Dolphin* that that dark night had produced its own hero: Dr. Jolly. He had made a swift recovery from the effects of his first disastrous entry into the engine room that night, appearing back in the control center only seconds after I had finished setting Ringman's broken leg. He had taken the news of Bolton's death pretty badly, but never, either by word or direct look, did he indicate to either Swanson or myself that the fault lay with us for insisting against his better judgment on bringing on board the ship a man whose life had been hanging in the balance even under the best of conditions. I think Swanson was pretty grateful for that and might even have got around to apologizing to Jolly had not a fire fighter come through from the engine room and told us that one of his team had slipped and either twisted or broken an ankle—the second of many minor accidents and injuries that were to happen down in the machinery space that night. Jolly had reached for the nearest closed-circuit breathing apparatus before we could try to stop him and was gone in a minute.

We eventually lost count of the number of trips he made down there that night. Fifteen at least, perhaps many more, by the time six o'clock had come around, my mind was beginning to get pretty fuzzy around the edges. He certainly had no lack of customers for his medical skill. Paradoxically enough, the two main types of injury that night were diametrically opposite in nature: burning and freezing, burning from the red-hot sheathing—and, earlier, the steam pipes—and freezing from a carelessly directed jet of carbon dioxide against exposed areas of face or hands. Jolly never failed to answer a call, not even after the time he'd given his own head a pretty nasty crack. He would complain bitterly to the captain, old boy, for rescuing him from the relative safety and comfort of Drift Ice Station Zebra, crack some dry joke, pull on his mask, and leave. A dozen speeches to Congress or Parliament couldn't have done what Jolly did that night in cementing Anglo-American friendship.

About 6:45 a.m. chief torpedoman Patterson came into the control center. I suppose he walked through the doorway, but that was only assumption; from where I sat on the deck between Swanson and Hansen, you couldn't see halfway to the door: but when he came up to Swanson he was crawling on his hands and knees, head swaying from side to side, whooping painfully, his respiration rate at least fifty to the minute. He was wearing no mask of any kind and was shivering constantly.

"We must do something, Captain," he said hoarsely. He spoke as much when inhaling as when exhaling; when your breathing is sufficiently distressed, one is as easy as the other. "We've got seven men passed out now between the for'ard torpedo room and the crew's mess. They're pretty sick men, Captain."

"Thank you, chief." Swanson, also without a mask, was in as bad a way as Patterson, his chest heaving, his breath hoarsely rasping, tears and sweat rolling down the grayness of his face. "We'll be as quick as possible."

"More oxygen," I said. "Bleed more oxygen into the ship."

"Oxygen? More oxygen?" He shook his head. "The pressure is too high as it is."

"Pressure won't kill them." I was dimly aware, through my cold and misery and burning chest and eyes, that my voice sounded just as strange as did those of Swanson and Patterson. "Carbon monoxide will kill them. Carbon monoxide is what is killing them now. It's the relative proportion of CO_2 to oxygen that matters. It's too high, it's far too high. That's what's going to finish us all off."

"More oxygen," Swanson ordered. Even the unnecessary acknowledgment of my words would have cost too much. "More oxygen."

Valves were turned and oxygen hissed into the control room and, I knew, into the crew spaces. I could feel my ears pop as the pressure swiftly built up but that was all I could feel. I certainly couldn't feel any improvement in my breathing, a feeling that was borne out when Patterson, noticeably weaker this time, crawled back and croaked out the bad news that he now had a dozen unconscious men on his hands.

I went for'ard with Patterson and a closed-circuit oxygen apparatus—one of the few unexhausted sets left—and clamped it for a minute or so onto the face of each unconscious man in turn, but I knew it was but a temporary palliative. The oxygen revived them, but within a few minutes of the mask being removed, most of them slipped back into unconsciousness again. I made my way back to the control room, a dark dungeon of huddled men nearly all lying down, most of them barely conscious. I was barely conscious myself. I wondered vaguely if they felt as I did, if the fire from the lungs had now spread to the remainder of the body, if they could see the first slight changes in color in their hands

195

and faces, the deadly blush of purple, the first unmistakable signs of a man beginning to die from carbon-monoxide poisoning. Jolly, I noticed, still hadn't returned from the engine room; he was keeping himself permanently on hand, it seemed, to help those men who were in ever-increasingly greater danger of hurting themselves and their comrades as their weakness increased, as their level of care and attention and concentration slid down toward zero.

Swanson was where I'd left him, propped on the desk against the plotting table. He smiled faintly as I sank down beside him and Hansen.

"How are they, Doctor?" he whispered. A whisper, but a rock-steady whisper. The man's monolithic calm had never cracked, and I realized dimly that here was a man who could never crack: you do find people like that, once in a million or once in a lifetime. Swanson was such a man.

"Far gone," I said. As a medical report, it might have lacked a thought in detail, but it contained the gist of what I wanted to say and it saved me energy. "You will have your first deaths for carbon-monoxide poisoning within the hour."

"So soon?" The surprise was in his red, swollen, streaming eyes as well as in his voice. "Not so soon, Doctor. It's hardly —well, it's hardly started to take effect."

"So soon," I said. "Carbon-monoxide poisoning is very rapidly progressive. Five dead within the hour. Within two hours, fifty. At least fifty."

"You take the choice out of my hands," he murmured. "For which I am grateful. John, where is our main propulsion officer? His hour has come."

"I'll get him." Hansen hauled himself wearily to his feet, an old man making his last struggle to rise from his death bed, and at that moment the engine-room door opened and blackened, exhausted men staggered into the control room. Waiting men filed out to take their place. Swanson said to one of the men who had just entered, "Is that you, Will?"

"Yes, sir." Lieutenant Raeburn, the navigating officer, pulled off his mask and began to cough, rackingly, painfully. Swanson waited until he had quieted a little.

"How are things down there, Will?"

"We've stopped making smoke, skipper." Raeburn wiped his streaming face, swayed dizzily, and lowered himself groggily to the floor. "I think we've drowned out the sheathing completely."

"How long to get the rest of it off?"

"God knows. Normally, ten minutes. The way we are, an hour. Maybe longer."

"Thank you. Ah!" He smiled faintly as Hansen and Cartwright appeared out of the smoke-filled gloom. "Our main propulsion officer. Mr. Cartwright, I would be glad if you would put the kettle on to boil. What's the record for activating the plant, getting steam up and spinning the turbo generators?"

"I couldn't say, skipper." Red-eyed, coughing, smoke-blackened, and obviously in considerable pain, Cartwright nevertheless straightened his shoulders and smiled slowly. "But you may consider it broken."

He left. Swanson heaved himself to his feet with obvious weakness—except for two brief inspection trips to the engine room, he had not once worn any breathing apparatus during those interminable and pain-filled hours. He called for power on the broadcast circuit, unhooked a microphone, and spoke in a calm, clear, strong voice: it was an amazing exhibition in self-control, the triumph of a mind over agonized lungs still starving for air.

"This is your captain speaking," he said. "The fire in the engine room is out. We are already reactivating our power plant. Open all water-tight doors throughout the ship. They are to remain open until further orders. You may regard the worst of our troubles as lying behind us. Thank you for all you have done." He hooked up the microphone and turned to Hansen. "The worst *is* behind, John—if we have enough power left to reactivate the plant."

"Surely the worst is still to come," I said. "It'll take you how long—three quarters of an hour, maybe an hour?—to get your turbo generators going and your air-purifying equipment working again. How long do you think it will take your air cleaners to make any noticeable effect on this poisonous air?"

"Half an hour. At least that. Perhaps more."

"There you are, then." My mind was so woolly and doped now that I had difficulty in finding words to frame my thoughts, and I wasn't even sure that my thoughts were worth thinking. "An hour and a half at least—and you said the worst was over. The worst hasn't even begun." I shook my head, trying to remember what it was that I had been going to say next, then remembered. "In an hour and a half, one out of every four of your men will be gone."

Swanson smiled. He actually, incredibly, smiled. He said, "As Sherlock used to say to Moriarty, 'I think not, Doctor.' Nobody's going to die of monoxide poisoning. In fifteen minutes' time we'll have fresh, breathable air throughout the ship."

Hansen glanced at me just as I glanced at him. The strain had been too much; the old man had gone off his rocker.

Swanson caught our interchange of looks and laughed, the laugh changing abruptly to a bout of convulsive coughing as he inhaled too much of that poisoned, smoke-laden atmosphere. He coughed for a long time, then gradually quieted down.

"Serves me right," he gasped. "Your faces . . . Why do you think I ordered the water-tight doors opened, Doctor?"

"No idea."

"John?"

Hansen shook his head.

Swanson looked at him quizzically and said, "Speak to the engine room. Tell them to light up the diesel."

"Yes, sir," Hansen said woodenly. He made no move.

"Lieutenant Hansen is wondering whether he should get a straitjacket," Swanson said. "Lieutenant Hansen knows that a diesel engine is never, *never* lit up when a submarine is submerged—unless with a snorkel, which is useless under ice —for a diesel not only uses air straight from the engine-room atmosphere, it gulps it down in great draughts and would soon remove all the air in the ship. Which is what I want. We bleed compressed air under fairly high pressure into the fore part of the ship. Nice, clean, fresh air. We light up the diesel in the after part—it will run rough at first because of the low concentration of oxygen in this poisonous muck—but it will run. It will suck up much of this filthy air, exhausting its gases over the side, and as it does, it will lower the atmospheric pressure aft and the fresh air will make its way through from for'ard. To have done this before now would have been suicidal. The fresh air would only have fed the flames until the fire was out of control. But we can do it now. We can run it for a few minutes only, of course, but a few minutes will be ample. You are with me, Lieutenant Hansen?"

Hansen was with him, all right, but he didn't answer. He had already left.

Three minutes passed; then we heard, through the now open passageway above the reactor room, the erratic sound of a diesel starting, fading, coughing, then catching again— we learned later that the engineers had had to bleed off several ether bottles in the vicinity of the air intake to get the engine to catch. For a minute or two it ran roughly and erratically and seemed to be making no impression at all on that poisonous air; then, imperceptibly almost, at first, then with an increasing degree of definition, we could see the smoke in the control room, illuminated by the single lamp still left burning there, begin to drift and eddy toward the reactor passage. Smoke began to stir and eddy in the corners of the

198

control room as the diesel sucked the fumes aft, and more smoke-laden air, a shade lighter in color, began to move in from the wardroom passageway, pulled in by the decreasing pressure in the control room, pushed in by the gradual build-up of fresh air in the fore part of the submarine as compressed air was bled into the living spaces.

A few more minutes made the miracle. The diesel thudded away in the engine room, running more sweetly and strongly as air with a higher concentration of oxygen reached its intake, and the smoke in the control room drained steadily away, to be replaced by a thin grayish mist from the fore part of the ship that was hardly deserving of the name of smoke at all. And that mist carried with it air, an air with fresh, life-giving oxygen, an air with a proportion of carbon dioxide and carbon monoxide that was now almost negligible. Or so it seemed to us.

The effect upon the crew was just within the limits of credibility. It was as if a wizard had passed through the length of the ship and touched them with the wand of life. Unconscious men, men for whom death had been less than half an hour away, began to stir, some to open their eyes. Sick, exhausted, nauseated, and pain-wracked men who had been lying or sitting on the decks in attitudes of huddled despair sat up straight or stood, their faces breaking into expressions of almost comical wonderment and disbelief as they drew great draughts down into their aching lungs and found that it was not poisonous gases they were inhaling but fresh, breathable air: men who had made up their minds for death began to wonder how they could ever have thought that way. As air went, I suppose, it was pretty substandard stuff, and the Factory Acts would have had something to say about it; but, for us, no pine-drenched mountain air ever tasted half so sweet.

Swanson kept a careful eye on the gauges recording the air pressure in the submarine. Gradually it sank down to the fifteen pounds at which the atmosphere was normally kept, then below it. He ordered the compressed air to be released under higher pressure, and then, when the atmospheric pressure was back to normal, he ordered the diesel stopped and the compressed air shut off.

"Commander Swanson," I said. "If you ever want to make admiral, you can apply to me for a reference any time."

"Thank you." He smiled. "We have been very lucky."

Sure we had been lucky, the way men who sailed with Swanson would always be lucky.

We could now hear the sounds of pumps and motors as Cartwright started in on the slow process of bringing the nuclear power plant to life again. Everyone knew that it was touch and go whether there would be enough life left in the batteries for that, but, curiously, no one seemed to doubt that Cartwright would succeed: we had been through too much to entertain even the thought of failure now.

Nor did we fail. At exactly eight o'clock that morning Cartwright phoned to say that he had steam on the turbine blades and that the *Dolphin* was a going proposition again. I was glad to hear it.

For three hours we cruised along at slow speed while the air-conditioning plant worked under maximum pressure to bring the air inside the *Dolphin* back to normal. After that, Swanson slowly stepped up our speed until we had reached about fifty per cent of normal cruising speed, which was as fast as the propulsion officer deemed it safe to go. For a variety of technical reasons it was impractical for the *Dolphin* to operate without all turbines in commission, so we were reduced to the speed of the slowest, and, without sheathing on it, Cartwright didn't want to push the starboard high-pressure turbine above a fraction of its power. This way, it would take us much longer to clear the ice pack and reach the open sea, but the captain, in a broadcast, said that if the limit of the ice pack was where it had been when we'd first moved under it—and there was no reason to think it should have shifted more than a few miles—we should be moving out into the open sea at about four o'clock the following morning.

By four o'clock that afternoon, members of the crew, working in relays, had managed to clear away from the machinery space all the debris and foam that had accumulated during the long night. After that, Swanson reduced all watches to the barest skeletons required to run the ship, so that as many men as possible might sleep as long as possible. Now that the exultation of victory was over, now that the almost intolerable relief of knowing that they were not, after all, to find their gasping end in a cold iron tomb under the ice cap had begun to fade, the inevitable reaction, when it did come, was correspondingly severe. A long and sleepless night behind them; hours of cruelly back-breaking toil in the metal jungle of the machinery space; that lifetime of tearing tension when they had not known whether they were going to live or die but had believed they were going to die; the poisonous fumes that had laid them all on the rack—all of these combined had taken cruel toll of their reserves of physical and mental energy, and the crew of the *Dolphin* were now sleep-ridden and exhausted as they had never been. When they lay down to sleep, they slept at once, like dead men.

I didn't sleep. Not then, not at four o'clock. I couldn't sleep. I had too much to think about: like how it had been primarily my fault, through mistake, miscalculation, or sheer pig-headedness, that the *Dolphin* and her crew had been brought to such desperate straits; like what Commander Swanson was going to say when he found out how much I'd kept from him, how little I'd told him. Still, if I had kept him in the dark so long, I couldn't see that there would be much harm in it if I kept him in the dark just that little time longer. It would be time enough in the morning to tell him all I knew. His reactions would be interesting, to say the least. He might be striking some medals for Rawlings, but I had the feeling that he wouldn't be striking any for me. Not after I'd told him what I'd have to.

Rawlings. That was the man I wanted now. I went to see him, told him what I had in mind, and asked him if he would mind sacrificing a few hours' sleep during the night. As always, Rawlings was co-operation itself.

Later that evening I had a look at one or two of the patients. Jolly, exhausted by his Herculean efforts of the previous night, was fathoms deep in slumber, so Swanson had asked if I would deputize for him. So I did, but I didn't try very hard. With only one exception they were sound asleep, and none of them was in so urgent need of medical attention that there would have been any justification for waking him up. The sole exception was Dr. Benson, who had recovered consciousness late that afternoon. He was obviously on the mend, but complained that his head felt like a pumpkin with someone at work on it with a riveting gun, so I fed him some pills and that was the extent of the treatment. I asked him if he had any idea as to what had been the cause of his fall from the top of the sail, but he was either too woozy to remember or just didn't know. Not that it mattered now. I already knew the answer.

I slept for nine hours after that, which was pretty selfish of me, considering that I had asked Rawlings to keep awake half the night; but, then, I hadn't had much option about that, for Rawlings was in a position to perform for me an essential task that I couldn't perform for myself.

Sometime during the night we passed out from under the ice cap into the open Arctic Ocean again.

I awoke shortly after seven, washed, shaved, and dressed as carefully as I could with one hand out of commission—for I believe a judge owes it to his public to be decently turned out when he goes to conduct a trial—then breakfasted well in the wardroom. Shortly before nine o'clock I walked into the control room. Hansen had the watch. I went up to

201

him and said quietly, so that I couldn't be overheard: "Where is Commander Swanson?"

"In his cabin."

"I'd like to speak to him and you. Privately."

Hansen looked at me speculatively, nodded, handed over the watch to the navigator, and led the way to Swanson's cabin. We knocked, went in, and closed the door behind us. I didn't waste any time in preamble.

"I know who the killer is," I said. "I've no proof, but I'm going to get it now. I would like you to be on hand—if you can spare the time."

They had used up all their emotional responses and reactions during the previous thirty hours, so they didn't throw up their hands or do startled double-takes or make any of the other standard signs of incredulousness. Instead, Swanson just looked thoughtfully at Hansen, rose from his table, folded the chart he'd been studying, and said dryly: "I think we might spare the time, Dr. Carpenter. I have never met a murderer." His tone was impersonal, even light, but the clear gray eyes had gone very cold indeed. "It will be quite an experience to meet a man with eight deaths on his conscience."

"You can count yourself lucky that it is only eight," I said. "He almost brought it up to the hundred mark yesterday morning."

This time I did get them. Swanson stared at me, then said softly, "What do you mean?"

"Our friend with the gun also carries a box of matches around with him," I said. "He was busy with them in the engine room in the early hours of yesterday morning."

"Someone *deliberately* tried to set the ship on fire?" Hansen looked at me in open disbelief. "I don't buy that, Doc."

"I buy it," Swanson said. "I buy anything Dr. Carpenter says. We're dealing with a madman. Only a madman would risk losing his life along with the lives of a hundred others."

"He miscalculated," I said mildly. "Come along."

They were waiting for us in the wardroom as I'd arranged, eleven of them in all: Rawlings, Zabrinski, Captain Folsom, Dr. Jolly, the two Harrington twins, who were now just barely well enough to be out of bed, Naseby, Hewson, Hassard, Kinnaird and Jeremy. Most of them were seated around the wardroom table except for Rawlings, who opened the door for us, and Zabrinski, his foot still in the cast, who was sitting in a chair in one corner of the room studying an issue of the *Dolphin Daze*, the submarine's own mimeographed newspaper. Some of them made to get to their feet as we came in, but Swanson waved them down. They sat silently, all except

202

Dr. Jolly, who boomed out a cheerful "Good morning, Captain. Well, well, this is an intriguing summons. Most intriguing. What is it you want to see us about, Captain?"

I cleared my throat. "You must forgive a small deception. It is I who wants to see you, not the captain."

"You?" Jolly pursed his lips and looked at me speculatively. "I don't get it, old boy. Why you?"

"I have been guilty of another small deception. I am not, as I gave you to understand, attached to the Ministry of Supply. I am an agent of the British government. An officer of M.I.6, counter-espionage."

Well, I got my reaction, all right. They just sat there, mouths wide open like newly landed fish, staring at me. It was Jolly, always a fast adjuster, who recovered first.

"Counter-espionage, by Jove! Counter-espionage! Spies and cloaks and daggers and beautiful blondes tucked away in the wardrobes—or wardroom, should I say. But why—why are you *here*? What do you—well, what *can* you want to see us about, Dr. Carpenter?"

"A small matter of murder," I said.

"Murder!" Captain Folsom spoke for the first time since coming aboard ship, the voice issuing from that savagely burnt face no more than a strangled croak. "Murder?"

"Two of the men lying up there now in the drift station lab were dead *before* the fire. They had been shot through the head. A third had been knifed. I would call that murder, wouldn't you?"

Jolly groped for the table and lowered himself shakily into his seat. The rest of them looked as if they were very glad that they were already sitting down.

"It seems too superfluous to add," I said, adding it all the same, "that the murderer is in this room now."

You wouldn't have thought it, not to look at them. You could see at a glance that none of those high-minded citizens could possibly be a killer. They were as innocent as life's young morning, the whole lot of them, pure and white as the driven snow.

12

IT WOULD BE AN UNDERSTATEMENT to say that I had the attention of the company. Maybe had I been a two-headed visitor from outer space, or had been about to announce the result of a multimillion-pound sweepstake in which they held the only tickets, or was holding straws for them to pick to decide who should go before the firing squad—maybe then they might have given me an even more exclusive degree of concentration. But I doubt it. It wouldn't have been possible.

"If you'll bear with me," I began, "first of all, I'd like to give you a little lecture in camera optics, and don't ask me what the hell that has to do with murder: it's got everything to do with it, as you'll find out soon enough.

"Film emulsion and lens quality being equal, the clarity of detail in any photograph depends upon the focal length of the lens—that is, the distance between the lens and the film. As recently as fifteen years ago the maximum focal length of any camera outside an observatory was about fifty inches. Those were used in reconnaissance planes in the later stages of the second world war. A small suitcase lying on the ground would show up on a photograph taken from a height of ten miles, which was pretty good for those days.

"But the U. S. Army and Air Force wanted bigger and better aerial cameras, and the only way this could be done was by increasing the focal length of the lens. There was obviously a superficial limit to this length, because the Americans wanted this camera to fit into a plane—or an orbiting satellite—and if you wanted a camera with a focal length of, say, two hundred and fifty inches, it was obviously going to be quite impossible to install a twenty-foot camera pointing vertically downward in a plane or small satellite. But scientists came up with a new type of camera, using the folded-lens principle, where the light, instead of coming down a long, straight barrel, is bounced around a series of angled mirrored corners, which permits the focal length to be increased greatly without having to enlarge the camera itself. By 1950 they'd developed a hundred-inch focal-length lens. It was quite an improvement on the old world war two cameras, which could barely pick up a suitcase at ten miles. This one could pick up a cigarette pack at ten miles. Then, ten years later, came what they called the Perkin-Elmer Roti satellite missile tracker, with a focal length of five hundred inches—equivalent to a barrel-type camera forty feet long. This one could pick up a cube of sugar at ten miles."

I looked inquiringly around the audience for signs of inattention. There were no signs of inattention. No lecturer ever had a keener audience than I had there.

"Three years later," I went on, "another American firm had developed this missile tracker into a fantastic camera that could be mounted in even a small-size satellite. Three years round-the-clock work to create this camera, but they thought it worth it. We don't know the focal length, it's never been revealed: we do know that, given the right atmospheric conditions, a white saucer on a dark surface will show up clearly from three hundred miles up in space. This on a relatively tiny negative capable of almost infinite enlargement, for the scientists have also come up with a completely new film emulsion, still super-secret and a hundred times as sensitive as the finest films available on the commercial market today.

"This was to be fitted to the two-ton satellite the Americans called 'Samos III'—'Samos' for 'Satellite and Missile Observation System.' It never was. This, the only camera of its kind in the world, vanished, hijacked in broad daylight, and, as we later learned, dismantled, flown from New York to Havana by a Polish jet-liner which had cleared for Miami and so avoided customs inspection.

"Four months ago this camera was launched in a Soviet satellite on a polar orbit, crossing the U.S. Middle West seven times a day. Those satellites can stay up indefinitely, but in just three days, with perfect weather conditions, the Soviets had all the pictures they ever wanted—pictures of every American missile-launching base west of the Mississippi. Every time this camera took a picture of a small section of the United States, another, smaller camera in the satellite, pointing vertically upward, took a fix on the stars. Then it was only a matter of checking map coordinates and they could have a Soviet intercontinental ballistics missile ranged in on every launching pad in America. But first they had to have the pictures.

"Radio transmission is no good, there's far too much quality and detail lost in the process—and you must remember that this was a relatively tiny negative in the first place. So they had to have the actual films. There are two ways of doing this: bring the satellite back to earth, or have it eject a capsule with the films. The Americans, with their Discoverer tests, have perfected the art of using planes to snatch falling capsules from the sky. The Russians haven't, although we do know they have a technique for ejecting capsules should a satellite run amuck. So they had to bring the satellite down. They planned to bring it down some two hundred miles east of the Caspian. But something went wrong. Precisely what, we don't know, but our experts say that it could only have been due to the fact that the retro rockets on one side of the capsule failed to fire when given the radio signal to do so. You are beginning to understand, gentlemen?"

"We are beginning to understand indeed." It was Jeremy who spoke, his voice very soft. "The satellite took up a different orbit."

"That's what happened. The rockets firing on one side didn't slow her up any that mattered: they just knocked her far off course. A new and wobbly orbit that passed through Alaska, south over the Pacific, across Grahamland in Antarctica and directly south of South America, up over Africa and western Europe, then around the North Pole in a shallow curve, maybe two hundred miles distant from it at the nearest point.

"Now, the only way the Russians could get the films was by ejecting the capsule, for with retro rockets firing on one side only, they knew that even if they did manage to slow up the satellite sufficiently for it to leave orbit, they had no idea where it would go. But the damnably awkward part of it from the Russians' viewpoint was that nowhere in its orbit of the earth did the satellite pass over the Soviet Union or any sphere of Communist influence whatsoever. Worse, ninety per cent of its travel was travel over open sea, and if they brought it down there they would never see their films again as the capsule is so heavily coated with aluminum and Pyroceram to withstand the heat of re-entry into the atmosphere that it was much heavier than water. And, as I said, they had never developed the American know-how of snatching falling capsules out of the air—and you will appreciate that they couldn't very well ask the Americans to do the job for them.

"So they decided to bring it down in the only safe place open to them—either the polar ice cap in the north, or the Antarctic in the south. You will remember, Captain, that I told you I had just returned from the Antarctic. The Russians have a couple of geophysical stations there, and, up until a few days ago, we thought that there was a fifty-fifty chance that the capsule might be brought down there. But we were wrong. Their nearest station in the Antarctic was three hundred miles from the path of orbit—and no field parties were stirring from home."

"So they decided to bring it down in the vicinity of Drift Ice Station Zebra?" Jolly asked quietly. It was a sign of his perturbation that he didn't even call me "old boy."

"Drift Ice Station Zebra wasn't even in existence at the time the satellite went haywire, although all preparations were complete. We had arranged for Canada to lend us a St. Lawrence ice breaker to set up the station, but the Russians, in a burst of friendly goodwill and international cooperation, offered us the atomic-powered *Lenin,* the finest ice breaker in the world. They wanted to make good and sure that Zebra was set up in good time. It was. The east-west drift of the ice cap was unusually slow this year, and almost eight weeks elapsed after the setting-up of the station until it was directly beneath the flight trajectory of the satellite."

"You *knew* what the Russians had in mind?" Hansen asked.

"We knew. But the Russians had no idea whatsoever that we were on to them. They had no idea that one of the pieces of equipment which was landed at Zebra was a satellite monitor which would tell Major Halliwell when the satellite received the radio signal to eject the capsule." I looked slowly around the Zebra survivors. "I'll wager none of you knew that. But Major Halliwell did—and the three other men who slept in his hut where this machine was located.

"What we did not know was the identity of the member of Zebra's company who had been suborned by the Russians. We were certain someone *must* have been, but we had no idea who it was. Every one of you had first-class security clearances. But someone was suborned—and that someone, when he arrived back in Britain, would have been a wealthy man for the rest of his life. In addition to leaving what was in effect an enemy agent planted in Zebra, the Soviets also left a portable monitor—an electronic device for tuning-in on a particular radio signal which would be activated inside the capsule at the moment of its ejection from the satellite. A capsule can be so accurately ejected three hundred miles up that it will land within a mile of its target, but the ice cap is pretty rough territory and dark most of the time, so this monitor would enable our friend to locate the capsule, which would keep on emitting its signal for at least, I suppose, twenty-four hours after landing. Our friend took the monitor and went out looking for the capsule. He found it, released it from its drogue, and brought it back to the station. You are still with me, gentlemen? Especially one particular gentleman?"

"I think we are all with you, Dr. Carpenter," Commander Swanson said softly. "Every last one of us."

"Fine. Well, unfortunately, Major Halliwell and his three companions also knew that the satellite had ejected its capsule—don't forget that they were monitoring this satellite twenty-four hours a day. They knew that someone was going to go looking for it pretty soon, but who that someone would be they had no idea. Anyway, Major Halliwall posted one of his men to keep watch. It was a wild night, bitterly cold, with a gale blowing an ice storm before it, but he kept a pretty good watch all the same. He either bumped into our friend returning with the capsule or, more probably, saw a light in a cabin, investigated, found our friend stripping the film from the capsule, and, instead of going quietly away and reporting to Major Halliwell, he went in and challenged this man. If that was the way of it, it was a bad mistake, the last he ever made. He got a knife between the ribs." I gazed at all the Zebra survivors in turn. "I wonder which one of you did it? Whoever it was, he wasn't very expert. He broke off the blade inside the chest. I found it there." I was looking at Swanson, and he didn't bat an eyelid. He knew I hadn't found the blade there; he had found the haft in the gas tank. But there was time enough to tell them that.

"When the man he had posted didn't turn up, Major Halliwell got worried. It must have been something like that. I don't know and it doesn't matter. Our friend with the broken knife was on the alert now, he knew someone was on to him—it must have come as a pretty severe shock—he'd thought himself completely unsuspected—and when the second man the major sent turned up, he was ready for him. He had to kill him, for the first man was lying dead in his cabin. Apart from his broken knife, he also had a gun. He used it.

"Both those men had come from Halliwell's cabin. The killer knew that Halliwell must have sent them and that he and the other man still in the major's cabin would be around in double-quick time if the second watcher didn't report back immediately. He decided not to wait for that: he'd burned his bridges, anyway. He took his gun, went into Major Halliwell's cabin, and shot him and the other man as they lay on their beds. I know that because the bullets in their heads entered low from the front and emerged high at the back—the angle the bullets would naturally take if the killer was

208

standing at the foot of their beds and fired at them as they were lying down. I suppose this is as good a time as any to say that my name is not really Carpenter. It's Halliwell. Major Halliwell was my elder brother."

"Good God!" Dr. Jolly whispered. "Good God above!"

"One thing the killer knew it was essential to do right away—to conceal the traces of his crime. There was only one way: burn the bodies out of all recognition. So he dragged a couple of drums of oil out of the fuel store, poured them against the walls of Major Halliwell's hut—he'd already pulled in there the first two men he'd killed—and set fire to it. For good measure, he also set fire to the fuel store. A thorough type, my friends, a man who never did anything by halves."

The men seated around the wardroom table were dazed and shocked, uncomprehending and incredulous. But they were incredulous only because the enormity of the whole thing was beyond them. But not beyond them all.

"I'm a man with a curious turn of mind," I went on. "I wondered why sick, burned, exhausted men had wasted their time and their little strength in shifting the dead men into the lab. Because someone had suggested that it might be a good thing to do, the decent thing to do. The real reason, of course, was to discourage anyone from going there. I looked under the floorboards and what did I find? Forty Nife cells in first-class condition, stores of food, a radio-sonde balloon, a hydrogen cylinder for inflating the balloon. I had expected to find the Nife cells. Kinnaird here has told us that there were a good many reserves, but Nife cells won't be destroyed in a fire. Buckled and bent a bit, but not destroyed. I hadn't expected to find the other items of equipment, but they made everything clear.

"The killer had had bad luck on two counts—being found out and with the weather. The weather really put the crimp on all his plans. The idea was that when conditions were favorable he'd send the films up into the sky attached to a radio-sonde balloon which could be swept up by a Russian plane. Snatching a falling capsule out of the sky is very tricky indeed: snaring a stationary balloon is dead easy. The relatively unused Nife cells our friend used for keeping in radio touch with his friends to let them know when the weather had cleared and when he was going to send the balloon up. There is no privacy on the air waves, so he used a special code. When he no longer had any need for it, he destroyed the code by the only safe method of destruction in the Arctic—fire. I found scores of pieces of charred paper imbedded in the walls of one of the huts where the wind had carried them from the met office after our friend had thrown the ashes away.

"The killer also made sure that only those few worn-out Nife cells were used to send the S.O.S.'s and to contact the *Dolphin*. By losing contact with us so frequently, and by sending such a blurred transmission, he tried to delay our arrival here so as to give the weather a chance to clear up and let him fly off his balloon. Incidentally, you may have heard the radio reports—it was in all the British newspapers—that Russian as well as American and British planes scoured this area immediately after the fire. The British and Americans were looking for Zebra: the Russians were looking for a radio-sonde balloon. So was the ice breaker *Dvina* when it tried to smash its way through here a few days ago. But there have been no more Russian planes: our friend radioed *his* friends to say that there was no hope of the weather clearing, that the *Dolphin* had arrived, and that they would have to take the films back with them on the submarine."

"One moment, Dr. Carpenter," Swanson interrupted in a careful sort of voice. "Are you saying that those films are aboard this ship now?"

"I'll be very much surprised if they aren't, Commander. The other attempt to delay us, of course, was by making a direct attack on the *Dolphin* itself. When it became known that the *Dolphin* was to make an attempt to reach Zebra, orders went through to Scotland to cripple the ship. Red Clydeside is no more Red than any other maritime center in Britain, but you'll find Communists in practically every shipyard in the country—and, more often than not, their mates don't know who they are. There was no intention, of course, of causing any fatal accident—and, as far as whoever was responsible for leaving the tube doors open was concerned, there was no reason why there should be. International espionage in peacetime shuns violence—which is why our friend here is going to be very unpopular with his masters. Like Britain or America, they'll adopt any legitimate or illegitimate tactic to gain their espionage end—but they stop short of murder, just as we do. Murder was no part of the Soviet plan."

"Who is it, Dr. Carpenter?" Jeremy said very quietly. "For God's sake, who is it? There's nine of us here and—do you *know* who it is?"

"I know. And only six, not nine, can be under suspicion. The ones who kept radio watches after the disaster. Captain Folsom and the two Harringtons here were completely immobilized. We have the word of all of you for that. So that, Jeremy, just leaves yourself, Kinnaird, Dr. Jolly, Hassard,

Naseby and Hewson. Murder for gain and high treason. There's only one answer for that. The trial will be over the day it begins: three weeks later it will all be over. You're a very clever man, my friend. You're more than that: you're brilliant. But I'm afraid it's the end of the road for you, Dr. Jolly."

They didn't get it. For long seconds they didn't get it. They were too shocked, too stunned. They'd heard my words, all right, but the meaning hadn't registered immediately. But it was beginning to register now, for, like marionettes under the guidance of a master puppeteer, they all slowly turned their heads and stared at Jolly. Jolly himself rose slowly to his feet and took two paces toward me, his eyes wide, his face shocked, his mouth working.

"Me?" His voice was low and hoarse and unbelieving. "Me? Are you—are you mad, Dr. Carpenter? In the name of God, man—"

I hit him. I don't know why I hit him—a crimson haze seemed to blur my vision—and Jolly was staggering back to crash on the deck, holding both hands to smashed lips and nose, before I could realize what I had done. I think if I had had a knife or a gun in my hand then, I would have killed him. I would have killed him the way I would have killed a fer-de-lance, a black-widow spider or any other such dark and evil and deadly thing, without thought of compunction or mercy. Gradually the haze cleared from my eyes. No one had stirred. No one had stirred an inch. Jolly pushed himself painfully to his knees and then his feet and collapsed heavily in his seat by the table. He was holding a blood-soaked handkerchief to his face. There was utter silence in the room.

"My brother, Jolly," I said. "My brother and all the dead men on Zebra. Do you know what I hope?" I said. "I hope that something goes wrong with the hangman's rope and that you take a long, long time to die."

He took the handkerchief from his mouth.

"You're a crazy man," he whispered between smashed and already puffing lips. "You don't know what you're saying."

"The jury at the Old Bailey will be the best judge of that. I've been on to you now, Jolly, for almost exactly sixty hours."

"What did you say?" Swanson demanded. "You've known for sixty hours!"

"I knew I'd have to face your wrath sometime or other, Commander," I said. Unaccountably, I was beginning to feel very tired, weary, and heart-sick of the whole business. "But if you had known who he was, you'd have locked him up right

211

away. You said so in so many words. I wanted to see where the trail led to in Britain, who his associates and contacts would be. I had splendid visions of smashing a whole spy ring. But I'm afraid the trail is cold. It ends right here. Please hear me out.

"Tell me, did no one think it strange that when Jolly came staggering out of his hut when it caught fire he should have collapsed and remained that way? Jolly claimed that he had been asphyxiated. Well, he wasn't asphyxiated inside the hut, because he managed to come out under his own steam. Then he collapsed. Curious. Fresh air invariably revives people. But not Jolly. He's a special breed. He wanted to make it clear to everyone that he had nothing to do with the fire. Just to drive home the point, he has repeatedly emphasized that he is not a man of action. If he isn't, then I've never met one."

"You can hardly call that proof of guilt," Swanson interrupted.

"I'm not adducing evidence," I said wearily. "I'm merely introducing pointers. Pointer number 2. You, Naseby, felt pretty bad about your failure to wake up your two friends, Flanders and Bryce. You could have shaken them for an hour and not woken them up. Jolly here used either ether or chloroform to lay them out. This was after he had killed Major Halliwell and the three others, but before he started getting busy with matches. He realized that if he burned the place down, there might be a long, long wait before rescue came, and he was going to make damned certain that he wasn't going to go hungry. If the rest of you had died from starvation, well, that was just your bad luck. But Flanders and Bryce lay between him and the food. Didn't it strike you as very strange, Naseby, that your shouting and shaking had no effect? The only reason could be that they had been drugged—and only one man had access to drugs. Also, you said that both Hewson and yourself felt pretty groggy. No wonder. It was a pretty small hut, and the chloroform or ether fumes had reached and affected you and Hewson. Normally, you'd have smelled it on waking up, but the stink of burning diesel obliterates every other smell. Again, I know this is not proof of any kind.

"Third pointer. I asked Captain Folsom this morning who had given the orders for the dead men to be put in the lab. He said he had. But, he remembered, it was Jolly's suggestion to him. Something learnedly medical about helping the morale of the survivors by putting the charred corpses out of sight.

"Fourth pointer. Jolly said that *how* the fire started was unimportant. A crude attempt to side-track me. Jolly knew as well as I did that it was all-important. I suppose, by the way, Jolly, that you deliberately jammed all the fire extinguishers you could before you started the fire. About that fire, Commander. Remember you were a bit suspicious of Hewson because he said the fuel drums hadn't started exploding until he was on his way to the main bunkhouse? He was telling the truth. There were no fewer than four drums in the fuel stores that didn't explode. The ones Jolly used to pour against the huts to start the fire. How am I doing, Dr. Jolly?"

"It's all a nightmare," he said very quietly. "It's a nightmare. Before God, I know nothing of any of this."

"Pointer number five. For some reason that is unclear to me, Jolly wanted to delay the *Dolphin* on its return trip. He could best do this, he decided, if Bolton and Brownell, the two very sick men still left out on the station, were judged too sick to be transferred to the *Dolphin*. The snag was that there were two other doctors around who might say that they *were* fit to be transferred. So he tried, with a fair measure of success, to eliminate us.

"First Benson. Didn't it strike you as strange, Commander, that the request for the survivors to be allowed to attend the funeral of Grant and Lieutenant Mills should have come from Naseby in the first place, then Kinnaird? Jolly, as the senior man of the party, with Captain Folsom temporarily unfit, was the obvious man to make the approach, but he didn't want to go calling too much attention to himself. Doubtless by dropping hints, he engineered it so that someone else should do it for him. Now, Jolly had noticed how glass-smooth and slippery the ice-banked sides of the sail were and he made a point of seeing that Benson went up the rope immediately ahead of him. You must remember it was almost pitch dark—just light enough for Jolly to make out the vague outline of Benson's head from the wash of light from the bridge as it cleared the top of the sail. A swift outward tug on the rope and Benson overbalanced. It seemed that he had fallen on top of Jolly. But only seemed. The loud, sharp crack I heard a fraction of a second after Benson's body struck was not caused by his head hitting the ice—it was caused by Jolly here trying to kick his head off. Did you hurt your toes much, Jolly?"

"You're mad," he said mechanically. "This is utter nonsense. Even if it wasn't nonsense, you couldn't prove a word of it."

"We'll see. Jolly claimed that Benson fell on top of him. He even flung himself on the ice and cracked his head to give some verisimilitude to his story. Our friend never misses any of the angles. I felt the slight bump on his head. But he wasn't laid out. He was faking. He recovered just that little bit too quickly and easily when he got back to the sick bay. And it was then that he made his first mistake, the mistake that put me on to him—and should have put me on guard for an attack against myself. You were there, Commander."

"I've missed everything else," Swanson said bitterly. "Do you want me to spoil a hundred per cent record?"

"When Jolly came to, he saw Benson lying there. All he could see of him was a blanket and a big gauze pack covering the back of his head. As far as Jolly was concerned, it could have been anybody—it had been pitch dark when the accident occurred. But what did he say? I remember his exact words. He said: 'Of course, of course. Yes, that's it. He fell on top of me, didn't he?' *He never thought to ask who it was*—the natural, the inevitable question in the circumstances. But Jolly didn't have to ask. He knew."

"He knew." Swanson stared at Jolly with cold, bleak eyes, and there was no doubt in his mind now about Jolly. "You're right, Dr. Carpenter. He knew."

"And then he had a go at me. Can't prove a thing, of course. But he was there when I asked you where the medical store was, and he no doubt nipped down smartly behind Henry and myself and loosened the latch on the hatch cover. But he didn't achieve quite the same high degree of success this time. Even so, when we went out to the station next morning, he still tried to stop Brownell and Bolton from being transferred back to the ship by saying Bolton was too ill. But you overruled him."

"I was right about Bolton," Jolly said. He seemed strangely quiet now. "Bolton died."

"He died," I agreed. "He died because you murdered him, and for Bolton alone I can make certain you hang. For a reason I still don't know, Jolly was still determined to stop this ship. Delay it, anyway. I think he wanted only an hour or two's delay. So he proposed to start a small fire, nothing much, just enough to cause a small scare and have the reactor shut down temporarily. As the site of his fire he chose the machinery space—the one place in the ship where he could casually let something drop and where it would lie hidden, for hours if need be, among the maze of pipes down there. In the sick bay he concocted some type of delayed-action chemical fuse that would give off plenty of smoke but very little flame—there are a dozen combinations of acids and chemicals that can bring this about, and our friend will be a highly trained expert well versed in all of them. Now, all Jolly wanted was an excuse to pass through the engine room

214

when it would be nice and quiet and virtually deserted. In the middle of the night. He fixed this, too. He can fix anything. He's a very, very clever man indeed, is our friend here: he's also an utterly ruthless fiend.

"Late in the evening of the night before the fire, the good healer here made a round of his patients. I went with him. One of the men he treated was Bolton, in the nucleonics lab —and, of course, to get to the nucleonics lab you have to pass through the engine room. There was an enlisted man watching over the patients, and Jolly left special word that he was to be called at any hour if Bolton became any worse. He was called. I checked with the engine-room staff after the fire. The engineer officer on watch and two others were in the maneuvering room, but an engineman carrying out a routine lubrication job saw him passing through the engine room about 1:30 a.m. in answer to a call from the man watching over the patients. He took the opportunity to drop his little chemical fuse as he was passing by the machinery space. What he didn't know was that his little toy lodged on or near the oil-saturated lagging on the housing of the starboard turbo generator, and that when it went off, it would generate sufficient heat to set the sheathing on fire."

Swanson looked at Jolly, bleakly and for a long time, then turned to me and shook his head. "I can't buy that, Dr. Carpenter. This phone call because a patient just happens to turn sick. Jolly is not the man to leave *anything* to chance."

"He isn't," I agreed. "He didn't. Up in the refrigerator in the sick bay I have an exhibit for the Old Bailey. A sheet of aluminum foil liberally covered with Jolly's fingerprints. Smeared on this foil is the remains of a salve. That foil was what Jolly had bandaged on Bolton's burned forearm that night, just after he had given him pain-killing shots—Bolton was suffering very badly. But before Jolly put the salve on the foil he spread on something else first, a layer of sodium chloride—common or garden household salt. Jolly knew that the drugs he had given Bolton would keep him under for three or four hours: he also knew that by the time Bolton had regained consciousness, his body heat would have thinned the salve and brought the salt into contact with the raw flesh on the forearm. He knew that Bolton, when he came out from the effects of the drugs, would come out screaming in agony. Can you imagine what it must have been like? The whole forearm a mass of raw flesh—and covered with salt? When he died soon after, he died from shock. Our good healer here—a lovable little lad, isn't he?

"Well, that's Jolly. Incidentally, you can discount most of the

215

gallant doctor's heroism during the fire—although he was understandably as anxious as any of us that we survive. The first time he went into the engine room it was too damned hot and uncomfortable for his liking, so he just lay down on the floor and let someone carry him for'ard to where the fresh air was. Later—"

"He had his mask off," Hansen objected.

"He took it off. *You* can hold your breath for ten or fifteen seconds—don't you think Jolly can, too? Later on, when he was performing his heroics in the engine room, it was because conditions there were better, conditions outside worse—and because by going into the engine room he was entitled to a closed-circuit breathing set. Jolly got more clean air last night than any of us. He doesn't mind if he causes someone to die screaming his head off in agony—but he himself isn't going to suffer the slightest degree of hardship. Not if he can help it. Isn't that so, Jolly?"

He didn't answer.

"Where are the films, Jolly?"

"I don't know what you're talking about," he said in a quiet, toneless voice. "Before God, my hands are clean."

"How about your fingerprints on that foil with the salt on it?"

"Any doctor can make a mistake."

"My God! Mistake! Where are they, Jolly—the films?"

"For God's sake, leave me alone," he said tiredly.

"Have it your own way." I looked at Swanson. "Got some nice secure place where you can lock this character up?"

"I certainly have," Swanson said grimly. "I'll conduct him there in person."

"No one's conducting anyone anywhere," Kinnaird said. He was looking at me, and I didn't care very much for the way he was looking at me. I didn't care very much either for what he held in his hand: a very nasty-looking Mauser. It was cradled in his fist as if it had grown there, and it was pointing straight between my eyes.

13

"CLEVER CLEVER COUNTER-ESPIONAGE, Carpenter," Dr. Jolly murmured. "How swiftly the fortunes of war change, old boy. But you shouldn't be surprised really. You haven't found out anything that actually matters, but surely you should have found out enough to realize that you are operating out of your class. Please don't try anything foolish. Kinnaird is one of the finest pistol shots I have ever known—and you will observe how strategically he's placed, so that everyone in the room is covered."

He delicately patted his still bleeding mouth with a handkerchief, rose, went behind me, and ran his hands quickly down my clothes.

"My word," he said. "Not even carrying a gun. You really are unprepared, Carpenter. Turn round, will you, so that your back is to Kinnaird's gun?"

I turned around. He smiled pleasantly, then hit me twice across the face with all his strength, first with the back of his right hand and then with the back of his left. I staggered but didn't fall down. I could taste the salt of blood.

"Can't even call it regrettable loss of temper," Jolly said with satisfaction. "Did it deliberately and with malice aforethought. Enjoyed it, too."

"So Kinnaird was the killer," I said slowly, thickly. "He was the man with the gun?"

"Wouldn't want to take all the credit, mate," Kinnaird said modestly. "Let's say we sorted them out fifty-fifty."

"*You* were the one who went out with the monitor to find the capsule," I nodded. "That's why you got your face as badly frost-bitten."

"Got lost," Kinnaird admitted. "Thought I'd never find the damned station again."

"Jolly and Kinnaird," Jeremy said wonderingly. "Jolly and Kinnaird. Your own mates. You two filthy, murderous—"

"Be quiet," Jolly ordered. "Kinnaird, don't bother answering questions. Unlike Carpenter here, I take no pleasure in outlining my *modus operandi* and explaining at length how clever I've been. As you observed, Carpenter, I'm a man of action. Commander Swanson, get on that phone there, call up your control room, order your ship to surface and steam north."

"You're becoming too ambitious, Jolly," Swanson said calmly. "You can't hijack a submarine."

"Kinnaird," Jolly said. "Point your gun at Hansen's stomach. When I reach the count of five, pull the trigger. One, two, three—"

Swanson half raised a hand in acknowledgment of defeat, crossed to the wall phone, gave the necessary orders, hung up and came back to stand beside me. He looked at me without either respect or admiration. I looked around at all the other people in the room. Jolly, Hansen and Rawlings standing, Zabrinski sitting on a chair by himself with the now disregarded copy of the *Dolphin Daze* on his knees, all the others sitting around the table, Kinnaird well clear of them, the gun very steady in his hands. So very steady. No one seemed to be contemplating any heroics. For the most part, everyone was too shocked, too dazed, to think of anything.

"Hijacking a nuclear submarine is an intriguing prospect, and no doubt would be a highly profitable one, Commander Swanson," Jolly said. "But I know my limitations. No, old top, we shall simply be leaving you. Not very many miles from here is a naval vessel with a helicopter on its after deck. In a little while, Commander, you will send a wireless message on a certain frequency giving our position: the helicopter will pick us up. And even if your crippled engine would stand the strain, I wouldn't advise you to come chasing after that ship with ideas about torpedoing it or anything of that dramatic sort. Apart from the fact that you wouldn't like to be responsible for triggering off a nuclear war, you couldn't catch it anyway. You won't even be able to see the ship, Commander—and if you did, it wouldn't matter, anyway. It has no nationality markings."

"Where are the films?" I asked.

"They're already aboard that naval vessel."

"They're *what?*" Swanson demanded. "How in hell's name can they be?"

"Sorry and all that, old boy. I repeat that, unlike Carpenter here, I don't go around shooting off my mouth. A professional, my dear captain, *never* gives information about his methods."

"So you get off with it," I said bitterly. My mouth felt thick and swollen.

218

"Don't see what's to stop us. Crimes don't always come home to roost, you know."

"Eight men murdered," I said wonderingly. "Eight men. You can stand there and cheerfully admit that you are responsible for the deaths of eight men."

"Cheerfully?" he said consideringly. "No, not cheerfully. I'm a professional, and a professional never kills unnecessarily. But this time it was necessary. That's all."

"That's the second time you've used the word 'professional,'" I said slowly. "I was wrong on one theory. You weren't just suborned after the Zebra team had been picked. You've been at this game a long time—you're too good not to have been."

"Fifteen years, old lad," Jolly said calmly. "Kinnaird and I —we were the best team in Britain. Our usefulness in that country, unfortunately, is over. I should imagine that our— uh—exceptional talents can be employed elsewhere."

"You admit to all those murders?" I asked.

He looked at me in sudden cold speculation. "A damned funny question, Carpenter. Of course. I've told you. Why?"

"And do you, Kinnaird?"

He looked at me in bleak suspicion. "Why ask?"

"You answer my question and I'll answer yours." At the corner of my range of vision I could see Jolly looking at me with narrowed eyes. He was very sensitive to atmosphere, he knew there was something off-key.

"You know damn well what I did, mate," Kinnaird said coldly.

"So there we have it. In the presence of no less than twelve witnesses, you both confess to murder. You shouldn't have done that, you know. I'll answer your question, Kinnaird. I wanted to have an oral confession from you because, apart from the sheet of aluminum foil and something I'll mention in a minute, we have no actual proof at all against either of you. But now we have your confessions. Your great talents are not going to be used in any other sphere, I'm afraid. You'll never see that helicopter or that naval vessel. You'll both die jerking on the end of a rope."

"What rubbish is this?" Jolly asked contemptuously. But there was worry under the contempt. "What last-minute despairing bluff are you trying to pull, Carpenter?"

I ignored his question. I said: "I've been on to Kinnaird for some sixty hours also, Jolly. But I had to play it this way. Without letting you gain what appeared to be the upper hand you would never have admitted to the crimes. But now you have."

"Don't fall for it, old lad," Jolly said to Kinnaird. "It's just some desperate bluff. He never had any idea that you were in on this."

"When I knew you were one of the killers," I said to Jolly, "I was almost certain Kinnaird had to be another. You shared the same cabin and unless Kinnaird had been sapped or drugged he had to be in on it. He was neither. He was in on it. That door wasn't jammed when Naseby ran to the radio room to warn you—the two of you were leaning all your weight against it to give the impression that it had been closed for hours and that ice had formed.

"By the same token, young Grant, the assistant radio operator, was in cahoots with you—or he wasn't. If he wasn't, he would have to be silenced. He wasn't. So you silenced him. After I'd caught on to the two of you, I had a good look at Grant. I went out and dug him up from where we'd buried him. Rawlings and I. I found a great big bruise at the base of his neck. He surprised you in something, or he woke when you knifed or shot one of Major Halliwell's men, and you laid him out. You didn't bother killing him: you were about to set the hut on fire and incinerate him, so killing would have been pointless. But you didn't reckon on Captain Folsom here going in and bringing him out—alive.

"That was most damnably awkward for you, wasn't it, Jolly? He was unconscious, but when and if he recovered consciousness, he could blow the whole works on you. But you couldn't get at him to finish him off, could you? The bunkhouse was full of people, most of them suffering so severely that sleep was impossible for them. When we arrived on the scene you got desperate. Grant was showing signs of regaining consciousness. You took a chance, but not all that much of a chance. Remember how surprised I was to find that you had used up all my morphine? Well, I *was* surprised then. But not now. I know now where it went. You gave him an injection of morphine—and you made damn sure the hypodermic held a lethal dose. Am I correct?"

"You're cleverer than I thought you were," he said calmly. "Maybe I have misjudged you a little. But it still makes no difference, old boy."

"I wonder. If I'd known about Kinnaird so long, why do you think I allowed a situation to develop where you could apparently turn the tables?"

" 'Apparently' is not the word you want. And the answer to your question is easy. You didn't know Kinnaird *had* a gun."

"No?" I looked at Kinnaird. "Are you sure that thing works?"

"Don't come that old stuff with me, mate," Kinnaird said in contempt.

"I just wondered," I said mildly. "I thought perhaps the petrol in the tractor's tank might have removed all the lubricating oil."

Jolly came close to me, his face tight and cold. "You *knew* about this? What goes on, Carpenter?"

"It was actually Commander Swanson here who found the gun in the tank," I said. "You had to leave it there because you knew you'd all be getting a good clean-up and medical examination when we got you on board, and it would have been bound to be discovered. But a murderer—a professional, Jolly—will never part with his gun unless he is compelled to. I knew if you got the slightest chance you would go back for it. So I put it back in the tank."

"The hell you did!" Swanson was as nearly angry as I'd ever seen him. "Forgot to tell me, didn't you?"

"I must have. That was after I'd cottoned on to you, Jolly. I wasn't *absolutely* sure you had a partner, but I knew if you had, it must be Kinnaird. So I put the gun back there in the middle of the night and I made good and certain that you, Jolly, didn't get the chance to go anywhere near the tractor shed at any time. But the gun vanished that following morning when everyone was out sampling the fresh air. So then I knew you had an accomplice. But the real reason for planting that gun, of course, is that without it you'd never have talked. But now you have talked and it's all finished. Put up that gun, Kinnaird."

"I'm afraid your bluff's run out, mate." The gun was pointing directly at my face.

"Your last chance, Kinnaird. Please pay attention to what I am saying. Put up that gun or you will be requiring the services of a doctor within twenty seconds."

He said something, short and unprintable. I said, "It's on your own head. Rawlings, you know what to do."

Every head turned toward Rawlings, who was standing leaning negligently against a bulkhead, his hands crossed lightly in front of him. Kinnaird looked too, the Mauser following the direction of his eyes. A gun barked, the sharp, flat crack of a Mannlicher-Schoenauer. Kinnaird screamed and his gun spun from his smashed hand. Zabrinski, holding my automatic in one hand and his copy of the *Dolphin Daze*—now with a neat charred hole through the middle—in the other, regarded his handiwork admiringly, then turned to me. "Was that how you wanted it done, Doc?"

"That was exactly how I wanted it done, Zabrinski. Thank you very much. A first-class job."

"A first-class job," Rawlings sniffed. He retrieved the fallen Mauser and pointed it in Jolly's general direction. "At four feet, even Zabrinski couldn't miss." He dug into a pocket, pulled out a roll of bandage, and tossed it to Jolly. "We kinda thought we might be having to use this, so we came prepared. Dr. Carpenter said your pal here would be requiring the services of a doctor. He is. You're a doctor. Get busy."

"Do it yourself," Jolly snarled. No "old boy," no "old top." The bonhomie was gone, and gone forever.

Rawlings looked at Swanson and said woodenly, "Permission to hit Dr. Jolly over the head with this little old gun, sir?"

"Permission granted," Swanson said grimly. But no further persuasion was necessary. Jolly cursed and started ripping the cover off the bandage.

For almost a minute there was silence in the room while we watched Jolly carry out a rough, ready and far from gentle repair job on Kinnaird's hand. Then Swanson said slowly: "I still don't understand how the hell Jolly got rid of the film."

"It was easy. Ten minutes' thinking and you'd get it. They waited until we had cleared the ice cap, then they took the films, shoved them in a waterproof bag, attached a yellow dye marker to the bag, then pumped it out through the garbage-disposal unit in the galley. Remember, they'd been on a tour of the ship and seen it—although the suggestion was probably radioed them by a naval expert. I had Rawlings posted on watch in the early hours of this morning, and he saw Kinnaird go into the galley about half-past four. Maybe he just wanted a ham sandwich, I don't know. But Rawlings says he had the bag and marker with him when he sneaked in and empty hands when he came out. The bag would float to the surface and the marker stain thousands of square yards of water. The naval ship up top would have worked out our shortest route from Zebra to Scotland and would be within a few miles of our point of exit from the ice pack. It could probably have located it without the helicopter but the chopper made it dead certain.

"Incidentally, I was being rather less than accurate when I said I didn't know the reason for Jolly's attempts to delay us. I knew all along. He'd been told that the ship couldn't reach our exit point until such and such a time and that it was vital to delay us until then. Jolly even had the effrontery to check with me what time we would be emerging from the ice pack."

Jolly looked up from Kinnaird's hand and his face was twisted in a mask of malevolence.

"You win, Carpenter. So you win. All along the line. But you lost out in the only thing that really mattered. They got the films—the films showing the location, as you said, of nearly every missile base in America. And that was all that mattered. Ten million pounds couldn't buy that information. But we got it." He bared his teeth in a savage smile. "We may have lost out, Carpenter, but we're professionals. We did our job."

"They got the films, all right," I acknowledged. "And I'd give a year's salary to see the faces of the men who develop them. Listen carefully, Jolly. Your main reason in trying to cripple Benson and myself was not so much that you could have the say-so on Bolton's health and so delay us: your main reason, your overriding reason, was that you wanted to be the only doctor on the ship so that it could be only you who would carry out the X-ray on Zabrinski's ankle and remove the plaster cast. Literally, everything hinged on that: basically, nothing else mattered. That was why you took such a desperate chance in crippling me when you heard me say I intended to X-ray Zabrinski's ankle the following morning. That was the one move you made that lacked the hallmark of class—of a professional—but, then, I think you were close to panic. You were lucky.

"Anyway, you removed the plaster cast two mornings ago and also the films that you had hidden there in oilskin paper when you applied the plaster to Zabrinski's leg the first night we arrived in Zebra. A perfect hiding place. You could always, of course, have wrapped them in bandages covering survivors' burns, but that would be too risky. The cast was brilliant.

"Unfortunately for you and your friends, I had removed the original plaster during the previous night, extracted the films from the oiled paper, and replaced them with others. That, incidentally, is the second piece of evidence I have on you. There are two perfect sets of prints on the leaders of the satellite films: yours and Kinnaird's. Along with the salt-covered aluminum foil and the confession freely made in front of witnesses, that guarantees you both the eight o'clock walk to the gallows. The gallows and failure, Jolly. You weren't even a professional. Your friends will never see those films."

Mouthing soundless words through smashed lips, his face masked in madness, and completely oblivious to the two guns, Jolly flung himself at me. He had taken two steps and two only when Rawlings' gun caught him, not lightly, on the side of the head. He crashed to the floor as if the Brooklyn

223

bridge had fallen in on top of him. Rawlings surveyed him dispassionately.

"Never did a day's work that gave me profounder satisfaction," he said conversationally. "Except, perhaps, those pictures I took with Dr. Benson's camera to give Dr. Carpenter here some negatives to shove inside that oiled paper."

"Pictures of what?" Swanson asked curiously.

Rawlings grinned happily. "All those pin-ups in Doc Benson's sick bay. Yogi Bear, Donald Duck, Pluto, Popeye, Snow White and the Seven Dwarfs—you name it, I got it. The works. Each a guaranteed work of art—and in glorious technicolor." He smiled a beatific smile. "Like Doc Carpenter here, I'd give a year's pay to see their faces when they get around to developing those negatives."

the gleam on the button on the f...... .... this yours, Murphy?" he said, and ⟨☞⟩ P9-BJC-981 I had to smack you so hard, bu........ ...... protect the boss around here."

"Thanks," I said. The tension drained out of the room and I returned my pistol to my pocket. "Now let's all of us be friends and tell me what I'm doing. You didn't get me down here and put on this show just for practice."

"Well, it's this way, Murphy," Muddy Track began. "Do you make much money selling that stuff you flashed on me this morning?"

"No," I said. "Do you?"

"Not a hell of a lot," he admitted. "But we will. You working with anybody?"

"No."

"How would you like to work with us?"

"Doing what?"

"Same stuff, only not those tubes. We've got a little coke, we're going to get a lot of heroin. A month ago we weren't making any money, the four of us. Now business is picking up. I'm going to need more guys to handle it, guys who can take care of themselves. You look like one to me, and I'll be better off having you on this side than starting an outfit of your own and fighting with me later on."

"What's in it for Johnny Murphy?"

"Plenty. The way I size you up, Murphy, you're working on a shoestring. Sooner or later, though, you'll get going. Well, I'm going now, and in a week or so I'm going to have more than I can handle. Why, we're getting . . ."

"Shut your big mouth, Muddy," growled Herman. "You talk too much."

"Don't tell me what to do, Herman," the little man spat angrily. "I told you guys before that Murphy spotted me this morning, and I was getting him down here to see whether we wanted to use him or . . ." and he drew his fingers across his throat.

"What do you do, Murphy?" asked Ciro.

"Yeah, what the hell *do* you do?" Cookie echoed.

"Wait a minute, boys," I countered. "Who's running this outfit? I like to talk to the head man when I'm making a deal, not to the hired help." That gun back in my pocket was a great little confidence-restorer.

"Take it easy, Murphy," Track cautioned. "I run this show, but the boys are right. Tell us a little what you do."

"Turn a buck now and then on the horses, bum my beer and cakes, pull twenty a week from Uncle Whiskers for doing nothing, and pick up a little here and there. I got a line on some of that juice you saw. I figure I'll be off the Bowery in a month or so," I told them, "and working uptown, and it won't be for peanuts. I won't be sleeping in flops, either, and I won't be sleeping alone. But if you guys got a proposition I'll listen to it. If I like it maybe I'll deal in. If I don't, I'll go home."

"You hot for any reason?" Track said.

"Cooled off. Why?"

"I thought maybe you were the same Johnny Murphy they were looking for two, three months ago on that drugstore job over in Queens."

"I said I was cooled off, didn't I? Anyhow, they can never prove I was there." Who, I wondered, was the Johnny Murphy that Muddy was asking about.

"Where did you get that morphine?"

"Off a guy who lifted it when he was in the Navy."

Muddy looked at the others. "Any of you guys got anything to say? I'm satisfied."

"He's okay by me, boss." The Puerto Rican smiled and stretched out his slender hand. "Glad to meet you, Murphy. I'm Ciro Valentino. Have another drink."

"Hiya, Ciro," I said. His grip was surprisingly strong. "That's a pretty fast draw you've got there." I poured whiskey into his glass and mine. "Good luck."

"I guess it's okay by me, too," growled Herman, "but I don't feel any too good about it." He snapped out his knife and went to work on his nails again. "And you better not turn out wrong, Murphy. What do you say, Cookie?"

"Anything the rest say. Give me a drink." He poured one for himself, one for Herman, and one for Muddy, in that order. "Well, here's luck to the Irish, Murphy." He raised his glass and drained it at one gulp.

My drink nearly stuck in my throat. I didn't like his tone. "What you got against the Irish?" I asked softly.

"Nothing." In the smoky room you couldn't tell whether it was a joke or whether it was something that wasn't funny at all.

"What do we do now, play some more poker?" he asked.

"The hell with poker," Herman said. "Let's all have another drink."

"What am I supposed to do, Muddy, and when do I start?" I asked when the bottle had been passed around.

"String along. Meet me every morning, and if I have anything I'll slip it to you and tell you where to take it and what to collect. You get a quarter of everything you take in for me and a third of any new business you can drum up for yourself. You'll do all right as soon as you start getting around, better when our big load comes in. But, for God's sake, don't get caught. I'll finger anybody I know for you, but keep your eyes open."

"Look, Muddy," I stressed, "I told you I was cooled off, didn't I? Do you think I got that way by walking around with my eyes shut?"

"No, probably not."

"And I got some contacts, too. How about this big load? What is it? Where's it coming from? When will it be here? I got to know how much I can handle before I go taking orders."

"Week or ten days. Herman arranged for a load of . . ."

"Shut up, Muddy," Herman growled.

"A load of heroin to come in from . . ."

"I said shut your trap, Muddy! God damn you. . . ."

"Don't tell me to shut up," Track barked at him. "I'm getting a bellyful of you and your lip!"

"You talk to me like that," Herman answered in a flat monotone, "and someday I'll kill you." The knife balanced in the half-raised hand.

And then a funny thing happened. Ciro's gun was out, covering Herman, and when Cookie's hand moved toward his pocket Ciro just smiled at him, and Cookie reached for the whiskey bottle and poured himself another wallop of booze.

It didn't look like one big happy family to me. "Go on, Muddy. I'm listening."

"That's about all." Either he had backed down or was one of the coolest customers I ever saw. "In a week or ten days we'll have plenty. Plenty. I tell you, Murphy, we're going to have a big thing here. Now let's have another drink."

"I'm going home," Herman said. "I've got stuff to do. Coming, Cookie?"

The two of them went into the back room, came out with their coats and hats, and left.

"I don't like those guys," I said to Muddy, rubbing the side of my head where Cookie had bopped me.

"Neither do I, but I can use them for a while," he confessed. "After that—who knows." He clicked his tongue.

VI.

MUDDY TRACK and Ciro Valentino and I finished what little whiskey was left in the bottle. Each of them seemed friendly enough, but neither was willing to give me much of a line on either Cookie or Herman—or on themselves for that matter. Ciro was a Harlem operator. He admitted that he ran a little travel agency up there as a front. Muddy let me know that he had worked with the old gang that Scabby Ruble ran before the war, which surprised me, because I thought they had been cleaned out. He had been just a little punk with them, running errands and answering the phone and stuff like that, and nobody ever bothered to pick him up. Ruble went to prison in '39 and was still there. After the gang was busted up, Muddy said, he went to some quickie business school and then got himself a job as an order clerk in a factory that went into war production, and Muddy got deferred. He waited the war out there, and as soon as the dope started moving into the States again he quit his job and started back to his old racket.

I still wasn't sure that he trusted me. It seemed he had invited me into the party on short notice, and whether he was fooled by my diving-across-the-table act or not, he'd probably be keeping a close eye on everything I did. And I didn't want to waste time on him. I wanted Rudolph Hoffmann, and the hell with a one-horse dope ring.

"When do I see you again, Muddy?" I asked.

"Tomorrow. About noon. Corner of Second Street."

"And the Bowery?"

"Yeah."

"Check. Now I'll go home and get some sleep."

"Where you live, Murphy?" Ciro inquired.

"Up on Second Avenue. Why?"

"I got a car down here. I'll drop you off on my way uptown. It's better than walking on a night like this."

"Thanks, friend," I said. This Valentino seemed to shape up as a pretty good guy, and since he was so hot with a gun it was better to play on his side. "Let's go. You coming, Muddy, or do you live here?"

"I live here. Housing shortage. Good hideout, though."

"Got a phone?"

"Yeah." He told me the number and looked oddly puzzled when he had finished. "Why don't you write it down?"

"I can remember numbers, Track. And what I keep in my head doesn't get lost or picked up, and you don't get bothered by a lot of calls from people you don't know."

"Good boy, Murphy," he smiled. "You'll do. Good night. See you tomorrow. About noon. Second and Bowery."

Valentino and I went down the dark stairs together and got in his big Buick sedan. "What kind of a setup is this, Ciro?" I asked as we pulled away from the curb. "Looks to me like two different outfits, with you and Muddy in one and Cookie and Herman in the other."

"That's the way it's getting to be," he admitted. "But Muddy's the boss. He has the contacts, at least down here. I've got them uptown, and he and I can work together without any arguments. He found the other two about four or five months ago. They had stuff to sell and could get more, he had places

45

to sell it, so they got together. Maybe he knew them when he was with Scabby Ruble. I don't know. None of us talk much." Ciro was a friendly sort of a guy, all right, but his last sentence was a hint.

I ignored it. "What did he deal me in for? He doesn't know me from nothing."

He turned the Buick up Second Avenue without saying anything, but I thought I knew the answers anyhow. If Muddy's gang was split down the middle for some reason or other, it would be a smart play for him to get a new man in, *on his side.* The easiest way to do it would be to let Cookie and Herman slap the new guy around a little. I felt the bump on my head.

On the other hand, maybe he knew I was a cop, and wanted me where he could keep an eye on me.

I wondered about that.

"If you don't know," Ciro Valentino remarked, "maybe you never will. Tell you one thing, though."

"What?"

"A taxi's been following us ever since we turned onto Second."

"You sure?"

"Yeah, it pulled away from the corner when we made the turn and has been a quarter of a block behind ever since."

"Who's in it?"

"Can't see. Too much reflection from the rain on the windshield to see what's inside."

"What are you going to do?"

"Nothing. I can lose them any time I want to. Where do you want to get off?"

"Anywhere along here." We were two blocks from my place, but there wasn't any percentage in showing Ciro, friendly though he might seem, exactly where his new pal Murphy lived.

He stopped for a red light and I opened the door and turned my collar up against the rain. "But just one little word, Murphy," he began as I stepped out. "Don't go around saying bad things when either of those guys are standing behind you —get it? Especially that goddamned Cookie. He's a killer. Now watch and see what this tail of mine does. Maybe he's tailing you."

The red light turned to green and the Buick jumped away

as I slammed the door and looked back. There was a taxi parked at the curb, about half a block away, but I couldn't see any sign of one following the Buick. I walked about a half a block and looked back again. The taxi was still by the curb, but it wasn't in the middle of the block any more. The damned thing was following me.

Rudy Hoffmann's got you now, Malone, I said to myself. *Lucky you turned around before you got it in the back, like your old man.*

Had Muddy put the finger on me? If not, who had? I thanked Valentino's quick eyes. I'd never have known Rudy was following me if it hadn't been for Ciro. The Puerto Rican had saved my life—temporarily, at least.

If I had used my head I would have ducked into a bar or a restaurant. I didn't stop to think, but turned and started to run back toward the taxi with my hand wrapped around the gun in my pocket, thumbing the safety catch up.

The taxi jumped the red light and took off on the cross street, and there wasn't another one in sight that I could grab to follow it. Excitement drained out of me and disappointment drained in. I pulled the safety catch down again and lit a cigarette. There wasn't any doubt in my mind that Hoffmann was on my trail.

But who the hell put him on it? That was the question. And how long had he been following me?

My mind was a muddle as I started to walk back to my room. Did he know where I lived? Did he know that I had been at Muddy's? Where had he picked up my trail? I didn't know the answers to any of those questions, but I did know that I better be pretty careful until I found out.

There weren't any more taxis that seemed interested in me as I walked along. Second Avenue was pretty well deserted at three in the morning. I opened the front door of the rooming house, stepped inside, and waited in the vestibule for about five minutes. Then, hand on gun again, I stepped out on the street and bumped into Herman.

He was surprised. "What the hell are you doing here?" I asked.

"Just walking along, getting a little air."

"Kind of wet, isn't it?"

47

"Not too wet."

"Where's Cookie?"

"I don't know." But his eyes glanced over my shoulder, and I looked back.

Cookie was standing on the corner.

"Hey, just what the hell is this? Are you two guys following me?"

"Not exactly. We just wanted to see where you lived. That's it, isn't it, Cookie?" he asked, as his friend came up. "We just wanted to see where Murphy lives, didn't we?"

"Sure," said Cookie.

"And why the hell do you care where I live? It's none of your goddamned business, as far as I can see."

"Just as a favor for Muddy."

"Favor for Muddy, my foot. You're a couple of sneaks, in my book, and if I catch you following me again I'll bust both of you in half. How did you get this far? You didn't walk up here." I was sore.

"Followed you and Valentino in a taxi."

"What!" The sense of danger passed, because these two guys were real and I knew I could deal with them. "What kind of a taxi?"

"A Checker, I think. We picked Val up when he turned on Second; he always comes uptown the same way."

"Why the hell did you lam out when I came back?"

"Christ, you were reaching for a gun. For all we knew you might think it was someone else in that cab and start shooting. The driver thought so. He lit out."

I thought that one over, and it made sense. "Listen," I told them. "Maybe Muddy did tell you to spot my hangout. I don't know. But if you want to know where I live, ask me, and don't go sneaking around like a couple of cops. Curiosity doesn't pay, in this league. Understand?"

"Yeah," said Cookie. "But don't act so damned snotty. You'll be following us one of these days to see where we live. Nobody takes anything for granted in this league, either. Right?"

He had a point there. "Right," I said. "And I live here and now I'm going upstairs and going to bed, and if anybody touches my door he's going to get shot. Good night!"

It was still raining at twelve o'clock the next morning when

Muddy Track came up to where I was shivering on the corner and gave me the eye. We didn't say a word, but I fell in behind him and followed as he walked along. There was a folded newspaper under his arm, and after a while he paused, looked around, and then carefully placed it on top of a trash can standing outside a hardware store. His derby-topped head nodded twice before he walked away, leaving me slouched against a wall under a second-story overhang that kept some of the rain away. When he was out of sight I picked up the paper, opened it enough to see that there was a small package concealed in the fold, and then ducked into the St. George Mission and headed for the men's room.

After waiting long enough to make sure that nobody was tailing me this time, and testing the flushing system to see if it was capable of removing the evidence in a hurry, I sat down with the paper and the prize that was in it. There were half a dozen little packages, neatly rolled pieces of white paper about half an inch wide and two inches long. Each was closed with a strip of scotch tape, and as I shook one of them beside my ear I could hear the contents rattling back and forth. All six had been wrapped in a sheet of the stationery Muddy sold, and there was a note written on the wrapping.

"TAKE TO GROCERY STORE. . . ." I read the penciled message just that far, stopped for a second, read the rest, and shoved it into my pocket with a hand that was shaking. And believe me, my heart was pounding with excitement as I left the St. George Mission and walked slowly to the saloon where the bartender knew me as a horse player.

"Gimme a beer with a shot on the side," I ordered.

"Hello, Murph," the bartender greeted me, drawing a small beer with the usual inch and a half head on it. "You shouldn't have hit it so hard last night. Bet you don't have a cent left, do you?"

My answer was to throw a buck on the bar, kill the drink in a hurry, and head for the phone booth. "This is Murphy," I said to the voice that answered my call. "I like 'Respingo' in the sixth race."

"Can do," the voice said. "How much. Two?"

"No. Four." I hung up.

"What do you like today, Murph?" the bartender asked.

" 'Respingo' in the sixth. Give me another drink."

"On me, Murph, on me." This time the beer only had a quarter-inch head on it.

Track's note told me to take the six papers of dope to a grocery store away over on West Sixty-first Street and collect ten dollars for each of them, which meant forty-five for him and fifteen for me.

It was a miserable place, dirty, smelly, and with an assortment of fly-specked canned goods that must have been three years old on the shelves. Some greasy salami hung in a moldy case, and a mangy cat lay on the counter with one eye open for the mice that plainly infested the place. A man in a filthy apron appeared from a back room as I came in.

"Can of beans," I said. "How do you like the weather?"

He reached for the beans. "Lousy," he muttered over his shoulder.

"Looks muddy to me."

Dirty apron put the beans back on the shelf. "We got some better beans back here," nodding toward the rear of the store. "Come and have a look at them." When we were in the back room he turned. "What looks muddy to you, Buster?"

"The track looks muddy. Give me sixty bucks and stuff the beans."

He peeled two twenties and four fives from a roll and handed them over, taking the six packages in return. "I'll take two dozen next week," he said. "Business is picking up. Lots of kids coming in here. I sell it to the boys and trade it to some of the good-looking chicks. Sixteen-year-old stuff. Yum-yum."

The son-of-a-bitch rolled his eyes and the sixty dollars in my pocket felt like sixty pounds of sewage as I mentally marked him for a good going over as soon as I could safely pick him up. The rain smelled nice and clean outside.

It was only about three o'clock, so I wandered into a movie down on Ninth Avenue to waste a couple of hours. First I sat in the back, and then after a while I moved farther down and on one side near an exit to see if anyone was on my tail. I didn't see anybody else changing seats. Ten minutes later I ducked out the side, caught an uptown bus, transferred crosstown, took a couple of subways, and at six I was going into Stratford's office.

50

Sixth race—six o'clock. Stratford, Hess, and Grallio were there. I made the fourth. Four guys—four dollars. I gave them a quick hello.

"'Respingo' finished third in a four-horse race, Malone," Stratford greeted me, "and didn't pay a cent. What's on your mind?"

"Look at this." My hands weren't too steady as I spread Track's delivery note on his desk. "Isn't that exactly the same printing as was on the warning letter?"

Stratford picked up his phone, dialed a number. "Bring me the latest letter from the Malone file, Burke," he barked. "The one we got just before young Malone went on the case."

Grallio and Hess moved around to study Track's delivery instructions over the Inspector's shoulder, and when Burke brought the other note in we didn't need more than a minute to see that each had been written by the same person.

"Where'd you get this, Malone?" Stratford asked. "Do you know who wrote it?"

"Muddy Track wrote it."

"Track!" Tony whistled. "You mean the guy I put you on yesterday?"

"Yeah. That's my unknown friend, it looks like from this. He's my new boss. He's the guy I'm working for."

"What do you mean, he's the guy you're working for?"

"I'm selling dope, Inspector. I sold sixty dollars' worth of it today to the slimy bastard who lives at that address. He sells some of it to young boys, he says, and some of it he trades to good-looking young girls, and it was all I could do to keep from strangling him with my bare hands. Here," and I pulled the sixty out of my pocket and separated three fives. "This is what I got out of those kids today. I don't want it. Put it in some fund where it will do some good."

The Inspector sealed the three fives in an envelope, noted something on the outside, and dropped it in a desk drawer. "You didn't manage to find Hoffmann during the course of your busy little day, did you?"

"No, but for a while last night I thought he had found me. By God, Inspector, I'm telling you now I was one relieved cop when it turned out to be a couple of other guys."

"Wait a minute, you're getting ahead of me and the rest of

the boys. Why did you think Hoffmann was following you last night, and who the hell were the other guys?"

Quickly I told them what had happened to me from the time Grallio sent me to the St. George Mission until I had walked into the station a few minutes before.

"You're a lucky cuss, Malone," Stratford said. "Of all the people who ever fell in a barnyard and came up smelling like a rose, you smell the sweetest. I don't quite see why you aren't dead." For a long while he regarded his cigar thoughtfully. "We can pick this Track up and coax him to tell us who Rudy Hoffmann is." The way he said "coax" wasn't very nice.

"No, let's take it easy, Inspector. If we bring him in, maybe he won't sing. Or maybe Hoffmann knows Track, too, and would scram out of town when Muddy turned up missing."

"You don't think one of these others, Cookie or Herman, is Hoffmann, do you?"

"Could be. That's an angle I want to work on."

"Yeah, and suppose one of them thinks you're Johnny Malone, what then? Maybe that's the angle they're working on."

"Maybe it is, but I think I'm a little smarter and a little faster than they are."

Stratford struck a match and held it to the dead cigar. "You mean you hope you are. There's a hell of a lot of policemen's widows living on pensions in this town because other cops thought they were smarter and faster than some crook. How long is it going to take you to get Track to tell you something?"

"Not too long, I hope. But when I bring somebody in here, sir, I'm not going to bring him in on suspicion or for carrying a gun. Not on this case. I'm going to bring him in the way they brought my old man in, you know that."

"Yeah. I know." Stratford planted his hands on his desk, palms down. "Now look. Hess, you get the hell down to the Bowery the first thing tomorrow morning. Pick up Malone and stay with him until he can put you on either Herman or Cookie. Grallio, you do the same thing. I want to know where those guys live, what they do, who they talk to, and what dames they run around with. Every damned thing about them. Now drift out of here, and for God's sake, Malone, don't let them find out who you are, or we'll have another 'Malone' file out there in the other room."

52

"How about Track and the Puerto Rican, boss?" Hess asked. "Do you want them tailed?"

"Hell no. Rudy Hoffmann isn't going around disguised as a Puerto Rican, and he isn't any four-foot-ten-inch character in a derby hat, either, unless he got pounded down somewhere. All I'm interested in right now is people who might be Hoffmann. This is the Homicide Squad, remember. Narcotics is somewhere else."

Charlie, Tony, and I started for the door, with me at the end of the parade. "Malone." The inspector's voice called me back.

"Yes, sir."

"I don't give a damn how you bring Hoffmann in, or how you bring any drug peddlers in the world in—just so they can't walk!"

VII.

THE BARTENDER at my favorite saloon wasn't too happy to see me walk in. "'Respingo,'" he snorted. "Four horses in a race and he don't win. Christ, my old lady could run around a track faster than that beetle." The beer had two inches of head on it.

"The word I got was it was in the bag. Anyhow, you can't win all the time. Give me a double rye."

"In the bag," he muttered. "In my foot." He poured me a double jigger—short. I drank it and went out to get some food.

Along about ten o'clock I drifted over to Rivington Street and found Muddy, Cookie, and Herman there. "Here's your forty-five bucks," I said. "I kept my cut. The guy wants two dozen rolls next week. He's a louse. I've been itching ever since I went in that place. Let Cookie go the next time."

53

"Go to hell," Cookie growled. "I've got my own places. Anyhow, I'm not a cheap shover."

"And another thing, Muddy," I continued, ignoring the crack, "did you tell these two guys to shadow me after Ciro and I left here the other night?"

"Shadow you? No. Why would I want them to do that?"

"That's what I want to know. You better tell them not to do it again. They might get hurt."

"Yeah." He took the cigar out of his mouth and studied it carefully. "I can see how that might happen."

"In fact," I said, "maybe I'll just take a few minutes and knock their heads together right now. I owe them a couple."

"Take it easy, take it easy." The authority in Track's voice surprised me a little. "You won't do anything of the kind, Murphy. And you two, I don't know why you were following Murphy, but you know it wasn't my idea. I know where he lives. And what's more, I don't want any arguing around here. Get it?"

Somehow or other we all got it. "I was only kidding," I admitted. There was a bottle of whiskey on the table. "Where do you keep the glasses? I'll get them and let's all have a drink." After all, if one of these guys was going to kill me, or if I was going to kill one of them, we might as well get along until we found out for sure who the other really was.

"Back room. The light switch is on the wall just inside the door."

"Thanks." I got four glasses and brought them in. Herman wasn't there.

"What became of your buddy, Cookie?"

"He went out for a while."

"What for?"

"Not that it's any of your business, Murphy, but maybe he has a date. It could be he went somewhere to see a girl. Any objections?"

"He can go to hell in a bucket, as far as I'm concerned." I put the glasses on the table, opened the bottle, and poured three drinks. "I was only asking. Here's to my first day's business," I said.

"Here's to tomorrow's," said Cookie.

"What do I do tomorrow, Muddy?" I asked. "More of the same?"

"A whole lot more. You're a pretty slick operator, Murphy. I like you. You sure lost me in that movie house."

Something jumped inside me. "What were you doing—following me, too? Maybe we should all get together and have me lead a parade up Fifth Avenue."

"Not exactly. I just happened to be up in that section about three this afternoon, and saw you come out of that grocery store and go into the show. I went in behind you, just to see why you were taking in that punk double feature. I found out."

"Well," I said, taking a slow drink, "it doesn't pay to get careless. Some of my best friends got careless and the first thing they knew they were run over by street cars, or somebody put the heat on them."

"In Queens, maybe," Cookie laughed. "Ice-cold Johnny Murphy from Queens."

My mental pencil made a mental note not to forget to find out who Johnny Murphy from Queens was and what he had done. He certainly had a reputation. "Ice-cold in Manhattan," I allowed. "But don't send me across the East River, Muddy. How about another drink, Cookie?"

"Thanks."

The three of us sat there and finished a couple more rounds without saying anything important. After a while I said to Muddy, "Do you want me to get out of the 52-20 Club? Sometimes they check up on guys."

"Might as well. You won't need that kind of money any more. It'll be peanuts. Glad you thought of . . ."

"What's the 52-20 Club?" Cookie interrupted.

"Where the hell have you been, fellow?" I wanted to know. "Didn't you ever hear of the G.I. Bill of Rights? Where were you during the war, anyhow, in the Boy Scouts?"

"I was in Mexico. Jumped ship there in '41, and couldn't see any reason for jumping back just to get torpedoed, so I stayed on the beach until the war was over. Give me another drink." He reached for the bottle.

"What navy were you in?" I asked him.

"I wasn't in any navy; I was in the merchant service. Tankers, mostly. I jumped off at Tampico."

"You don't look like a guy who had spent much time at sea."

"What do you mean?" he flared. "I went to sea for damned near twenty-five years. You don't know anything about it, Murphy. You're just dumb."

"Where'd you meet Herman? On a boat?"

"On a boat! Say 'ship,' Murphy. No, I met him in Mexico, if it's any of your business, which it isn't."

"When's he coming back?" I looked at my watch.

"Pretty soon."

"Where did you say he went?"

"I said he stepped out for a while."

"Is he out with Ciro?"

"Hell, no. They wouldn't be seen dead with each other. He's with his girl." He drained his glass and I poured him another.

"He's too damned crazy about women," Muddy said. "They'll get him in trouble one of these days. They're just as crazy about him, too. I don't know what he's got, but all he has to do is snap his fingers and they come running."

"Can't afford them, myself," I said.

"I'm too old," Track admitted.

Cookie took half his drink at one swallow and helped himself to one of my cigarettes. He was a little tight.

"Why don't you give me my job and deal me my decks tonight, Muddy?" I scratched a match and held it for Cookie.

"Then I won't have to meet you tomorrow."

"Don't keep it here, in the first place. This apartment is clear. Got to spend the morning lining up the delivery schedule, too. What did you do with that note?"

"Burned it and flushed it down the can in the mission. Why?"

"Just wondered. I'll meet you tomorrow, about one. Corner of Hester Street and the Bowery. You'll have money tomorrow night, Murphy. I got something in mind."

"I'll have a new suit the next day, then. I'm tired of this thing I'm wearing." I reached for my hat and started to get up. "You coming, Cookie? I'll buy you a drink." The bottle was empty.

"Aw, hang around for a while until Herman gets back. We can find a cab and go up together. There's more whiskey in the back room. I'll get a bottle." He stood up and lurched through the door.

All of a sudden I didn't want to go uptown in a taxi with

56

Cookie and Herman. "No more for me," I said to Muddy, and left before Cookie returned.

It was midnight. Rivington Street was deserted, black, and ugly. As I came up to the corner where I had waited the night before a spark flashed in the recessed doorway. Then a voice muttered, "No good cigarette lighter!" Then, louder, "You got a light, fella?"

Giving lights to strangers in dark corners of tough neighborhoods is one of the best ways in the world to get a bump on the head, especially at midnight. My hand dropped into my pocket.

"Don't shoot me, Johnny, you bum. It's Tony. Just give me a light while I talk to you."

My hand shifted from the gun to a package of matches.

"Anybody home?" Tony asked.

"One." The flash of the match glowed in the doorway.

"What do?"

"I'll turn right on Delancey, cross Ridge, and be in the first bar that's open."

"Check. Thanks for the light."

I flipped the match stub away and walked off without another word. Tony was starting his day's work early, and I wondered where Charlie Hess was and what he was doing.

Grallio joined me soon after I reached the first bar on the other side of Ridge Street. We got together at a corner table away from the other customers and ordered a couple of ryes and water.

"Which one's there?" Tony asked.

"Cookie. He's half tanked. Herman's out with some girl, but he'll be back later. Cookie's waiting for him. Where's Charlie?"

"He's lying in a doorway across the street—looking very drunk. You should have seen him move in. He fell five times before he got where he wanted to go. We tossed a coin to see who'd get the dirty job and he lost. He poured half a pint of whiskey on his coat and spilled salad dressing all over himself to look like he'd thrown up. He stinks like a pig. Where are you going?"

"Home. I meet the boss at Hester and the Bowery at one tomorrow afternoon. Will you be there?"

"If we don't get on the trail tonight."

"Okay. Let's shove."

I took a bus uptown, went three blocks past my place, got out and walked back, making sure I wasn't being followed this time. I didn't need to worry. Instead of being followed I had been anticipated. There was something wrong with the room when I went in. Nothing seemed to have been disturbed, but there was just that feeling of something—something you couldn't put your finger on. The money was still inside the window-shade roller. The spare automatic was still in the coat pocket, but when I took it out with a handkerchief and held it in the light there were fingerprints on it that weren't there when I had last looked at it, because I had wiped it clean.

"Nuts to you, Herman," I said to myself. "Sneak around until your feet blister, you won't find out anything about me." I shoved the bed around so that anyone who had scouted the room wouldn't be able to get me with a blind shot through the door, jammed a chair against the knob, brushed my teeth and went to sleep, wondering what Charlie and Tony were doing.

They told me the story later. Grallio went back, after he left me, and sat in a car he had parked a few doors up the street from Muddy's flat. Hess lay uncomfortably in his cold doorway and cursed the day he ever decided to go on the force. Along about two o'clock, a taxi drove up and Herman got out, said something to the driver, and entered the building. The taxi parked with the meter running and after ten minutes Herman and Cookie came out. Cookie was having a little trouble with his feet, but Herman steered him into the taxi and they drove away.

Tony couldn't start up and follow without tipping his hand. He waited until the taxi disappeared around the next corner, probably heading back to Delaney Street. Then he quickly backed his own car to the Willett Street intersection and took off for Delancey himself. If the taxi doubled back to Delancey, as he hoped, he had a good chance of picking it up there.

Hess, on the other hand, gave a few moans and struggled to a sitting position, wobbled to his feet, and staggered away. The farther he got from the doorway the better he could walk. Inside of two blocks he was sober. He tossed his filthy coat in a dark doorway, revealing himself surprisingly well dressed beneath it, except for his trousers, and entered the first place that had a pay

58

telephone. When he left the phone booth his shoes were rubbed clean, the wrinkled trousers had been removed to disclose another pair, and the phone call had disclosed where Herman's taxi was garaged. He jumped into another cab and hurried away.

"Keep this under your hat," he told the night foreman at the garage. "I want to get hold of the driver of Number 2642, as soon as I can. I'm from Headquarters." He flashed his badge and then quickly returned it to his pocket.

"You're in luck tonight, Chief." The foreman thumbed through a sheaf of papers. "That would be Frankie Epstein. He called in about ten or fifteen minutes ago and said he would work his way back here to get his brakes looked at. Why don't you sit down and wait? How about a cup of coffee?" He lifted a pot from a hot plate, poured into a huge cup, motioned toward tin cans of sugar and condensed milk.

"Thanks." Hess settled into a chair, shoveled sugar into the black, fragrant brew. "I can use this. It's damned chilly tonight. Wish I was home and in bed. No fun being a cop when you have to be out all night, and every night at that." He shook out a pack of cigarettes, offered them to the foreman, helped himself. "When this driver comes in can I talk to him alone—in here?"

"Sure. I'll go take a look at his brakes. If the phone rings, though, I'll have to come back and answer it."

"That's all right." A shiny cab rolled into the garage, blew its horn. "That looks like 2642 now."

"Yeah." The foreman stepped to the door of his little office. "Hey, Frankie," he called. "Leave the hack there and come in. Guy wants to see you."

The driver walked over. "This is Frankie Epstein, Chief," the foreman said. "Sit down, Frankie. This guy wants to ask you some questions. I'll look at the brakes. Which ones?"

"Left rear." Then Epstein looked at Hess again. "Whatcha wanta know?"

"Tell me about that fare you took down to Rivington about an hour ago."

"You a cop?"

"Yeah."

"Thought so. Nobody else would be around askin' questions dis time of night." The driver stuck a cigarette in his mouth, poured himself a cup of coffee. "Well," he began, "there ain't much to tell. I picked up the single about quarter t' two on the corner of Bleecker and MacDougal."

"What did he look like?"

"Nothin' special. Blond, about five eleven or six feet, I guess. Regular business suit, dark topcoat, white shirt, gray hat. See a million of 'em. Every day. He wants to go to Rivington Street. I forget the number but I got it on th' card. I'm thinkin' that's a hell of a place to go at two in the morning, but I got a livin' to make, so I don't say nothin'." He sipped the coffee.

"What then?"

"We get there okay and he gets out and tells me to wait. He has to pick up a friend. I don't much like sittin' down there alone, but there ain't a soul anywhere except a bum sleepin' off a binge in a doorway across th' street, and I figure he ain't goin' t' bother me."

Hess smiled to himself. "Go on."

"After a while, him and his friend come out and get in the cab and the first guy tells me to drive to an apartment house up on East Ninetieth Street. The second guy looks like the first one, only kind of sloppy because he's half canned. So I takes them up to this place in the Nineties and the first guy gives me ten bucks and tells me to keep the change, which I figure ain't too bad."

"Did you hear anything they said?"

"Not much. The one that was a little tight was singing something when he got in, and then I heard him say was Murphy all right and the first guy said yeah, he guessed so. Then they pulled the glass shut and I couldn't hear nothin'."

"That's all right." Hess finished the notes he had been making on a sheet of paper from the foreman's memo pad. "That's just what I wanted to know. Don't tell anyone you were talking to me, understand."

"Yeah, I get it. But what are them two guys doing?"

Hess looked around carefully, folded his notes and put them in his pocket, and lowered his voice to a whisper. "Terpsichorean interpretations," he confided.

"Chee," said Epstein. "I'd never of picked them up if I'd knowed that."

"There's a whole gang of them in this town," continued Hess.

"We think the head guy is named Arthur Murray. Don't breathe a word of it."

Amazed as Epstein was by the revelation, he would have been even more surprised if he had followed the detective after that. For Charlie Hess quickly walked across town until he came to a main avenue, hailed a cab, and directed the driver to the address on East Ninetieth Street. There he got out, paid the fare, and as soon as the cab had driven off he walked across the street and entered the sedan that Tony had been driving.

"Hello, you bum," he greeted the other detective.

"What took you so long, Charlie?" Tony asked. "I've been sitting here for an hour."

"You can damn well sit there until nine o'clock, too. I'm going home and get some sleep. Are they in there?" He nodded toward the apartment house on the other side of the street.

"Would I be here if they weren't? What did you find out?"

"The one guy got the cab down on the corner of Bleecker and MacDougal. . . ."

"That's Herman."

"Who's telling this story, you or me? As I was saying, Herman gets the cab and comes down to pick up his friend. . . ."

"Cookie."

"Cookie. Cookie is drunk. All the cabby hears him say is that Murphy is all right, and Herman says he guesses so. Then they come up here. I had a stroke of luck finding the driver in a hurry. Now I'm going to get some sleep and you can sit here and wait for them. They say the sunrises are wonderful at this time of the year; be sure to remember so you can tell me about it. Good night, you bum."

"Good night, Charlie. If I'm not here in the morning, you know where to find me."

In spite of the fact that someone had been through my room while I was down at Muddy Track's, I got more sleep that night than either of my two detective friends. I cleared out of the room the next morning at about eight, had my breakfast, read the morning paper, and wasted two hours. Then I walked into a little drugstore and asked the clerk for some colorless nail polish. He looked at me and simpered. "The 'Spring Rose' shade is just

61

the very, very slightest pink. Wouldn't you rather have that? It's lovely."

I didn't catch on. "No, thanks. Just give me a little bottle of the colorless kind."

"Oh, well, if you insist." He shrugged his shoulders and started wrapping the little bottle. "We have an excellent bargain in bath salts today. 'Tulip Time.' It's lovely, too."

"No, thanks. How much is the polish?"

"Thirty cents." He leaned over the counter, and I smelled the perfume he was wearing. "I bet you look nice when you're dressed up," he whispered. "Would you like to go to the ballet with me tomorrow night?" He handed me my change, brushing his fingers against mine.

Damned fairy. I pushed the palm of my hand into his face and gave him a quick shove. He stumbled over something and fell down behind the counter as I walked out, his high-pitched voice screaming curses at me.

My room had been cleaned up and the bed made when I got back. I pulled a hair out of my head and glued it across the crack between the door and the frame, on the outside, down near the floor. The nail polish was invisible, and you had to look very carefully to discover the hair. But I knew where it was, and if it was broken when I came back I would know that somebody had been in my room again.

At one o'clock I picked up Muddy Track, followed him into the Elevated, watched him get off and leave a small package on the seat behind him. I got five hundred dollars when I delivered it to a midtown hotel room. When I left the hotel, I dodged on and off a subway a couple of times, in case the boss had tried to follow me again, and finally wound up in a Times Square store.

My shoulders are wide enough so the rest of my hundred and ninety-or-so pounds slopes down to my feet in a fairly orderly manner, but you should have seen me when I came out of that store. They specialized in padding, and belted backs, and a half a dozen other tailor's tricks to make little jerks look solid. The most conservative material they had was a dark blue with a chalk stripe about an eighth of an inch wide. Ordinarily I go to a more conservative store, but I figured a bit of flashiness would be more in character with my new identity. But I sure had a set of shoulders and chest muscles when I came out wearing that new suit, a pale pink shirt, and an imitation hand-painted tie.

VIII.

At nine o'clock on the same morning, I learned later, Charlie Hess came around the corner and walked west on Ninetieth Street. As he passed a small sedan parked there, the driver started the engine and drove around the next corner. When Hess caught up to him, Grallio stepped out.

"She's all yours, pal," he said.

"They still in there?"

"Far as I know. I'll be back as soon as I get some breakfast and a shave."

Hess drove the car around the block and parked it a few yards from where it had been before. After about two hours, a good-looking, well-dressed young man with black hair and the build of a light heavyweight walked slowly toward him, leading a small Scottie on a leash. Hess started the car and drove away, winking at the dog walker as he went.

Strange things happened on Ninetieth Street that day. Two men drove up in a gas-company truck and placed a little fence around a manhole, after which one of them disappeared down the hole and the other sat on the curb. The man on the curb was a stocky blond with short-clipped hair. The dog walker passed his way, the curb sitter patted the Scottie, the two men exchanged a few words, and the dog walker moved off again.

He soon reappeared, without his dog, and entered a tap-room across the street from the open manhole. There he took a seat at a table which gave him a clear view through the front window, ordered a whiskey and water, muttered something about waiting for a friend, and sipped slowly at the drink.

His friend joined him as soon as he could get away from the manhole and change his clothes.

"What do you think, Charlie? Are they going to stay in there all day, or did they sneak out the back way?"

"I don't know, Tony. But they didn't come out the front, not together, at any rate."

"Maybe we missed them. Neither of us knows exactly what they look like."

"We'll get an awful growl from Stratford if we missed them. How long do you want to stay here?"

"Until it gets dark. Where's the car?"

"Parked up the street. I got a newer one." Hess took a drink, stopped midway, slowly replaced the glass on the table. "I think we'd better be going, Tony."

Two men had come out of the apartment house. Each was wearing a gray hat, a dark topcoat, a sober business suit. One of them stepped into the street and hailed a taxi. It passed him. They got another.

Hess and Grallio followed carefully through the increasingly heavy traffic, keeping the cab always in sight as it hurried down First Avenue, skirted the Stuyvesant Town and Peter Cooper Village developments, headed west on Fourteenth Street, turned again and wormed its way into Washington Square and the heart of Greenwich Village.

"Well, what do you know," said Hess. "Bleecker and Mac-Dougal. Right where they started from last night. We could both have stood in bed all this time."

The taxi stopped in front of a cellar night club, one of a dozen or more in that section of town. Some of them are all right; most of them are sucker traps, operating only to separate the unwary tourist from his bankroll as quickly as possible. Cookie and Herman got out of their taxi, paid the driver, and walked down a short flight of steps into the open door of Sophie's Place.

". . . and then entered place called Sophie's Place near corner of Bleecker and MacDougal Streets at"—Tony glanced at his watch—"5:31 p.m." He snapped the notebook shut, tossed it in the glove compartment, kicked the door. "What do we do now? Go in after them?"

64

"Let's just one of us go and the other can sit in the car and get some sleep." Hess took a coin from his pocket, flipped it in the air.

"Heads," called Grallio.

"Tails," announced Hess. "You go. I'll wait here. Step softly when you return, please, so as not to awaken the sleeping detective you will find stretched across the seat." He had stopped the car a good half block from Sophie's Place. Now, after his partner left, he drove around the block and parked nearer the cellar club. There he promptly went to sleep.

Tony Grallio, on the other hand, was very wide awake as he went down the steps into the poorly lighted room. A small bar, with six stools, stretched along the right side of a narrow passageway. Farther on, there was a larger room, half filled with small, red-calico-covered tables. The other half of the room contained a piano and some chairs and music racks on a low platform. Beyond the room were four doors, one marked "Men," one "Ladies," one "Exit," and the last evidently led to a kitchen.

The two men he had followed the night before were sitting at one end of the bar talking to the bartender when the detective entered and sat on a stool by himself. "Rye and water," he ordered as the bartender looked his way, and when the drink was mixed he raised his glass. "Happy landings, gents," he offered.

Herman and Cookie raised their glasses and sipped in return, and Grallio studied them carefully as they went back to their conversation. The one with the once-busted nose, he knew, must be Cookie. He catalogued them carefully so he would never forget what they looked like, saw that they were drinking beer, listened for scraps from their talk.

"Day after tomorrow," he heard Cookie say. "You told Muddy yet?"

"I'll tell him when I get good and ready," the other replied. "And you keep sober and keep your mouth shut. I don't want to see you like you were last night until we're finished. Get it?"

Cookie muttered something unintelligible, swallowed his beer, and motioned to the bartender for a refill. "Don't be so damned Christly," he said, draining the glass.

Herman looked at the watch on his wrist, then at the bartender. "It's six o'clock," he announced. "Where's Billie?"

"Aw, give her a chance, Herman," the bartender replied. "She didn't get to sleep too early last night, you know that, even though we did have to say goodby to you two before twelve." He leered stupidly.

"The customers can go to hell." Herman finished his beer and slid the glass across the bar. "Cookie and I were home by two-thirty, and I had to pick him up." He looked at his watch again. "She better be here soon so she can have dinner before the first show."

Tony motioned for another drink. "You got a show here?" he asked the bartender.

"Well, we call it a show. We got a chanteuse—a singer, you know. Billie Bloomer, she calls herself, only she don't wear bloomers. She plays the piano a little and sings almost anything the customers ask for. Hang around."

"When does she go on?"

"About eight. Depends on when the place starts to fill up. We generally have a dinner crowd here."

"Is that all the excitement you got?"

"Aw, Billie's not bad. She's got good looks and good legs and everything's in the right place. Say, you're new around here, ain't you?"

"Yeah, I just got in from Buffalo and thought I'd come down to Greenwich Village and look around."

"Well, this is as good a place to look as any, I guess. Them drinks are seventy-five cents each," he added, as Tony dropped a bill on the bar. "Plus tax."

Tony smiled to himself as he looked at the shot glass. Thick sides, heavy bottom, less than an ounce at the very most. The whiskey was watered, too, and would be watered even more as fast as the bartender figured he could get away with it. "Gee whiz," he said. "This is a swell place. I always wanted to see Greenwich Village."

The door marked "Exit" in the back room opened just then, and a tall striking blonde walked in. "Hello, you sweethearts," she called. "Set 'em up for the stellar attraction!" Her eyes were blue, properly accentuated with mascara, and her red mouth was the kind shipwrecked men dream about on desert islands. The long full skirt she wore swished intimately around her thighs and, as she removed the short fur jacket she was wearing,

66

Tony saw that, if she was the Billie Bloomer who was expected, the bartender's observation of "everything's in the right place" was entirely correct. There was plenty of it, too, so much that Tony mentally asked himself, "True or false?" She dropped one of her gloves on the floor as she hung her coat in the almost empty check room. As she bent over to pick it up, he saw the answer was "true."

"A good detective," Tony told me later as he described the incident, "has to be able to size up situations quickly. You know that, Johnny. These were Lucky Strike size—so round, so firm, so fully packed."

"Where you been, Billie?" Cookie asked. "Herman's been wearing out his watch looking at the time. What you drinking?"

"He ought to know where I've been," the girl smiled. "Right where he left me. Gosh, I haven't had my breakfast yet." She moved between the two men, linked her arm with Herman's, stroked his hand with her long fingers. "Give me something with two shots of brandy and an egg in it so I can get my strength back. And give me a cigarette, too."

Tony watched as Herman took a pack of cigarettes from an inside pocket and Billie placed one between her lips. He noticed that her hand shook a little, and the cigarette was unsteady while Herman struck a match and held it for her. Herman returned the matches to his coat pocket, and when he put his hand back in the girl's the detective saw that he transferred something white to her eager grasp.

"Excuse me, gents," he heard her say, and then she walked quickly across the dining room and disappeared behind the door marked "Ladies." Cookie glanced at Herman. Herman merely shrugged his shoulders.

The Waring mixer behind the bar hummed and swished the brandy-and-egg concoction until the bartender flipped the switch, removed the mixing glass, and poured the frothy yellow stuff into a glass. Billie came back just in time to take it from him, and drained half of it immediately. "Ah," she purred. "Good. A little of this and a little of that and a girl can manage to get along all right in the big city."

"How about dinner, Billie," Cookie reminded, "now that you've had breakfast? We're hungry."

"Me, too," she replied without looking at him. "Send another one of these things back to the table, will you?" she called over her shoulder as they walked into the dining-room section.

"That's a hell of a breakfast, if you ask me," Tony commented as he motioned for another drink. "She must get more than that to keep her looking so healthy, and I bet that guy she called 'Herman' is giving it to her—huh?"

The bartender stopped in the middle of cracking an egg. "Listen, Buster-from-Buffalo," and he leaned across the bar, "we've got free speech in this country and all that, but I wouldn't go thinking right out loud around here if I was you and valued my health. Not that way, I wouldn't."

"Oh." Tony's black eyebrows arched. "Umm. I get it. Thanks, I'll keep my big mouth shut. Good thing they were around the corner and couldn't hear me, I guess. Say, when does she start to sing? I'll bet she's pretty good."

"In about an hour and a half. There won't be many people here until then." The bartender took the girl's drink into the dining room, returned.

"Is that piano in tune?" the detective asked. "Reason I want to know is that I used to play and sing a little in a couple of clubs in Buffalo and Rochester. Maybe I could do a song or two now, while the place is empty. If the boss heard me he might take me on. I'd like to get a job in New York."

"I'm the boss here," was the answer, "and I'm not thinking about hiring anybody. Billie's good enough for us. But go ahead, if you want to. I'll tell you how bad you stink."

The piano faced so that Grallio could watch the three diners. They gave him a quick glance as he ran his fingers over the keys, expertly playing a few chords from "Clair de Lune," and then improvising a musical bridge which he followed into "Let Me Call You Sweetheart." He played it through to the end, then picked up the melody of the chorus and began to sing, softly but in a clear true tenor ". . . for I'm in love with you." A wide smile crossed his handsome face as he tilted his head back and went on. "It says here that I'm falling in love with you."

Billie gave him a quick smile, the bartender nodded approval, Cookie and Herman continued eating without paying any attention to the performance. "I will take you home, Kathleen," he began to sing, and when he had finished the ballad he started another.

> "In Dublin's fair city, where girls are so pretty,
> It was there that I first met sweet Molly Malone."

There was an immediate reaction—the reaction that Tony had been hoping for when he first had the idea of playing and singing to the small audience. Cookie and Herman stopped eating, set their knives and forks down carefully, and looked at each other. Tension rolled into the room like a fog.

"She pushed a wheelbarrow through streets wide and narrow. . . ."

Cookie came over to the stage, placed his hand on the end of the keyboard. "Why don't you shut up and go back to the bar, mister? You're bothering me and my friends."

"I like to play the piano, cousin. What bothers you, the playing or the particular selection?"

"I just said it bothers me, that's all. I don't have to spell it out." The words were soft, but there was nothing soft in Cookie's eyes.

"How would you like to go to hell?" Tony asked, and picked up the theme of his interrupted song.

"Singing, 'Cockles and muss— . . .'"

Cookie's heavy hand banged down discordantly on the bass keys, bringing the music to an abrupt end. At the same time he grabbed Grallio's coat, pulling the detective toward him.

The result of his impetuous action surprised him. Tony struck him squarely on the jaw and knocked him sprawling into a table. Cookie crashed against the chairs and fell heavily to the floor.

"Alive o-o-o-oh!"

Herman and the bartender reached Tony at the same time. "I'll kill you," he heard the former hiss, while the latter, an empty beer bottle in his hand, said, "That's enough trouble, buddy. You sing well, but you better sing somewhere else. Go away, Herman, I'll take care of this. Get out, Buffalo, and be quick about it." The empty bottle moved threateningly.

"Okay, okay. I just didn't like what that guy said, that's all."

Tony started for the door. "I was singing all right. I don't see what he had to get sore about."

"And don't come back!" the bartender shouted.

The door slammed shut behind him, and Detective Tony Grallio rubbed his knuckles reflectively as he walked away, smiling to himself.

"Hey, Charlie." He shook his sleeping partner. "Those guys don't even like *Molly* Malone. They're mad at the whole family."

IX.

I WAS HAVING a drink with Charlie Hess the next day. "So," I said, when he had told me Tony's story, "Cookie wanted to know if something was the 'day after tomorrow' and, whatever it was, Muddy didn't know about it. That's probably the big shipment of stuff Muddy has been expecting for some time. Far as I can figure, Herman's job is to make arrangements and pick it up. I don't know what Cookie does—and I don't like to guess."

Charlie and I were sitting together in a little saloon over on Eighth Avenue. I had had another pretty good day, so far as business was concerned, with a couple of hundred dollars in the pocket of my new suit. Hess had told me I was to keep it. Stratford had said I might as well let the crooks I was working with pay their own funeral expenses, and give the Mayor just that much less to worry about when he tried to balance the city budget.

The Inspector hadn't been too pleased, though, that Tony had taken a poke at Cookie. It fingered him, but good, as far as any future work on the case was concerned. "That was a bonehead play, Grallio," he had frowned. "And I don't know what

the hell to do with you now. Malone and Hess will have to carry on by themselves for a while. Lucky they're close enough to the finish line so they can do it alone. You come in here tomorrow morning. By that time I may be able to figure out something new for you. Kids are swiping bubble gum from each other in some of the public schools, I hear—that ought to be a good job."

According to Charlie Hess, Tony just sat there and took it. "On second thought," Stratford had continued, "maybe you can still do something on this case. See what you can find out about that girl—Billie Bloomer. There may be an interesting angle there."

"I told him it sounded as though there were more curves than angles," Hess laughed to me, "and Stratford threw us the hell out of the office. And that's the whole story as we know it. They live up on East Ninetieth Street, they seem to travel together, they hang out at Sophie's Place, Billie Bloomer is Herman's girl, he feds her dope, and they don't like Molly Malone. What are you going to do now?"

"Go back to Rivington Street and see what's going on."

"Well, take it easy. You leave here first and I'll make sure there isn't a tail on you."

I worked my way back and forth across town a couple of times and ended up at Muddy Track's place. Ciro Valentino, Cookie, and Herman were there too, and I gave them the big hello. Much to my surprise, Herman warmed up, a little. Maybe it was because he hadn't found anything when he had searched my room; maybe it was just a trap. I never knew.

"Muddy tells me you're doing pretty good, Murphy," he volunteered. "And that's a pretty snappy outfit you're wearing."

"Thanks. I'm not doing too bad for a growing boy," I allowed. "Hope we've got a good supply on hand. Got a couple of leads today that ought to pan out all right. Bought a couple a bear traps, too, to stick inside my room just in case some bears come sneaking around when I'm out."

"You hear that, Cookie?" he laughed. "Be careful if you drop in on Murphy or you'll lose a leg."

"I used to go hunting in the forest near our place when I was a kid," Cookie said. "I'll be careful."

"Where was that?" I asked. "Europe?"

"It wasn't Peru, Murphy, I'll say that much. Have a drink. You know where the glasses are."

So Cookie had lived near a forest—not a woods—when he was a kid. That was interesting. I got myself a glass.

"Pull up a chair, Murphy," Track said. "We've got business to talk about tonight. Do you still have those lousy clothes you were wearing before you got that new suit, or did you burn 'em?"

"They're still up at my place. Why?"

"Put them on tomorrow night. You'll be able to use them. Tell him the rest, Herman."

"We've got a nice little deal all arranged, Murphy. Couple of kilos of pure heroin, and I mean pure. It'll be worth a million dollars to us when we get it and cut it down. It came in from Turkey this morning, and right now it's on a ship over on the Hudson River. I talked to the guy on the phone, but he's scared to try to bring it across the dock."

"I don't blame him," I said. "From what I read in the papers they're keeping a pretty good watch on the docks. A flock of guys have been picked up in the last month."

Herman wasn't kidding when he said two kilos—that's about sixty-six ounces—of pure heroin would be worth a million bucks. You can cut one ounce to twenty, and each of those twenty makes five hundred capsules, and a capsule sells for at least two dollars. This wasn't a kids' game.

"Yeah," Herman went on. "That's the trouble. But this guy's pretty smart. He's been on this ship for a long time, and I've known him for about twenty years, and he's never been caught yet. The way it's going to work is like this. Some workmen have been doing some work around the end of the dock. They've got a little rowboat that they keep tied up at one end of the pier, though, and that end ain't guarded. Tomorrow night this boat-swain I know is going to slip off the ship over the stern, get in the rowboat, and drift down the river. You know that place where they keep the fireboat, down at the end of Thirteenth Street?"

"I got an idea where it is."

"It's where all those markets are, the West Washington Market, they call it, where they bring in lettuce and stuff."

"You mean the old chicken market."

"Maybe that's what they used to call it. It's below the Cunard docks. Anyhow, this fellow is going to drift down there, past the fireboat docks, until he comes to that long pier where people are always fishing in the summer. He'll have the stuff in a tin can with a strong string tied to it, and the first chance he gets he'll tie the other end of the string to the dock."

"And what do I do?"

"You're sitting on the end of the dock, fishing," Muddy chimed in. "Looking like a bum, looking hungry, and fishing. If any strangers come along you either get rid of them or else, when the boat shows up, you give him the sign and he goes away and comes back the next night."

"That's a hell of a place to sit alone at night trying to catch fish," I objected.

"You won't be alone, Murphy," Herman continued. "I'll be there. Cookie will be there. Valentino will be there. The way we plan it now, Val has his car parked on the street, and he's in it. Cookie is sitting in the market. A guy we know has let him in earlier. Cookie keeps his eye out the window to make sure there's nobody around we don't like."

"And what do you do?"

"I'll be there. Don't be surprised when you see me."

"And when do I start fishing?"

"Along about nine o'clock. Keep on fishing until midnight. Now let's play some cards for a while. I got a date later on."

We played a couple of hands of poker and had some more drinks. Came a time when Cookie and I dropped out early on the same hand. "You get home okay the other night?" I asked.

"Yeah, but I had a big head the next day." He held his hands out about a foot from his ears.

"You got some soot or something on your chin now." The bruise that Tony's fist had made showed up plainly in the light.

"That's not soot," Cookie admitted. "Some wise dago sneaked in a punch while I wasn't looking over at Sophie's last night. Damn near busted my jaw."

"Yeah? What did you do to him?"

"I didn't do much of anything." He smiled painfully and fingered his chin. "When I crawled out from under the table where I had landed, the guy was gone."

I laughed. "What did he hit you for?"

73

"He was singing a song I don't like."

"What song's that?"

"That goddamned Molly Malone thing."

"Hell, Cookie, that's a good Irish song," I said. "What's the matter, don't you like Irishmen?"

"Some I do, some I don't. One time . . ."

Herman won the hand. As he raked in the pile of quarters and dimes he looked up and interrupted whatever Cookie was going to tell me. "I don't think any of us should be going over to Sophie's for a while. I don't like that act last night. The more I think about it, the less I like it."

"Nuts, Herman," his friend told him. "You're too damned cautious."

"That's the way I've managed to keep alive. When something out of the ordinary happens where I am, I leave—if I can. We're leaving Sophie's."

"Maybe you are. But I've shot myself out of a couple of spots and I can do it again. And anyhow, what about Billie?"

"Billie will be all right. She can take care of herself."

"Until quitting time. I know who will take care of her after that." Cookie laughed loudly at his own joke. "Give me two cards."

It got to be about three.

There wasn't any work for me the next day so I took in a couple of movies, ate a big dinner that evening, and at eight o'clock I was changed into my old clothes and walking across town. There was a piece of fishline in my pocket, together with a couple of hooks, a hunk of cork, and some ends of bacon rind for bait.

Nine o'clock found me sitting on the end of the dock, fishing and having fun doing it. There weren't many other people around. About ten minutes after I got there a car drove down and parked, with its lights out, but nobody got out. I figured there was a pair of lovers in it who wanted to be alone, so I lit a cigarette, whistled, and finally took my fishing line around where they were and started fishing there. Pretty soon they got tired of having me for an audience and moved off. I felt like a heel, interrupting love's young dream, though from what I heard they weren't dreaming. If I had been the guy in the car I would have been sore as hell.

74

Just before a clock somewhere in the distance struck ten, I caught a fish. It was a dismal little thing, about seven inches long and without much flesh on its bones. I took it off the hook and threw it on the dock to prove that I really had been fishing.

Then some kids came along—you can see I wasn't lonely and didn't lack company. Kids at night in New York can be friendly or they can be vicious little beasts, just as likely to knock you over the head as not.

These were undecided. There were five of them wandering around town at night looking for something to steal. I watched them out of one corner of my eye as they came down the dock, and hoped I wouldn't have any trouble with them.

"You won't catch any fish here," one of them volunteered, after they had studied me for a while.

I picked up the one from the dock. It wriggled feebly.

"That's no good to eat," another kid told me. "They're poison." He threw a handful of gravel into the water.

"Knock it off," I ordered. "What are you trying to do, scare all the fish away?"

"Aw, go to hell," the first one growled. "We'll throw all the stuff we want to in the water. You don't own it."

"Not if I blow this whistle and get a cop down here you won't." I stuck my hand in my pocket. "I know what you kids are doing, you're swiping stuff and breaking windows. I heard you."

"Who's afraid of cops?" he challenged. "They can't catch anybody." Nevertheless, they began to edge away from me, and pretty soon they were gone, leaving me alone again. The lights on a barge moored to the next pier blinked out and I went back to my fishing, undisturbed by anything except the gentle noises made by little waves rolling in from ships going up and down the river.

It must have been about eleven-thirty when I saw something black floating on the dark water. Slowly it moved in toward me until I recognized it as a man in a small boat. I lit a cigarette to give a spot of light that the rower could use as a beacon. In a few minutes the boat was bobbing against the pilings. The rower threw a piece of line around a mooring bitt, steadied himself carefully, and looked up at me.

"Got a match, buddy?" he asked. "Mine got wet."

"Sure." I reached down and handed him a paper of safety matches. "Keep 'em. I got more."

"Thanks. How's your fishing tonight? Catching much?"

"I caught one a little while ago. I may get a big one later."

"You will." The stranger released his mooring line, not from the bitt on the dock but from a cleat on the gunwale of his own small craft, shoved out into the tide, and rowed softly away. The line trailed back to the dock for a while, then it went slack from his end and settled under the dirty Hudson, all except the short length that stretched from the dock to the water's edge.

In a little while I heard footsteps behind me, and a tall figure appeared through the darkness. It was Herman. "Any luck?" he asked.

"There may be something on the end of the line now, but I haven't pulled it in."

"When did you catch it?"

"Little while ago."

Herman produced a tin can tied to a heavy string. "Live bait," he commented as he threw it into the water and fastened the free end of the string to another bitt on the dock. "Are you sure it was the right man?" he asked, sitting down beside me.

"He said his matches were wet."

"Guess it's all right, then. But you know, Murphy, you can't always be sure about things like that. You don't know who he was. You don't even know who I am. I don't know for sure who you are, do I?"

I hoped he didn't know who I was. "You ought to have a pretty good line on me by now," I said. "After going through my room the other night."

He lit a cigarette. "How did you know about that?"

"Somebody left fingerprints on the gun in my coat pocket. I had wiped it clean when I put it there."

"Yeah?" He drew away a little. "How did you know they were mine?"

"I didn't. I just knew they weren't mine, and guessed the rest."

"You guess too damned well, Murphy." He took three or four long drags on his cigarette before he said anything else. "How long do you guess a man could last in the river tonight?"

"Half an hour. Why?"

76

"You're crazy as hell. Two minutes, maybe. After that they could stick you in a furnace or stack you between half a dozen hot blondes and you'd never thaw out. That water's cold."

"I could yell loud enough to get that fireboat down here in less than two minutes."

"Yeah." He flipped the cigarette butt into the water. "You probably could."

Believe me, my feet were wedged against some timbers at the end of the dock. It would have taken a good shove to get me into the water.

"I don't think you're going to catch anything else tonight," he continued. "Why don't you go home and let me fish a while?"

"All right." I knew he would wait there until he figured the city was sound asleep, then he would pull up the line the boatman had left behind, retrieve the can of heroin at the end of it, and the night's business would be over. The fish I caught went back in the water, and I started the long walk back to Second Avenue alone.

The ancient brick buildings of the market houses were as cold as old mausoleums when I passed them, and it was hard to keep from shivering when I walked down the centers of the narrow alleys. There was no traffic on West Street, under the elevated highway. A few lights gleamed in the windows of an all-night diner on the corner, and a fat little man came out of a dark building on Gansevoort Street and lost himself in the shadows there while I walked up to Fourteenth Street with its welcome lights and neon signs. I wondered if I had passed the window where Cookie was watching, and whether he had been holding his gun on me as I walked by.

On the way across Fourteenth I got to thinking about Mary Kieran, and how long it had been since I had seen her. Certainly she couldn't object to my appearance now that I had new clothes and all the outward signs of prosperity. For a moment, there on the corner of Seventh Avenue, I was tempted to walk down to St. Anthony's Hospital on the chance that she was still up. A stray wind which had passed by a fish market changed my mind. Mary wouldn't welcome me with open arms, smelling as I did of fish. Anyhow, it was long after midnight and no time to go calling on a girl, no matter how much I wanted to see her.

The hair on my door was loose when I got home. I knocked softly. No answer. "Hey," I whispered. "Hey, did he come in yet?"

There wasn't anybody there. There wasn't even a sign that anybody had been there, except the unstuck hair.

The next afternoon, about three, the gang met at the place in Rivington Street. I got there first, to find Muddy with his feet on the table, a big cigar in his mouth, looking pleased with the world.

"It went off without a hitch, Johnny, without a hitch," he exclaimed. "Herman brought it in late last night. We're in the money, I'm telling you, in the money. We've got a million dollars' worth of stuff here, easy. Oh, that Herman, he's a honey. With his connections and my brains we're all going to be rich."

"Who the hell is Herman, anyhow?" I asked. "And who is Cookie? That Herman's a smart operator. Last night went off like clockwork. But I never heard of either of them around town. What're their names?"

Muddy looked at me. "They're pretty new in town, Johnny. Cookie came to me a couple of months ago. Said he had been in Mexico where he had known another guy from Scabby Ruble's mob who was still hiding out from the Treasury Department men. Maybe he did, I don't know. Anyhow, he knew where to find me. I was just about out of business materials, you might say, and I told him so. The next day he came back with Herman, and they had about half a kilo of heroin with them. That was enough to keep me and Val going, and Herman said he could get more."

"They surely know their way around town for a couple of strangers."

"Yeah, they do. Maybe they've been here before, for all you know. Me, I wouldn't ask too many questions. They had it, I know where to sell it, now we all work together."

"What's their last names?"

"Cookie's name is Adler. Herman says his is Holman. I wouldn't know for sure. Herman and Cookie are good enough for me, I don't pay them by check." Footsteps sounded outside. "Here they come now."

Herman and Cookie came in without knocking, and Herman came directly to the point. "Is it ready?" he asked.

"It sure is." Muddy got up and went into another room, came back with a cardboard box that said "Post Toasties" on the side. "Here you are—twenty grand, and if you're paying more than ten I don't think you're so smart. Want to count it now?"

"Stick it in the closet, Cookie," Herman ordered. "We'll count it later. And it better all be there."

X.

CIRO VALENTINO came in a few minutes later, and then Muddy gave him and Cookie and me a thousand bucks a piece for our work the night before. We sat around shooting the breeze and drinking for a couple of hours. Finally, about seven o'clock, somebody suggested going out to eat. "No," said Herman. "That's not a good idea right now. No use for all of us to be together where people can see us until I finish my job."

"What's that?" I asked.

"I got to see the guy who was in the boat last night, Johnny," Herman answered. "I'm supposed to meet him later tonight and give him his cut. But there's always the chance the harbor police or the Coast Guard or somebody picked him up. If they did, and if he talked, then maybe we shouldn't all be together out in the open."

"That makes sense to me." I didn't want to go out and eat with them anyhow, and felt much happier when the party broke up and we all left, one by one.

As soon as I was clear of the place I ducked into a phone booth and called Mary. "Hello," I said. "This is Johnny. Remember me?"

"Johnny!" It sounded as though she *did* remember me, and had forgotten how sore she was the last time I had seen her.

"Where have you been? I was wondering whether you had forgotten all about me."

Her voice made me feel all nice and warm inside. "Have you had dinner yet?" I asked.

"No."

"Neither have I, and I'm hungry enough to eat a raw horse. Are you off duty tonight?"

"Yes."

"Well, let's have dinner together. I'm wearing a new suit, and I don't need a shave. Let's go somewhere special."

"That would be fun, Johnny. When can you get here?"

"Well, I don't know. I don't particularly want to come over to that section of town right now, because I'm still on a case. How about meeting me up in the lobby of the Hotel Pennsylvania?"

"All right. How soon will you be there? I'll have to change my clothes."

"I'll be there when you get there, darling. And hurry."

"I'm coming as fast as I can, Johnny. Goodby."

I walked up Delancey Street whistling "Eileen Oge," and just as I started down the subway steps Cookie came up behind me. "Hello, Murphy," he said. "Going some place?"

"Yeah. Where are you going?" I was as glad to see him as I would have been to catch smallpox.

"Up to Fourteenth Street. Where are you going?"

"Up to the Garden to catch the fights," I improvised.

"That's funny," he said. "I thought there was a basketball game in the Garden tonight."

"For someone who hasn't been in New York too long, chum, you certainly seem to know your way around. What's the idea of following me this time?"

"I'm not following you, Murphy. What makes you think I am? Should I be following you for some reason or other?"

We were walking along the subway platform, threading our way in and out among the fair-sized crowd, and just as the train came roaring in Cookie lurched heavily against me. For a moment I teetered on the edge of the platform and almost fell under the first car. But somehow or other, and I'll never know how I managed it, I grabbed him by his sleeve and pulled myself back to safety.

I was ready to kill him with my bare hands, but the expression on his face stopped me. He turned and began to curse a stupid-looking woman. "You goddamned dumb cow! I almost knocked my buddy under the train!"

The woman didn't say anything, just turned white and stood there.

"Come on," I said. "Let's get in the car. I'll feel safer there."

He apologized over and over again, until he got off at Fourteenth Street. I rode up to Fiftieth Street, then doubled back to Thirty-fourth and walked over to the Pennsylvania Hotel. And I never found out whether Cookie had tried to shove me under the train or whether it was an accident. Maybe that dame had bumped him and pushed him against me. But I wasn't very happy about the whole thing.

Mary and I had dinner in the Cafe Rouge, and she was the prettiest person there, in a blue dress with a wide, swishing skirt and a low neckline that came down to the soft hollow between her full young breasts. Dick Jurgen's Orchestra was playing, and we danced without realizing time could go by so quickly.

Once, between dances, she looked at me. "Happy tonight, Johnny?" she asked.

"You know I am, Mary." My hand reached across the table for hers. "Happier than I have been for a long, long time."

"But there's something wrong, somewhere, isn't there?"

"Not a thing."

"Yes, there is. You're worried about something." Then, as she noticed my bewildered expression, "I don't mean about us, Johnny. I don't think anything's going to go wrong there again. But what is it? Is it the case you're working on?"

"Maybe," I admitted. "It's a dope ring, and dope's a horrible thing, enough to worry anybody. It'll be wrapped up in a week or so, I hope. Don't tell that to anybody—some of your best friends may be hopheads." I forced a little laugh. "There goes the music again, let's dance."

Hoffmann and Cookie and dope and the dirty grocer on Sixty-first Street faded from my mind as I held Mary close in my arms on the dance floor. But when the clock struck twelve she thought, like Cinderella, that she should be getting home.

We rode down to her place in a taxi and I kissed her good

night before we got out, because there wasn't any sense in my standing around in Village doorways where I might be seen. For all I knew Herman was going to meet his boating friend somewhere down there, and I didn't want him to think I was following them. But the street was clear when the taxi pulled up at Mary's door, so I ducked out and took her across the sidewalk, jumped back in the cab, rode over to the corner of University Place, got out, and walked the rest of the way to my room.

Nobody had been fooling around the door this time.

I had an appointment to meet Muddy at ten in the morning, so I was up and having breakfast and reading a tabloid before nine. Suddenly a short item caught my eye.

MURDER SUSPECTED IN SEAMAN'S DEATH

Boatswain Peter Arranto, whose body was found in a hallway on West Eighteenth Street at 3:30 this morning, was murdered, according to information from the Homicide Squad. The dead man, who was identified as a member of the crew of the *SS San Stefano,* which arrived in New York from the Mediterranean three days ago, had been stabbed in the back of the neck, according to the police.

There was more to the story than that, but I didn't need to read any further. In a few seconds I was in a phone booth and talking to Inspector Stratford. "About this guy Peter Arranto that was found on West Eighteenth, Chief—when did he get killed?"

"About eleven o'clock last night, as near as we can figure."

"What killed him?"

"Somebody stabbed him in the back of the neck, right at the bottom of his skull, straight through his spinal column."

"What with?"

"That's a funny thing. The medico says he never saw a wound like it before. Must have been made by a smooth spike of some kind, about three inches long. Not an ice pick, though, it's a little bigger than that. About as big around as a pencil at the thick end. Why? Do you know something about it?"

"Not a thing, Chief. Not a thing," I lied. "I thought maybe

I did, but from what you tell me I must have been wrong. Did Tony find out anything about that girl?"

"He says she's a hophead and a nymphomaniac—and he had a hell of a time finding out that she uses dope." The Inspector laughed. "He picked her up as she was coming out of Sophie's the night before last."

"Tell him to look out. That's all."

I shouldn't have lied to Stratford. When he described the hole in the dead man's neck, I knew who had struck him. It was Herman, with his spiked knife. And the dead man had been the guy who rowed the boat and bummed my matches. And Herman was in twenty thousand dollars.

But if I had told Stratford he would have picked Herman up, busted the gang, and I might never have found out who and where Rudy Hoffmann was.

That's what I thought.

Muddy kept me waiting almost half an hour, but we finally made our contact. This time I found myself with a candy box to deliver, and when I saw the note with it I whistled in spite of myself. Business *was* picking up. The address impressed me so much I stopped and had my shoes shined before I hailed a taxi and gave the Park Avenue number.

A doorman wearing a uniform that would have shamed a five-star admiral in the Balkan Navy opened the taxi door, and I tipped him a dollar before I entered the imposing lobby of the apartment house. Another flunky, who must have been at least a three-star Balkan admiral, greeted me with an "I-smell-horse-manure" expression and finally condescended to ask me whom I wanted to see.

"The Countess de Callene."

"And whom shall I say is calling, please?" he whined through his thin nose. I felt like giving him a poke in his frozen face. He pushed a little gold button and picked up a white telephone.

"Tell her it's Murphy."

Something clicked in the phone, and frozen-face stuck his nose in the mouthpiece. "A Mr. Murphy to see the Countess. Thank you." He fondled the phone in its holder. "Elevator number four to Suite Forty-seven, *Mister* Murphy."

What I guess you call a French maid—at least, she was wearing black stockings and spoke with an accent—opened the door of Suite Forty-seven when I rang the bell.

"Wait a meeneet, please," she told me, and disappeared. "Thees way, monsieur," she said when she came back, and I followed her through a hallway that was papered with black-and-red stripes and had a black rug on the floor. White-framed pictures that I couldn't make head or tail of—they looked like someone had thrown paint at them without caring whether it stuck or not—hung all over the walls.

Finally we came to a pair of doors and the maid knocked. From somewhere on the other side came a husky "Come in." The maid pushed the doors open and announced, "Monsieur Murphee."

"Come in, Mr. Murphy," said the same husky voice. "You may go, Marie. I'll ring when I want you again."

Now just because I'm an orphan and a cop and was brought up the hard way in New York doesn't say that I've never been around. I've seen a lot of swell layouts—tony gambling rooms and hundred-dollar-a-night cat houses, and when I was in France during the war I went through some of those old places the French kings used to build to keep their girl friends in. But I never walked into a room like that one. It must have taken up a quarter of one floor of the whole building. The ceiling was at least thirty feet high. And glass—my God, there were mirrors all over the place, and crystal jugs and other glass stuff on the tables and shelves. One whole side of the room was windows. Heavy draperies kept out most of the light, but there were a couple of lamps here and there. The walls were colored kind of a pinkish gold, a soft color like the complexions of some of the good-looking high-yellow girls you see in Harlem night-clubs.

The furniture was gold and pink, and the biggest thing in the room was a couch, about twelve feet long and stacked with golden pillows, over in one corner about a half mile from the door. I didn't see a soul in the place.

"You have something for me, Mr. Murphy?" the same husky voice asked, and by looking for it I discovered there was some-body stretched out on one end of the couch. I started that way.

The Countess de Callene was lying flat on her stomach on the long sofa, tanning herself under an ultraviolet light, and she didn't have a stitch of clothes on. She was about twenty-eight, I'd say, and her skin was soft and firm and dark gold in color from the tips of her toes up over her rounded buttocks and her shoulders to where a cascade of light brown hair fell across one arm. The ultraviolet light made her face look green where it reflected from her make-up.

"Pardon my informal attire, Murphy. Is that padding in your coat, or are your shoulders really that broad? How much do you weigh?" She raised up on her elbows to look at me.

"About two hundred pounds, Cou . . . your high. . . ." I was tonguetied.

"Just call me Callie, Murphy, and reach over to that switch and turn off this goddamned light, it makes me look like hell. And throw me that sheet from the end of the bed, will you? I can see in your big blue eyes that you think I'm a loose woman."

When I had done all that, she wrapped the sheet around herself, as well as anyone could, and sat up. "Do you think I'm pretty?" she wanted to know.

Well, she was. For all I could tell, she was a dope taker and a tramp and God knows what, but she looked darned good, sitting there in that room wearing nothing but a sheet, and I told her so. Her red lips opened in a bright smile, showing a row of shining white teeth. "What's your first name, Murphy?"

"John."

"Well, Johnny, darling, why don't you go right over to that table where the bowl of ice is and mix a round of drinks. I'd like a martini, with hardly any vermouth in it. You can have one, too, if you promise to be good."

I stirred a shaker full of about ten-to-one martinis, picked up two glasses, and brought them and the mixer over to the couch, where I filled the glasses, put the shaker on the cocktail table and sat down beside her. "Good morning," I said, lifting my drink.

"This is a game preserve, Johnny," she said, putting her glass down and grabbing me by my ears until I thought they would pull loose from my head. She pressed her mouth up against mine, hot and moist and demanding. I let the glass

85

fall and dug my fingers into the soft flesh just below her armpits, clutching her closer to me and forcing her backward.

She let go the grip on my ears and pulled the sheet between us again, shaking her lips loose. "You better pour yourself another drink, Johnny," the deep voice purred in my ear, "and let me get mine. I need one, I think."

A martini seemed like a poor idea at the time, but I poured myself one and drank it, jolting myself back into a sober state again. That's a funny thing to say, I guess, but that kiss had knocked me off my base, and I didn't care.

"Who sent you up here?" the countess—if she was one—wanted to know.

"Muddy."

"What's his last name?"

"You tell me, Callie."

"His last name's Track, and you know damn well it is, and you've got a Barracini chocolate box, and if I give you ten thousand dollars you'll give it to me, is that right?"

"Yes."

"You'll find the money in that envelope over there on the table, right where the ice was. Go and count it and then stick it in your pocket and come back here and have another drink."

Ten thousand dollars it was, a wad about an inch thick, and nothing smaller than a fifty. "You don't look like you used this stuff," I said as I put the candy box on the table and pocketed the money. "I can tell by your eyes."

"You don't think I'm a goddamned fool, do you? I'm not, any more than I'm a countess. But a girl has to find some way to pay the rent if she wants to live in a layout like this. I know a hell of a lot of bums in this town, Johnny Murphy, and most of them are bored stiff and have more money than they know what to do with, and little Callie Rogers from Brooklyn is going to pry as much of it away from them as she can while she still has her health."

"Were you born in Brooklyn?" I asked. "So was I."

"That makes us practically cousins, so we can't get married. All our children would be idiots, or Ptolemies, or born with two heads, I can't stand two-headed kids. Come over here and have another martini."

This time, when I saw her put her empty glass on the table,

I put mine down, too. And what do you think she had in mind as she dropped the sheet again and put her hands up behind my head?

That's right—she thought she was going to get all that heroin for less than ten grand. Keep away from the fire, Johnny, I said to myself, or you're going to get a bad burn.

And when I left I still had the Countess de Callene's ten thousand dollars in my pocket, and felt quite up to snooting the inside doorman when I got out of the elevator and walked through the lobby.

XI.

A BOTTLE of whiskey sat on the table in front of Herman, but it was only half full, and I hadn't been in Muddy Track's place more than twenty minutes before it was empty and Herman had stepped into one of the back rooms and returned with a full one. Cookie and Muddy and I had one drink to start the evening, and another to help it along, but Herman was slugging them away one after another.

Muddy wanted to hear about the Countess de Callene, and I told him as much as I wanted him to know and forked over his share of the ten grand. He peeled off some of the bills and tossed them to Herman, who stuck them in his pocket and kept on drinking.

"Herman's contact," Track explained to me. "I don't know where he found her."

"Guy that brought the big load over told me about her," Herman said. "He had been bringing it in for her, too. I told him we would take care of her deliveries. Then I called her and explained that from now on she was to deal with Muddy."

"How did the guy like that?" I asked.

"Not much." He took his rigger's knife out of his pocket and opened the spike. Something at the base caught his eye and he scraped it loose with his thumbnail, smiling to himself. Then he started cleaning his fingernails, just like he had done the first time I ever met him.

"I thought maybe one of you guys had met her in Brooklyn. She comes from there, she told me. Her name's really Rogers. She's no more a countess than I am."

"How old did you say she is?" Cookie said.

"About twenty-eight, I'd guess."

."Naw. Too young," Herman said.

"I wouldn't know her either," added Cookie. "You ain't a Brooklyn boy, are you, Johnny?"

Before I could answer Ciro Valentino came in with a copy of the *Daily News* under his arm and a nasty look on his face. He pulled a thick wallet from inside his coat, counted out some money, and gave it to Muddy. Then he looked straight at Herman.

"You stupid bastard!" The rest of us sat up a little straighter in our chairs. "You dumb mucker! You don't have any more brains than a wet duck!" He threw the copy of the *News* on the table. "What the hell are you trying to do, Holman, queer us all? You didn't have to kill the guy, did you? And don't move your hands, Cookie. I'm faster than you are."

I glanced at the paper and saw it was open to the story about Peter Arranto. Muddy saw it, too. He picked up the paper and read while Valentino stood there, rocking slowly on the balls of his feet. Herman didn't even glance up from his finger-nails. Cookie placed his hands on the table, one on either side of his drink, and slowly patted the glass with his fingers.

Finally Muddy spoke. "Sit down, Ciro. Have a drink and cool off." Then, to Herman, "You didn't have to kill Pete, did you?"

"I told you he was running some deals of his own, didn't I? You don't want every bum who comes in here starting in business for himself, do you?" There wasn't any answer. "If you do, you're all a bunch of goddamned fools, that's all I have to say!"

Still nobody said anything. Val kept rocking. Cookie kept petting his glass.

Herman gulped a quarter of a tumbler of whiskey. "All

right, you bastards, say something! Sure, I killed him. He's not the first one, and he won't be the last! What if I did? I'll run my end of this business any way I damn please, and if you Christers don't like it Cookie and me will get out! What do you have to say to that?" he shouted. "Say something! Go ahead, say it!" He looked widely around the room until his eyes fixed on something by the door. Then he threw his hand back with a quick motion, threw his knife so that it whirled around and around and finally ended up impaling the spider that had ventured onto the door frame, ten feet away.

"Get the knife, Cookie," he ordered, "while I listen to what these *verdammte Schweine* have to say." Cookie walked over to the door and got the knife, wiped the spider off against the seat of his pants, and came back to his chair.

"Calm down, Herman. Take it easy." Muddy Track relit the dead cigar in his mouth. "Nobody said anything about busting up the gang. Only thing is that we're all doing so well now that it would be a shame if we had to lay off for a while. You sure you didn't leave anything behind? Nobody saw you?"

"Muddy." Herman sounded as though he were explaining something to a child. "Nobody saw anything. I didn't leave my calling card. I was wearing gloves. I've done the big job before, you don't need to worry about me. Just tell me, do you want me to keep on working with you or do you want me to scram?"

"I don't know what anyone else thinks," I said, "but as long as you can dig up countesses for me to visit you can rub out a new guy every day."

"You got sense, Murphy," he acknowledged. "Anybody else got anything to say?"

"I say we better all keep our eyes open for a couple of weeks," Muddy said, "until we're sure the cops don't tie this thing together. Just regular customers for a while. Nobody new. Is that all right with everybody?"

You had to hand it to Muddy, he knew what to say and how to say it, and I could feel the tension die down. Cookie picked up his glass; Ciro sat down, reached for the bottle, and poured a round for everybody. Nothing more was said about the late Peter Arranto while we sat there for an hour, talking and drinking. After a while the conversation came around to people who had so much money they didn't know what to do with it, like the customers the Countess had told me about, and I had to retell my story for Valentino's benefit. "She was a good-looking thing," I said, "with that sun-tan and those beautiful . . ."

"Do you think she's home now?" Herman interrupted. His voice was a little thick, and I realized he was beginning to get tight. It wasn't surprising, he had been drinking steadily, and nobody can keep it up forever without showing it.

"Why?"

"I'll go up and see her now. I just feel like having something like that around right now." The pupils of his eyes narrowed, reflecting tiny pinpoints of light, and a vein began to throb in his temple. "Let's go see her, Johnny, you and me. Huh?"

"Nuts," I said. "Let's not. Anyhow, she drinks martinis and it isn't good to mix whiskey with gin, you know that."

But the little vein kept throbbing there on the side of Herman's head. He was thinking about women, any woman, a woman stretched out under a sun lamp, and the idea was beginning to get him.

I knew a guy once who wrote stories for magazines, and every time he sold one he would get out a big Buick roadster he owned, put the top down, and drive from New York to Pittsburgh and back just as fast as he could go. He got a bang out of selling the story, but he had to pile a bigger bang on top of it. The way he did it was to drive ninety miles an hour.

There was another case I read about that happened somewhere in France. A man was nuts about women. He'd meet some girl and start courting her. Finally he would propose, be accepted, and marry her. Then, every time, right after the wedding night he'd cut his bride's throat. He had to kill the girl to bring the whole thing to a perfect climax, as far as he was concerned.

The same kind of a thing was happening to Herman. He had killed a man, and killing gave him such a kick that he couldn't stop there. So he started drinking heavily to keep the kick going, and when alcohol began to let him down he wanted a woman.

"I'm going over and get Billie. Got to have Billie. Get a big kick out of Billie," he mumbled. "Big kick. Won't give

90

her any dope 'till mornin'. Jus' promise. Get a big kick out of Billie," He lurched to his feet.

Cookie stood up, too. "Wait a minute, Herman. You said we shouldn't go over to Sophie's for a while. Remember? That big wop that was playing the piano the other night, remember him? You said to stay away."

"Th' hell with him. Stick 'im inna head with m' knife. Gotta see Billie."

"Wait until the show's finished, Herman. You can see her then."

The crafty, silly look that drunks get came over Herman's face. "Gotta eat, though, don't I? Can't go hungry. Can't drink on an empty stomach. Bes' place to eat is Sophie's. Come on, le's go over to Sophie's an' have a little bite to eat. Only kiddin' about Billie, just want a little bite to eat."

"You can eat at a thousand other places besides Sophie's," Muddy volunteered.

"No good. Going to Sophie's. Everybody come with me and we have a big party. Wunnerful party. Throwin' wunnerful party at Sophie's." He staggered into the next room.

"What about it?" I asked. "How long before he falls over on his face?"

"About an hour," Cookie told me. "I've seen him like this a couple of times before. Then he'll sleep for another hour, and when he wakes up you'd never know he had a drink."

"He won't stay here for an hour, will he?"

"No, he's set for Sophie's and Billie now. I better go along with him."

"You better all go with him," Muddy suggested. "I don't want him to pass out and get picked up by any cops. Go over to Sophie's with him, give him some more drinks, keep your eyes on him all the time. When he goes to sleep let him sleep, and when he wakes up turn him over to his girlfriend and let her take him home."

Herman weaved back into the room with his hat in his hand. "Wait a minute," we told him. "We're going with you."

Muddy stayed home, but the rest of us piled into Ciro's car and drove across town to Sophie's place.

The fresh air seemed to sober Herman a little. He was steadier when he got out of the car, and led the way evenly down the steps to the club's entrance. The bartender nodded a greeting, and we went through the dining room to a corner table and sat down. Herman called a waiter.

"Where's Billie?" he wanted to know.

"She's out in the john."

"Tell her to come in and have a drink with us. Pull up a chair for her and bring us something to drink." He fished in his pocket, came out with a handful of money, dumped it on the table. "Give everybody a drink!"

There must have been better than a thousand dollars in the pile, but it wasn't there long. Ciro grabbed it as fast as I had seen him grab his gun, and had the money out of sight. "You goddamned fool! What the hell are you trying to do, get every crook and cop in the Village in here after us? Put the money away."

"Hello, Cookie. Hello, Herman, honey." A musical voice came over my shoulder and I turned to find myself looking down inside some female's dress, all the way to her navel. From Tony Grallio's description I knew it must be Billie Bloomer, and after I got my head twisted around I saw that she was leaning over and kissing Herman. Across the table from me Valentino smiled and winked.

She sat down and snuggled up to Herman, running her fingers across his hand. Finally Cookie introduced us all around, a waiter came with a tray of drinks, and Herman tossed his down neat. Billie didn't want any supper. She kept looking at Herman while the rest of us ordered. You could see she was wondering when he was going to slip her the little white powder so she could go out to the ladies' room and dope herself up.

But her boy friend didn't do anything of the kind. The waiter brought some more drinks, and Herman poured his down.

"Sing us a song, Billie," he said. "Sing me a nice li'l song."

"I don't want to sing a song, honey."

"Go sing a song, Billie. Then we'll go home. Gettin' late. Time to go home." His head nodded. "Go sing a song."

Billie went over to the piano, threading her way between the tables filled with people, and began to play a few chords. She had a good voice, but I don't remember what she sang because

I was watching Herman. Slowly his head dropped to the table until it rested on his outstretched arm, and he went to sleep.

"He'll wake up in an hour and feel fine," Cookie prophesied.

Scattered applause marked the end of the song, and Billie came back to the table. "What's wrong with him?"

"He's just a little sleepy. He'll be all right."

"Let me take him out to the back room where he can lie down. I'll take his shoes and his coat off and make him comfortable." You knew she was figuring to go through that coat before she ever took it off, hunting for the junk she needed so badly.

"Don't bother him, Billie. Let him have a little nap. Inside of an hour he'll be a new man. Drink your drink." The waiter arrived with antipasto. "Are you sure you don't want anything to eat?"

She insisted she wasn't hungry, so we started eating while she sat there and took little sips from her glass. Finally she decided to work another angle.

"All you guys in the same racket?" She glanced at Ciro and me.

"Yeah," Cookie told her, "we work together. Why? Looking for another job?"

"No," she said. "I was just thinking about something."

I knew she was wondering whether she could get Ciro or me to give her a capsule of dope. Evidently she knew that Cookie didn't have any with him. I didn't have any on me, and I don't know whether Ciro did or not.

Five musicians came in while we were sitting there, tuned up their saxophones and trumpets, and started hitting out a tune that set my feet tapping on the floor.

"Do you dance, Johnny?" She turned to me.

"Nothing I like better, Billie, and that sounds like music for dancing, if I ever heard it."

"Come on." Her hand grabbed mine. "Dance with me."

We took a few steps before the dance floor filled up with other couples, and as soon as there was a crowd around us that dame gave me the works, but good. She wanted dope, and she wanted it bad, and if I had any she was dead set to get it away from me.

"I've got such a headache, honey," she whispered in my ear,

"and my nerves are all shot. You got anything for nerves, honey?" I felt her fingers tickling the back of my neck and wriggling around my ear.

"Nothing I can give you here, Billie. Too many people around."

"Let's go somewhere else. I can get away." She rounded her lips and blew a thin stream of her hot breath into my ear while she pressed her abdomen against mine. "Come on."

"Aw no," I said. "You're Herman's girl, aren't you? You don't want him to wake up and find us gone, do you?"

"He won't wake up, Johnny." She caught my leg between hers as I took a step backward and threw her weight against the top of my thigh. I almost tripped. "I live just around the corner, honey. We can be back before he wakes up." The soft cushion of her breasts was hot against my chest.

"Maybe he isn't really sleeping," I suggested. "We better not go. I don't want him to get sore at me."

She tried a few more tricks that had me sweating, but it was no dice. Finally the music stopped and we went back to the table and sat down. Cookie and Ciro looked up to greet us, then went back to whatever they had been talking about while Billie and I had been dancing. The bartender came to the table, looked at Herman, and shook his head. "Pardon me, fellows." He turned to Billie. "Tear yourself away, kid. You get paid for singing around here, and the other customers are hollering for you."

Billie stuck her tongue out at him, but she got up and started toward the orchestra. As she left the table her elbow smacked me alongside the head.

"Ouch!" I rubbed the spot she had hit.

Ciro and Cookie dropped their forks and started laughing like hell. "What's so damned funny?" I wanted to know.

"You. Johnny, you." Ciro was laughing so hard he could barely talk. "She's so-o-o sweet to you on the floor, and then she bangs you on the head. Maybe you don't say the right things to her, Johnny. I think Ciro better dance with her the next time."

94

XII.

LIKE THE little girl said—when I dance, Mama, I sweat. And when I've been drinking and dance, I sweat a whole lot of alcohol out of my system. The three of us, Cookie and Valentino and I, had been drinking pretty heavily. We kept on having more drinks during dinner, and after a while Cookie and Val started arguing.

"I don't see how that bum can sleep like that, after sticking a guy in the back with a knife," Valentino muttered, nodding at the still sleeping Herman. "That's a yellow way to do a guy in."

"What do you mean, yellow?" Very deliberately Cookie placed his fork on his plate. "You got enough guts to do it?"

"I got all the guts I need. I don't shiv guys in the back."

"I never heard you had so much guts. You don't have enough to call him yellow to his face, I noticed."

"No? Wake him up, errand boy." Ciro leaned forward. "That's all you are, sonny, an errand boy for a yellow back-stabber. Unless you're in love with him, you dumb queer!"

A red flush started behind Cookie's ears and spread over his face while he wondered whether he could beat Valentino to the draw.

"Not in here, for God's sake," I growled at them. "Do you want the place full of cops? There's probably a detective somewhere in this joint; there usually is in these cellar clubs."

That's the truth, although I was taking a chance on tipping my hand when I said it. But Ciro and Cookie were so sore, and so full of booze, that they probably never noticed it. A shooting wasn't what I wanted, although I knew something was going to break tonight. I felt it in my bones.

Everything so far seemed to point to Cookie being Rudolph

Hoffmann. He had been a merchant sailor for twenty-five years. So had Rudy. Cookie had been near a forest when he was a kid. Hoffmann was born in Meiningen, and that's near the Thuringian Forest. Neither of them had any love for Irishmen named Malone. Cookie had said he wouldn't have known Callie Rogers. Hoffmann wouldn't have known a young kid like that, either.

But I wanted to hear him say that he was gunning for Johnny Malone—and then I wanted to plug him myself.

"Go to hell, you shanty Irish, you," he snarled at me. "You don't need to get in this. Keep out if you want to keep healthy. I've got no quarrel with you, Murphy!"

"Are you sure?" I chanced.

"You don't cheat at cards," was his surprising reply. "You don't know the difference between a ship and a boat."

It stopped me. I couldn't figure it out. "That's the truth," I admitted. "Anyhow, nobody cheats at cards and nobody's yellow and nobody's queer. Let's wake Herman up and go home. We're all tight."

"I'm not tight, Johnny," Ciro said. "I'm not so tight I don't know what people are saying. But you're right, this creep joint is probably full of cops. Call the waiter and let's have another drink."

It's no use arguing with drunks, especially drunks who carry guns, so we had another round of drinks brought to the table. "Now let's forget this crap," I suggested, raising my glass. "Let's shake hands all around. Both of you guys are good guys. Come on, shake."

Well, they finally shook hands, but you could see they didn't mean it. Damn it, if I hadn't been so sure Cookie was Rudolph Hoffmann I would have coaxed them into shooting each other right then and there. It would have saved the city a lot of money.

Herman stirred a little, sat up, rubbed his eyes, and asked for a cigarette. "What did I do, go to sleep?"

"You sure did."

"You guys eat?"

"Finished just a little while ago."

He motioned to the waiter. "Bring me a steak, rare, and a double brandy to go with it." Looking at him, you would never have guessed that he had been drunk an hour before.

"I see you've been dancing with Billie, Johnny."

"How the hell did you know. You were asleep."

"Lipstick on your collar."

"I'll be damned. She's a pretty good dancer, Herman."

"Yeah." He took a taste of the double brandy. "But don't get any cute ideas about her, Murphy. That's mine."

It was a good thing he hadn't seen Billie and me dancing together, and I wondered what he would think if he heard of Tony Grallio's report to Inspector Stratford, but I kept my trap shut. Billie came over, ignored me, and sat down beside him.

"How you feeling, honey?"

"I'm feeling fine, and as soon as I get a good steak inside me we'll be set for the night." The music started again. "How about a dance?" he asked her, and they got up together and walked away.

"Look at that thing wiggle, Johnny," Valentino winked at me. "She's giving him the same going over she gave you. Boy, I knew I should have danced with that dame."

"Stop picking on Billie, will you?" Cookie rasped. "You talk too much."

I smelled danger again. "Let's get the hell out of here. It's after one o'clock and Herman doesn't need anyone to take care of him any more."

"Suits me." Ciro led the way. "Who pays for this?"

"Herman will pay for it," Cookie said. "The party's always on him in here."

"He doesn't pay my bills." Valentino threw twenty dollars on the table and walked away. Cookie and I followed him, and Ciro didn't say anything more until we were on the street and standing beside his car. Then it was so low that I was the only one who heard it.

"I pay my own way," he whispered to himself. "I don't need any yellow Nazi to pick up my check." He was a little drunk. "Get in, I'll drive you home," he said, louder, and opened both the doors on his side.

"I'll sit in the back," Cookie announced, stepping in and closing the door behind him. I knew perfectly well he intended to shoot Valentino as soon as I got out, or maybe if I sat beside Val on the front seat he would shoot both of us in our backs at the first red light. He rolled the window down from the inside. "Wonder how Herman's making out?"

"That yellow Nazi. . . ." Ciro began, in a loud voice.

"Who the hell are you to call anybody yellow!" Cookie shouted. "You're nothing but a nigger yourself!"

It happened so fast I didn't get all of it. Valentino yanked the back door open with his left hand at the same time he started shooting with his right. I heard people shouting as I started to walk rapidly away, looking for a dark doorway to hide in. A glance over my shoulder told me that Cookie's body had toppled out on the sidewalk. Then I heard an engine start up; gears screamed, Valentino's car raced past me, took a corner on two wheels, and disappeared. I turned the corner myself, only in the other direction, and went down the first subway entrance I came to.

Half an hour later I was somewhere out in the wilds of Brooklyn; then I switched trains and came back to Manhattan and went to bed, sore at Ciro Valentino for blowing the whole setup to pieces the way he had. If Cookie was Rudy Hoffmann, and if Cookie was dead—and he probably was—then my big chance was gone, and I'd be a little ashamed to wear my old man's potsy after that. And if Cookie wasn't Hoffman— that crack about cheating at cards had me a little doubtful—the gang was certainly split wide open.

I'd have to start all over again to find Muddy and, through him, Rudy.

Maybe I could find one of the others, though. I might be able to locate Herman in some station house or down at Center Street, held for questioning. An open shooting, like this one, couldn't be covered up like the stabbing of Peter Arranto. Too many people were there right after it happened. I wondered, too, if Ciro had been picked up. If he managed to get back to Harlem he could hide out in the crowded Puerto Rican section for months without being caught.

As I dropped off to sleep, I wondered where the cops were looking for me.

The first thing in the morning, after I had shaved and

stuck the hair on the door on my way out, I grabbed a paper. The headlines were on the second page.

GANG SHOOTING IN VILLAGE

I was glad to see that Cookie—Charles Adler, the paper had it—wasn't dead, although he had four holes in him and the doctors at St. Anthony's, where he had been taken, listed his condition as "critical." He couldn't talk.

An automobile, with bullet holes through the back seat, had been found abandoned on Lafayette Street. It answered the description of the getaway car, and the police were tracing the license plates. They were also looking, the paper said, for two other men who had been seen with the wounded man and his assailant earlier in the evening.

I called Stratford and he told me to get over to West Twentieth Street as fast as I could. Twenty minutes later we were together in his office.

"Tell me what happened."

"In a minute. Tell me first—has Adler talked?"

"No. Not yet."

"Is he going to die?"

"I don't know."

"You know what I think, Inspector?"

"What?"

"I think he's Rudolph Hoffmann."

"Yeah? What makes you think that?"

Quickly I ran through the little pieces of evidence I had collected. "If it hadn't been for that crack about not cheating at cards and not knowing a ship from a boat, I'd have got him myself last night. But that stopped me. I still can't figure it. That's why I decided to wait a few days more."

"You must be nuts. I'd say you had a good enough case."

"But don't you see, Chief, I have to be sure. If I wasn't, I'd never know when some other guy who looked like that would walk up behind me and let me have it. Did you manage to pick up his pal Herman yet?"

"No. Can't find him. Or your friend Valentino, either."

"Find Muddy Track?"

"Charles Hess has been watching the house but he hasn't reported anything."

"Any dope on what Herman did after the shooting? I got to get back in touch with one of them."

"Not much on Herman. According to the best stories we have, half the people in Sophie's ran out on the street when they heard the shots, and all the rest of the people crowded up toward the bar. There was a policewoman there, out of uniform and having dinner with some boy friend, and she gave us the best report. A lot of the customers remember that Herman was dancing with that girl Billie Bloomer, but nobody remembers seeing him leave. All we know is that all of a sudden he was gone."

"How about Billie? Did she fade out, too?"

"No, she stayed until the place closed up. We questioned her, naturally, because she had been at the table with the rest of you. But she said the only members of the party she knew were Herman and the guy who got shot, and the hired help backed her up by swearing they had never seen either of you in the place before. She admitted that she had been introduced to you, and had danced once with 'the fellow with the broad shoulders,' but that was all we could get out of her."

"What did she say when you asked her where Herman had gone?"

"Only that when they heard the shots he started for the front door. We took her name and address and told her not to leave town."

"Did anyone go around to her apartment and look for Herman there?"

"Not that I know of. Why? Do you think he went there?"

"I know damned well he went there. The way he felt earlier in the evening, he was going to spend the night there no matter how many people got shot. I bet he's still there, hiding out right under your nose and enjoying every minute of it."

"I'll be damned. Malone, if I don't believe you're right. Wish I had someone to send over. Wait a minute. I'll call Westman and get him to send one of his boys." He reached for the phone.

"Hold it, Inspector." He dropped the phone back on its stand. "What are you going to do when you find him? He didn't shoot Adler. All he has to say is that he had a date with the girl and didn't want anything to interfere with it. He can say he was too drunk to know what was going on—and he can get a lot of people to back him up on that story, including me. He drifted out the back way and went up to her place. Unless going to bed with night-club singers has suddenly become a crime in New York, you can't hold him for anything. He didn't even see it happen."

"What the hell is he, a buddy of yours?"

"No. I hate his guts. But I'm in that gang and I want to stay in until this thing is settled.

"I got an idea he did that Pete Arranto job."

"You do? What makes you thing that?"

"Nuts, Malone." Stratford chewed savagely at his cigar. "You know he did it, and I know you know he did it. You just want to make a big splash and get the whole gang yourself, your own way." He threw the soggy butt into a wastebasket. "I don't know that I blame you, I was a rookie dick myself once, but I can't go along with you forever. My job is to catch crooks. No matter what you say I'm going to get Valentino. And I don't see any reason for not getting Holman, too, right away."

"You don't have a good enough case on the Arranto deal to burn him, Inspector, you know that."

"All right, so I don't. What do you suggest?"

"Let's pick him up and then let him go. Then pick me up. You can tell the papers that my story agrees with his. Let me go, too. Don't look for Muddy Track—call Charlie off. That way we'll all come out in the open again. I can check on Cookie while he is in the hospital. It will seem okay because I'm his friend. If he doesn't pan out to be Rudy I'll still be able to find out from Muddy where Rudy is. The whole deal will tie us together like a band of ever-loving brothers."

"I'll give you a week, Malone. Then I'm going to bring the whole kit and kaboodle in and sweat everything out of them that we can. I'll make Holman sing about the Arranto job if I have to break every bone in his body, and Track'll sing, too, or I haven't been on the force for twenty years."

"Thank you, sir."

"Now I'm going to have the Eighth Precinct pick up Holman. Check in with them so you know when they have him, and then make arrangements to have them nab you in Sophie's

Place. That'll look good. Suspect returns to the scene of his crime."

"Okay with me, sir. Who's going to look for him? Maybe we should get Charlie Hess, he knows him when he sees him."

"No, I don't want him to know Charlie. Right now I'll tell them to send anybody up to that girl's apartment and bring in any man they find there. You don't think he'll come out shooting, do you?"

"No. Cookie carried the gun, all Herman ever used was a knife, and he's probably ditched it long ago. Anything else?"

"That's all. Remember, you've got one week. Get along—and good hunting!"

They found Herman in Billie Bloomer's apartment, and didn't have any trouble with him. He played it pretty smart. Sure, he said, Adler was a friend of his. They both lived in the same apartment house on East Ninetieth Street. He had met Adler in Mexico. Both were refugees and had fled there in 1941, and if the police didn't believe it all they had to do was check with the Mexican authorities. No, he didn't know what Adler did for a living. As far as he was concerned, he had investments in Mexico that paid him a small but comfortable income, and they could check that, too.

Why had he disappeared when he heard the shots? Well, he had a date that he didn't want to miss—you fellows know how it is sometimes. Who were the other people at the table? He wasn't quite sure. He and Cookie had been drinking in his apartment most of the afternoon, and had stopped in a few other places before they wound up at Sophie's. Somewhere they had met Valentino and Murphy, he couldn't remember just where. No, he couldn't go back to the place, he had been pretty drunk, so drunk he had gone to sleep at the table and didn't even know what might have caused all the trouble between Cookie and Valentino.

Any good detective could have picked holes in the story and tied Herman into a dozen knots, but they had the word from Stratford and finally let him go with the warning to stay around town for a while. They didn't even put a tail on him.

Herman didn't know it, but I was sitting upstairs in the detectives' room at the Eighth Precinct while they were questioning him downstairs. My old sidekick Dennis had been in

102

on the examination. As soon as Herman left he came upstairs and told me what had happened.

"Do you think we ought to get in touch with the people in Mexico, Johnny?"

"Sure, but let somebody else do it. He wouldn't have told that story if he didn't have himself covered down there, and if you don't check him he may find out about it and wonder why. But how about you going over to Sophie's and waiting there for me? I'll be along in a while and you can have the fun of bringing me in. I'll park my gun here until I get back."

An hour later I walked into Sophie's and sat down at the bar. Dinny was sitting there sucking a short beer. "Billie around?" I asked the bartender, ignoring his frantic frowning as he tried to tip me off that a detective was sitting three stools away.

"Naw," he said, making more faces. "She won't be in 'til later."

"I can't hang around that long. When she gets here tell her Johnny Murphy wants to see her, will you?"

The bartender gulped. Dinny slid off his stool and stepped toward me, one hand on his hip. "Did you say your name was Johnny Murphy?"

"Yeah. What about it?"

"Is this the guy who was in here last night, bartender?"

"Uh-huh."

"All right, Murphy." Dinny pulled his badge from his pocket. "Police. We've been looking for you."

"What the hell for?"

"You'll find out. Stand up here, and don't go reaching for anything." Expertly he patted my pockets and the sides of my chest, looking for guns. "Don't make no trouble, Murphy." He snapped a handcuff on my right wrist, locked the other cuff to a pipe along the wall. "Wait here while I phone for a wagon. Where's your phone, bartender?"

The bartender motioned toward the counter behind his bar. "Gee," he whispered when Dinny was phoning, "I tried to tip you off."

"Thanks. Forget it. They don't have anything on me. I'll be back for the drink I didn't get."

Dinny unsnapped the handcuff from the pipe and locked it over his own left wrist. "We'll just wait here for the car,

Murphy. No use standing out on the street collecting a crowd. I hope you come quiet." We waited. "Here it is now," he said, as a police sedan drew up outside. "Come on, bum, let's go and see the chief."

XIII.

As soon as the police car with Dinny and me in the back was around the corner, he started to laugh until I thought he would choke. "Oh oh oh. Ha ha ha—wasn't I good, Johnny? Didn't that look like the real McCoy?" He doubled up on the seat. "Come on, bum, let's go and see the chief! Oh, me aching back!"

"Shut up, you silly mick," I laughed, too. "Sit up and stop clowning before somebody sees us and knows the whole thing's a fake. And take these damned bracelets off, will you?"

He pulled himself back on the seat beside me. "Oh, no, Johnny. I'm takin' you into the station house with me gun in me hand. You're a desperate character, hobnobbin' with killers of all kinds, I hear, and I can't be takin' a chance."

He did, too. Marched me right out of the car with the cuffs on me, his hand on his hip, and the driver standing by with *his* hand on *his* hip. Everybody kept a straight face as he took me upstairs to the detectives' room. Half a dozen of the boys were there—Lynch and the others. They were getting a big kick out of it.

"What you got there, Dinny?"

"Work him over. . . ."

"We know how to make guys talk, tough guy. . . ."

After the ribbing Dinny unlocked me, and we all sat around for an hour or so before I got my gun and left. The first thing I wanted to do was to get in touch with Herman, but I didn't want to go straight up to his place on Ninetieth Street because he didn't know that I knew where he lived.

There was another little thing that needed attention, too. I picked up an evening paper and caught a taxi, told the driver to take me up Third Avenue to Seventeenth Street, and began looking in the paper for the latest news about Cookie as we rode along. I had moved back to page four in the *Telegram,* and the story still said that Cookie couldn't talk. But it also gave his address.

The cab dropped me off at the corner and I walked up the avenue until I came to a small saloon. There was nobody at the bar except the bartender, polishing glasses. I went in and asked for a rye and water, drank it and had another, and threw a twenty on the bar.

"How would you like to keep the change?" I asked as the bartender reached for the money.

He glanced at me suspiciously. "Doing what? No knockout drops. My license is worth more than change from a twenty."

"Nothing like that. Some of us are rigging a gag for a friend. He got so drunk last night he pulled a blank, and doesn't remember where he was."

"Yeah?"

"Well, he wasn't here, I know that, but in this gag we're fixing up we want him to think he was somewhere along here, you understand. He's a tall blond guy, with blue eyes, dresses like someone who works in an office. He's about forty-five, fifty, and he pals around with another man who looks and dresses about the same. His name is 'Herman' and he calls the other fellow 'Cookie.' "

"Yeah?"

"Now what I want you to do, for the rest of this twenty, is this. If he comes in here and wants to know if he was here yesterday afternoon with Cookie, you tell him that he was. And if he wants to know what he did, you tell him that he met me and a tall dark man here and that the four of us left together. Get it?"

"Yeah. Don't sound like much of a gag to me, but if he comes in I'll give it to him." He picked up the twenty, rang up two drinks on the cash register, and started to pocket the change.

Then he came back. "This smells like an alibi to me, Mac. You sure it ain't?"

I handed him a ten spot. "What do you care what it is?"

"I don't." The ten followed the change into his pocket.

Another taxi took me up to Ninetieth Street and dropped me in front of Herman's address. I pushed the little button beside his name on the mail boxes until finally the door latch clicked and I went in.

When I got up to the proper floor, Herman opened his door as soon as he heard me knock. "What are you doing here, Murphy?" he asked. "The cops are looking for you. Don't you know that? Come in and have a drink."

I followed him into the little one-room-and-bath. It was furnished simply. There was a studio couch, a couple of chairs, some uninteresting prints on the wall, and a desk full of old newspapers in one corner. He went over to a little alcove, got some ice from a refrigerator, put it in a glass, splashed some water in the glass from a tap over the sink, and brought it back to me. A bottle and his own glass were standing on a table beside his chair and he motioned to me to help myself.

"I've just left the Eighth Precinct," I said, pouring a drink in the glass. "They picked me up at Sophie's and gave me a bad half hour before they let me go."

"What were you doing over there?"

"Looking for Billie to find out what happened to you."

"Find her?"

"No. There was a cop in the place and he nabbed me."

"You might have known there'd be one there. That wasn't very smart, Murphy. That was dumb."

"What did I care? They were going to get me sooner or later, and I figured I might as well let them get away with it and think they were bright boys. And anyhow, they caught you, too."

"How did you know that?"

"I was coming around the corner when they came and took you away. Hell, Herman, I've been trying to get in touch with you all day, just so we could get our stories straight."

"What happened last night?"

"Cookie and Ciro got snapping at each other—both of them were drunk—and Cookie finally called Ciro a nigger. Ciro shot

106

him. I faded out. I told the cops we had separated at the door and I had gone one way while they went the other and thought the shots were backfires." I stopped talking long enough to light a cigarette. "And I did another little job this afternoon, too, after I saw them nab you. I went to a joint down on Third Avenue just above Seventieth and fixed up a story for the bartender to tell. If anybody wants to know how we got together, you and Cookie and Ciro and me, he'll say we met there. I don't know what you told, but that's what I told the cops who picked me up, and the story's all ready. Cost me twenty-nine dollars and twenty cents, too, which I figure you owe me."

He refilled our glasses and told me what had happened to him at the station house, none of which was news to me.

"How's Cookie?" I asked him then.

"They won't let me in to see him. I went around to the hospital this afternoon, but they said he was still unconscious."

"Is he going to live?"

"I don't know. He got one in the shoulder, one in the arm, and two in the belly." His eyes blazed. "Maybe he isn't going to die, but I know one guy who is—that goddamned Valentino! He shot Cookie in the belly on purpose," he snarled, "and I'll get him if it's the last thing I ever do. Do you know where he is?"

"Hell, no, I don't know where he is. Last time I saw him he was tearing around the corner in his car."

"How did you find out where I live? Have you been following me?"

"Nuts, Holman. Why should I follow you? I saw in the paper where Cookie lived, knew you lived in the same place, came up, and saw your name on the mail box downstairs. No trick to that."

Herman went back to the refrigerator for more ice, returned and began pacing back and forth across the floor. "I've got to find Valentino. I'll kill that dirty nigger," he mumbled. "Have you got a gun on you, Murphy? Let me have it. I'll find him somewhere."

"Oh, no," I said. "You don't get my gun. I ditched one last night, this is the only one I got left and if I gave it to you I wouldn't have any. I don't like to walk around that way. Where's your knife?"

"I threw it out of Billie's window last night, into a bunch of trash in somebody's back yard. It won't be found."

"Go get another."

"Aw no, not now. Not since I let Pete Arranto have it with a knife. That's too much of a trade-mark right now." He pulled a couple of keys from his pocket. "No," he said to himself, "that's mine." He dropped the keys on the table, opened a drawer of the desk. "Here we are. Here's a key to Cookie's apartment, and I know where he has a spare gun hidden. If the cops haven't found it I can use it. Wait here, I'll be back."

As soon as he was out of the room I grabbed the keys he had dropped on the table, selected the one that opened his door, laid a piece of paper over it and rubbed it with a pencil until I had a clear impression. Herman came back.

"Got it," he exclaimed, patting his pocket. "Now watch me find that son-of-a-bitch." He went into the closet, dragged out his topcoat, slapped his hat on his head. "I'll hunt for that black bastard Valentino until I find him. And if you tell him I'm looking for him, Murphy, I'll kill you, too. Don't think I won't. Now let's get the hell out of here."

"How about that twenty-nine-twenty you owe me?"

"For Christ's sake! Here!" He threw thirty bucks on the table. "Don't bother to give me any change, I can stand it. Come on!"

We separated on the street. Herman went uptown to look for Ciro. As soon as his bus was out of sight I headed for a telephone booth. Not to call Stratford this time—I didn't care whether Herman found Valentino or not—but to call Mary and see what she was doing for supper.

She wasn't doing anything special, so we decided to do it together and I promised to hurry down to her place and meet her there. If Herman was going to be up in Harlem we weren't likely to meet him in the Village. Anyhow, it didn't matter any more whether we bumped into each other outside of business hours or not.

"I want to talk to you, Johnny," Mary said, when we had finished eating and were enjoying cigarettes after coffee. "About a whole lot of things."

"Go ahead, this is as good a place as any." There was only candlelight on the table, only a few other diners in the room.

"I don't want to talk here."

"Well, we can't very well go over to that dump of mine."

"I know. . . ."

"Wait," I said. "Little Johnny has the makings of an idea. Just sit here while I get on the phone."

"Hello. Bill Jackson?" I asked. "This is Johnny Malone, your landlord. Remember me? What are you and Peggy doing tonight?"

"Johnny!" his voice came back. "Where the hell have you been? We've been trying to get in touch with you for two weeks. We even called the Police Department, but they say they've never heard of you."

"What did you want?"

"Why, there was a man came around here asking Peggy where you were."

"Yeah? What did he look like?"

"She said he was maybe six feet tall, blond, blue eyes, busted nose. Ugly-looking beggar."

"Let me talk to her."

"She isn't here. She went up to Connecticut to visit her folks. I was just going out to catch a train and go up there too when you called. You were lucky to catch me."

"What did Peggy tell this guy?"

"She said she didn't know where you were, that we had rented the place through an agent and she thought maybe you had gone to California. So he told her not to tell anybody he had been around or else, and went away."

"Any sign of him since?"

"Not since then. Look, Johnny, I've got to hurry and catch a train. Was there anything else you wanted?"

"Yeah. If you're going to be out tonight, do you mind if I come over and sit in my chairs for a while?"

"What have you got, a date?"

"Sure. Something special."

"It's your apartment, Johnny. Drop in any time you want to, we won't be back for a week. So long."

"Thanks a lot. Goodby."

Mary and I walked over to Sullivan Street and built a little fire in the fireplace before we settled down against a bunch of cushions on the studio couch.

It took a while to get started with the conversation, though.

You know how things are. All the time I had known Mary we had never been any place where we wouldn't be bothered. We were always in restaurants, or the movies, or in taxis, and that's a hell of a way to court a girl. But there in my own apartment it was different, and I held her close against me, just as hard as I could, and she wasn't able to do much talking for a while because I didn't give her a chance.

But you have to come up for air eventually, and then Mary started to tell me what was bothering her, though I hadn't suspected what she had on her mind until she began.

"Johnny, just what is this case you're working on? Can you tell me?"

"Why, darling, I can't tell you much more than I did the other night. I'm trying to catch a dope ring, that's all."

"Well, do you have to dance the way you were dancing at Sophie's last night to catch them?"

"Were you there?" I stalled a little for time. "I didn't see you."

"No, I wasn't there, but I heard all about it. One of the other nurses was there and she told me. She said you were dancing with the girl who sings, and the way she described it and the language she used was disgusting."

"Did she tell you who else I was with?"

"She said you were all drunk."

"Listen, Mary." I reached for her hand and was glad when she didn't pull it away. "You know I love you, more than anything else in the world. You know I've got a job, too, and sometimes I have to do a lot of things that I don't like to do. Last night was one of them. I never saw that girl before, but just to explain, Mary, she's a dope fiend and last night she thought I had some and that she could get me to give it to her if she acted that way. What else did your tattle-tale friend have to tell you?"

"They brought a man into the emergency ward last night, Johnny. His name is Charles Adler. He's shot. He may die. Do you know him?"

"Sure, I know him. He's one of the gang I'm trying to catch. I was sitting at a table with him when I wasn't dancing with that girl. Did your friend tell you that she saw us together?"

"Yes."

"Did she see him get shot?"

"No, she left before that. She said it would open my eyes if I knew the sort of company you kept. Oh, Johnny, I don't like her, and she doesn't like me, and she tells me things just to hurt my feelings. You know I trust you, darling. Only . . . only. . . ."

"Only I wish you had a job where you came home at nights to a nice little place like this, and that I could be here to meet you, and that we didn't have to go along seeing each other the way we do now, and . . ." I felt something wet against my cheek. Tears were rolling from the corners of her eyes.

"Don't be worried, my darling. Don't cry." My fingers tried to brush the tears away. "It won't be much longer before I have all the evidence. Then things won't be like this."

"Why don't you arrest them now?"

"There's more to it than dope, Mary. I can't tell you, honestly I can't. You'll have to trust me, that's all. Just trust me. And don't let that other nurse worry you. . . ."

A sudden, sharp thought crossed my mind. "How did she know about Adler if she left before he got shot?"

"She saw him this morning. She's on duty for emergencies."

"Did she tell him who I am—that my name is Malone?"

"I don't think so. He's unconscious."

"Don't let her do it, Mary, don't let her anywhere near him! Does he have a police guard?"

"Certainly, there's a man on duty in the room all the time, you know they'd do that."

"Get that girl transferred, Mary, or tell the guard to do it. It's important. Is she on tonight?"

"No, she goes on in the mornings. I don't think she'd tell him who you are. She wouldn't do that, even if she doesn't like me."

"There's always the chance she might let it slip. . . . Listen, Mary, do you know how my father died?"

"You told me, Johnny, when we first started going together. Why?"

"Because I think Charles Adler is the man who killed him, and I can't let anything happen to Adler until I can prove it. He mustn't even be allowed to die there in the hospital, you understand?"

111

"Yes." Her tone was very low and thoughtful as she reached in my pocket for a cigarette. "I can see it all now. I wish you had told me before. I'll have that girl taken off duty. I'll take care of him myself; maybe I can find out if he is the man you're looking for. Is his name really Adler?"

"No. It's Hoffman. Rudolph Hoffman. Look out for him, Mary, he won't do you any good."

"He isn't very dangerous now, Johnny. He's a sick man, very sick. And there's always a guard in the room."

"Hospital guards have gone to sleep, or out to take a smoke." My arm went around her shoulders again; she tossed her cigarette into the dying embers in the fireplace and turned her face up to mine. "Be careful, my darling, be very careful," I murmured.

We talked about entirely different things after that, and sometimes we didn't talk at all. Finally the clock on the mantel said it was time to go, and we walked slowly back to Mary's front door.

"Good night," I whispered. "Be careful, because I love you very much."

"I will," she promised. "Are you going to kill him if he gets well?"

"I don't know. It all depends. First of all, I have to find out who he really is."

"As soon as he's able to talk I'll be there to hear what he says," she decided. "Can you call me from time to time, so I can let you know?"

"Yes, and I'll come around, too. After all, it isn't any secret that I know him. It's perfectly natural for his friends to drop in and see how he is getting along, as far as the hospital is concerned."

"Maybe I can find out if his name isn't Adler." There was a thoughtful little crease between Mary's twinkling eyes, as though she were considering some brilliant and wonderful new idea. "I may even be able to find out what his real name is."

"I wish you could," I confessed, "but I've been trying to do that ever since I met the guy. Just let me know when he can talk, and I'll come over and have a word or two with him. Good night again."

"Good night." Her lips met mine for an instant, and then the door shut behind her and I started my long walk home. It wasn't as lonely as it had been before, because this time I knew that Mary was walking with me, and would never be very far from me again. That was one of the things we had talked about.

XIV.

THE POLICE didn't find Ciro Valentino's body until a week later, when a Harlem janitor uncovered a human arm in his coal pile and ran screaming for the nearest cop. When they dug the rest of the body out there he was, dead with the top of his head bashed in. Nobody will ever know exactly how it happened, but the police investigation turned up enough information so the story can be pieced together reasonably well.

When Herman left his apartment, he headed uptown to Valentino's little travel agency. It was still open—in fact, it usually stayed open until late at night to take care of the Puerto Ricans who same in after work to arrange transportation for their families still on the island, and to pay the weekly installments they owed for their own fares.

Ciro wasn't there, of course, and none of the clerks or other people in the place would tell Herman where the boss was. He offered fifty, a hundred, and finally a thousand dollars to anybody who would tell him, but they all kept their traps shut. Finally he left the agency office.

He was standing on the sidewalk outside wondering where to go next when one of Ciro's swarthy fellow islanders came up to him.

"You looking for somebody, mister?" the Puerto Rican inquired.

113

"Yes. Do you know where he is?"

"Seems like a lot of people looking for him today."

The stranger lit a yellow cigarette with shaking hands. "Lots of cops looking for somebody around here. You wouldn't be another cop, would you?"

"I'm not a cop and I'm looking for Ciro Valentino. I'll pay a hundred dollars to anyone who can tell me where he is."

"How do I know you're not a cop?"

Herman had noticed the shaking hands, and now he took a chance. "Listen, I can show you I'm not. I can show you I'm in the same business he is. You need a shot pretty bad, don't you?" The stranger nodded. "I thought so," Herman continued. "You tell me where he is and I'll give you enough to keep you happy for the rest of your life."

"And money, too?"

"Yes, god damn it, a thousand dollars. Where is he?"

"I don't know, but I know where his girl friend lives, and I bet she knows. I bet he sneaks in there at night. Don't nobody else but me in all Harlem know where she lives, either. But I know, mister. You give me a thousand dollars and the junk for that?" The man's hands were trembling badly now.

"Yes!" Herman almost shouted. "I'll give it to you. Where is she?"

"Give it to me first."

"I don't have it with me. I'll get it. I've got the money but I don't have the dope. Tell me where she is and I'll get it for you as soon as I can."

"I'll tell you after I get it, mister," the Puerto Rican purred. "I don't want promises. Let's go get it together, then I'll tell you." He whistled for a cab, stepped in with Herman, and together they drove back to Ninetieth Street where Herman picked up a pocketful of the precious capsules.

The informer's uncontrollable craving for the drug increased as they drove back to Harlem. "Give me a shot now, mister," he whined. "Just one little whiff. That's all I want. I don't want no money." He told Herman where the girl lived, what her name was. "There, mister, I told you. Now give it to me, please."

"Shut up! I won't give you a damned thing until we get there, except this!" He slapped the hophead cruelly across the

114

face until his nose started to bleed. "Shut up or I'll break your nose next time!"

The taxi stopped at the address the Puerto Rican had mentioned, and the two passengers stepped out.

"Is this it?" Herman demanded.

"This is it," the bloody-nosed man said. "See, here's her name on the mail box. Now give it to me." Herman handed him a package. "That isn't all you have. There's more in your pocket. Where's the thousand dollars?"

In reply Herman slapped the man again. "That's enough for a while. You get the rest when I make sure you're not double-crossing me. I'll meet you on the corner when I come out. If you tell anyone that I'm in here I'll kill you. Now go away." The Puerto Rican shuffled off and disappeared.

Herman knocked on the door of the second-floor apartment, leveled his gun at the slim and beautiful mulatto girl who opened it. He grabbed her wrist in his strong hand.

"Let me in," he hissed, "or I'll break your arm. Keep quiet, or I'll kill you." The girl silently opened the door; Herman stepped through and closed it behind him. "Where's Valentino?" he asked.

"He's not here."

"We'll see." He twisted her arm behind her and, keeping her in front of him, carefully walked through the other rooms of the apartment, looking in closets and under the bed.

"You're no cop," she said, when the search was completed and he had released her. "Who are you? What do you want?"

"I want Valentino."

"He isn't here. He won't be here. Go away, I don't like you."

"He'll be here, I think. When he comes I want to see him."

"Why?"

"Because I'm going to break his pretty nose, and knock out his pretty teeth, so no other girls will ever fall for him again!"

"What other girls?" The dark eyes flashed and the full red mouth tightened against the flawless olive skin of the girl's beautiful face.

"My girl, for one. The girl he took away from me. The white girl with the golden hair that he slept with last night, and bragged this morning that white girls were lovelier than the island wenches he was used to!" Herman cursed. "No girls will

115

want to sleep with him when I've finished. He won't be able to sleep with other girls when I'm done!"

"Where he sleep with this other girl last night?" Her breasts rose and fell rapidly as her jealous rage mounted. "I wonder why he not come home last night!"

A telephone rang. "Answer it, but if you say that I'm here I'll fix you, too."

"Be still." She walked over to the ringing phone while he followed, pistol in hand. "I think I want to hear the talk between you and Ciro about this white girl." She picked up the phone. "Hello, honey . . . no, nobody has been here . . . no, I see nobody outside . . . yes, I wait for you."

"He says the police are after him," she told Herman. "He says he has to hide and must stay here for a little while. He'll be over, then we talk. Now I get you a drink, yes."

"Yes, we'll both have a drink, from the same bottle." He watched her closely while she poured rum into two glasses, waited until she took the first sip, then downed his at a single gulp. "Now I think I better tie you up. You might change your mind about wanting to watch me talk to Ciro." He forced her into the bathroom where he knotted a towel around her wrists and stuffed another into her mouth. Then he carried her into the bedroom and threw her on the bed. In the drawer of a dressing table he found several pairs of nylon stockings with which he bound her ankles and, after removing the towel, her wrists. He went back to the bathroom and returned with a roll of adhesive tape and a hypodermic needle that he found in the medicine cabinet.

"I see you use this stuff, too," he said, removing the gag from her mouth. "I suppose Ciro kept you well supplied." The girl said nothing; glared at him. "I left you enough for about ten days. Your boy friend won't be around for a while. In ten days I'll call you up and, if you behave between now and then, I'll bring you some. When Ciro heals up maybe he'll bring you more, but that will be the only thing he can bring you. If you ever tell anybody that I was here I'll find out about it, and you'll never get another shot as long as you live. You know what that means. You'll get old and ugly overnight, old and ugly and no man will ever want you again. Do you understand?" He

116

plastered a piece of adhesive tape across her mouth without waiting for an answer.

With a sudden sweep of his hand he pulled her skirt above her thighs, where hundreds of little red marks told a story of drug addiction, and plunged the needle into her leg. "Sleep tight." He pressed the plunger down. "Happy dreams." The girl lay still, only her eyes moved. "You'd be a lovely thing if it wasn't for those needle marks," he mused. "Maybe I should think of some way to take you with me when I go."

The level of the rum in the bottle had dropped when Herman, waiting in the living room, heard footsteps on the stairs. He stepped behind the door with a heavy candlestick poised in his hand. A key turned in the lock, the door opened.

"Felicidad, where are . . ." The candlestick crashed, and Ciro Valentino fell slowly to the floor as Herman closed the door again. Once more he raised the candlestick and beat it into Valentino's skull. Only a little bit of blood oozed out.

The murderer muttered something to himself, took the candlestick into the bedroom, and carefully washed the blood away. Then, with a handful of toilet paper, he proceeded through the apartment, removing fingerprints from the rum bottle, the glass he had used, and anywhere he might have touched. Finally he mopped the few drops of blood from the floor and wadded paper into the hole in the dead man's head.

A visit to the bedroom told him the girl still slept. He untied her wrists and for a moment stood there, looking at her face, her body, and the long olive legs so promisingly exposed. He leaned toward her again, licking his lips and swallowing the flood of saliva that suddenly began to form in his mouth, then he turned out the light and went away. With a single motion he lifted Ciro's body to his shoulder, listened carefully, opened the door, and carried the dead man down the stairs to the cellar. Swiftly he shoveled a hole in the rear of the coal pile, removed the tissue paper from the wound in Valentino's head and threw it in the furnace, dumped the body in the grave he had dug, and tossed the coal back over it.

An hour later he was sitting at the bar in Sophie's Place, drinking steadily and quietly, waiting for Billie to finish her last song.

I knew he was there. Charlie Hess saw him come in, sat beside him as he drank, watched him go out with the girl.

He was probably with her as I walked home that night, after I said goodby to Mary, but I wasn't worrying about Herman Holman and Billie Bloomer then. In a day or so, I thought, Cookie would either be dead or else he would be able to talk, and I felt sure that when he started he would tell me a lot of things I wanted to know. My plan was to walk in on him, cold, and say, "All right, Rudy, the doctors tell me you're going to croak. There's only one thing I want to know. Where did you go after you killed Greg Malone?" And if he stalled I would just push him gently in the belly until he told me.

The hair was still stuck between the door and the frame when I got to my room, and no strangers bothered me during the night; at least, if they did I didn't know about it. It was ten o'clock in the morning when I woke up, later than I had wanted it to be. I called Muddy Track's place but nobody answered, and there didn't seem to be any reason for going down there. Muddy, I figured, would be out of business soon. Cookie was in the hospital, Valentino was on the lam, and Herman was hunting for Valentino—so I thought.

After breakfast I walked across town to the hospital. Maybe a telephone call would have been just as good, but then I wouldn't have had a chance to see Mary, which was what I really wanted to do.

"Johnny," she said, when the receptionist had located her and she had come down to the waiting room to see me. "Come over here in the corner, I've something to tell you." She took me by the hand and led me where nobody could see us—I promptly kissed her—and sat down on a hard settee.

"What is it?"

"Johnny," she whispered, "that man's name really is Charles Adler. He isn't Rudolph Hoffmann at all!"

Something kind of curled up inside of me and died, and I slumped back in the settee and darned near cried with disappointment. The prize was gone. The wheel had stopped on somebody else's number. For a while I didn't even ask Mary how she knew—she had said that Cookie wasn't Rudy and there didn't seem to be any reason to question her any further.

118

Finally, though, the little ray of hope that refused to go out forced me to open my mouth.

"How did you find out?"

"Oh, I did an awful thing, Johnny, really I did."

"What did you do, hit him with a club?"

"Worse than that. I'd be dismissed if anybody ever knew. You won't tell a soul, will you? Ever?"

"Cross my heart and hope to die."

"Well, this morning when I went on duty, after I had arranged to take care of him myself and had that other nurse taken off, I went in to see him. The girl I relieved told me he had been tossing and mumbling for more than two hours. His fever was down and his pulse was closer to normal than it had been so far. He was probably going to regain consciousness any minute. So I brought his chart up to date and then I went back to the pharmacy."

"The pharmacy? Why?"

"You'll see later. Then I went back to Adler's room and straightened out the bed and talked to the guard, until all of a sudden Mr. Adler opened his eyes and asked for a drink of water.

Mary gave him a few sips of water, she told me, and asked him how he felt. His stomach hurt him, he muttered, his shoulder hurt, and his head ached. What had happened to him?

"You've been in an accident," she said. "You're a very sick man."

"Did Ciro shoot me? I remember I was going to shoot him."

"Somebody shot you, and you're still very sick. Now I have to give you some penicillin." She picked up a hypo she had brought from the pharmacy. "This won't hurt you, and it will help you get well." Her practiced fingers found the proper spot in his thigh and he winced slightly as the needle pierced his flesh. "There, there. That didn't hurt, you know it didn't. Now, do you want to tell us who shot you?"

"Wait a minute, lady." The police guard had dropped his paper and was standing on the other side of the bed. "This guy ain't supposed to talk to you. He's supposed to talk to the police. My orders is to call the Station when he's ready to talk, and have another detective come over here to take down whatever he says. Don't you go asking him questions. Wait until we're ready."

"You better go call, then," she snapped. "He's already mentioned one name and you weren't fast enough to get it. Go down to the first floor, on the other side of the building. The telephone's there."

"Gee, are you sure that's the closest one?"

"Yes. You better hurry."

"But I'm not supposed to leave this guy. He might get away."

"You'll be getting a two months' leave without pay if you don't hurry and make that call." She looked back at Cookie, noticed that his face was beginning to turn redder than it had been. A touch on his wrist told her that his pulse had quickened. The worried policeman left the room.

Cookie began to mutter again, and he writhed slowly on the bed.

"What's your full name?" Mary asked him gently. "What's your name? It isn't Adler, is it? What's your name?"

XV.

"Mary," I said, "that wasn't penicillin you gave him, was it?"

She shook her head. "No. It was sodium pentothal."

My eyes opened wider and I whistled. "You little devil," I grinned gleefully. "I thought I recognized the symptoms—a flushed face and a rising pulse. You didn't get caught, did you?"

"Not yet I didn't. You're the only person who knows or ever will know, I hope."

"What did he say when you asked him his name?"

"He tried to sit up, but I held him down, and then he said, very clearly, 'My name is Charles Wilhelm Adler, Charles

120

Wilhelm Adler, Charles Wilhelm Adler.' Three times, Johnny, it must be his real name, he couldn't say that if his name was something else. You can't tell a lie when you're full of sodium pentothal, you just can't."

"No, I don't think he could. Did you ask him anything else?"

"Yes, but first of all I gave him an injection of morphine in a vein in his arm to put him back to sleep in a hurry. I was afraid the guard would come back, or that one of the doctors would drop in. Then I asked him if he knew Rudolph Hoffmann.

"And he said?"

"He said, 'No,' and went back to sleep."

All my carefully laid plans went out the window. If Cookie Adler wasn't Rudy Hoffmann—and there didn't seem to be much doubt about it after what Mary had told me—it meant the search had to begin all over again. I was only vaguely aware of what Mary was saying.

". . . the guard was awfully angry that I had put Mr. Adler back to sleep, but I told him the penicillin had caused violent reaction and that I had to do it, so there wasn't much he could say. Two detectives came over, but when they found out what had happened they went away again."

"Is Cookie still asleep?"

"He should be. He was when you came in, just before I left the room."

"I think I'll go up and see him. Will that be all right?"

"It won't do any harm, but I don't think he will be awake."

"It doesn't matter. I just want to establish the fact that I saw him, in case anybody wants to know what I was doing over here."

We took the elevator and walked around to Cookie's room together. "I have a visitor to see Mr. Adler," Mary told the guard. "He's a personal friend and it's all right. Did Mr. Adler wake up yet?"

"Not that I know," the guard answered, "and I've been watching him pretty close. I don't want him to go back to sleep this time." He settled back to reading his paper, then suddenly dropped it and looked at me. "Say, I know you," he blurted. "You're Johnny Malone, the guy who got Steinsky and Bogar . . . !"

"Shut up, you damned fool!" I almost shouted, and turned to see if Adler could possibly have heard. Mary looked, too; she even raised one of the wounded man's eyelids and touched her finger to the eyeball to see if he was awake, then let the lid drop back and shrugged her shoulders.

I stepped out into the corridor, motioning to the guard to follow me. "Look, stupid," and my face must have been red with rage, "of all the dumb tricks I ever heard of, that was the worst. What are you trying to do, anyway. Get me shot?"

"Gee," he fumbled, "I'm sorry. I didn't think. You . . . you won't report me, will you?"

Whatever answer I was going to give was cut off by a voice from the hospital call system. "Nurse Kiernan, Nurse Kiernan, call the reception desk, call the reception desk."

"Get back in there, and keep your big mouth shut from now on," I ordered, "and remember that my name is Murphy and you never saw me before today." Mary came out, looking worried, but didn't say anything until she made the call to the reception desk.

"Did he hear that?" I asked.

"I don't know," she said. "He's just about halfway out of the morphine. Some of his reflexes are normal. He may be able to hear what is said without being able to make any response. There's another visitor for him downstairs, and I have to go and see who it is."

We went down in the elevator, and seeing it was self-service and gave plenty of privacy I had a chance to tell Mary how wonderful she was, and to kiss her again.

Cookie's latest visitor was Herman. "Hello, Johnny," he said, surprised. "What are you doing here? Visiting Cookie? How is he?"

"Still unconscious," I said. "But Miss Kiernan tells me that his fever is down and his pulse is coming back to normal."

"Well, that's good news." He turned to Mary. "I judge that you're the nurse who's taking care of my friend? My name is Holman—Herman Holman."

"Sorry," I fumbled. "I should have introduced you. Miss Kiernan, this is Mr. Holman."

122

"I'm very glad to meet you, Miss Kiernan. Certainly Mr. Adler should improve rapidly under the care of one so pretty as you." He bowed slightly, with Old World courtliness, then looked at me and smiled. "Murphy," he asked, "are you sure you came here just to see how Cookie was getting along?"

"What do you mean?"

"I hate to be anything less than gallant, but there is lipstick on your upper lip. I had no idea. . . . I'd say you are a very fortunate young man. May I offer my congratulations?" He stuck out his hand and there wasn't much I could do but accept it. "We'll all have to get together, when Cookie's well again, and have a little celebration, won't we?"

I could have shot him. He had backed me into a corner and found out something I certainly didn't want him to know. I rubbed the lipstick off my lip. "Well," I said, "I guess I better be going, and let you see Cookie. Goodby, Mary."

You had to hand it to Herman; he could turn on the charm and manners and polish when he wanted to. It was a sour Johnny Malone who walked out of St. Anthony's after that meeting. And if I had known what was going to happen next, my disgust at being caught off guard would have changed to something else.

Fear, maybe. But not for me.

But right then, as I walked aimlessly along the street, I was in a stew. After my own dumb play, I didn't have the heart to call Lieutenant Westman and get the guard transferred to Flatbush. I didn't feel like calling Inspector Stratford, either. He had given me a week to close what I thought was an airtight case against Adler. Now one of those precious days was gone, and for all the practical ideas that were in my head, the whole week might as well have been finished.

Herman was the only other possibility I could think of, and what evidence did I have on him? Most of my time and work had been spent trying to trap Cookie. But Cookie was the wrong man, for I didn't doubt the evidence Mary had obtained. A truth-drug confession won't stand up in court, but it was good enough for me. And I had been a dope all along, because suddenly I saw that all the other evidence I had collected against Cookie wasn't evidence at all, but just wishful

123

thinking on my part. He'd never said or done a single thing that was real evidence against him.

Slowly my wits sorted themselves out. Rudy Hoffmann was probably either Cookie or Herman. He wasn't Cookie. Could he really be Herman, or was I starting to fool myself again with more wishful thinking? What had Herman ever said or done? Not a darned thing.

But Muddy Track knew. Muddy had written a letter to the Police Commissioner, warning me to be on my guard. How did Muddy know? I could only guess that he had seen Rudy somewhere probably in one of his business deals, and recognized him. Yet he must have met hundreds of shady characters in his time.

Maybe, if I could find Muddy, he would tell me. A dangerous plan began to form in my mind. I would go to Muddy and arrest him for selling dope, and then I would make a deal with him. If he would tell me who Rudy was, and where I could find him, I would intercede in any way I could. I might even let Muddy get away, out of the country, or at least give him a half-hour start for freedom.

Those were dangerous thoughts for a young detective. They meant dismissal from the force or, at the very least, suspension and demotion. It seemed worth the price.

I called Muddy's telephone number again. Nobody answered.

Somehow or other, walking along, I found myself up around Twentieth Street. There I had another idea, and walked over to the station house. Avoiding Stratford and any other Homicide men, I turned the little automatic I was carrying back to the Ballistics clerk and strapped my own Police-Model .38 under my arm. Then I got my old man's badge, shined it up a little against my sleeve, and dropped it in my pocket.

"Going shooting?" the clerk asked.

"Going to bring in a couple of surprises for Stratford. Don't tell him I checked them out, you hear?"

"Not a peep, Johnny. You can trust me."

Feeling like a cop again, with a man-sized gun under my arm and a potsy in my pocket, I drifted down to Rivington Street. Muddy wasn't home. I searched the flat from one end to the other. There was a case and a half of whiskey in one room, some dirty dishes and some stale coffee in the sink, but there wasn't any dope. The pockets of some suits yielded little except tobacco crumbs, and the few pieces of linen in a table drawer didn't bear any laundry marks at all. In other words, I drew a blank.

Muddy never did show up, even though I sat and waited until long after midnight. There wasn't even a telephone call.

Finally I gave up and went home, more disgusted with myself than ever. Angrily I tramped up the stairs to my room, took the key, and started to jab it into the lock. The little whiskers on the back of my neck began to tickle.

The hair on the door was unstuck at one end!

Silently I dropped to my knees, crawled away from the door with the .38 in my hand.

"Come on out, Rudy!" I yelled, "or I'm coming in shooting!"

A shot crashed through the door, waist high, and I fired three quick ones back while I was jumping to my feet and retreating to the other side of the hall. Someone in another room screamed as I charged and hit my own door with my shoulder, tearing the lock loose from the frame. As the door flew open, I dropped flat, firing another shot blindly into the dark room as I fell.

Nothing happened, except that acrid powder fumes blew back in my face as a draft came in through the open window. Whoever had been waiting for me was gone. And now there was a crowd in the hall outside, jabbering and clattering like a flock of geese. "Go away," I growled, and slammed the door in their faces.

It didn't take long for the cops to get there, just long enough for me to turn on the light and reload the .38. "In there, in there," the outside voices said, and then there was a hard knock on the lockless door, enough to push it open about two inches.

"All right, all right. Come out with your hands up!"

"Who is it?" I backed into the corner away from the door.

"Police!"

"Kick your badge under the door to prove it. Somebody tried to get me a minute ago. Let me see your badge and you can come in without any trouble." My gun was in one hand, my own shield in the other.

125

"The hell with that. Come out with your hands up!"

"Easier to do it my way, copper. When I see your shield, I'll throw my gun on the bed where you can see it."

The door was pushed open a little further, and then I saw a patrolman's cap appear through the opening, with the big bright shield above the visor. I tossed my gun on the bed with a sigh of relief, held my hands out at my sides with my own badge face up in one of them.

"Come in," I invited. The door was kicked open, and a husky cop stepped through and did a quick turn to bring his pistol aimed squarely at my chest. Then he saw the gleaming bit of metal in my hand. "Shut the door, please." I tossed the shield to him and he caught it, reluctantly it seemed, as he shoved the door shut with his foot.

"G.A.M.," he read the initials on the back of the shield. "J.F.M. . . Who the hell are you?"

"John Francis Malone, detective third, Homicide. The other initials are my father's. He wore that badge before I did."

"Yeah? How do I know you didn't steal it? What's going on in here, anyhow? Who's been doing all the shooting?"

"Me. All except the first. Somebody else did that."

"And where might that somebody be, if I might ask?" His politeness was entirely assumed.

"Out the window."

He walked over to the window and looked down at the sidewalk below. "He ain't there now."

"You didn't think he'd stay around, did you, waiting for us to ask him up for a drink?"

A siren sounded outside. "I gotta take you in. Your story sounds sorta fishy to me." He lifted my revolver from the bed. "Where'd you get this?"

"You'll find it's mine, and registered in my name."

"Huh," he grunted as he slipped my gun into his pocket. "Stand up here while I see what else you've got." His big hands patted me thoroughly. "What else you got in this room?"

"Another gun, some dope, and a couple thousand dollars."

A second patrolman appeared at the door, gun in hand. "What's cookin', Buzz?" the newcomer asked.

"This guy's been shooting holes through the door." He tipped my shield so only the other patrolman could see it, which was pretty smart since it didn't give the curious neighbors any clue that I was a detective. "I don't know what to believe. What do you think?"

"Better take him around to the Station."

"Yeah," said Buzz, "I guess I better. Come on, let's go."

"How about somebody hanging around until I get back?" I asked. "I like to have some of my stuff here when I return."

"All right," said the other cop. "I'll keep an eye on it for you."

Buzz and I went out together, pushing our way through the chattering crowd on the stairs, and got in the patrol car that was waiting outside with its driver. Buzz was still suspicious, and you couldn't blame him.

"What Precinct did you say you worked out of?" he asked.

"None. I said I was with the Homicide Squad."

"Yeah? Who's head of it?"

"Stratford. Know him?"

"Naw. That don't prove nothing. You could of read it in the newspapers." The car stopped. "Let's get out here and see who knows you." We walked into the station house together. "What did you say your name is?"

"John Francis Malone, detective third grade." Miscellaneous characters watched us as we walked past the desk and the night sergeant sitting there.

"Taking this guy in to see the skipper," Buzz explained. "Book him later." We passed through a door and entered an office where a police lieutenant sat at a table, reading reports. "Here's one for you, boss," my escort said. "He's been shooting holes through his door, and when I find him he shows me this"—he tossed my shield on the desk—"and this." My gun followed the shield.

The lieutenant picked up the badge, looked at it, and dialed a number on his telephone. "Hello. Got a shield here"—he read the number—"with the initials G.A.M. and J.F.M. on the back? . . . What?" He wrote something on a scratch pad. "What does he look like? . . . Yeah. What's his gun number?" He wrote again. "What's his fingerprint classification? . . . yeah . . . yeah . . . yeah I got it. Thanks."

He pushed an ink pad toward me, and I rolled fingers over it and then over the piece of paper on which he had been making his notes. He studied them for a while, then he turned to Buzz and asked. "Did he tell you what his name was?"

"Yeah. Malone. John Francis Malone."

The lieutenant handed me my shield and my gun. "Here you are, Malone," he grinned. "Or at least if you aren't Malone you're something new in police work, because your number and your prints match up. How much do you feel like telling me?"

"Aw, nuts," Buzz exploded, striking a match across his trousers and lighting a cigarette. "And I thought I had made a pinch. No hard feelings, though. My name's Haggerty." He extended his hand.

"Mine's Broadbent," the lieutenant introduced himself, and I shook hands with both of them. "How about it?" Broadbent repeated. "Can you tell me what's cooking?"

"A little," I admitted. "I'm working on a narcotics deal that I ran into while hunting a murderer. One of the gang must be wise—at least, it wasn't a good friend of mine who was waiting for me in that room."

We sat around in Broadbent's office and chatted for a little while longer, but they didn't learn anything they didn't need to know. After a while we drove back to my place with a couple of their specialists, who looked around the room for fingerprints—they didn't find any—and dug the bullet that had come through the door out of the wall across the hall. It was smashed too much to be any good.

While they were doing that I gathered my stuff together— what little there was—dug the morphine out of the mattress, and my cash out of the window-shade roller. The landlord was hanging around, so I paid my rent and gave him an extra ten to fix the door.

We went back to the station house where they gave me a locker to stick my stuff in, and checked my little automatic and most of my money in the strong box. Then, since it was about four o'clock in the morning, I turned in on a cot and went to sleep.

XVI.

There were only four people in the world who knew where I had lived on Second Avenue and who also could have had any reason to kill me. One was Muddy Track. If he had found out I was a cop he might have tried it. He could have followed me home any time without my knowing about it, just as he had shadowed me into that movie when I went out on my first delivery job. Ciro Valentino had driven me close to my place, and he might have found out where the room was if he had wanted to. Herman and Cookie certainly knew. I had told them.

Of all the four, the one that I had suspected the most was Cookie. But it was a dead cinch he hadn't been there when somebody had fired a shot at me, because he was in the hospital.

Ciro wasn't much of a possibility. So far as I knew, he was hiding somewhere, with the law after him, and wouldn't be taking chances while the heat was on.

That left Muddy and Herman—and Muddy wasn't a killer. So Herman was trying to kill me either because he knew I was Johnny Malone, or for some other reason that wouldn't make much difference to me after I was dead.

It was interesting to think about, but I went to sleep instead.

There was a different lieutenant on duty when I crawled out of the cot in the police station in the morning, and he sent one of the boys to get a key made from the tracing I had made in Herman's apartment. While that was being done, I shaved and had a cup of coffee and some doughnuts. When the man came back with the new key, I was ready to go.

The key fitted the main door to the apartment house on Ninetieth Street evenly and cleanly. I took the self-operated

129

elevator to the floor above Herman's apartment, walked down, and listened carefully outside his door. Now and then I seemed to hear the faintest of sounds. It could have been someone breathing heavily, or it could have been the street traffic below. I rapped gently on the door.

No answer.

I rapped again, louder this time.

No answer—or was there a little noise inside? If there was, it wasn't repeated.

The key slid silently into the lock and I pushed the door open slowly, my gun ready, my body bent low to the floor.

Something—somebody—was lying on the floor inside, and there was a dark brown stain that had spread ominously over the rug. As I closed the door quietly behind me, a wheeze came from the prone figure, its shoulders heaved, its head turned a little.

I tiptoed into the room and bent over the body. "Muddy, Muddy," I whispered. "What's wrong?"

He heard my voice, struggled to rise, fell back on the floor with blood drooling thickly from his lips. Very gently I turned him over on his back, ripped his shirtfront open, but when I saw the purple-lipped hole in his chest, where a wide knife had been slipped between his ribs, I knew there was nothing I could do except make the poor guy comfortable for the next twenty minutes or so. I propped some pillows around his head, opened his collar, and got a wet towel from the bathroom to sponge his sallow face while he followed my movements with dull, pained eyes.

"Doctor?" I asked, softly.

He nodded his head slowly from one side to the other, started to speak, but was choked as a fresh throatful of blood, from God knows where, gushed into his mouth. I wiped it away.

"Thanks . . . Johnny," he mumbled. "Too . . . late . . . now."

"Who did it? Herman?"

He nodded a slow yes.

"Why? Why did he try to kill you?"

"I . . . know . . ."—another hemorrhage choked him, and

130

I had to wipe more of the crimson froth from his lips before he could go on—"too . . . much."

"What do you know, Muddy? What do you know?"

"Tell the cops, Johnny, tell the cops for me. . . ." Only by putting my ears close to his mouth could I understand his tortured whispers.

"What should I tell the cops, Muddy? Tell me, I'll tell them."

He looked at me through the gray haze that was forming over his eyes. "Cigarette. . . ." I lighted one for him, held it between his lips while he took a long, gurgling drag. His eyes closed.

"Muddy! Muddy! Don't go now. Why did Herman kill you? What should I tell the cops?"

"Tell Johnny Malone . . . Malone . . . a cop . . . J-j-j. . . ." The weak voice trailed off to nothingness again.

"I'm Johnny Malone, Muddy. I'm a cop. I'm Johnny Malone, do you hear me? I'm Johnny Malone! Do you hear me, Muddy? Do you understand? I'm Johnny Malone!"

His weak hand moved to touch mine. "Hello, Johnny . . . Malone. Herman said . . . you were. . . . Didn't know . . . your old man . . . good to me . . . I was a kid. Should have listened . . . what he said. Too late . . . now . . . goodby."

I thought he had died, he lay so still, but there was one little spark left in his heart.

"Johnny," he breathed. "Herman . . . is . . . Rudol . . . you know?"

"I know who you mean, Muddy. Thanks."

"Saw him kill your father, Johnny . . . cigarette. . . ." He took another horrible drag. "Get him . . . Johnny."

"I will, Muddy, I'll get him now." I stood up.

"Wait until . . . I go, Johnny," the dying man's thin voice floated up to me, and I bent down beside him again. "Not afraid . . . just don't want to . . . be alone, that's all."

"Sure, Muddy," I said. "Sure, sure, I'll stay. Cigarette?" But his lips were too weak to hold it, and he couldn't control the bubbles in his throat. I wiped his face again.

The red mouth moved. "Music," it said. "Going now."

There was a little radio set on the table, and I turned it on and waited beside Muddy while it warmed up. An orchestra was playing a selection I didn't recognize. Muddy's fingers curled around mine; his breathing grew fainter and fainter.

"That was a recording of Beethoven's Symphony Number Three, in E Flat Major, commonly known as the 'Eroica Symphony,' as played by the London Philharmonic Orchestra under the direction of Serge Koussevitzky," the announcer intoned. "And now for your ten o'clock weather report." I started to go and tune in something else, but Muddy's fingers held me. "This afternoon and this evening will be cloudy, with light rain and heavy fog over most of New York City and vicinity. Clearing tomorrow and warmer. In Connecticut and . . ."

The fingers fell away from my own.

I turned off the radio and its weather reports and started for the door, but then I came back, slowly. Muddy had never done me any harm. He had been a pretty good guy, for a dope runner. I pulled the cover off the studio couch, took one of the sheets and spread it carefully over him, crossed myself.

"Hail Mary, full of grace. . . ."

Then I remembered something else, and stepped over to look at the dusty old newspapers lying in a pile on Herman's desk. Each one contained the story of Probationary Patrolman John Malone and how he had killed two men caught sticking up Meyerowitz's Jewelry Store.

I wondered how many times Herman had read and reread those papers, looking for some clue that would lead him to me. Finally he had learned, from Cookie, and now he was somewhere in New York searching for me. Maybe he was standing outside the door of his apartment. Maybe he was on the street below. Wherever he was, he was looking for Johnny Murphy . . . Johnny Malone.

Did he know that I knew he was Rudolph Hoffmann? Probably not. That was the only advantage I had as I swung the apartment door open and stepped into the hall.

It was empty. I walked down two flights before I pushed the button to bring the elevator to the floor, rode down to the street level, and walked out on the sidewalk. The bright morning sun was already covered by dark clouds scudding across the sky, foretelling the rain and fog the weather forecaster had promised. It looked like the beginning of a dirty day, a day that had started with one murder and might well end with another.

There was only one place I could think of to start my search —Billie Bloomer's apartment. Her man had gone to her after the murder of Peter Arranto. He might go there again.

No familiar figure was waiting for me anywhere I could see as I walked carefully across town to Madison Avenue and boarded a downtown bus. Looking back to that day, I have to smile to myself and wonder why somebody didn't report the suspicious character who kept his hand inside his coat, like Napoleon, and who stopped so often to fix his shoelaces or simply lean against a wall to study his surroundings before he walked on. And I sat in the rear seat of the bus, too, where I could check every person who entered after I did.

Billie, hollow-eyed, haggard, and shaky, opened the door when I knocked. "Hello, fella," she said, drawing her negligee together at the neck. "Fancy meeting you at this time of the day." Then she spotted the gun in my hand. "Hey, what the hell goes on, mister?"

"Keep your voice down," I whispered. "Is Herman here?"

"No."

"Any cops around?"

"Hell, no. Do I look like I was entertaining cops?" She looked like she was entertaining a bad hangover.

I pushed her back through the door and followed her inside, closing the door behind us. "The cops are looking for all of us. They caught Muddy Track. I gotta find Herman and tell him. He wasn't at his place, maybe he'll show up here."

"I don't know where he is. I haven't seen him since the night before last. Jeez, I wish he'd show up, I need a shot." She looked at herself in a mirror on the wall, then turned again toward me. "I met you the other night, what's your name?"

"Johnny Murphy."

"You got any snow on you, Johnny? Just a little? I need it bad this morning."

"Not me, sister, not today. Didn't you hear me say the cops caught Muddy? They're not catching me with any stuff, not Johnny Murphy."

She walked across the room and took a bottle of whiskey from a cupboard, brought it toward me with two glasses. "Don't mind if a girl has a drink, do you?" She poured one glass about a third full, tossed it down in a single swallow, held the bottle

133

and the other glass toward me. "Help yourself, Johnny, and get your mind off your troubles."

"When do you think Herman will be here?" The raw liquor burned my tongue.

"I don't know. After I'm finished with my show tonight, maybe. Maybe he won't be here at all. I told you I didn't see him last night."

"I'll wait. You got anything to eat in here?" The one-room apartment didn't seem to offer too much in the way of banquet facilities, but there was a hot plate, a sink full of dirty dishes, and a small icebox in one corner. The rest of the room was furnished with a studio couch, unmade and the sheets disheveled after a night's use, a single armchair, the cupboard which also seemed to serve as a dressing table, and a worn rug on the floor. One door led into a closet; through another I could see stockings and lingerie hanging in a small bathroom. I sat down in the chair.

"Coffee and eggs." She poured herself another drink. "I was just about to get myself some breakfast when you knocked, though God only knows what good food will do me. Are you sure you don't have any stuff with you, Johnny? I'd do anything for a little shot, honey." The negligee dropped open slightly.

"Coffee and eggs will do, toots. Cover yourself up before you catch a cold. I came here to see Herman."

She moved over to the hot plate, filled a coffee maker, while I lit a cigarette and poured myself another drink and wished Herman would show up before I got fidgety.

"You don't mind if I fix myself up a little, do you? Herman might get a wrong idea if he came in here and found us like this." She gathered some clothes from the closet and disappeared into the bathroom. "Don't let the coffee boil over," she warned as she closed the door. In a few seconds I heard water running in the shower.

When she reappeared she had accomplished a minor miracle. Make-up hid the lines around her eyes and the corners of her mouth, her hair was neatly arranged, her dress was clean and up-to-date and as modest as anything she could wear would ever be. Only the slight shaking of her hands and the pupils of her eyes showed that she was a drug addict, and you had to be pretty good to spot it. A lot of guys would have said she was a knockout.

Eggs went into a skillet and were sizzling away, when there was a rap at the door and I jumped out of the chair and into the bathroom. "See who it is," I whispered. "Don't say I'm here, no matter who it is, even if it's Herman—there may be cops behind him." Through the space between the door and the frame, I watched her walk across the room.

She turned the lock while I waited, my finger tight on the trigger of the .38, blood pounding in my head.

A roughly dressed young punk with an armful of paper bags pushed his way into the room, looked around, and then put his bundles on the table and kicked the door shut behind him. "Hyah, Billie," patting her on the fanny. "Here's the stuff you ordered yesterday, except we don't have no lamb chops. How about a little kiss or somethin', huh?"

"Go away." She pushed him toward the door. "I'm expecting company for breakfast." The delivery boy followed her glance toward the eggs frying in the skillet, shrugged his shoulders, muttered something I didn't understand, and left.

I stepped out of the bathroom. "You seem to have a lot of affectionate friends," I smiled.

"Damned fresh kids." She passed it off. "Who does he think he is, anyhow?"

The eggs and coffee were just what I needed. We ate silently, Billy mixing whiskey with her food. Finally, when the eggs were gone and there was no more coffee I offered her a cigarette, lit one for myself, and relaxed for the first time since I left Herman's apartment and the murdered Muddy.

"It doesn't look as though you were expecting Herman very soon. Too bad I had to be here when the butcher's boy dropped in. Did I ruin your morning?"

"Nuts." The tone was scornful. "Good thing you were here. That guy would want to be marrying me soon if I didn't get rid of him. Have another drink."

"What do you want me to do, get drunk before Herman gets here?"

"Hell, maybe he'll never show up. You and me might as well get acquainted. Pour one for me, too, I've gotta go to the john."

XVII.

BILLIE BLOOMER and I sat
there until about five o'clock, batting the breeze and drinking
whiskey. She could drink more than any human being I ever
saw. She must have had almost two fifths compared to the four
or five little shots I fiddled with during the afternoon. But by
five o'clock she was definitely drunk. Her make-up was smeared
where she had wiped her mouth with the side of her hand, and
her hair was tumbled over her face. Liquor had spilled down
the front of her dress.

"You're a bum, Johnny Murphy." Whiskey sloshed into her
glass again. "Jus' a bum. Why di'n you bring me jus' one little
powder? Tha's all I need, jus' one little powder. Go get some,
honey. Go 'head, get me jus' one weensie little bit, a teensy-
weensie little bit for Billy." Her mouth hung slightly open and
she was having trouble focusing her eyes as her head bobbed
back and forth. "You know where some is, go get some for
me. Gotta sing tonight, y' know. Can't sing this way, Johnny.
Go on, do it for Billie. Billie'll be here when you get back."

She settled back on the couch, looked at me with one eye,
patted the sheet beside her. "Come here an' let me give you a
great big kiss, Johnny, and then you'll get me a teensy-weensie
little shot, won't you, honey . . . honey . . . honey." The
next thing I heard was snoring. She was a very ugly sight when
she was drunk *and* asleep.

A glance at my watch said it was six o'clock, but there was
no way to tell how soon Herman would show up, if ever.
Maybe, I began to think, maybe he won't come at all. If he
thought that Muddy's body had been found in his apartment.
. . . Then I kicked myself for being a stupid fool!

Of course, that was what had happened. Herman had come

back to his apartment and found Muddy with the sheet over him, propped up with pillows. He knew damn well Muddy never did it himself, so someone else had been there. Who? Maybe Herman might guess it had been me, but he couldn't be sure. Somebody else knew that Muddy had been killed, that somebody might have told the police, who might have gone to Billie's to see if he was where they had found him before. No matter what he thought, any dope could figure that he wouldn't come knocking at the door I was watching, at least not for a long, long time.

I tried to put myself in Herman's place and figure what I would do, but I was so sore at myself I couldn't think clearly. The whole afternoon had been wasted sitting there drinking cheap whiskey with a cheap blonde floozy and, instead of being the great detective, Malone was nothing more than a great oaf. I kicked the table and sent the glasses crashing to the floor.

"All right," a heavy voice on the other side of the door called out. "I know you're in there. Come on out."

I fired two shots through the door, heard a muffled cry of pain followed by a stream of cursing, and started for the lock to finish Rudolph Hoffmann once and for all. A fusillade of shots from the other side changed my mind, darned near forever, and, as bullets whistled by my head and cracked into the wall above the oblivious Billie, I jumped for the bathroom window, kicked out the glass, and lowered myself until I was hanging from the sill by my fingertips. The apartment door splintered open as I twisted my head to see what was below me, and, just before I dropped, a brilliant spotlight stabbed against my shoulders and a bullet from somewhere knocked little pieces of brick from the wall beside my face.

My right leg hit an ashcan in the alley below as I fell. Pain grabbed the ankle and I turned over, striking the back of my head on rough, wet cobblestones. It didn't knock me out, but there wasn't any fight left in me as I lay there with the slow rain falling on my face, wondering what the hell was happening. It didn't take long to find out.

A uniformed cop, with more guts than brains, came running down the alleyway, blew his whistle, and a spotlight from a squad car searched along the dark walls until it found me.

The patrolman approached cautiously. "I've got you!" he shouted. "Don't move, or I'll shoot!"

"Aw, shut up, hero, and put that gun away." I moved my hand to get the detective's shield from my pocket, but he aimed his cannon at me and I froze. "You'll find a potsy in my pocket, copper. Name's Malone. Homicide Squad."

"Pipe down," he growled; and then, as two other policemen came running up to him, "This guy says he's on the force. Keep an eye on him while I look in his pocket."

He leaned over me, keeping his pistol stuck in my ribs, shoved his free hand into my pocket, and came out with the little leather case. "Nuts," he said, and tossed the badge to one of the other cops. "Take a good look at this in the light and make sure it ain't out of a box of Nifties." Again he leaned over, ran his hand across my chest, and then removed my pistol from its holster. "You can get up now."

"Give me a hand, there's something wrong with my ankle."

The third cop helped me get up. "Now let's get out of the rain and sit in the car while we get this thing straightened out, boys," I said, stepping gingerly on the bad leg. "I've got a lot of work to do tonight and I don't want to waste time."

Finally the whole gang of us—patrolmen, detectives, three or four squad cars—wound up at the station house. The cop I had shot through the door of Billie's apartment wasn't badly hurt, all he had was a little scratch across the upper part of his left arm. After he got it disinfected and bandaged he was as good as new. We shook—it was just one of those things you're liable to run into in police work—and I promised to pay for mending the holes in his coat.

Sitting there in the Station, I found out that Herman had darned near outsmarted me permanently. At least, I guessed it was Herman. Somebody had reported that there was a murdered man in an apartment on Ninetieth Street—Herman's apartment—and that the murderer was a guy named Johnny Murphy and he was hiding, armed and ready to shoot, in Billie Bloomer's place. Of course, the cops had gone up to Ninetieth Street to take a look and there they found Muddy Track. That didn't leave much doubt in their minds as to the truth in the rest of the story, so they had surrounded Billie's place.

Some of them had sneaked up the stairs to catch me in the

room, and when I kicked the table over they made their move. It was only luck that I didn't kill one of them when I let fly through the door, and only a whole lot more luck kept them from killing me. If I hadn't turned my ankle when I hit the ground, and had tried to make a run for it, I would have been a dead duck.

We were getting the story straightened out and my ankle taped up so I could walk without too much trouble when all of a sudden the conversation stopped and all the guys who were sitting stood up, and those who were standing stood a little straighter. I looked over my shoulder and saw my boss, Inspector Stratford, come into the room. He didn't look too pleased.

"God damn it, Malone!" he roared, chewing his cigar. "What the hell are you doing, anyhow? I've been trying to get you ever since last night, and all I find is holes shot through doors all over the city, Christ knows how many people killed or dying in hospitals, and you trying to shoot it out with half a Precinct!"

"Yes, sir, but . . ."

"Don't 'but' me, Malone. What's happened to that dope gang you had sewed up, and what's happened to Rudy Hoffmann?"

"The gang's pretty well done for, Inspector. Cookie Adler's still in the hospital with a belly full of holes. Valentino's on the lam, I guess. Track got killed this morning. Except for me there's only one person left, and that's Herman Holman. Holman killed Track." I paused for a breath. "Holman, sir, is Rudolph Hoffmann. I think. As soon as I get this ankle strapped up I'm going out and look for him some more."

"Where the hell is he?"

"I don't know, sir, but if I look around enough I bet I can find him."

"You *hope* you can find him, you mean. What's all this shooting that's going on this evening?"

"Hoffmann must have found out that I was in his girl's apartment, waiting for him, so he called up the fellows here and told them where I was and that I was the guy who had killed Track. He probably figured I'd do just what I did, shoot through the door, and then the police would kill me and save him the trouble."

"You're too goddamned lucky to live, Malone. Lieutenant Broadbent tells me you were shooting through doors over on the East Side last night. Who were you shooting at then, Hoffmann?"

"That's my guess, Inspector."

"Guess? Guess? By God, Malone, you're not paid to guess—don't you *know?*"

"I'm sure Holman is Hoffmann, sir."

"Christ Almighty, two days ago you were sure this other guy, Cookie, was Hoffmann. What made you change your mind?"

"Muddy Track told me, just before he died."

"That kind of evidence ain't worth a gust of gas in a high wind. I bet we can't prove that Hoffmann killed your friend Track, or Peter what's-his-name, or that he was ever in the dope racket, or even that he killed your old man—and what the hell are you going to do about it? I'm asking you."

His jawing was beginning to get under my skin and I felt my face grow redder and redder. "I'm going to bring him in," I retorted, "in a sack. The D.A. won't have to spend any time or any money proving anything. Hoffmann will be dead when he sees him."

"Yeah, or else Malone will be dead. I gave you a week to get that guy when you had them all eating out of your hand. There's still a couple of days left, but I'm putting out an alarm to the whole department to pick him up. If you want to get him first you'll have to work fast, because there are some guys on this force who've got brains." He threw the chewed-up butt of his cigar in a cuspidor, turned toward the door, then reached in his pocket and faced back to me again. "If you get in trouble, Malone, use this." He tossed something shiny toward me and I caught it as he walked out.

It was a police whistle.

The other policemen kind of stood around on one foot for a while and then most of them drifted away. They didn't know me personally and they were all embarrassed because the Inspector had chewed me out in front of them. I was embarrassed, too, and sore.

"Give me my gun and my old man's badge," I said to the sergeant at the desk, "and check me out of here."

He was a wise and understanding old-timer. He handed me my stuff and watched me leave without saying a word.

Since then Stratford has told me that the whole thing was

140

deliberate on his part, just to make me sore. He knew I was disappointed and all fouled up with my thinking, and rather than let me get down in the dumps he gave me a verbal boot in my tail to keep me moving.

It worked. A dirty, drizzling rain was falling when I walked out on the street to begin my hunt again. It trickled down the back of my neck, but I didn't even feel it. The only thing that surprises me is that it wet me at all—I was so burned up by the Inspector's bawling out that the rain should have sizzled into steam as fast as it fell on me.

There wasn't a clear idea in my mind, not a clue. For a while all I did was walk along the street, peering intently at the faces of all the people I passed, hurrying to overtake other pedestrians ahead of me so that I could turn and make sure they were not Rudy. None of them were.

The rain soaked my cigarettes as fast as I lit them, one after another. Taxis came toward me and I tried to fade into shadows, for I never knew when one of them would belch a stream of lead from the rear seat. But gradually I calmed down and made an effort to systematize my thoughts. The calmer I got the wetter I got.

Finally I stepped to the curb and hailed a taxi, told the driver to take me to Hoffmann's place on Ninetieth Street. There didn't seem to be much chance that he would be there, but it seemed as good a place as any to start over again.

There was a plainclothesman loitering in the lobby. He merely nodded when he saw my shield and learned where I was going. Another opened the apartment door when I knocked. Muddy's body was gone but the rug with its dark stain was there to remind me of what had happened only a few hours before.

"Malone. Homicide Squad. Find anything worthwhile?"

"Naw. Wasn't even a fingerprint. Everything in the place was wiped clean, even the handle on the john."

"Anything in the desk drawers?"

"Nothing but some underwear and a couple of shirts and some dirty socks that belonged to the guy who lived here."

"He was in the dope racket, you know, and he had a lot of cash somewhere. You find anything like that?"

"Gee, I don't think anybody said anything about dope. But

we didn't find any money or other stuff. Just some clothes, like I said, and those old newspapers, and a couple of suits in the closet. You can look around if you want to, you seem to know as much about this case as I do. Who the hell killed the little guy, anyhow?"

"The fellow who lived here. Herman Holman, he called himself." Carefully I inspected the suits in the closet, didn't find anything in particular.

"Jeez," the guard went on, plainly glad to have someone to talk to. "He sure did a good job with a knife. Only thing I can't figure, how was the little guy able to prop himself up with pillows, and smoke cigarettes, and who put a sheet over him after he was dead?"

"I did. I sat here and watched him croak." There was an old pair of shoes on the closet floor, but although the soles had a foul odor they were scraped clean and I couldn't find anything on them that told me where Hoffmann went walking. "Better have these sent down to the lab," I said, tossing them out. "Maybe a microscope can find something on them."

"You say you were here?" The guard regarded me suspiciously. "How do I know you're on the force? Maybe you killed the little fellow yourself."

I was busy going through the desk drawers by that time, so I picked up the old newspapers and handed them to him. "Here, cousin, read about me and stop worrying. I didn't kill him; all I'm trying to do is find the guy who did." There wasn't anything in the desk, except old clothes, nor could I find anything in the whole apartment to aid the search for Hoffmann.

"Gee," the guard said, putting the papers back on the desk. "I didn't recognize your name at first, Malone. Sorry I said what I did."

"Forget it." I sat down in the chair and lit a cigarette, felt my ankle beginning to throb again. "Half a Precinct made the same mistake a couple of hours ago, so you're excused." The smoke felt good in my lungs. "But I wish to God I had some idea where that fellow Holman is," I added. "I'm looking for him, and for keeps."

When I finished the cigarette, I left and went down to the hospital. Maybe Cookie could tell me something.

It was about ten o'clock when I got there, long after visiting

142

hours, and I had to argue with the girl at the desk before she would even call the duty nurse to find out if Cookie could have a visitor—even one from the Police Department. But finally she told me to go up.

The nurse, somebody I didn't know, looked at my wet clothes with evident distaste, as though she was sure I was carrying an epidemic of pneumonia around with me. "Mr. Adler is awake," she said, "but he's still a very sick man, and I can't allow you to disturb him. The police were here this afternoon, talking to him, and his fever went up considerably until an hour or so ago. You'll have to be very careful."

"Yes, ma'm. I won't bother him. I only want to ask him where I can find his friend, Mr. Holman."

"Don't take more than fifteen minutes."

Cookie was pale and thinner than he had been before he was shot, but he didn't look too badly to me, not for a guy with a belly full of holes. He was reading a newspaper when I walked in.

"Hello, you goddamned cop," he snarled. "What the hell do you want?"

"How did you find out I was a cop?"

"By keeping my eyes shut and my ears open, stupid. I heard that dumb dick call you 'Malone' when you came in here the other day."

"And you told Herman, huh?"

"You'll never know." His eyes glared their hatred at me.

"Where's Herman now?"

"Don't make me laugh, Malone, I've got stitches."

The policeman who had been guarding the wounded man was standing beside the bed. "Close the door," I said. "I don't want them to hear this guy screaming." He grinned, pushed the door shut.

XVIII.

I̲T̲ ̲D̲I̲D̲N̲'̲T̲ scare Cookie one little bit. He knew darned well I wasn't going to lay a finger on him there in the hospital, unless I wanted to get thrown off the force.

"What are you going to do now, Dick Tracy? Comb my hair?"

"I'm going to bust you one right in the belly if you don't tell me where Herman is!"

"Oh, no, you're not. This is a hospital, bud, not the back room at headquarters."

"Listen, Adler. I've got enough on you to send you up the river for the rest of your life, and before you go I'll have a chance to talk to you in one of those back rooms you seem to know so much about. Where did you learn, anyhow? With the Nazis?"

"I'll bet I don't get more than a couple of years, if I get anything. You don't have a damned thing on me except carrying a gun." He had me there.

"We can send you back to Germany."

"That'll break my heart," he sneered. "Why don't you go away, little boy, and play detective while I finish reading my newspaper."

"One more chance, Cookie." I leaned over him, my fist clenched above his abdomen. "Tell me where Herman is or I'll break you open!"

"Aw, shut up!" I jerked my fist down about four inches, just grazing the sheet, but the newspaper in his hand never even shook. What the hell are you going to do with a guy like that?

"Open the door," I told the cop. "I'm just wasting my time

here. If I want to find his buddy I better go out and look for him."

"I never seen 'em come any tougher," he volunteered. "We had three guys in here this afternoon and he didn't tell them anything, either. If we hadn't found his name on them papers he had with him when he got shot we'd probably be thinking he was Mr. Hush's brother, for all the news he gives out."

"Yeah. Well, goodby, Cookie. I'll be waiting for you when you get discharged." He didn't return my farewells, and I walked over to the elevator, went downstairs, and around the corner to see if Mary was in.

She wasn't, and nobody seemed to know where she was, except that she had gone to some kind of a party. I remembered the party Herman had said he would throw to celebrate Cookie's recovery, and wished he was throwing it that night so I could walk in and shoot the host.

The next place I visited was Sophie's. The bartender jumped like he was seeing a ghost when I came in and sat down at the bar.

"Come here," I ordered, paying no attention to the other customers. "Where the hell is Herman? Have you seen him?"

"What are you doing here?" he stammered. "Herman told me . . . I thought . . . didn't the cops get you this afternoon?"

"No, the cops didn't get me. What made you think they did?"

"Herman said you were over at Billie's when we had all the shooting this afternoon."

"What made him think I was there?"

"Gee, I don't know. But they caught somebody and took him away."

"It wasn't me, buddy. Where's Herman now?"

"I don't know. He left after that."

"Did he see who it was the cops took away?"

"He went out. He didn't come back."

Can you imagine the nerve of that Hoffmann guy? He called up the police, told them I had killed Muddy and where to find me, and then he came down and was probably standing on the corner to see what happened. It was a wonder he didn't put on a uniform and drive up in a squad car.

"Where's Billie?" I wondered.

"She got creased when the bullets were flying around and they took her over to Bellevue."

"Hurt bad?"

"I don't think so. Somebody told me she would be wearing an adhesive-tape brassiere, that's all I know. She was out cold, they said."

"Tough. You sure you don't know where Herman is?"

"No. He didn't say where he was going."

"Maybe he went over to Bellevue to see Billie?"

He shrugged his shoulders, drew a beer for a customer. "Could be."

I slid into the telephone booth and called Bellevue Hospital. "Give me the police emergency ward," I told the operator. "Hello. This is Detective Malone, Homicide Squad." I gave my shield number. "Did you get a girl who goes by the name of Billie Bloomer in there about six-thirty today? Shot in the . . . you did? . . . Did anybody come in to see her, or did anybody call for her? . . . They didn't? . . . How is she, all right? . . . Oh, she is? Thanks, that's all."

Billie was still drunk, and nobody had tried to get in touch with her.

So all I knew about Herman—or Hoffmann—was that he had been in the Village at six-thirty. It was now eleven, and he could have been halfway to Mexico in the time that had passed. "If Herman comes back tell him to wait for me," I told the bartender. "I'll be back about one."

Only a little rain was falling by that time, but a chilly, dense fog was slowly settling over the city. Steamship whistles sounded deep notes over on the Hudson River, their throaty tones punctuated now and then by the shriller toots of tugs. I walked up through Washington Square Park, aimlessly and in a fog of my own, through the little street between the park and Eighth, and turned to the left.

"Hello, Johnny," a voice greeted me. Surprised, I turned my hand jumping inside my coat, and I breathed out in a long sigh when I saw it was only Dinny. "What's the matter, Johnny? You act kinda jumpy, boy."

"Dinny! You damned near got yourself shot, fella. I'm as nervous as the Sultan's bride tonight."

"Well, take it easy," he said. "Cool off. You were walking along there like you were asleep, and that's no way to be. You better go home and go to bed."

"Wish I could, but I can't. The Inspector's riding my tail to bring in Hoffmann, but quick."

"Who?"

"Didn't you hear? Rudolph Hoffmann, the guy who shot my father fifteen years ago. There's a general alarm out for him."

"The hell you say. I didn't hear about it. Who is this Hoffmann anyhow?"

"What do you mean, you don't know? He's the same guy you picked up a couple of days ago—the fellow who called himself Herman Holman."

"Herman Hol . . . !" Dinny's eyes rounded with amazement. "Why, for Christ's sake, Johnny, I was just saying hello to him and some girl, not more than twenty minutes ago!"

"You were *what!*" I grabbed him by the lapels of his coat. "Where, Dinny, for God's sake! Where was it! I've been looking for him for thirty hours! What did the girl look like?"

"Cute little thing. Pretty as a picture. Maybe five feet six inches tall. Black hair. I think I've seen her over at the hospital a couple of times."

"That's my girl! Where were they!"

"Walking up Sixth Avenue. He nodded to me and I nodded to him and said hello. I didn't know you were looking for him."

"Jesus," I said. "Why didn't I tell you all about it the other day. Which way did they go, Dinny? I've got to get them!" I remembered how Hoffmann got when he had killed—now he was somewhere with my Mary.

"I looked back and saw them turn and go down Tenth Street, so I figured he was walking her back to the hospital. Gee, Johnny, I wish I had known about it, I'd . . ."

I didn't wait for his answer before I started running. The twisted ankle slowed me down and hurt like hell, but I limped and dodged between the people on the sidewalk as fast as possible. There wasn't any fog in my brain any more, nothing except red Irish rage, and that didn't interfere with my thinking. Once I slipped on the wet pavement and went down, but

147

I was up and hurrying on in another second, nothing but my dignity bruised.

There were no couples walking anywhere near the hospital, and Mary hadn't checked in. Slowly and limpingly I retraced the route they might have used, asking everybody I met whether they had seen a tall man of forty-five or so with a pretty black-haired girl.

Nobody had.

There are a lot of little drinking and eating places around that part of New York, most of them down in cellars, like Sophie's. I started to search through them one by one.

When you leave the fog and the gloom and the outside darkness and step through a door under the bright light that shines in front of the hatcheck booth, you wish you were invisible. You couldn't be a better target for someone you can't see, but who may be sitting in one of the dark booths. "Check, please," the girl says, but you're too busy trying to probe back into the half light to pay any attention to her. The hair stands up on the back of your neck, and those aren't raindrops on your forehead—that's sweat.

Cold sweat. And you can't keep it back, because it pours naturally when you're looking for a man who wants to kill you, and you know he'll see you first. You're scared silly, but there isn't anything to do except walk down that line of dimly lighted booths and between the tables while the juke box dins in your ears so loudly you wonder if you could hear a shot or a woman screaming, "Look out, Johnny!" before it hits you in the back. And you want to put a cigarette in your mouth but you don't dare use your hands to open the pack or light a match or do anything with them except be ready to grab your gun at the same time you're dropping flat on the floor so you'll be harder to hit.

There must be some better way to make a living, but you don't have time to think about that, either. All you think of is that a guy whose hands are bloody and red and who wants only two things—you and a woman—is somewhere with the girl you love, the girl you want to marry, and you keep praying that you can find him before he can have either of the things he wants that night.

He isn't in the first place you visit, or the second, or the

148

third, or the next or the next or the next. Then you get to wondering maybe he's got her in a hotel room, or an apartment, or in some alley over by the waterfront, choking off her screams with those bloody hands of his, laughing in her face when she begs him, promises anything, only don't . . . don't . . . and you hear her dress ripping down the front and you only hope she faints or maybe dies before she knows what finally happens.

You're praying and cursing and you walk down some more steps and open another door. . . .

"JOHNNY! LOOK OUT!"

Splat! Something hot and sharp stung me across the left shoulder, and I dropped to the floor with the gun in my hand, trying to find a target somewhere in that dark room as I wriggled out of the light.

"Come out, Rudy, god damn you, I see you!" I shouted. *I couldn't see a thing.* Somebody had upset a table in front of me, women were screaming and crowding under the booths along the walls, and another bullet splintered through the table top beside my head. Cautiously I peered around the corner, and then I saw him standing against the back wall, holding Mary in front of him for a shield while he waited to get another shot at me.

I knew Mary wasn't big enough to cover him completely, and I could hit him, but I was afraid to try it. There was one chance in a million that I might miss and hit her as she struggled to get away from him. But I could see his legs, as my eyes became more accustomed to the half light, and I slowly brought my revolver to bear on one of them, hoping Mary wouldn't kick as I fired. The .38 boomed and echoed through the room and I rolled over and over until I rolled into some of the huddled customers, waiting for an answer from Rudolph Hoffmann.

None came, and when I looked back to where he had been he and Mary were gone. I raced to the back of the room and into the kitchen. "Where did he go? Where's the girl!" I shouted.

There were two cooks and a dishwasher in the kitchen, and if they had ever known how to speak English they certainly had forgotten it by the time I crashed in. *Jabber jabber jabber.*

149

First they pointed to the door I had come through, then they pointed to some broken dishes and spilled soup. The dishwasher fainted when he saw blood on the floor, a heavy stream that told me I hadn't missed somebody's leg. The blood trail led through a back door into a little yard.

Mary was there, unhurt. "Did he hit you, Johnny?" she sobbed, throwing her arms around me. "Oh, darling, darling, my darling, I thought he had killed you when you fell down." Hysterical tears wet my face. "Oh, Johnny, you shot him— you shot him—right in the leg. He can't get very far."

"Where did he go, Mary. Are you hurt? Are you all right? Did I get here in time?"

"Oh, yes, yes, but I was scared. He's Rudolph Hoffmann, isn't . . ." She stopped and looked at her hand. "He did hit you, Johnny. You're hit! There's blood on my hand."

"It's nothing, only a scratch." But as I lowered my left arm a little red trickle came down over my wrist. It didn't hurt, and when I took off my coat even Mary could see it was only a little cut, not more than a quarter of an inch deep and maybe an inch long. We padded a handkerchief over it so my undershirt would hold it in place for a while.

"Wait until the police get here, Mary. Tell them what happened and make them take you back to the hospital and stay with you until I get back. And I'll be back as soon as there isn't any danger from Rudy Hoffmann ever again. You understand?"

She nodded. "He said we were going to meet you and have a party, Johnny. He said you knew. And then you didn't come and didn't come. . . . Be careful, Johnny. . . . I'll be waiting for you."

I was through the back yard and over the fence as she called to me, following the red trail through another yard and in the rear door of an apartment house. It led me out the front door to the sidewalk, up the street and then, all of a sudden, it disappeared.

It was plain that Hoffmann had found a taxi to pick him up. I looked to the right and saw a yellow automobile through the fog. It was about two blocks away. Suddenly it skidded crazily to a stop, a door opened, there was a little orange flash, and then it drove away again, leaving a dark shadow lying in the middle of the street. The taxi turned toward the river.

In spite of my bad ankle, nobody reached the wounded driver before me. He had been shot through the left arm—sooner or later Hoffmann was going to miss left arms and really hurt someone—and while the poor devil's bone was broken there didn't seem to be much permanent damage.

"What happened?" I asked the cursing driver as I looked at his wound.

"Big guy comes running out, stops me, gets in and says to hurry up to Pier 57, he's gotta catch a boat," he gasped. "I look back and see he's tyin' up a hole in his leg, and that there's blood all over the floor. So I asks him what the hell and slam on the brakes. Next thing I know he's out of the cab with a gat in his hand. He shoots me, yanks me out on the street, and drives off in my hack." He struggled to his feet. "Call a cop, for Christ's sake. I gotta get my hack back!"

"I'm a cop. Take it easy. We'll get your cab back, but wait until you get that arm fixed. Hey, you," I called one of the dopey-looking kibitzers who had gathered around by this time, "get on a phone and get an ambulance for this guy, he's been in an accident. And sit down, you," I ordered the driver, "before you fall down. What was the number of your cab?" I never got an answer, the poor guy fainted dead away and I lowered him to the sidewalk.

"Take care of him, he's not dead. Don't move him around until an ambulance gets here. I've gotta go. Police." I flashed my badge. "Don't let anybody touch him!"

XIX.

But I had no idea where to go. Hoffmann's commandeered taxi had disappeared toward the west and the riverfront. I hurried blindly after it until another cruising cab came along, showed my shield to the driver, and together we started looking for the wounded Rudy. "Pier 57" —that was where he said he wanted to go. We went up there, fast. It's a Grace Line pier, usually busy, but no ships were alongside. The pier guards hadn't seen anyone who looked like Hoffmann.

Telling my driver to shove off, I called Headquarters and asked them to get the number of the wounded driver's cab as soon as he woke up and then start looking for it. Then I leaned against the wall to wait for Hoffmann just in case he should show up at Pier 57.

Where would he go this time, I wondered. Not to Ninetieth Street. Not to Billie's. Not to Muddy's place on Rivington Street. He knew I was alive, he knew I was a cop, he would be sure half the Police Department would be looking for him in every place I could think of.

The fog rolled in from the ocean, carrying with it the mournful tolling of hundreds of bell buoys rocking back and forth all the way from Ambrose Light to Albany, the muffled siren and foghorn calls of the river traffic, the spicy, sour, and undefinable smells of warehouses, fish markets, and strange cargoes from all over the world. I slouched there against the entrance to the pier, watching the fuzzy yellow headlights of passing trucks, feeling something that told me to move on but not saying exactly where or what it was.

Were the little bells trying to say that Hoffmann had gone back to sea? Were those foghorns sounding from a ship which even then was carrying him out of range? It didn't seem so. The only floating thing he might have boarded on the spur of the moment would have been a ferryboat, but that would be crowded with passengers who would have been sure to spot a wounded man with a bloody leg.

A shift in the wind brought in a section of fog with a decayed and rotten odor from some part of the harbor and set it down in front of me. It smelled of dead flesh, of wet feathers—it smelled like the soles of the old shoes in Hoffmann's closet—it smelled like a chicken market.

I knew where Rudy was.

Do you remember when we planned to get the big shipment of heroin from the man in the rowboat, and Herman said that Cookie would be inside the market, looking out? "A guy we know has let him in . . ." he said.

Those markets would be deserted now. Nobody would be there for another hour or so, and Rudy could hide, if he could get in, until the guy he knew arrived. Then, I supposed, if he was Rudy's friend he could manage to move Hoffmann to a better hiding place, one that I would never be able to discover.

It's only four and a half blocks from Pier 57 to the market buildings, and in that many minutes I was there, squinting through the fog and straining my ears to catch the slightest suspicious sound. The old buildings, built in 1887, are ideal for hiding but they aren't good for hunting. Narrow little alleyways, just wide enough for a truck to drive through, separate two-story brick structures, so covered with soot and grime that you can't see where the walls stop and the shadows begin. Rows of windows, the lower sills waist-high, either broken and boarded up or else with glass as dirty as the walls, screen whatever may be inside. They're wonderful to crouch behind.

Rudy Hoffmann, a hole in his leg and a loaded automatic in his hand, was crouching patiently behind one of those windows, waiting.

Which shadow? There were hundreds of them and any second a sharp *splat* and an orange flash and a little hunk of lead might come from any one.

It wasn't only the fog and the damp air that made me shiver —I was scared, and I'm not ashamed to admit it. But something made me start down the first alley alone, instead of calling the nearest precinct and asking for a squad of cops to ring the place.

This was more than a murder case. This was a family affair. Maybe I was going at it the hard way but when it was over nobody else was going to be able to take the credit for killing the rat who had shot my old man in the back.

I wanted to kill him with my bare hands, if I could, but a .38 slug would do.

"Cookie will make sure there's nobody around we don't like," he had said. Nobody around where? The waterfront? That would limit the search to the windows facing the pier where I had gone fishing.

153

Down to my hands and knees I went, below the level of the windows. At every one my fingers cautiously tapped. At every door I slowly turned the knob and gently pushed to see if it was unlocked.

Two dim blobs of light loomed through the fog, coming toward me down the narrow street, and I rolled into a deep shadow and lay still, hoping whoever was in the car wouldn't be able to see me, wondering who was driving down there at that hour of the morning.

Maybe it was Herman, still in his taxi, and I had beaten him to his hiding place.

The car came closer. There weren't any top lights on the roof. It couldn't be a taxi.

It wasn't a police car.

It was an old Chevvy coupe, dirty, one fender tattered and rusty, and nobody in it but a man who peered slowly from side to side as he passed. I watched the red taillight fade into the fog and turn the corner. The noise of the exhaust and valves long overdue for grinding died away.

Back to tapping and door-testing I went, finding nothing as the minutes ticked away. My throat was dry and sandy, my ankle ached again, my clothes were damp and filthy as I inched my way along the rough sidewalk, window after window. A shot from the other side, or the sudden crash of glass down on my head, would have been a welcome relief from crawling and tapping . . . tapping and crawling . . . watching and waiting.

Then I heard the same Chevvy coming back again, but it was somewhere behind me and the lights didn't show. Quickly humping under the next two or three windows and past another door, I ducked around the corner and crouched in a narrow street beside a pile of junk. The chevvy, lights out this time, crawled slowly by my hiding place and stopped. A man got out. I couldn't see what he was doing because the corner of a building hid him from me, but I heard a knob turn, heard a door creak open, didn't hear it close again.

Slowly and quietly I slid across the street on my belly, the .38 heavy and reassuring in my hand, and wriggled up to the half-open door. Through the gloom inside I could make out the dim shadows of tables and boxes. There was a taller shadow on the other side of the room, moving slowly toward an open stairway.

"Herman," a voice whispered. "Herman. Where the hell are you? It's me, Fred. Are you here?"

Three measured knocks answered him from somewhere on the second floor.

"Herman. Are you upstairs? Is that you, Herman? Come on down, I've got the car here."

I couldn't understand the answer.

"No, there's nobody around," Fred whispered back. "I drove around once and there wasn't a soul. What? All right, I'll look."

Before I could duck he was at the door. If I hadn't risen to my knees he would have stepped on me.

"Shut up!" I rasped in his face as I leaped to my feet. "Tell him to come down or I'll drill you!"

If he had the brains God gives to little green apples he would have done just what I said, but instead he suddenly opened his big mouth and yelled, "Look out, Herm . . . !"

I smacked him one in the jaw with my left hand and he went down like a log.

"Who's there?" Hoffmann called softly. "What's up, Fred?"

"Come on down, Hoffmann, or I'm coming up. You can't get away this time."

"Come up and try to get me, Malone, god damn you, if you've got enough guts!"

"Easier for you to come down, Rudy, with your hands up, and let me take you in."

"And fry for killing your old man? Go to hell!"

"I can't prove you killed him."

"Don't make me laugh, you son-of-a-bitch. I killed him and you know it. You don't intend to take me in. Come on upstairs if you want me."

I tiptoed over to the foot of the stairs and looked up. Something hit me on the arm, knocking the gun out of my hand. I had forgotten Fred. I thought he was out cold, but he wasn't. While I had been chattering away he got to his feet and threw a chicken box at me. He dove before I could recover the pistol from the floor, carrying me up against the wall, flailing at me with his big fists and hollering, "Herman, Herman, I've got him, I've got him!"

He didn't have me, not by a damned sight, but he gave me a bad ten seconds. First he hit me in the stomach, and for a moment I thought I was going to lose my lunch—only I didn't have one to lose. Then he clipped me alongside the eye. The sudden sharpness of the pain told me he had split the skin open and I would have an unlovely shiner in the morning. It didn't worry me then—I was too busy throwing punches myself and trying to get rid of Fred before Rudy decided to lean over the top of the stairs and take a couple of shots at me.

My right hammered him below the heart, and a left uppercut straightened him out, throwing his head back for a split second. That's all the time I needed. Swinging my right like an axe I let him have it right across his Adam's apple with the heel of my hand and he went down to the floor again, gasping and choking for breath. As he went I grabbed the .38 from the corner where it had fallen and tested the trigger and hammer carefully to make sure it hadn't been damaged. It worked fine.

"Are you ready, Rudy? I'm coming up. This is your last chance!"

"Go to hell, Malone, and come and get me if you think you can!"

I picked up the chicken crate Fred had thrown at me, and held it above my head with my left hand as I started up the stairs. Blood from the cut in my cheek was running down my face, salty to my lips where it trickled by.

The stairway was open, there wasn't even a handrail, and all I could see was the open space in the ceiling above me. Everything else was black, and somewhere in the blackness was Rudy Hoffmann, still waiting.

The chicken crate was about three inches above the second-floor level when Rudy fired—at the crate. At the same time I shoved my pistol up and chanced a shot into the darkness, and the quick flash disclosed a solid wall of chicken crates stacked on the floor above my head.

With a crash they were pushed over, and I fell to the bottom of the stairs as they hit me. In the midst of their banging and bouncing came the sharp snaps from Rudy's gun as he leaned over from the upper floor and fired at the mess of boxes and me. Splinters flew in my face.

He didn't manage to hit me, somehow or other, and I threw the crates off and was starting up the stairs again when the sound of breaking glass told me that Hoffmann was moving out.

It didn't take me more than a second or two to get up the steps, through the crates scattered around the second floor, and over to the broken window, but Rudy was gone. I stuck my head between the jagged edges of glass—suddenly realized my shoulders wouldn't go through and that the hole wasn't possibly big enough to let a man out. I dropped back to the floor as a bullet whipped over my head. Glass tinkled down beside my shoulder.

And there we were, together in a black room, separated by no more than twenty feet, barricaded behind nothing more substantial than a couple of chicken crates, not daring to shoot at each other because we couldn't afford to miss. There were five shots left in the chamber of the .38. Rudy couldn't have more than two or three in the clip in his gun, unless he had reloaded after firing down the steps at me.

The stinking floor steamed under my nose and I strained to catch the faintest sound from across the room, and wondered why I couldn't hear his heartbeats. Certainly he ought to be able to hear mine pounding away—*thump, thump, thumpthump.*

Had anybody heard the shots? Hoffmann's automatic didn't make much noise, but my Smith & Wesson boomed like the crack of doom, and it should have echoed through the old market houses, attracting some attention.

An hour seemed to go by.

There was a stirring and shuffling below, then I heard the Chevvy's noisy engine cough into action, gears meshed together, and Fred drove rapidly away. Where? To get help? Or maybe he was performing the old military maneuver known technically as getting the hell out of there. But suppose he was bringing help?

All he had to do was get a cop, tell him two guys were shooting it out in his shop, and he would have a platoon down there to clean up the whole thing. Somebody might get hurt. My left hand silently searched the floor for something to throw and attract Rudy's attention, maybe make him move.

157

All it found was a piece of glass, and I silently arched the fragment across the room. It clattered to the floor.

Nothing happened. Nothing except more and deeper silence.

Perhaps the fog had thinned out a little, or dawn was just around the corner. At any rate, it seemed that I could see a little better, a little farther, than when I first dropped beside the window. Maybe two or three feet ahead of me. Not the whole way. My one leg was against a wall, with the other I explored until my toe touched a crate. Drawing the leg back about six inches I kicked out and set the box skidding across the room.

Hoffmann's shot plowed into the wall above my heel.

I sent four back—*Bang! Bang! Bang! Bang!*—carefully spaced in a short arc five inches above the floor, covering the space where the orange flash of his gun had marked his hiding spot a moment before. A little cry of pain mingled with the third bang—the sweetest music I had heard for a long time, and then he dropped over the stair opening and stumbled into the boxes below.

I knocked the remaining glass out of the window and crawled onto the steeply sloping roof, holding the window frame with my left hand as my toes felt for the gutter. Dawn was coming fast, and there on the roof I was a helpless target that anyone could see for a hundred feet. My toes found some support, snail-like I squirmed until my free hand found it too, then I lowered myself from the gutter and dropped to the sidewalk. There was no trash can this time, only about five feet of space, and I caught and steadied myself without doing much more than flexing my knees. The doorway was half open in front of me, and there stood Rudolph Hoffmann.

His face was pale and haggard in the morning light. He was supporting himself with his left hand, holding so fiercely to the door frame that his knuckles glowed as white as little dabs of phosphorus. A thin trickle of blood ran down his right hand, along the barrel of the little automatic he held, and dripped on the ground. It must have been the last blood left in him, for the pallor of his face made him look like a man long gone. The always pale lips were blue and lifeless and sagging, as though the supporting muscles had finally grown weary of standing at attention for all the years they had been kept in line. Except for his eyes he was tired and old, worn out by hate. The eyes still bored ahead, black and cold and bitter. Somehow or other long-forgotten words that I had read in school—"Tiger, tiger, burning bright . . ." started going through my head, over and over again, with the deadly monotony of telegraphic tapping.

It seemed a shame to waste my last bullet on a guy who was so close to the end of the line, but that bloody right hand slowly lifted and the narrow black pupils kept glaring from the pale, sagging face. . . .

THE END

Take Your Pick from These Hard-to-Get Best-Selling Books!

Now you may enjoy many hours of exciting reading pleasure at a small fraction of the original cost. These POPULAR LIBRARY books are complete, full-length editions of successful novels formerly priced at $2.00 or more.

If your bookseller or newsdealer cannot supply you, order by mail from POPULAR LIBRARY, INC., 10 East 40th Street, New York 16, N. Y. Enclose 30c (which includes cost of mailing and handling) for each book ordered. If you order 4 books or more, we pay the postage and you need only enclose 25c per book.

Please order by number. Mail in your list promptly, as only a limited number of copies of each of these select titles is still available.

Mysteries

Westerns

Novels and Specials